The Choking Game

To Slippery Rock
Community Library —
Remember to
breathe!
M E Reed

A John and Sarah Jarad
Nantucket Mystery

MARTHA REED

THE CHOKING GAME
A John and Sarah Jarad Nantucket Mystery
Copyright © 2014 by Martha Reed

ISBN-13: 978-1502813602
ISBN-10: 1502813602

First Buccaneer/KMA Pittsburgh ePub and trade paperback print edition
Published December 2014
Cover art by Karen Phillips
Printed in the United States of America

Available from Amazon.com, CreateSpace.com, other retail outlets, Kindle, and other devices.

DEDICATION

with gratitude

to

Dorothy L. Sayers

Who showed me the way.

ACKNOWLEDGMENTS

Heartfelt thanks to:

Sisters in Crime, Inc.

The Mary Roberts Rinehart Pittsburgh Chapter of Sisters in Crime, Inc.

Lee Lofland, and the Writers' Police Academy

Generous mentors and friends:

Nancy Martin, Annette Dashofy, Tim Esiais, Ramona DeFelice Long,

Hank Phillippi Ryan, Hallie Ephron, Marcia Talley, Susan Meier.

Insightful editors: Susan Gottfried and Ramona DeFelice Long

Graphic designer Karen Phillips for the amazing cover design.

Beta readers: Jeff Boarts, Mary Sutton, Holly Dynoske,

Sue Em Davenport, Laura Seebacher, Betty Kubina,

Jody Clarke Walter, and the Women Who Read Too Much.

With special appreciation to the members of The Mutinous Crew:

Randy Walkowiak, Nancy Holsinger, Ginger Thomas, Stephanie Salo,

Joan Widdoes, Sarah 'Boo-Boo' Reed, Reed Widdoes, and Molly Widdoes.

The beatings will continue, until morale improves.

CHAPTER ONE

Sunday, May 29, 2011
2:17 AM

Candy hugged herself for warmth. She should have brought a sweater. As fabulous as her new Toshiro Geta dress was, May was way too early for sleeveless linen. Rubbing her arms briskly helped, but nothing was going to warm her tone as long as Skip insisted on ruining their night by acting like such a complete jackass.

Polpis Road was as deserted as an unlit stage. Skip kept flicking the headlights from high beam to low beam and back again, trying to follow the road's nearly invisible surface. She should never have given him the keys. His driving style was making her feel car sick.

"High beams won't help, Skip, you just lose your night vision. Keep them on low and follow the center stripe home. If you go off the road you'll feel it; the tires will go soft. It's sand."

"How'd you like to drive?" he snarled. "I didn't ask to play chauffeur, you know. I got told."

"Oh no, please. Carry on." Sarcasm trilled an arch into her voice. "You're doing such a fine job."

"Then quit bitchin' about it, will you?"

"Why do you always make things so difficult? But no, why listen to me? I've only lived on Nantucket my entire life."

She caught Skip's grimace from the corner of her eye. It was the only warning she had before he wrenched the steering wheel hard right and deliberately drove toward the bushes. She raised her hands to protect her face. "Skip! What are you doing?"

"That's it!" The car skidded sideways as he stood on the brake. "I have had enough!"

"You asshole!" Clawing at the door, Candy scrambled into the night. The car's high beams illuminated pine trees scant inches off the front bumper. As she moved unsteadily hand over hand around the trunk of the car, her heeled sandals sank into the loose gravel. She struggled to keep her balance. "Give me the keys, Skip! I have had enough of your crap."

He slipped from behind the wheel, and hefted the keys in one hand. "You want the keys, bitch?" He hurled them into the pines. "Then fetch. Go find them."

"No! Don't do that!" Candy clenched her fists. "Why do you have to act like such a child?"

Skip strolled onto the road, clapping his hands. In the stillness of the watchful night, the claps made sharp, flat sounds like gunshots. "How 'bout that? Now you get to deal with me for a change." His laughter mocked her through the darkness. "Enjoy the walk home, bitch."

"Asshole!"

Candy shivered as the night air kissed her bare collarbones. Stepping into the trees, she pushed aside dead lower branches, seeking the keys. Hopefully, they hadn't fallen too far in. One prickly branch scratched the back of her hand. She licked the scratch to ease the pain. Her saliva felt thick against her skin, and she realized she was losing her buzz. Great, just great. Now she would have trouble falling asleep. That bastard had ruined her entire night. Straightening up, she looked for Skip, and saw him marching unsteadily toward town. He was finally taking her advice and following the center stripe home. Cupping her hands, she hooted. "Enjoy the walk home, jackass! It's only six miles. And don't look for me. I am not coming to pick you up!"

Candy returned to her task, sure that Skip had tossed the keys over by the big dead pine. Stepping along a sandy path, she moved deeper into the trees. Wouldn't it be a laugh when she finally found them? And even though it would be going the wrong way, she would definitely have to drive back into town now, just so she could flip Skip off when she passed him on the road. Have a nice walk home yourself, asshole. Ha!

A branch snapped in the darkness to her left. It was a big snap, too, a deliberate snap, not the sound of a dead branch cracking in the breeze. She cocked her head to listen. The sound wasn't repeated. Candy decided it was probably a deer. Everyone knew these woods were full of them.

The second snap stopped her in her tracks.

Candy stood alone in the night, feeling panic sparkle up her spine. She fought it back. If Skip thought he could scare her, he had another think coming! Besides, hunting in the dark for her keys like this was stupid, a waste of time. She should go back to her car, and use her cellphone to call for a cab. She had a spare set of keys at the house. She could come back in the morning and pick up her car when it was light out. Now that was smart thinking! She started back to her car. She was almost out of the trees. This whole episode was silly, really, all of this childish panic over a deer. How she would laugh about this in the morning over her cappuccino! She was nearing the edge of the trees, she was almost home free, when she caught a toothy sound carried on the very breath of the wind. It was a soft sound, almost tuneless. Someone nearby was whistling Yankee Doodle Dandy.

Candy dropped to her knees. Holy shit! It's The Whistler! She clutched her hands to still her thudding heart. Her skin slicked with sweat as she studied the man crossing through the headlights of her car. Whoever he was, it wasn't Skip, playing a prank. Skip was slim. He had been wearing khakis with a sports coat. This guy was stockier. He was in jeans and sneakers. The Whistler reached into the car, and clicked off the headlights. She was plunged into darkness.

Blinking rapidly to adjust her eyes, Candy trembled with indecision. What should she do? Stand up and confront him? Scream for help? Run like hell? She hated feeling defenseless, but her cell phone and her mace were stashed in her purse in the front seat of the car. If she needed to use them, she would never reach them in time. Struggling to stay calm, Candy realized she had another option, one The Whistler wouldn't know about. She'd grown up nearby in Polpis Harbor. As a kid, she had memorized every bridle path and sandy track that crisscrossed the heart of the island. She was willing to bet ten to one that if she could slip away without being seen, she could lose this creep out on The Commons. Slowly slipping her sandals over her heels, Candy retreated into the deeper shadows of the trees. This whistling son of a bitch wasn't getting the best of her!

She headed inland. The pines thinned out where the mounded landscape of The Commons began. She had to slow down to work her way around a couple of the bigger mounds, since they wore splayed crowns of cockspur hawthorn and there was no way she was fighting her way through that kind of thorny brush. At the same time, she felt grateful for the cover the hawthorn provided, because anything that camouflaged her moving silhouette from the night sky had to be a bonus, right? In spite of her pounding heart, Candy chuckled. See? Having three older brothers teach you Sharks and Minnows had been a good thing.

The eroded trail suddenly emptied into a manmade gravel path. Candy felt such a rush of pure vindication that she had to fight to keep from raising her arms in victory to the sky. This was the lane that led to Altar Rock, and the path that would lead her to Polpis Harbor, and home. She cut left, and when Candy considered her fright, she felt her anger grow. The cops would certainly hear about this once she reached a phone! What did those guys get paid for, anyway, letting this Whistler creep run around scaring people? Indignation helped Candy pick up her pace. She broke into a steady jog, supporting her heavy breasts on her forearms as she ran.

The lane up ahead split into a Y. Candy moved left again, knowing that the right fork circled back toward Altar Rock. Truthfully, she hoped to run across Polpis Road soon. The gritty sand was punishing her feet, and her pedicured heels were sore. Noting an earthier undertone to the air, she was even more satisfied with her sense of direction. That peaty smell was the Windswept cranberry bog. She would have to skirt it on her way home. She began to dream of the downy comfort of her king-sized pillow-top mattress, of the softness of her 800-thread count linen sheets, of the relief of simply closing her eyes and putting this godforsaken night behind her, when The Whistler stepped out of the thicket to her right.

Candy flinched at his unexpected proximity. Her toes snagged a fox grape vine and she tripped, flinging her sandals wide and windmilling her arms in a flailing attempt to maintain her balance. Falling was the strangest thing. It felt like slow motion until she landed flat on her face with a splash. Pushing herself back up, Candy spat a mouthful of water so bitter the taste seared her tongue. The vegetative mat she was lying on undulated slowly before flooding with six inches of runny mud.

"Shit!" Remembering childhood warnings, she rolled onto her back. Everyone knew that cranberry bogs were shallow, only eight inches deep. To get out, all you had to do was stand up. So Candy stood up, and her slim legs broke through the peaty organic crust. She found herself treading cold deep water instead. Fear iced her stomach as she realized the truth: she wasn't in a shallow cranberry bog, she'd tripped into Satan's Tub, one of Nantucket's bottomless kettle ponds. Desperate, her eyes stinging from the acidic water, Candy dug her manicure into the bog's rubbery surface. Groping, increasingly frantic, she scrabbled for purchase, feeling for a branch, a root, a trailing vine, anything that might help her pull free of the sucking mud. Bog water clouded her eyes like milk. She blinked them clear to see The Whistler standing on the bank, watching her struggle.

"Help me! Why won't you help me?"

The Whistler reached into his jacket and unwrapped a pack of cigarettes. Shaking one free, he placed it carefully between his teeth. A small flame illuminated his broad smile before he blew the match out with a slow and controlled exhalation.

"Fucker!" she screamed as root systems began to snarl her ankles. Their itchy touch made her skin crawl. Clay began to coat the back of her tongue. Candy tried spitting the taste from her mouth, but only swallowed another gulp of bitter bog water instead. Coughing, choking, Candy realized she only had one chance left. Like everything else in this world, she was going to have to do it herself.

Raising her knees, she pulled her feet free of the clinging roots. Rolling out flat on her belly, Candy floated, her lips barely bubbling clear of the bog. Slowly, oh-so slowly, she swam toward a line of bulrushes, knowing that they defined the edge of the bog. Extending her arms forward, she sank her fingernails into the soggy bank, ignoring the puddled mugwort clinging to her ears. Digging her toes into the peat, Candy leveraged her legs, heaving herself up, up, forward and up, clawing for every inch. Greenbrier thorns tore her hands. She ignored the pain. Digging in with her elbows and knees, she wormed forward through the slime. Spent, exhausted, but finally on firm ground, Candy collapsed. The puddle she lay in stank like cheap leather. Strands of luminous algae hung from her eyelashes. Pushing herself up on her elbows, she puked her stomach clean. Wiping her mouth with the back of her hand, her teeth began to chatter, a skeletal clicking sound she couldn't control. Candy looked around. The Whistler had vanished.

"Ohmigod," she sobbed, blowing muddy snot from her nose. She cradled her hands, her fingers curled like apostrophes in pain, her manicure ripped into the quick. "What a fucking train wreck."

She felt his presence even before she heard anything. Looking up, Candy found him standing by her shoulder. She tried to smile, and failed. "Ohmigod-"

CHAPTER TWO

Lieutenant John Jarad checked his watch. 07:17, and the sun was already two fingers above the horizon. Because Nantucket rested at 70 degrees West longitude, dawn broke early on the island. It was their first duty call of the day, but if what he suspected was true, John already had serious misgivings about the way this day was shaping up.

Less than an hour ago, a jogger had dialed 911 to report that something had disturbed Satan's Tub during the night. At first, John had hoped that one of the island's all too numerous deer had decided to go for a midnight swim, but finding the abandoned car by the roadside had quashed that idea. He turned to see how Detective CJ Allamand was holding up under the burden of unplanned overtime. He had already released CJ from her overnight shift, but she was the force's certified crime scene investigator, and she had insisted on attending the call anyway. CJ looked as unruffled as always, with her wide-spaced eyes recording every detail. He did detect a certain firmness around her mouth, though, that warned him CJ was suppressing some anger. He flicked the driver's license in his hand. "Candy Kane. Unusual name."

"I can't imagine what her parents were thinking, naming her that. Sounds like a stripper."

"She was a pole dancer." Sergeant Ted Parsons scratched his jaw. "Met her at a cousin's stag party once. Looks like a young Pam Anderson. Has a nice act, too. Classy, not what you would think. Told me she usually worked The Combat Zone over in Boston. Took the shuttle over on Friday, and flew back on Sunday morning. Seemed nice enough, too, and smart."

"Smart enough to earn a living working two days a week," John noted.

"Sure," CJ scowled. "If you call dancing naked in front of a roomful of strange men earning a living." She raised an evidence sleeve and thumbed the chrome police whistle it contained. "I hate it whenever The Whistler leaves one of these. It's like he's taunting us, the prick."

"He wants to make sure we know he's back at it again." John shifted his

6

weight, and the ground squelched beneath his boots. It was a marshy, unpleasant sound. He had already asked the FBI to profile The Whistler, but their report hadn't narrowed the field by much. It suggested looking for an intelligent white male in a position of authority who exhibited control issues. That description fit ninety percent of the men living on Nantucket. "I don't like seeing this new level of aggression. Judging from the tracks, the vic was running before she went in. What's The Whistler up to this year?"

"Escalating violence in a psychopath is never a good thing." CJ stomped the crusted clay off her boots. "Not to mention he's broken from his regular pattern. Always before, he stuck to south of town. This, no, this is something new."

"Maybe last night he got lucky?" Ted said. "Maybe Polpis Harbor is his home range, and last night he happened to find her out here?"

"Lucky for him, then," CJ said. "Not so lucky for her."

When John thought of what they might recover from Satan's Tub, he felt his heart flutter against his ribs like a trapped bird. This incident was going to be his first real test as the new Lieutenant-Commander for the Nantucket force. The team was looking to him to present a strong and confident lead. He knew he could keep the anxiety from showing on his face; he prayed it wasn't reflected in his eyes. "Ted? I'll need you to cover traffic detail by the car."

"Traffic detail, sir?"

John swallowed, hard. Presenting orders to the older officer continued to be a challenge. As much as he liked the guy, Ted's constant questioning of his assignments kept tripping John up. Second thoughts and second guesses were distractions he couldn't afford right now, when his new command was still so green. Maybe a more conciliatory tone might work? "We'll need to keep traffic moving to avoid a gawker's block. Plus, Paul is on his way. Someone will need to direct him to the site. I can tell you he wasn't thrilled to get a call from us this morning."

"I'll just bet he wasn't. Sir."

Ted's tone was carefully neutral. That was probably as good as it was going to get. John returned his focus to the hive of activity by the bog. He watched a young diver pull a black wetsuit up over his shoulders. A second diver, a female with a long blonde braid, had already suited up. She stood by, checking the tubes and tanks and gauges. John wasn't entirely convinced of the suitability of this idea, but the Salty Dogs were licensed divers, and since they donated their time it kept expenses down and the Board of Selectmen out of his budget and off his back. Doubtful, still dubious, he crossed his arms. "You be careful down there, Toby. We don't want to lose you."

"Don't worry about me, Lieutenant Jarad. This is awesome." Toby

Talbot stuffed his mop of bronze curls into his neoprene headgear before shouldering his heavy tank. "I've been wanting to dive Satan's Tub for years, but the Conservancy wouldn't let me."

"You won't see much down there, Toe." The female diver threaded a nylon line through his dive belt. "Bog water's not great for clarity. Remember, though, if you do find something, you'll come upon it pretty quick. If it gets to be too much, tug on the line. We'll haul you out."

"Don't worry about me, Meg. I'll be fine, but thanks." Spitting into his mask, Toby worked the warm saliva around the glass with his fingertips. After testing his flashlight, he adjusted his mask, gave a quick thumbs up, and stepped off into the bog.

John winced as the low-tide tang of marsh gas puddled the air. The stench brought tears to his eyes. He wasn't alone; even CJ pinched her nose until the gas cloud dissipated. Looking up, John noticed Paul Jenkins marching up the path. Paul was Nantucket County's sole Medical Examiner, a compact man built of wiry muscle. As John had suspected, Paul did not look pleased to be called out so early. Nevertheless, Paul was here. He knew his duty, as did they all.

Paul's voice was pitched surprisingly low, and as always, he spoke with great deliberation. "Morning, John, CJ. Ted said I'd find you here. What've we got?"

"We think she's in the bog." John extended the victim's license. "The Whistler left his usual calling card."

Paul placed his medical bag carefully between his feet, and slid his wire-rimmed glasses up his nose. "You're sure about that? The Whistler's never been physical before."

"We'll find out soon enough," John said. "We just sent Toby down to check."

"Good Lord, I hope you're wrong about this. Satan's Tub would be a terrible place to end up." Paul returned the license. "I've often wondered why they didn't fence the Tub off when they built the path?"

"I know why." CJ crossed her arms. "The Conservancy wouldn't allow it. Fence post lumber is Wolmanized. They were concerned the chemicals might upset the natural environment."

"My word, folks are certainly going green these days. Of course, they might have to reconsider their policy, once the lawyers get through with this one."

Ted reappeared around a bend in the path. John frowned until he noted that Ted was escorting a stranger who even looked like a washashore: pale, rumpled, almost cadaverous when compared to the sergeant's stockier, muscular build. "What've we got, Ted?"

"Found this guy by the car, sir. Says he's the boyfriend."

"Fiancé, actually." The man smiled uncertainly. "Skip Pedders. What's going on, Officer?"

"Lieutenant Jarad, Mr. Pedders. What brings you out so early?"

Skip's eyes followed the line leading into the bog. His jaw fell open. "My God! You think Candy's in that pond?"

The man's surprise seemed genuine. It was difficult to fake the drop in blood pressure that could cause someone to turn even paler. "Have you known Ms. Kane long, sir?"

"Candy?" He stuttered. "Since Labor Day. I met her at a C-Stack convention. I moved to Nantucket to be nearer. My God, do you really think she's down there?"

"C-Stack?" CJ interrupted. "What's that?"

Skip waved off CJ's question, but answered it anyway. "Computer programming. I write access codes for automated data feeds. You've heard of Bingley ProTech? I'm their consultant."

"Got it," John said, although he didn't. He wanted to keep the questioning focused on the missing woman. They could confirm the man's employment history later. "When was the last time you saw Ms. Kane, sir?"

"We had dinner last night, but I don't know anything about this." He pointed a shaky finger. "She was fine when I left her with the car. Jesus!" His eyes tracked the perimeter of the bog. "I can't believe this is happening. How did Candy end up here?"

"Let's back up a bit, sir. What time did you stop the car?"

"Around two, two-thirty?"

"And why did you stop the car, sir? You didn't run out of gas; the tank's half full."

Skip swiped the sweat off his lip. "Okay, listen. Candy and I were having this fight and I pulled off the road and I–I threw her keys in the bushes. That's all I did, I swear, and then I walked back to town. It took me over an hour. You wouldn't believe how deserted this friggin' road gets that late at night. I only saw one car the whole time I was out here, and he wouldn't stop to give me a ride. I tried flagging him down, but he almost ran me over. I had to jump out of the way."

John held his breath. Had that driver been The Whistler? It made sense. The Whistler would need some form of transportation to get around the island. Were they this close to getting a lead that might help them nail the stalker? He checked on CJ. Her eyes were shining with the same anticipation and hope. "Can you describe that car for us, sir?"

"Describe the car? No, not really. All I saw were the headlights. I do know it was a convertible, though, because I heard his music blasting as he drove by, the son of a bitch."

A convertible. Now that was an interesting detail. Convertibles were comparatively rare on Nantucket.

"Did you catch the license plate?" John asked.

"Seriously? It was pitch dark, and he went flashing by."

"Every detail is helpful, Mr. Pedders. Now, tell me, again. Why did you throw the keys in the bushes?"

"I know how stupid that sounds, Lieutenant, but really, that's just what happened." Skip stuck his hands in his pockets. "And then, this morning, I realized what a jerk thing I had done, so I texted Candy to make sure she got home okay, but she wouldn't reply. I tried calling her, but she wouldn't pick up. So I figured she was still pissed, and screening her calls. Then I thought it might be better to come out to her house and apologize, you know, in person, face to face. That's when I saw her car still parked by the road and I stopped, and I ran into you guys. I swear, that's all I know."

That explanation of the night's events sounded lame enough to be true, but John needed to be sure. "You said you tried calling Ms. Kane this morning, sir? Did you try calling her house?"

"Yes, and I tried her cellphone, too, but like I said, it kept rolling to voicemail."

John waved Ted closer. "Ted? Did you find a cellphone in the car?"

"No, sir. Just the purse."

Curious, John thought. *If Ms. Kane had her cellphone with her last night, why didn't she use it to call for help?*

"That's the funny part about all of this," Skip volunteered. "Candy's cellphone was the reason for our fight. She kept leaving the table to go talk to a 'girlfriend,' only I know it wasn't any girlfriend, it was some other guy, and that sucks because we were supposed to be out celebrating my birthday. Sweet way to get treated on your birthday, don't you think?"

Join the club, buddy. John quickly studied his boots. Apparently, he wasn't the only one having relationship issues. Carefully keeping his face blank, he raised his eyes. "So, you and Ms. Kane have been having problems?"

"Well, yeah, maybe, a little. Candy expects too much from me. With her lifestyle, you know, she hangs out with a lot of players, guys with real money to burn. There's this one Russian dude, he buys a bottle of Dom every night, and he sprays it on her as part of her finale. That shit costs three hundred bucks a bottle! I can't compete with that, and Candy knows it. She used to be okay with it, but lately? I'm not so sure. She hasn't seemed happy. But I would never hurt her, never! If she wants it to be over, then fine. But I would never hurt her. You gotta believe me."

Strike two. John continued his silent count. The stats were starting to stack up against Skip Pedders. Over eighty percent of violent crimes committed against women were perpetrated by someone they knew from a domestic situation. It was a mind-numbing statistic, but true.

The bog burped a flat muddy bubble. Meg staggered forward. She almost tumbled in before Ted reached over to take the line from her hands. He removed the slack loops that threatened to snarl their feet by expertly coiling the line around his elbow and his thumb. John got ready to remind Ted of his properly assigned duty when Toby resurfaced.

He pulled off his mask. "I found her, sir! Lieutenant Jarad? I found her. I've tied her off."

"Nice work, Toby." John moved to the edge of the bog. "Okay, haul it in, Ted. Let's see what we've got."

Ted grimaced as the prickly nylon line bit into his fingers. Slowly, steadily, against Ted's insistent pull, a pale female form emerged from the dark pool. The naked body broached the surface face down. It bobbed gently, the line looped around her left wrist, her right arm stretched out in graceful counterbalance, fingers curved. With each tug of the line, her long hair ebbed and flowed like eel grass caught in a strong tidal current.

"My God." Skip strained forward. "Candy? Is that her?"

CJ held him back. "Where are her clothes?"

"Here, put these on." Paul handed John a pair of blue nitrile gloves. "Make sure Ted gets a set. I'm going to need your help with this."

Toby crawled out of the bog and stood. Excited and breathless, he stripped off his headgear. "I tried to be careful down there, Lieutenant Jarad, but I had to cut her loose. She was tied to a cinderblock."

"I'm sure you did fine." John waited impatiently for Ted to finish rolling on his gloves. Finally, in tandem, they reached down to grasp an arm. Together, they hauled the corpse up the clay bank. Hot bile scorched the back of John's throat. He had to clench his stomach to keep from vomiting. *Sweet Jesus! The arm he held felt as gelatinous as a squid. What in God's name had happened to this woman's bones?*

Paul stooped to examine the cord knotted around the victim's purple ankles. He ran his thumb up her muddy calf. "This is odd. The skin shouldn't be affected like this. Yes, bog tannin does color tissue, but generally, it takes time." Grasping a shoulder, Paul rolled the corpse over.

Flaccid breasts submitted to the law of gravity and fell away to both sides. The nipples were colored a deep ruby red. Her bristling pubic patch and the nests of hair growing in her armpits were tinted an even darker shade of mahogany. Her open, staring eyes were garnet, although her pupils remained a milky gray. Her gaping mouth revealed an oddly pointed tongue that protruded from between her hennaed teeth and burgundy lips.

"Crissakes!" Ted sputtered. "I'm gonna dream about this one!"

Paul crouched lower. "I see bruising on the neck that may be ligature marks. She may have been strangled." His fingers explored the back of the skull. "This feels like a fracture, but I'll have to autopsy to be sure." He scraped a blob of clay off one shoulder. "Why does this tattoo look familiar? Where I have seen this before?"

"Tattoo? What tattoo?" Skip pushed forward. "Candy doesn't have any tattoos."

"Doesn't have any tattoos?" John repeated, stunned into pointless repetition.

"Holy shit." Skip hiccupped. "That's not Candy!"

"I was afraid of that." Paul pushed up off his knees. "Toby? Any chance you missed finding a second victim down there?"

Toby looked ashen. "No way, sir. She was the only one in that bog, I'd swear to it."

John felt his world flip upside down. Anticipating a homicide was bad enough, but not knowing who the victim was seemed even worse. *Who was this woman? Did she have any friends or family searching for her?* He blinked and snapped back into the immediacy of the moment. First things first. They needed to contain the crime scene. Skip Pedders was one civilian on site too many. "Sergeant Parsons, take Mr. Pedders back to his car and wait for me there. Mr. Pedders, please return to your car, sir. Sergeant Parsons will take your contact information. We appreciate your cooperation."

Paul was a seasoned pro. He knew the drill. He waited until the two men were out of earshot before continuing in a murmur, "We may have some trouble with this one. I won't be able to present an accurate time of death. There's been no tissue decomposition because of the bog tannin. She may have been in there for fifty years."

John lifted his eyes from the corpse and scanned the rolling moor. It stretched out distant and visible for miles. "It's more than that now. Because if this isn't Candy Kane, then where is she?"

CHAPTER THREE

John ran the variables for the missing woman through his mind. Candy Kane could be dead, her corpse hidden nearby. In that case, he would need to send to Methuen for the cadaver dog team. She could be dead, with her corpse still in The Whistler's possession. There wasn't much he could do about that particular variable right this minute. Or, Candy Kane could still be alive and The Whistler's captive. He sent up a silent prayer. God help the woman if this last variable was true.

In any case, he needed to split the team to maximize the effectiveness of their response. He would leave CJ to finish processing the site. He could trust her to be thorough. He would take Ted back to the station, and initiate a BOLO bulletin on Candy Kane. That sounded like a plan. He discarded the gloves into Paul's medical bag and began to breathe easier. "She's all yours, Paul. Do what you can for us."

"I should have some kind of preliminary report for you first thing tomorrow morning-"

"Lieutenant?" CJ interrupted. She was listening intently to the personal radio strapped to her shoulder. "John? I don't believe this. Candy Kane is at Cottage Hospital. Some good Samaritan found her crawling along Polpis Road, and brought her in."

John felt his decision tree snap like a splintered mast. It was such an intense sensation he wanted to throw up an arm to protect his head. *Candy Kane, alive and independent?* He hadn't even considered that variable. The morning's events had triggered such a hurried response that he'd rushed right into the biggest rookie mistake of them all: making assumptions ahead of your data. That was especially galling because he knew that investigative success came in keeping your mind open to all the possibilities, and in not making any knee-jerk responses or decisions.

He willed himself to slow down, to think things through properly, to resist the prodding insistence to hurry up. Candy Kane was in skilled hands at Cottage Hospital. She would have fresh information about The Whistler.

She should be their primary focus. *Game on.* He knew what he needed to do. He felt his revised response compel him forward as firmly as if he had a pissed-off ten pound bluefish hooked on a line. He only needed to follow this out to see where it lead. This, this was his favorite feeling in the whole world, and the reason he had entered law enforcement in the first place.

"CJ, come with me," he said. He was so eager to get to the hospital that she had to trot to keep up.

"Do you think this new vic is one of his?"

"I'm not sure. Paul seems to think she's been in the Tub for years. The Whistler's only be active for three summers. If Paul's right, the timing doesn't fit. Plus, this vic may have been strangled. That's not The Whistler's M.O. I'm thinking these two events may be unrelated."

"What are you saying?" She stopped dead in her tracks. "We have a killer on the island? One we didn't even know about?"

He shivered as CJ spoke his thoughts out loud. Of course, accidents occurred on Nantucket all the time. No one was immune to tragedy; look at what had happened to Chief Brock. But to suggest that a homicide had taken place on Nantucket felt alien, as if he had looked up into the sky and suddenly seen two moons. Somehow, in his mind, homicide only happened back on the mainland. Murder didn't happen on Nantucket, where everyone knew their neighbors only all too well, or did it? Suddenly, he had his answer, and he felt as provincial as a hired carriage horse with clip-clop blinders on.

And Paul had suggested strangulation as a cause of death. Throttling someone was an intensely personal act. It was purposeful, deliberate, physically demanding. Both the victim and the actor would see death coming. Death by strangulation could take five minutes, with the victim fighting for life for as long as consciousness remained. How much hatred did one person have to feel in order to crush someone's windpipe for five interminable minutes? "We may have to face that possibility with this investigation."

"Holy crap," CJ breathed.

Ted saw them coming. He was standing next to the cruiser with Skip Pedders. John noted that Skip was smoking a cigarette badly. Skip could barely hang on to it. He added that detail to his list of observations about the man. And, although he was willing to grant that the corpse in Satan's Tub had apparently surprised Skip as much as it had the rest of the team, Skip was still a person of interest in a possible assault. He wouldn't be cleared until after they had interviewed Candy Kane.

He strode forward. "Good news, Mr. Pedders. Ms. Kane is safe, at Cottage Hospital."

"Candy's alive?" Skip dropped his cigarette in the sand. "Quick! What's the fastest way there? Point me in the right direction."

The man was agitated. Was he upset because Candy was still alive? Was that good news he heard, or the worst possible outcome he could have imagined? Skip wasn't giving the answer away. He just looked jittery.

"I suggest that you wait until Ms. Kane sends for you, sir," John said. "The doctors may not let you in to see her."

"They'll let me in, Lieutenant." Skip dug for his keys. "I'm her fiancé."

It was probably best to keep Skip nearby until after the Kane interview anyway. "Why don't you follow us to the hospital, sir? That would be the quickest, and safest, way."

"Fine by me. Can we please get going?"

"One moment. Ted? Take charge of the site. Do one final old school sweep. Make sure we didn't overlook anything."

"But, sir!" Ted blinked. He glanced covertly at CJ standing nearby. "Why are you taking her with you to interview the stripper? She's the CSI."

John had the answer at hand simply because it was true. "She's also detective-grade, plus I think Ms. Kane may appreciate having a woman officer to talk with."

"That's bull, sir, pure bull! Why am I always assigned to grunt duty lately?"

John hit his limit. He was through justifying his every action. "Because I can count on you to be thorough, Sergeant Parsons. I'll expect your report on my blotter by the end of day. Is that understood?"

Ted's neck flushed an ugly mottled red. He dropped his eyes and studied the ground. "Yes, *sir*."

Reaching into his pocket, John removed his Ray-Bans. He turned to face the rising sun. "Ready, Detective Allamand? Let's roll."

* * * * * * *

CJ studied her boss from the passenger side of the speeding cruiser. She had to admit that even after six months, it was still hard to think of John Jarad as their new field commander. It had nothing to do with either John's abilities or his qualifications. He had already proven his competency beyond all doubt, plus he had more education than any two other officers combined, and that included Chief Brock. No, it was more about her perception of him as a person than in his abilities because somehow, when she wasn't looking, her childhood chum Johnny Jarad had morphed into a seriously studious man.

CJ wasn't entirely convinced that this was a good thing. In fact, it worried her. Sometimes the heart could see better than the eye, and her heart was telling her there was something seriously wrong with her good friend John. For instance, she couldn't remember the last time she had seen him laugh.

She studied his profile as they sped northwest. What about John had changed? Physically, he looked the same. He still had that headful of unruly hair, which he kept trimmed short in a futile attempt to control the indefatigable Jarad curl. CJ had to admit that having hair that thick was becoming something of a rarity among the other men in their thirty-something age group. John had also inherited his long, straight nose from the Jarad side of the family, as well as the forehead that was just a tad too wide to be called truly handsome. His chocolate brown eyes dipped up out of that same gene pool although his smile, which in her humble opinion he didn't share with the world nearly often enough, came straight from his mother's Winspear side of the family.

CJ considered John to be one of her closest friends. She had known him since that first day of kindergarten and, if she remembered right, she was the reason he had missed a front tooth through most of the second grade. She still carried the scar from that punch on the middle finger of her right hand. Their friendship had grown because they shared a common passion and they knew it: they loved the pursuit of justice. After graduation, CJ had moved off island to earn her degree in Criminal Justice at UMASS. John was made of sterner stuff. He had stayed away two years longer to earn his Masters degree from Bridgewater State before buying his ferry ticket home. Because of that commitment, CJ knew that John had earned every bit of his recent promotion from Sergeant Major to Lieutenant-Commander and yet, sometimes CJ wondered if John really believed he was up to the task.

And yes, his promotion had surprised the team. John was young to be L-C, but he had been the Council's first pick once Chief Brock had opened his eyes from the coma, and it had been obvious to them all that the chief would not be returning to active duty. Ever. That traitorous understanding had been underscored when hospital scuttlebutt revealed that the chief had been admitted to Emergency carrying a blood alcohol load of point two-three percent. The Council, desperate to avoid any whiff of scandal that might spook the tourist herd, had eased the chief into a newly-created public relations post so that he could finish out his service term and collect his thirty-year pension.

CJ agreed that was the only decent thing to do. The chief seemed content with his new duty, and John had accepted the promotion. Still, CJ wilted a little each time she passed the shattered tree when patrolling Wauwinet, and she had to avert her eyes whenever she caught sight of the chief's dented skull and his still livid scar. CJ hated feeling that way, but there it was. She knew it was uncharitable, but she often wondered why the man didn't simply wear a cap. And on really grim days, when her bad ankle was throbbing and she felt more than unusually cranky, she even caught herself devising clever ways to surprise him with one, as a gift.

She rubbed her eyes. It was almost 9 a.m.. The overtime was catching up with her, but she wouldn't have missed this interview for the world. Candy Kane might be able to offer fresh insight into The Whistler, plus Satan's Tub was outside of his regular range. That meant The Whistler had changed his stalking pattern, and a change in pattern meant The Whistler might have made a mistake they could capitalize on this year.

Chief Brock and Pete Simpkins had been in charge of the investigation so far, and a flat nothing had come of it, but the chief was out of the picture now and Simpkins had opted for an early retirement. It was her turn to be on deck as Detective, and she was determined that she would not drop the ball. She would stay alert for two days straight if it meant nabbing The Whistler. She was sure that John felt the same way. One persistent thought kept bobbing to the surface of her mind. "I've been helping Joe Curley digitize the archive. I don't recall any report of a missing woman on island."

John tightened his grip on the wheel. "I don't recall seeing one, either."

"So where did this vic come from? She didn't fall out of the sky. I suppose, if she was a visitor who came over by herself, then maybe no one would miss her that way?"

"True, but I sincerely doubt she got into Satan's Tub by herself. And tying a cinderblock to your ankles makes a tough sell for a suicide."

"Homicide, then." CJ repeated the word just to hear it spoken. "Homicide on Nantucket." She found it surprisingly hard to wrap her mind around the suggestion. They hadn't recorded a homicide on Nantucket since the Great Lobster Pot War back in the seventies before she was born, and yet here she was, smack dab in the middle of this one. "What do you make of it?" She caught John's rueful smile before he caught himself. His smile blinked out.

He pointed a finger down the road. "I think we should interview Ms. Kane, and wait for Paul's preliminary report, before we make any assumptions."

And there it was again. John's defensive shell clicking shut like a scallop as he retreated into process and formality. Where was all of this new defensiveness coming from? John used to be more open about discussing conjecture. He had been almost fearless about exploring probability theory. It was one of his greatest strengths. Stubbornly, CJ decided she wasn't going to let him get away with this behavior. She would crack this shell. No way was she going to let this defensiveness harden into a fresh bad habit. "Thanks for assigning me to the interview. I know you could've brought Ted as backup, just as easy."

"Ted was the wrong approach." They had moved under the shade of the town trees. John dropped his sunglasses into the console and scanned the rearview mirror. "God knows what Ms. Kane went through last night. Get ready, CJ. You may need to take the lead on this one. This may need a woman's touch."

"I'm on it." She accepted the suggestion with Yankee practicality, and decided to risk a plunge to see if John was open to any other suggestions she might make. "I've noticed you've been riding Ted pretty hard lately. You should get to know him better. Ted's a good guy. He has a lot to offer."

"Ha," John scoffed. "Give me a for instance."

"Like assigning him to traffic detail this morning, instead of calling in a secondary unit. Or, when you left him just now to field the site. I saw Ted's face. He was hurt."

"He'll get over it."

"No, John, I'm serious. You need Ted to be a part of the team. I get that you're L-C now, but you can't do everything by yourself." She turned to face him as much as the seatbelt would allow. "Sure, you can still leave the grunt work to us. We'll man the oars, but we need you sitting higher and acting as mate, and being fair, or else morale is going to hit the shitter."

"Comment duly noted, Detective Allamand." He quirked a grin.

CJ relaxed. At least he was still receptive to her suggestions. That was something. She stopped picking at her cuticle and decided to push the conversation one step further, to test her theory as to why John had so recently changed. She had a private suspicion that his new defensiveness stemmed from one singular and exceptional bitch. "Besides, I had to come with you today. No way was I going to let you two knuckleheads go interview a stripper, alone."

"Why do you say that?"

"Ted with his big, soft heart, and with you on the rebound? No fucking way. The only thing worse than making a mistake is making a bigger mistake in the opposite direction."

"Drop it, CJ." John scowled. "I'm not going to talk about Ava. That subject is closed."

CJ rejoiced. Her surmise had been spot on. Damn that Ava Descartes if she had ruined this good man. "What the hell, John? I understand that you're still sore about Ava. Who wouldn't be? You've been through a lot since Christmas. I'm sorry to say I've been through it a couple of times myself, but I'm telling you, Ava Descartes was the wrong woman for you. You need to find someone less structured, not more. Someone to help loosen you up. Help get you out of your rut."

"Now I'm in a rut?"

"Don't mind me saying so, but yeah."

"Dating a stripper would get me out of my rut," he countered.

She delighted to see the flash of his old playful spirit. "Oh, sure! Like Jenny would ever let you date a stripper."

"I'm old enough now not to worry about what my mother thinks of my love life." He pulled in next to an idling diesel ambulance and tipped his head to study the side mirror, watching Skip Pedders pull his Prius into an opposing slot. His eyes darkened. "I don't want to discuss this right now. Actually, I don't want to discuss this at all. What do you say we focus our attention on the investigation at hand, Detective Allamand? What do you say that we try doing that?"

And just like that, he shuttered his eyes to become Lieutenant-Commander Jarad again. CJ realized with a flutter of despair that the opportunity to counsel her friend Johnny was gone.

* * * * * * *

John hesitated before the automatic door. He hated hospitals. He always had. His nose crinkled at the antiseptic tinge that always seemed to hang in the air. That metallic smell reminded him of the last time he had seen his father alive, being wheeled away on a gurney. He suddenly felt twelve years old again, bereft and helpless. His boots slapped the linoleum as he walked toward the Admission desk. There was nothing he could do to pussyfoot the sound. He had already learned to discount the gazes from curious civilians whenever he showed up dressed in his Lieutenant's uniform, but today he felt even more conspicuous compared to the lax cotton pajamas the hospital staff seemed to be wearing to work nowadays.

"Lieutenant Jarad?" R.N. Nancy Mentor stood behind a counter. "Over here, please, sir."

Skip dodged CJ's blockade. He trotted ahead. "Candy Kane? Is she here? Is she alright?"

Nancy laid her pen against a clipboard. "And you are?"

"Skip Pedders. I'm Candy's … friend. I'm a friend of hers."

"I'm sorry, Mr. Pedders, but I can't give out information without Dr. Murray's express permission."

"How long will that take?"

"I have no way of knowing. In any case, you'll need to take a seat in the waiting room until Dr. Murray gives the okay."

Skip slowly turned. He tapped his lip. "I suppose you're going in there now? To see Candy?"

"I'm sure we will, sir," John said. "Once Dr. Murray says we can."

"Can I talk to you a second, Lieutenant?" Skip started pacing. "I've been thinking about what you said on the way over. I don't really see a need for me to stick around, as long as Candy's fine. I'm not even sure she'd want to see me. She might still be mad. I think I'll wait until she wants to talk to me. That way, I'm not stepping on her toes. Candy likes her space."

John watched Skip wilt into pure cowardice before his eyes.

"Do me a favor, and give Candy a message? Tell her I'll call her, later.

She'll understand. I really do need to go check the server." He backed away. "This is way more than I bargained for."

Skip wanted to be away from the situation so badly he didn't even wait for a reply. He turned on his heel and headed for the door.

"Where's he going?" CJ said.

"He decided to wait until she sends for him."

"You're letting him walk away?"

"We don't have anything to hold him on, yet. Don't worry. If we need to pick him up, we know where he lives."

"Hello, Cuz." Dr. Annabel Murray walked up, almost silent on her rubber shoes. Tall and trim with a stork-like stoop earned from a career habit of stuffing her hands in her lab coat pockets, Dr. Annie had an honest face with warm brown eyes shining with intelligence, and a mane of naturally auburn hair. She could have amassed a fortune treating mainland pediatrics, but Nantucket had desperately needed a year-round G.P., so Annie had returned to the island to develop her practice instead. "Glad to see you, too, CJ. You'll need to get set for this one. It isn't pretty. She's been severely assaulted. Someone did a real number on her."

"Severely assaulted?" CJ paled. "Was she raped?"

"There's no evidence of sexual trauma, but someone did beat her badly. She's also being treated for exhaustion and severe dehydration. I've given her a sedative. She won't be awake for much longer." She lowered her voice. "Was it The Whistler? Did he do this?"

"Has she said anything about it?" John asked.

"No. All she's done is cry, and ask for the police. What she really needs most is sleep. It's the best thing for her." She tapped her clipboard. "I'll give you ten minutes with her today, but that's it, and I mean it. We're moving her off the ward into a private room. I want her to stay overnight for observation. It's important that she feels protected, and safe. That's half the battle." She studied them over the rim of her tortoiseshell glasses. "Get the guy who did this, John. He needs to be locked up." She shoved the double doors open and led them down the hall. "She's in the last cubicle on the left. We tried to give her as much privacy as possible."

As they crossed the length of the thirty-foot ward, John prayed that Candy Kane was lucid enough to give them fresh details for the investigation. If she was unresponsive, they would have to wait until this evening to follow up. He hated the idea of losing a full day's pursuit. Dr. Annie reached up to tug the privacy curtain back, and he cringed at the metallic hiss the curtain rings made against the rod.

"Ms. Kane, the police are here."

John was appalled by the sight that met his eyes. He felt physically sickened, as if someone had slugged him in the gut. Candy Kane lay on a raised bed, a blanket folded neatly across her knees. She had an IV drip taped into the crook of one arm. She had been beaten mercilessly. Her nose was flattened. Both eyes were blackened, and they had swollen into purple slits. Finger-shaped bruises cross-hatched her throat and her upper arms. Both hands were splinted. He could see the bloody exposed nail beds on her fingers from where he stood. His knees buckled, and almost gave way. Whatever else had occurred at Satan's Tub, Candy had put up one helluva fight.

"Holy hell," CJ muttered, sounding equally dazed.

Candy turned her head. Stitches as thick as black ants marched across her crushed lips. She gently ran her tongue across her teeth. "Took you cops long enough to find me."

"Ms. Kane?" John pulled a chair closer, and sat. "I'm Lieutenant Jarad. This is Detective Allamand. We're here to help. Can you tell us what happened?"

Candy sighed, and shut her eyes.

John held his breath, and his silence. What Candy had experienced last night meant more to her now than the simple fact of survival. Physical violence may have seared her mind, altering her permanent memory and her perception as to the actual passage of time. He rested his hands in his lap. Sometimes it took a steady listening silence to coax horrified memory out of the shadows, and back into the light.

"I got out of the bog." Candy swallowed. Her shredded voice was barely louder than a whisper. "All I wanted to do was go home." She swallowed again, and grimaced. "I looked up. He was there. I don't know where he came from. I didn't see him, before. I asked for help. To use his phone, to call you, to call the cops. He touched me, like he was afraid of me, like I wasn't real. Then he freaked out. He kept screaming: 'Stay dead, Katie. Stay dead. You're supposed to stay dead'. He choked me. I dragged him into the mud." Tears pooled along her swollen eyelids. "He kicked me to get free. He kept kicking me. I tried to make him stop. He stepped on my hands. Look what he did to my hands."

John's mind snapped to hyper-alert. Candy was describing a level of pathological brutality he had feared might come from The Whistler someday, and here it was. Some event had triggered the stalker into developing a horrifying new level of physical behavior over the winter. But she had given them a name. *Katie.* Maybe she had more to offer. "Can you describe The Whistler for us? What did he look like?"

"He looked like you." She shifted in the bed and groaned. "Maybe taller. But it was dark. I stopped making noise. He pushed me back in the bog. Then he left. I didn't see him leave."

CJ was staring. John knew she was thinking the same thing. Dealing with a serial stalker was one thing. Dealing with an escalating psychopath with a limited police force was something entirely different. Maybe it was time to call the FBI and ask for ground assistance. "Is there anything else about The Whistler, Ms. Kane? Anything at all would be a help."

"Yes." Twin creases appeared between her eyebrows as she made the effort to concentrate. "The Whistler didn't do this. It was someone else."

John thought his ears had played a trick on him. *Could she be right? Had there been a second actor at Satan's Tub last night?* "I'm sorry. Could you repeat that?"

The sedative was taking effect. Candy's soft voice grew even softer. "The Whistler was there, but he left. Then the other one showed up. They weren't together. We fought. He left, too. I found the road. I don't know how." She raised a splinted hand to her forehead. "Why can't I remember this?"

CJ pushed off the wall. "Ms. Kane, did Skip Pedders do this? Did he beat you?"

"No, it wasn't Skip." Candy shuddered. "But this was his fault. He left me there, alone. Where is Skip? Where is he?"

"Dr. Murray said he could see you later," CJ lied.

"You tell him to go fuck himself. Fucker. Don't let Skip in here. I don't ever want to ever see him again."

John was relieved that Candy didn't want to see her faithless lover. How on earth could they explain that Skip had taken the first chance he had to duck out on the encounter? Did Candy really need to know that, too, on top of everything else?

"Time's up, officers." Dr. Annie returned, stepping between the curtain. "You can interview Ms. Kane more, later. Right now, she needs to rest."

John stood, grateful for the interruption. Weeping women left him feeling powerless, ineffective, and weak. He hated feeling that way. He'd seen way too much of that with Ava. He put that bitter memory back in the box where it belonged, and focused on the task at hand. Maybe it was a coward's response, but he used it because it worked.

"Dr. Murray's right, Ms. Kane. We'll be in touch." He got halfway down the corridor before he paused so quickly that CJ jostled his elbow. "Dr. Annie? You'll keep us posted of any change? We'll need to talk with her again, when she's more coherent."

"It would be best to wait until tomorrow, John, if you can." Dr. Annie picked up another clipboard. "She needs to be given the time to heal."

Don't we all? He pondered. He still felt the nasty aftereffects of his breakup with Ava, and they'd split up six months ago. How much longer until he started feeling more like his regular self? He still felt hollow, and disconnected. What if this emptiness was permanent, like a scar? *When I told Ava I wasn't ready yet to commit to marriage, did I do the right thing? Or should I have just kept my mouth shut, and gone ahead with her plans, hoping that someday my feelings would firm up?*

Holy hell, John started. *I've got to stop beating myself up like this!* He shoved the questions aside. Time was the only cure for this shit, and it was well past time to jog on. He had an investigation to run, dammit!

"Let me get this straight," CJ said. "Now we have two actors? The Whistler we knew about, but now there's a second one, who might be a killer?"

"It's only confusing because the two events overlapped at Satan's Tub. Having a shared crime site has blurred the line. Candy was a victim of both The Whistler and this new actor, who I think is connected to the bog victim we found. And, if what Candy said is correct, we've got both of them on the island with us this summer."

"Shit. My head is spinning. I'm not smart enough to keep track of this. But here's a thought: If the victim has been in Satan's Tub for as long as Paul thinks she has, then that means her killer has been running around on the island free and easy for decades, maybe?"

"That's what it sounded like to me."

"Crissakes!" CJ sputtered. "Where do we even start with this one?"

"Let's start by identifying the bog victim. From what Candy said, her first name may have been Katie, plus she had that tattoo." John headed down the cement steps that led to Paul's domain, the county morgue housed in the Cottage Hospital basement. "Paul may have a set of crime scene photos ready for us. I want to take them out to Madaket, and show them to Billy Bear. Billy may be able to help us with an ID, because if he didn't ink that tat, then he may at least know who did. These tattoo artists can recognize each other's work. It's a good place to start."

CJ studied him with unabashed admiration. "You know what, John Jarad? That's not half bad. But do me a favor. Take Ted with you when you go."

"Why would I do that?"

"Because Ted's on deck, my shift officially ended four hours ago, and your budget can't afford more overtime." She yawned hugely. "Besides, Ted and Billy are old fishing buddies. You'll get more information out of Billy, if you take Ted with you, instead of me."

"That sounds like pretty sage advice, Detective Allamand."

"I know it does." CJ grinned crookedly. "It's so sage, you probably won't take it."

CHAPTER FOUR

John was glad he had insisted on driving. In the past, whenever he had worked closely with Ted, he had sensed an undercurrent of disapproval wafting off the guy that always seemed to lead them into a strained and uncomfortable silence. It didn't help matters that John could easily remember repeated instances of Ted whispering "college boy" behind his back when John had first joined the force. That grudge still rankled, but at least the act of driving removed some of the constraint by giving John something active to do.

The cruiser was traveling west on Madaket Road, about to cross the Long Pond bridge. Ted had one hand out the window, playing with the breeze blowing inland off the salt marsh. He flicked a finger toward Long Pond. "Saw the biggest turtle I ever saw in my life right there, sir. Crissakes! Size of a diesel tire. Just swam up out of the mud. I ran and got my dad. He grabbed his .22, but the turtle was gone by the time we got back. Never saw it again. Can't imagine where it got to. Gave me turtle nightmares for a month." He chuckled. "Gram told us to kill it and bring it home, and she'd make a pot of turtle soup. By God, she was a tough one. That friggin' turtle was bigger than she was." He cleared his throat. "Excuse my French."

"I'm learning all kinds of things about you today, Sergeant. So, Madaket is home?"

"Near enough." Ted pointed vaguely south. "Grew up on Hither Creek. Great place to grow up, too, a great place. A whole pack of us kids running wild as red Indians all summer long. We never came in for lunch, neither, just built a fire and grilled a mess of blue right there on the shingle." He snapped his fingers. "This one time, Otis' sister Ruthie brought a sack of peanut butter sandwiches. We looked at her like she was nuts. Why eat peanut butter, when you could eat fresh grilled blue instead?"

"I'm with you on that one. There's nothing better, with a couple of cold beers to wash it down."

"Yes, sir. Beer-thirty is my favorite time of day." Ted studied the surrounding marshland. "Some of this has changed since we were kids, but by God, not much. Of course, they built that godawful Landing back in the sixties. My dad almost popped a cork over that one. I was afraid all of this was going to change by the time I got back from my tour, but thank God someone had the nuts to fight the developers. I'd hate to see them pave this marsh the way they did the Haulover breach." He scratched his chin. "Why do people have to fuck with everything? Why can't they leave well enough alone?"

Recognizing the rhetorical nature of Ted's questions, John maintained his silence. He scanned the meadow of marsh grass that lipped the road. This end of the island had no firm shoreline to it, only the raised roadbed and the acres of gray-green grass that rustled over pools of brackish water. John quickly turned the wheel to avoid a stunningly deep pothole. The cruiser swayed in response. "I'm against over-development as much as the next man, but maybe we could ask the County to fix the road?"

Ted brayed a laugh. "You'd be surprised, Lieutenant. Folks in Madaket want to keep the road this way. Potholes keep the tourists in town, where they belong." His fingers beat a jittery tattoo against the door. "I can remember the day Billy got tagged. Old Chief Rawlins tagged him proper, too."

"That was before my time. What did Chief Rawlins tag Billy for?"

"Insurance fraud, plus theft of marine property. Billy got sentenced seven to ten. He was out in two and a half for good behavior."

"Where did we send him?"

"MCI-Norfolk, medium security." Ted settled back. "Billy still swears he never meant to do it, but I'm not so sure. I mean, he had to know what he was doing, right? At some point you have to know when you're stepping over the line."

"What did Billy say?"

"He says one thing led to another. See, first Billy bought a gray boat at an abandoned boat auction. It was a hulk, a real mess. I think it set him back fifty, maybe a hundred bucks? Then he went around telling everyone he was going to restore it, you know, fix it up. The boat came with a clear title, and that's what made the auction so important, because with Billy's name on the title and the title clear with the Commonwealth, that lined everything up, and made it legit."

"I'm with you so far."

"Okay. So Billy goes to work on this hulk on weekends and on days, you know, when the weather's foul and he can't go fishing or tend his garden. And that's when Billy's luck heads south because one day, the insurance adjuster stops by, and she notices that Billy's got two boats going in his shed, and that both boats share the same hull ID number, plus the new boat matches the description of a boat that just got boosted out of Glouchester harbor. She figures that Billy stole the new boat, and then copied the HIN off the old one, so he could register the stolen boat in his name, which technically it already was, since the HIN on the stolen boat matched the registration with the clear title. All Billy had to do next was to junk the old boat, and sail away."

"That's pretty clever."

"Clever enough to earn Billy a prison jacket, and that's where his luck really headed south because the Commonwealth had just gotten strict over that kind of thing. They made insurance fraud a Class I felony. Billy Bear was their first felony candidate. Ding, ding. We had a winner."

"Ouch." John winced. "Billy's never been in trouble since, has he?"

"Not even a DUI. I tell you what, that one tag scared him straight. Besides, Billy has a kid to take care of now, a son, Ozzie. His ex-wife split as soon as Billy got out of prison. She left Oz behind. Billy loves that kid more than anything." Ted paused to scan a solitary house built high on pilings in the center of the marsh. "Funny thing, though. It turns out that MCI-Norfolk wasn't all that bad of a place for Billy. They offered some kind of half-assed liberal arts program. The teacher there recognized that Billy had real talent. He does. I've seen it. He can draw like Michael Angelo. So after he gets out, Billy moves himself and Oz to Kansas City to earn a degree in dermographic art, and Lieutenant, that's what they call it, too, sir: Dermographic Art with a capital *A*. Billy is a tat artist, and his place is called a studio. Don't call it a tattoo parlor or you'll really piss him off."

"Thanks for the heads-up. That's good to know."

A boulder painted with the number 12 stood at the end of a weedy, overgrown lane. John turned in. The cruiser bounced down a hummocky driveway desperately in need of a fresh layer of crushed shell topcoat. The driveway opened into a narrow mowed lot. Ted pointed toward a street legal Kawasaki motorcycle.

"Pull in next to the rice-burner, Lieutenant. Mind the ditch. It surprises some people."

"Thank you, Sergeant. I see it."

A picket fence separated the lot from a marshy ditch filled with peeping frogs, bushy scotch broom, and cattails. Tucking the manila folder filled with Paul's photographs under his arm, John left the car, closing the door softly out of long and cautious habit. As he surveyed Billy's farmstead, his orderly mind was delighted with what he saw. Billy had been busy. He had cleared more than an acre of scrub and planted a vegetable garden that even included grapevines and a row of young fruit trees. A faded red barn still stood on the highest point of land although the barn's siding was so warped out of true that you could see into the barn through the chinks in its planked walls. What surprised him most of all was the state-of-the-art solar grid panel mounted on the barn's roof.

Ted paused with his hand on the gate. "You do know Billy's gone seriously green, right, sir? He even made Island Electric come out and rip out any lines that crossed his property. He's also the one who led the harbor breach protest last summer."

"I remember that event, Sergeant. I'm the one who signed the original parade permit."

Ted grinned. "Still taking heat for that, sir?"

"Nothing I can't handle." John noticed that, for the first time that day, Ted's smile had actually reached his eyes. Was that sympathy he saw there? If it was, it would be a first. As Ted fiddled with the lock, John turned to read the plywood sign tacked up next to the fence:

Studio Hours: Usually 1PM to 6PM.
Tuesday thru Sunday (Hours may vary)
No parcel deliveries before 1PM! I mean it!
Homeland Security provided by Smith & Wesson.
Must present photo ID to be tattooed or pierced.
No children under age 16 permitted in studio AT ANY TIME.
If you're drunk or high, come back later. I won't touch you now.
All food must be eaten outside and Yes, this includes your fucking latte.
Absolutely NO smoking! Cigarettes = Cancer.
These rules are simple and must be followed.
NO EXCEPTIONS!
!!!!!!!!

"Hear that sound, Lieutenant?" Ted cocked his head to listen to a persistent buzzing. "ZzzZZZZzzzz, ZZZzzz? We're in luck. Billy's working on someone." He opened the gate but before they could step through it, an enormous wolfhound ambled out of the barn. Seeing them, the wire-haired dog stopped short and took two stiff-legged steps forward. The coarse hair along its spine began to stiffen, and the dog began to emit a menacing growl. Ted very carefully latched the gate as John unsnapped his holster.

"Hold up a minute, Lieutenant. That dog is new." Cupping both hands, he shouted. "Billy! Hey, Billy! C'mon, man. Call off the dog."

The buzzing abruptly stopped, and a shadow appeared behind the studio's screened door. The door was batted open. Billy Bear stood framed in the doorway, his hands encased in black latex gloves. John was momentarily startled until he realized Billy held a tattooing gun in his left hand. He let his own hand drop to his side.

"Tyson!" Billy commanded. "Stand down."

Whining a soft protest, the wolfhound settled back on its haunches.

"Ted? Something wrong? It's not Ozzie, is it?"

John stepped forward. "Nothing's wrong, Mr. Bear, but we would like to ask you some questions."

"Can't it wait? I'm with a client."

"No, sir. I'm afraid not. It won't take long, but we would like ten minutes."

"Let me check." Billy spoke over his shoulder to his unseen client. "Charlie, the cops are here to ask me some questions, whatever the fuck that's supposed to mean. Do you mind company?"

"Doesn't bother me, Billy. I'm riding clean."

"Come on in." Billy propped the screened door open with his hip. "If it doesn't bother Charlie, it won't bother me."

* * * * * * *

"Hey, Ted. Take a seat." Billy gestured toward a pair of worn oak chairs. "You know the drill. Make yourselves comfortable. I'm almost done, then I'll be right with you."

Ted felt more than a little guilty. He hadn't seen Billy since the last great bluefish run back in November. He was glad to see that his friend had held up through the winter, although he knew that Billy was pushing the wrong side of forty the same way he was. Billy had always stood half a head taller, and he was built more on the slender side, but Ted noticed that Billy was beginning to show a bit of a belly that he was doing his best to hide by letting his Led Zeppelin T-shirt hang outside the waistband of his jeans. Billy's cobwebby hair was pulled back into a braid as usual, and his eyes were lined with deep crows' feet wrinkles that suggested that Billy had pretty much seen everything the world had to offer, and he wasn't particularly impressed with much of it.

"Tyson?" Ted asked.

"He's big, he's bad, and you don't want to mess with him."

"He's new."

"He is. I've chased off some odd trespassers lately."

Billy set the tat gun down and reached over to lower the volume on his CD player, realizing, too late, that he had just contaminated his gloves. Disgusted, he stripped the gloves off and tossed them in the hazardous waste bin.

"Bonehead," he muttered. "I hate when I do that. These gloves aren't recyclable, but there the best ones on the market. You gotta keep an eye on that Hepatitus C. It is some seriously wicked shit. There's no vaccine for it, yet."

Ted stepped aside to let the lieutenant move forward into the room. "Billy? You remember Lieutenant Jarad?"

"Actually, we met last summer, Mr. Bear. At the harbor parade."

"Ah, yes, the harbor *protest*," Billy corrected. "I do remember you, Lieutenant Jarad. Only, weren't you Sergeant Jarad then? Congratulations on the promotion. I'm sure it was well deserved. Sorry you ended up swimming in the Sound. I can promise you that wasn't our original intention. We were targeting the Feds, but someone must've got over-enthusiastic when they saw the uniform."

"No harm, no foul."

Ted faked a cough to hide his grin behind his fist. He was surprised to hear the lieutenant sound so reasonable under Billy's needling, especially when you considered the amount of guff he still took from the force over that particular swim. Maybe he needed to give the guy some credit for holding his temper. The lieutenant then nodded to Billy's client who was stretched out on a vinyl chair that looked very much like the one you'd find in a dentist's office.

"How're you doing, Charlie?"

"Hey, Lieutenant Jarad. I'm good." The extremely tan kid laughed nervously. "Thanks for letting Billy finish me up. I only get an hour for lunch. We're trying to finish this sleeve before my parents get back from Mykonos." He displayed an elaborate tattoo running the length of his right arm. "They can't fight what's already done, right?"

"No one can stop you, as long as you're of age. You are eighteen, right?"

Billy glanced up sharply. "I ID all my clients before I start any work, Lieutenant."

"I'm sure you do. I saw your sign. So, Charlie? I hear you're working for TB May this summer. Did you get your carpenter's union card?"

"Whatever it takes to get the work, you know how that goes, Lieutenant Jarad. I'm a paid-up hammerhead now." He tapped a piece of wrinkled graph paper laid out on the table. "That's why I picked out this design."

The lieutenant rotated the graph paper with his fingertips and shared the improved angle. Ted noted a crudely drawn hammerhead shark swimming through a school of vaguely tropical fish. When he compared the sketch in front of him to the full-blown tattoo developing along the kid's arm, he felt a warm flush of jealousy. This tattoo was art with a capital *A*. His own service tat paled in comparison because Billy's tat work was three-dimensional and stunning.

"That's some design." The lieutenant admitted. "How much does a tattoo like that cost?"

Billy tugged a fresh pair of gloves from a cardboard box. "I can usually work out a payment plan for something this elaborate. A sleeve like Charlie's can run to a thousand bucks before it's done." Billy smoothed the latex across his knuckles. "At least Charlie knew what he wanted. That helps. Some clients have no idea what they want, or they bring in something they picked up off the street. One guy I know brought in a tribal he pulled off a dry cleaning bag he found in Hyannis."

"What's a tribal?" the Lieutenant asked. "Does it have something to do with gangs?"

"Not that I'm aware of." Tearing open a foiled packet, Billy swabbed Charlie's arm. "A tribal is a tat with one color, usually solid black. There's no shading involved." He stretched the skin on Charlie's arm with his thumb. "See how I'm laying the color in around the fins on this shark right now? That's shading. A tribal is flat black." He flipped a switch and the nervous buzzing began again. Ducking his head, Billy got back to work.

Ted rubbed his forearm and recalled the first time he had met the needle in Hamburg during leave. That tat had almost cost him an arm when the dirty needle had pushed a staph infection under his skin. His CO had even offered to cut the tat out of his hide without an anesthetic since tats were not in keeping with the tradition of the Corps. Ted had politely thanked the man and declined the offer. Even so, Ted had admired the guy enough to add his initials to the tat later when the CO caught a sniper round while on patrol in Kuwait City.

Luckily enough, Chief Brock had understood the importance of that respectful gesture when it came time to land a civilian job, because the chief had grandfathered Ted's tat in when he had joined the Nantucket force. Since then, though, Ted had been repeatedly warned that fresh ink was strictly forbidden. Ted didn't know if that fascist policy had come from the Council or if it had come from the new lieutenant, but it sure sounded like something the new lieutenant would cook up. He was one stiff little prick.

Speaking of the lieutenant, Ted turned to see what the guy was up to now. Usually, the lieutenant couldn't sit still for five minutes without getting into some new kind of busy-ness. The guy would be hell to live with if he was ever confined to a boat. True, Ted had to admit it really wasn't the lieutenant's fault. He was a Jarad, after all, and that family was famous for its twitch gene. Not one of them knew how to relax, and the lieutenant was no exception. Case in point. Even now the guy was at it again, flipping through the owner's manual for an EagleAlert scanner on the desk by the door. The guy was so intent on figuring the scanner out that he didn't realize he kept bumping a stack of discarded packaging material in the recycle bin. If that bin tipped, it would fling green Styrofoam peanuts across the studio floor. Neat freak that he was, Billy would just love that. It might even be worthwhile to see it happen but no, Ted admitted, he was an officer of the peace. He needed to do what he could to honor that charge.

He was about to warn the lieutenant about the potential for disaster when the monitor next to the scanner flashed an image of a shapely mermaid that caught Ted's eye. True, she was a little more than naturally ample, but he supposed that being a mermaid probably helped her in the buoyancy department. The image of that sexy tat was replaced by one of a ravening Doberman chained between two flaming skulls. Thankfully, this tat also caught the lieutenant's eye, and he found something in it to occupy his busy little badger mind. He finally put the manual down and stepped back to admire the slideshow, too.

"That's certainly impressive."

"Ozzie put that together." Billy smiled proudly. "It's a slideshow of all my tats. He's a smart kid."

"Takes after his dad," Ted said.

"Don't I wish." Billy gave a mock salute. "Kid's better than I'll ever be."

The lieutenant idled over now to watch poor Charlie stuck in the chair. He watched Billy use a dry paper towel to blot the excess ink running down the kid's arm.

"Doesn't that hurt?"

"Outlining's a bitch," Charlie confessed. "Shading doesn't hurt so much. It feels more like a massage."

"Don't shrug." Billy leaned back on his stool. "I'd hate to make a mistake, but you'd hate it more." Never losing his focus, Billy ducked back down, intent as a bird of prey. "I've never heard that it felt like a massage before but Charlie might be right. You do get an endorphin high with every tattoo. By the end of the day, when we're done, Charlie will feel like he drank a twelve-pack, all by himself." He blotted another long drip. "Pain does three things, Lieutenant. One, it raises your blood pressure. Two, it raises your heart rate, and three, it raises your body temperature. In short, it turns you on. I've even had some clients say they feel more alive after one of my tats and you know what? I believe them."

"Some of your clients come back for more than one tattoo?"

"Get one of my tats and you'll never look back. I have a book of repeat customers. Some clients say my tats help them connect more to life because with a tat you're creating a reminder of one particular moment in your life, a memory of that one special time or a special group of people, or that one special lover. Take Charlie here. I'll bet he remembers this moment for the rest of his life."

"You bet I will, because right now, it hurts like hell!"

"Easy there, hoss. We're almost done." Billy studied the design spreading out beneath his fingers. He lifted the tat gun again, and raised his voice over the electric buzzing. "I've even heard some people get addicted to the pain because of the endorphin high. And why not? You can get addicted to pain, like anything else." Finishing the border, Billy switched the gun off and placed it on the table. "Okay, Charlie. That's enough for today. Come back on Tuesday. We'll finish her up."

Charlie sat up quickly. He admired his tattoo in a mirror. "That looks wicked awesome, Billy. Hey, do you have any more of that ointment? I'm out."

"Glad to see you're using it." Billy retrieved a tube from a cubbyhole. He tossed it to the kid. "Best thing you could do for yourself. Remember to keep the tat moist and, oh yeah, I'll need to see another fifty, before you go."

"Got it right here." Hopping in place, Charlie struggled to remove his wallet from his right hip pocket using his left hand. "I'm so pumped we're almost done!"

The lieutenant frowned. "Shouldn't you put a bandage on that?"

"You only need a bandage if you go to a butcher," Billy said. "I'm an artist, Lieutenant. If you go to a tat artist, and the tat's done properly, you shouldn't even bleed."

"Here you go, Billy." Charlie handed across two crumpled twenties and a ten. "Thanks again, man. See you on Tuesday."

"Let me know if anything changes." Billy held the screened door open as Charlie sprinted for his bike before he laughed softly. "He'll be sleeping on his side for the next couple of days." Folding the bills neatly, Billy pocketed the money. He began to tidy up his workstation, spritzing the chair and the surrounding area. The scent of chlorine bleach clouded the air. "I'll give you credit for patience, Lieutenant. What can I do for the Nantucket police?"

* * * * * * *

John pulled the set of crime site photographs from the envelope. He found the one he wanted and held it out. "Is this tattoo a tribal, like the one you mentioned?"

Billy studied the photograph carefully. "Before I answer you, Lieutenant, I think I need to know why you're asking. Tattoos are personal. Some of my clients prefer to keep them private. I need to respect that."

"Fair enough." John lowered the envelope to the tabletop while he decided how much information he could share. Most of the crime site details would eventually get reported in the *Inky Mirror*, but he didn't want to give anything away too soon. Still, he needed to tell Billy something to earn his trust. He decided to start with a high-level fly-by and see where that got him. "We discovered a woman's body in Satan's Tub this morning. She had no ID on her other than that tattoo. I'm hoping you can help us ID it since that tattoo might give us a line on who she is. Then we can return her to her people. Someone, somewhere, is missing her."

Billy retreated to his workstation, flicking the photograph with his fingers. Setting the photograph down, he opened a bottle of mineral water and swished it through his teeth, nodding slowly as he made his decision. "I heard something about that this morning at the Java Hut. They were saying she was murdered. Is that true?"

John silently cursed the hyper-efficient island grapevine he constantly struggled against. Nantucket was such a tight-knit community it took virtually no time at all for any titillating bit of news to make the rounds, and the gossip generally got more lurid as it went. "That is still being determined."

"Was it The Whistler? Did he do this? Is that what you cops think?"

"Billy." Ted stepped forward. "If you can help us catch the prick who did this, you need to say so, straight out. Can you ID that tat for us or not?"

Billy snatched the photograph back up. He marched to the desk, flipping the PC monitor off along the way. "Let's try to save some energy wherever we can." The slideshow winked to a bright pinpoint of light as Billy lifted a fat album. He started rapidly flipping through its pages. He stopped near the middle, and matched the image there to the photograph he held in his hand. "What you have is a triquetra. It's an ancient symbol found in many of the world's cultures. The early Christians appropriated it to symbolize their Trinity, but most scholars agree that the triquetra actually predates Christianity. It may have represented the triple Goddess to the Celtic cultures, or even Odin, but there's no way to know that for sure."

"What do you mean when you say Celtic cultures?" John asked. "The victim might be Irish?"

"I wouldn't go that far, Lieutenant. Like I said, the triquetra is universal." Billy flipped the album open to another page. "See? Here's the Navajo version, and this one's Mesopotamian. The design is more than five thousand years old." He paused at the blatting sound of an approaching motorcycle. Tyson began to bark. The dog's warning pitch turned to an eager whine, and then to a series of happy yelps. Billy frowned as the screened door burst open to admit a rangy teenager carrying a chrome motorcycle helmet shaped like a skull.

"Dad?" Ozzie wondered, breathless. "What's going on? Why are the cops here?"

"Take it easy, Oz. You remember Ted Parsons? This is his boss, Lieutenant Jarad. They're here to ask me about this tattoo."

"What about it?" Ozzie dropped the helmet to the floor. He pulled up a stool and sat down. Ozzie had shaggy brown bangs that kept falling into his eyes. He bristled with concern. "What do they want to know?"

Billy tapped the album. "They were asking me about this design-"

"Sure," Ozzie offered. "It's the tribal-"

"And I told them it's a triquetra, but it's not my work."

Ozzie dropped his eyes to the floor. "No way. That tat is way too crude for you."

"Honestly, Lieutenant," Billy volunteered. "That tat could have been done by anyone with a gun. I can tell you it was done professionally, and not by a kid with a pin. See how refined the edges are? You'll only get that level of definition with a top drawer gun and a steady hand. That tat did not come from an amateur. That's pretty much all I can tell you."

"You could probably even pull that design off the Internet," Ozzie said. "It's not that rare."

"Oz? Go take care of Tyson. He's ready for his dinner."

"What? Okay, Dad."

"Alright." John stood. "We'll search the Internet and see what we can find. Something there might point us in the right direction. If you think of anything more, Billy, give us a call. Either way, we'll be in touch."

"Will do." Billy passed the photograph over. He held the screened door open. "Sorry I couldn't be more help."

John led the way as they trudged passed the barn in silence. Ted leaned against the passenger side of the cruiser. He rested his arms across the roof, tapping it repeatedly while he cleared his throat. "I'm not happy about this at all, sir. I've known Billy all my life. I'd swear that he is lying to us."

"Let's take it easy on him. We hit Billy with a lot. Let's give him a day to think it through. I'd prefer that the next time, he came to us."

"You know he inked that tat, sir." Ted thumped the roof to emphasize his point. "You know that tat was one of his."

"I do know that because I saw it listed in Ozzie's slideshow before Billy turned it off." John squinted into the sun, a shimmering orange globe half-hidden behind the trees. "I also noticed that Billy bought a brand-new scanner this morning. The packing slip was still in his recycle bin. Why would Billy Bear the tattoo artist suddenly take such an interest in overhearing police transmissions? Got any ideas about that?"

Ted turned his head. He studied the studio door. "Sonofabitch."

****

Ozzie watched the two cops leave, hiding in the shadows of the barn. A trickle of sweat traced a line down his spine like a ghoulish finger. He pulled his T-shirt free from his skin and exhaled. At least the cops hadn't been here asking about him and his friends and the wicked great trick they were playing on island developers by moving surveyor's stakes during the night. That awesome bit of sabotage was getting blamed on townie kids up to no good. But the cops had been here to talk to Dad, and the thought of Dad in trouble again tightened Ozzie's chest to the point he couldn't breathe. Dad had sworn that he would never do anything that might get him sent back to prison and yet here they were, cops with questions, and inside Dad's studio, when he had tried to help out, Dad had shut him down. What the fuck was going on?

"Oz?" Dad had followed him outside. He stood in the sun, holding up a hand to shade his eyes from the glare. "Son? I know you're there. Could you come back inside? We need to talk, Oz. It's important."

"Sure. I guess." Ozzie slipped between two loose boards. He followed Dad inside. Not knowing where to start, he just did. "Dad? You know that tribal was one of yours. You won first prize for it at the Meeting of the Marked." Lifting the remote, he switched the monitor on and flicked rapidly through the slideshow. "October 31, 2007. Fan choice, first prize. What? You think the cops won't find out about that? What are you, stupid?"

"Please don't talk to me like that, Oz. I need your help."

Dad opened a desk drawer and hid the album in it before selecting a three-tiered trophy off the shelf. He tried stuffing that sideways into the drawer, too. Oz felt rattled. Dad was usually so smart. What he was trying to do now defied geometry. It was futile, and ridiculous.

"I need you to remove any traces of that tat that might lead the cops to me. Delete it off your slideshow and ... shit! Did you load the image to our website?"

"I think I only loaded color gifs, but I'll have to check to make sure. But Dad, if the tat's loaded on the convention's web site we're hosed! I can't pull it off someone else's FTP. When the cops do an image search, they'll find it, easy." He clutched his father's arm. "What's going on?"

Dad sighed, and smoothed his hair. "You're right. You deserve an explanation. I've never made a secret of the fact I've been to prison, Oz. Prison is my jacket, and I accept that because that's the way the shit broke. A man makes his decisions and he takes his licks. But I learned something in prison, and that's to never trust a cop. Don't do it, son, because if they have to choose you will lose, I guarantee it. So, another part of my jacket is that I'm not a rat. I'm not going to give something up to the cops just because they ask me to bend over and take it nicely."

"But Ted Parsons is your friend! You guys drink beer together!"

"But Ted is still a cop. Use your God-given intelligence for one minute, Oz, and think: what if the cops are wrong? They don't know what's going on any more than we do. They're just nosing around, and guessing."

"So why were they asking you about that tat?"

"Because they found it on the body of a dead girl this morning."

It took Oz a moment to process what Dad had said. A dead girl? "What the fuck?"

"Okay, Oz, listen. What if, say, what if that girl died from an overdose or something and someone panicked and hid her body? You hear about shit like that happening all the time."

Oz felt time stand still. "Dad? Is that what happened to her?"

"I can't tell you anything right now, son. No, Oz, no, I swear, I need to check one thing and then I'll tell you everything I know. But here's the important thing, Oz. Not telling the cops what I know is my choice, but it doesn't have to be yours. You're seventeen, you're a man now, and you need to make up your own mind about what you're going to do because that's the jacket you're going to have to live with for the rest of your life. I promise I won't be pissed at whatever you decide to do, but Oz, I need to know if you're going to tell the cops about that tat because I need to figure out the best way to protect you."

"Protect me? Protect me from what?"

"I can't tell you that, either. I know! I know! Oz, wait! Listen, let me make one call and we'll know where we stand. But first, before I do, I need to know what you're gonna do."

"I …" Ozzie felt light-headed. Dad had never spoken to him so directly before, like he was an equal, as an adult. "I'm going help you, Dad. Tell me what you want me to do."

"Thank you, Oz." Dad rubbed his eyes. "Don't worry, son. We'll get through this. We always do. You just need to hang tight for a little while, okay? Now, get out of here. I need to make a call."

Ozzie hit the screened door so hard it slapped back into its frame. He didn't know what to think. Sure, Dad had been in prison. That was no secret like Dad said, but Dad also said that if you were going to change the system, you needed to change it from within. That's why Oz had never mentioned his crew and their midnight mischief. Now, here was Dad hiding information about a dead girl from the cops! How did that fit into changing the system from within? It was so messed up that Oz didn't even know what to think.

He dropped to the stoop as Tyson loped up. The big ugly dog licked the side of Ozzie's face with his sandpaper tongue. "Oh, fuck, Tyson. Yuck. That's disgusting." Oz threw his arms around Tyson's neck. He buried his face in the dog's wiry hair. Oz could hear his father's voice carrying through the studio walls. He had no idea who his dad was talking to, but he could overhear every word of Dad's side of the conversation.

"Hey, it's me. About time you answered your phone! You know they found the girl in Satan's Tub? Fuck no, I'm not overreacting! Are you shittin' me? You said she overdosed. In town, they're calling it murder."

Murder? Ozzie stopped breathing. In the sudden awful silence, the blood roared in his ears.

"Because she has your tattoo on her, that's why! I don't believe in coincidence and neither will they. I know that wasn't mentioned in the paper, but the cops were here, and they sure as shit mentioned it to me now."

There was a lengthy pause. "Listen, that's enough out of you. I need to see your face. I need to see your eyes. No, I can't, I've got another client coming. I just said I can't. Fine. What time tomorrow? Seven? Alright. I'll meet you in the Tap Room tomorrow at seven. Make sure you're there. Now, what about Kurt? What's his take on things?"

There was an even lengthier period of silence. For a moment, Ozzie thought that Dad had hung up the phone until Dad spoke again, and this time Dad's voice carried such a threatening tone in it that gooseflesh scrabbled across Ozzie's arms.

"Don't play games with me, you manipulative bitch. I don't give a shit if Kurt's in Hyannis, you go find him. You're supposed to be his keeper. Listen! You'd better warn Kurt about this shit because if this goes deep, I will give him up to the cops. Don't think I won't. I am not going to prison for Kurt Stockton. Did I make that clear enough for you? What's it gonna be?"

CHAPTER FIVE

Sarah Hawthorne clutched the steel railing, feeling more than a little nervous. True, she had taken *The Good Ship Lollipop* to a Steelers game back in Pittsburgh plenty of times, and *The Eagle* was certainly a big enough ship for a ferry, but Sarah had never been out of the sight of land before. She assumed the purple smudge on the horizon was Nantucket, but everywhere else she looked, all she could see was the turquoise sky darkening to an azure horizon and then the rolling, ultramarine sea.

In spite of her unspoken fear, she found the ferry ride to be as easy as pie. The steel deck swayed like an easy rocking chair, and the warm May breeze kept tickling her ears. The ferry made a swishing sound like a giant washing machine as it sliced through the waves, and its long, trailing wake sparkled pure white the way a bride was supposed to. As she stared into the water, Sarah felt the tension ease off her shoulders. Each watery mile carried her further away from the life she had known back in the 'Burgh. It felt great to get away. If Mason really wanted to find her now, he would have no idea of where to look.

She snorted, dismayed by her profound new negativity. She liked to think of herself as a positive and outgoing person, but lately, somehow, all of that had changed, and not for the better. For more than a year, she had been living her life under what felt like a soggy brown blanket. She felt constricted, purposeless, lost. Now, she was moving her whole life to Nantucket, determined to make a fresh start. The past was done with. It was time to move on.

Turning her back on the rising sun, she pulled out her cellphone and cradled the Sidekick in her hand. Who would ever guess that a cell phone could keep you connected to so much sorrow? It was the last link to her old life. Sarah tossed it over the rail, watching it tumble thirty feet until it slid into a wave without a splash. Her heart started racing. She felt frightened and exhilarated at the same time. *Is this what freedom feels like?* There was no one left she needed to call. She was finally alone.

She settled into a chilly steel chair behind a windscreen of painted pipes. After Mason's latest incomprehensible outburst, she had filled her beloved beater Cavalier with everything she owned and she had driven eleven hours straight to Grand Pap's farm in Vermont, only to have Mason track her down and show up there, unannounced. It had been an ugly, hate-filled scene. Sarah shuddered to remember it. Mason had threatened to kill her if Sarah didn't get into his car and return with him to Pittsburgh right then and there. Grand Pap, a Korean War veteran and no slacker when it came to recognizing a genuine threat, had pulled out the shotgun he normally reserved for snakes. He had run Mason off with one look. Sarah had thought she would never sleep again, but she must have dozed that night because Grand Pap woke her up in the middle of it to tell her to quickly pack her things; he was driving her to Vernon to catch the Boston bus. Sarah knew this was a true sacrifice on Grand Pap's part because he never, but never left his dairy herd unattended.

Groggy and confused, all she could see on the way to the bus depot was the back country lane bracketed by the truck's dim headlights. Sarah had listened carefully as Grand Pap directed her to continue on from Boston to a town called Hyannis. There, she could catch a ferry to another place called Nantucket, an island some thirty miles to sea. Grand Pap said they were always looking for good summer help on Nantucket, and she could find a job and escape from Mason all at the same time. As frightened as Sarah was, it had sounded like a plan.

A Craigslist posting had helped her land a barmaid's job at Cap'n Clancey's Clam Shack and Tap Room, a local watering hole. Sarah had taken the job sight unseen in spite of its minimum wage because the job came with room and board, which she had learned on overbooked Nantucket was key. She also learned that Nantucket was home to a thriving East Coast arts community. For the first time in what felt like months, she felt an unfamiliar flicker of hope. *Perhaps this new audience might be more receptive to her artwork?* It had been so long since Sarah had trusted in hope that she wasn't even sure she still could, but she was willing to give it a try and that tiny, tiny baby step alone was something refreshingly new.

Tucking her hands into her hoodie pocket for warmth, she studied her fellow passengers braving the air on the open deck below her. A middle-aged mom kept checking the shopping bags at her feet while her two girls played a shrieking game of tag between the rows of bolted steel chairs. Three teenagers were smoking some cheeb behind a canvas-strapped lifeboat while a nervous friend posted a nervous lookout by an oval steel door. Alone at the stern, an older man leaned against the railing. Although he looked a little short for her taste from this angle, he was undeniably attractive. He had a bag with a Greenbok's Artist Supply logo on it slung over one shoulder, and he looked vaguely familiar. *Was he someone famous?*

Should she know who he was? The ferry began a slow turn and the changing breeze ruffled his rather long, sable hair. Sarah felt a pang of recognition and then a blush of shame. Of course he looked familiar. From this angle he sort of looked like her dad.

The man turned his back on the ocean. He pulled a sheet of paper from his jacket. Holding the paper stiffly in both hands, he began to tear it into thin strips, releasing each strip to catch the breeze. The strips fluttered across the deck like confetti before drifting into the water on the other side. Sarah scowled. *Litterbug.* She despised people who disrespected the environment.

The teenage lookout jumped a foot in the air as the steel door clanked and a blonde woman stepped on deck. She was wearing a fabulous tangerine mohair coat. She lowered her oversized Jackie-O sunglasses as she strolled toward the man like a predatory jungle cat.

"Hello, darling. I see you got my note."

Darling grabbed the woman by the arm. He pulled her into an alcove directly beneath Sarah's feet. She felt trapped by their redirection and flinched at their sudden physicality. *Should she let them know she was there?* By the time she made up her mind to cough, it was too late to act without appearing stupidly obvious. Sarah hated feeling conspicuous. It was her pet peeve. Shrinking deeper into her hoodie, she curled up and remained silent.

"Dammit, Sally! What were you thinking, leaving a note like that on my car? Anyone could have seen it."

"What else did you want me to do, Kurt? You weren't returning my calls. It's lucky I knew where you usually like to park. Darling, what have you done to your hand?"

"It's nothing."

"It doesn't look like nothing. Have you seen a doctor?"

"I don't need to see a doctor. I slammed it in the trunk when I was unpacking, that's all. Looks worse than it is."

"You should be more careful. Your right hand, too! How are you going to paint?"

"Stop fussing, woman. I can still hold a brush."

"Fine. What were you doing in Hyannis, anyway? Enjoying another illicit rendezvous? Does Melissa know what you've been up to?"

"Leave Melissa out of this. Dammit, Sally, cut the crap. You told me to meet you on the ferry and here I am. What do you want?"

"It's easy enough. You've heard that Katie's resurfaced? That's why I wanted to see you, to ask what we're going to do about it."

"What do you mean 'what are we going to do about it'? I don't see that we have to do anything. Let the police take care of that. It's their job."

"True, but sooner or later they're going to snoop around and ask questions."

"Let them. I didn't do anything wrong."

Sally's laughter was musical. "You really don't remember what happened, do you?"

"What is it that I'm supposed to remember this time?"

"Oh, darling, never mind. I'll take care of things like I always do. I just wanted to make sure we're on the same page. You can trust me, Kurt. I'll always look out for you, but this one might be a little tricky. It may take some finesse."

"Trust you? Ha! Like I ever have a choice."

"We all have choices, Kurt. For instance, I saw that new painting of yours down at the Arts Guild. '*Chasing Rainbows*' is very nice. I need to add it to my collection."

"You go to hell! That piece is worth forty thousand, easy. It took me most of the winter!"

"I'm not going to fight over it, darling. How about this? You give me that painting, and I'll take care of the Katie situation. Do we have a deal?"

"Fuck you."

Sally laughed again. "But darling, you already have. Or don't you remember that, either? I have to say that's not very flattering. I like to think I'm at least memorable." Stepping out of the alcove, Sally strolled toward the door, smoothing her gloves. "You really should cut down on the booze, Kurt. It's hell on the memory, not to mention performance. But then, you'd know all about that, wouldn't you?"

"Bitch! Someone should do the world a favor and strangle you."

"I might like that." Sally paused. "Did you bring your sale book with you? Why don't we go down to your car and take care of the transfer now? You won't even have to crate it; I'll have it delivered straight to my house. How easy is that?"

"Sally, you know that I despise you, right? I seriously, seriously despise you."

"Don't be so dramatic. If you're going to keep playing with young girls, sooner or later, you're going to get toasted. You're lucky I'm here to put their little fires out. Come on. Let's take care of business. I need to get back to my car. I'm first in line. You know the rule: first in, first out."

Kurt yanked the steel door open and the couple disappeared inside. Sarah deflated. She found herself feeling surprisingly dejected. Maybe she was naïve, but she had hoped that Nantucket would somehow be different, somehow be a better place than the one she had left behind. Evidently, Nantucket was just like everywhere else. She wasn't even off the boat yet, and she had already discovered a man cheating on his wife, and a woman blackmailing him over his adultery. She knew it was childish, but she felt cheated. Was the honeymoon with her new life over so soon?

An overhead air horn released a blast so tremendous it rattled the fillings in her teeth. Looking up, she realized the ferry was entering the harbor. As Nantucket unfolded before her eyes, Sarah fell in love. The island was even more charming than she had hoped it would be. Of course, she had Googled Nantucket on the bus ride down but the images hadn't captured the scale of the place or the fact that the whole town was monochromatic. Every building she saw was a slightly different shade of gray. As *The Eagle* cruised by a stubby lighthouse stuck all by itself on a spit of land, a pod of children dropped their sand pails to wave. The cottages on her left were built on stilts, their decks littered with beach toys and striped towels hung over the railings to dry. Distant churches pointed white steeples at the cerulean sky. Sarah breathed it all in. She had made it to Nantucket, her new home. She was finally safe.

The Tap Room's address was 101b Straight Wharf. Sarah hoped that it was close enough to walk to save on cab fare since her life savings consisted of the folding money in her wallet. After purchasing her ferry ticket she had stopped counting it because knowing the actual pathetically low dollar amount only made her even more nervous.

The airhorn released another thundering blast, startling a flock of gulls. They took off in a squawking spiral above her head. Hefting her duffle, Sarah took her place in the gangplank line. As *The Eagle* repeatedly nosed the pier, the passengers in the queue jostled like dominos, and Sarah smiled with delight. Apparently, sea legs or not, it didn't really matter: old hand or island newcomer, every one of them was staggering around like a drunken sailor.

The ferry's gigantic maw opened with a protracted clanking groan. A gangplank swung over on a chain as passenger cars began to leave the hold. Each car made a *ka-thunk, ka-thunk* sound as it moved from the floating ship to the concrete pier. Sarah trotted down the gangplank and crossed a parking lot to follow a gravel lane into the center of town. The gravel under her shoes crunched oddly, making a sound like poker chips. Looking down, Sarah realized she had entered another world. The path wasn't paved with gravel; she was walking on scallop shells. Who on earth would waste these beautiful shells like this? Couldn't they find something better to make with them?

The homes she passed had signboards on them with names like *Omega, Zenas Coffin, Edward Carey*. Sarah wasn't sure if these were the names of the houses or of their owners. She would have to find someone and ask. She began to feel the thrill of having an entirely new place to explore. Everything she saw was fresh and uncertain, and Sarah was surprised to find that she felt okay with that. The constant flutter of anxiety that seemed to pressure her heart was gone. She felt a tiny suggestion of untried possibility with every step. Maybe, just maybe, Nantucket had enough magic in it to fix her messed up life.

Turning a corner, she started looking for a shingled building with red trim. It was a good thing she knew about the red trim because every building Sarah looked at had shingles on it. Turning right, she saw it. Cap'n Clancey's Clam Shack, dead ahead. Her directions said The Tap Room was through a separate door on the left. The Tap Room looked deserted, its windows dark, but the door opened when she pushed on it. She lugged her duffle inside. The Tap Room was cool, dim, and inviting, the way a good bar should be. The L-shaped room was narrow, with a low, timber-framed ceiling and what looked like a new stage built along the interior's exposed brick wall. Solid oak chairs clustered around circular tables, and a mahogany bar back created a safe haven station for the wait staff. She assumed the darkened hallway on the right led back to a kitchen. A well-built man in a Red Sox jersey was leaning over the register, talking to a girl with a mane of curly hair. Both of them were backlit by the light from the bar.

"Sorry, miss," he said. "You'll have to go next door if you're looking for food. We don't open 'til five."

"Actually, I'm looking for work. I'm Sarah Hawthorne. Are you Steve? I answered your ad?"

"Sarah, I hoped that was you." Reaching out, he grasped her hand. "Steve Barnett, the manager. I also tend bar and keep an eye on the place for the owners. Perfect timing! Meet Alien, your roommate."

"Jackass. It's Eileen. Don't mind him. I learned last year Steve likes to think he's funny, even when he's not."

Sarah's heart wilted. *Roommate?* She had assumed room and board meant that she'd be getting a room of her own. She would have no privacy at all with a roommate. Gathering her tattered courage, she spoke up. "Maybe I misunderstood? I thought I'd be getting a room to myself?"

"Fat chance!" Alien brayed. "You're lucky you're even getting a room! I waited too long last year. I had to share a house with sixteen other people. We slept in shifts on the floor. It's a miracle the plumbing held up. Don't take it personal, Steve. She doesn't realize how lucky she is. Sharing a room with only one other person is a bonus."

Sarah struggled to keep a smile on her face. What had she gotten herself into if this, this was considered lucky?

Steve stepped from behind the bar. "Let me show you The Dorm. The quickest way is through the kitchen and across the alley. It's not very private, but like Alien said, you can't beat the price."

Alien followed them across the greasy kitchen floor. "Need a hand with that duffle?"

"No, thanks." Sarah said. "I've got it. It balances me out."

Steve led the way through a screened door and across an alley paved with Belgian block. "Sorry about the stink. Not much I can do about it. The good news is the breeze blows most of it across the harbor, so you won't get this upstairs. And don't be surprised when they come to empty the dumpsters in the morning. It can make a racket like the roof's coming off. You'll get used it eventually."

Sarah caught a flicker of movement under a dumpster. She flinched. "Was that a rat?"

"Yes." He continued up a set of splintery stairs. "You'll have to get used to them, too. You're living on top of a wharf. Bastids eat poison like it's saltwater taffy. Personally, I think the poison only makes them stronger. Watch the railing, girls. It could use a nail or two."

Steve opened another screened door at the top of the stairs. Sarah waited for Alien to enter and then followed them down a shotgun hallway with doors staggered along both sides. One of the doors was open and Sarah peeked inside, being all nebby. The room held two twin beds and the debris of occupancy. Continuing on, Sarah noted that the doors had multiple index cards thumb-tacked to them, evidently some kind of messaging system. A few of the cards had the words *I'm in town, call me. Sally* scrawled across them in lurid red marker, signed by what looked like a lipstick kiss. Sarah gave a passing thought to her discarded electronic voicemail system, now deep in its watery grave. All these changes were going to take some getting used to.

"Here we go. Room number eight." Steve pushed a door open. "Alien, I told you this morning you should keep the door locked."

"Why bother? It's not like I have anything worth stealing."

The room was identical to the tiny rooms Sarah had already passed. The only difference was this one had a dusty sheer curtain on the single window and a particleboard nightstand between the two beds that was painted mustard yellow.

"I called dibbies on this one this morning." Alien plopped on the bed by the window. She tested the mattress with her palm. "Not bad at all. Beats sleeping on a floor."

Steve filled the doorway. "Here's the drill. Your room key is on the nightstand. It's a good idea to lock up every time you leave although, as you can see, no one does. If you have any valuables, leave them with me. I'll lock them in the safe. Do not leave any money lying around; I guarantee it will vanish. If anything does disappear, don't come crying to me, I don't want to hear about it. You've been warned." His smile took the sting from his words. "Once you've settled in, come back down and we'll fit you with a uniform. Your shift starts tonight at five; our daily staff meeting is in the dining room at four-thirty. Other than that, the rules are pretty simple." He ticked the points off on his fingers. "One: No smoking in The Dorm. I'd hate to see how fast this place goes up if it ever catches fire. Two: Do your partying somewhere else. These walls are paper thin and I do not want to get a late-night call because you're keeping everyone else up. Three: You share the bathroom, so don't be a pig. The bathroom is at the end of the hall. Alien can show it to you. It's pretty basic. We'll take care of linens and your uniform each week, but you're responsible for your personal laundry, including your towels. Any questions?"

It seemed simple enough. "I think I got it."

"Great! Welcome to the Tap Room crew. I can promise a summer you'll never forget. Come see me when you're ready for your uniform. I'll be in my office. It's the storeroom behind the bar."

"Thank you." Sarah lowered her duffle. It completely filled the gap between the beds. Taking a slow breath, she let it all out, trying to wrap her head around her new reality. Evidently, this narrow bed was her new home.

Plumping her pillow, Alien made herself comfortable. "So, where are you from?"

"Vermont," Sarah said. The idea of lying made her squirm, but she couldn't think of another option.

"I thought so. Your accent sounds kinda funny. I'm from Providence via Long Island, myself. You certainly picked an exciting time to visit the far-away isle. Have you heard about The Whistler yet?"

The bedsprings squeaked as Sarah sat down. "What's The Whistler?"

"The Whistler's not a what, he's a who." Alien leaned forward. "See, every summer there's this guy, a real wackjob, who chases girls home from the bars. He's a real stalker creep. The Whistler's been stalking girls for years now, and the cops can't catch him. The thing is, he's already made an appearance this year and it's not even part of the real season yet. And yesterday, the cops found a girl, a dead girl, somebody's nanny I heard, floating in Satan's Tub. Word was she was murdered. Can you believe that?"

"What?" Sarah felt an echo of all of her earlier fears roll over her like a thundercloud. A stalker on Nantucket targeting girls? Why hadn't she heard about this before? She clenched her fists in frustration, feeling ready to scream. All of this effort to escape Mason's insanity and now here she was, back in the same boat again? "Alien? What's up with this stalker?"

"Isn't it insane? Of course, no one talks about The Whistler because they're afraid he'll scare the tourists, but all of that's going to change now because of the dead girl. There's no way the cops can hush this one up." Reaching for her purse, Alien scrabbled through it. She came up empty. "Snap! I'm all out of ciggies. Do you have any on you?"

Sarah blinked. What was Alien asking for? Did she say *ciggies*? "I don't smoke."

"I didn't think so. You're thin enough, but you don't look like a smoker." Alien scrambled up. "I need to get to The Hub before our shift starts. Can I get you anything while I'm out?"

Sarah shook herself from her daze. "Are you going to smoke in our room?"

"Only when I want to." Alien paused. "Why? Is that a problem?"

"No," Sarah lied, again. Evidently, Alien was going to ignore all of Steve's rules, and lying was becoming Sarah's unhappy new habit.

"Great! Be right back."

Sarah leaned against the wall and ran her fingers through her hair. She felt like her life was one chaotic scramble lately, and she knew she wasn't through with changing yet. She was going to have to adapt to even more changes, even faster. She didn't feel nearly nimble enough. Instead, she felt brittle, fragmented, insufficient. The petulant voice inside her head wailed *I can't do this*! She dialed the voice down, knowing from experience that listening to it never solved anything. She needed to keep her focus on plowing ahead. Grand Pap said that he survived Korea by taking everything that came at him and keeping his knees bent. That sounded like solid advice. If Grand Pap had survived a war, she should be able to survive one summer.

Yes, discovering there was a stalker loose on Nantucket had been a nasty shock, but she would study it out and do what she could to avoid crossing his path. Maybe there was a silver lining in all of her troubles with Mason; at least she had learned how to defend herself against a stalker threat. Alien, her new smoker roommate, was another issue. Maybe she should have confronted Alien right away about smoking in their room, but the truth was Sarah felt spent. The last forty-eight hours had been grueling. She didn't have the pop left in her for another argument this day. She just wanted to be left alone.

All of her earlier joyful anticipation began to dribble away. The void it left filled back up with the persistent prickling anxiety that trapped the breath in her chest. When she considered how truly alone she was now, Sarah felt fear blossom across her soul like frost. And then, just when she was beginning to doubt the strength of her courage, she recalled Grand Pap's words as she had boarded the Boston bus. "You remember this, Missy," Grand Pap had said. "Courage isn't about being fearless. Courage is about being strong in spite of it. Don't you forget you come from a long line of strong women. My own mother was one of them, and God help me, I married another. Not one of them was a quitter, and neither are you." And then, Grand Pap had dried his eyes across his knuckles and kissed her goodbye.

Reaching for her pillow, Sarah hugged it close. Curling tight into a ball, she closed her eyes. *Sweet Jesus, help me*, she prayed. *I need to be strong about this. This is my new life starting.*

CHAPTER SIX

Seven o'clock and The Tap Room crowd was already going wild. The bar was packed wall to wall with customers, the room so full that every time a table opened up, the dartboard players had to pause their game to let even more newcomers through. Raising her tray, Sarah sidled through the massed bodies, having already learned that the mob always stood thickest right in front of the waitressing station. Steve was in his glory behind the bar, spinning his cocktail shaker like a gunslinger. He had warned them at their staff meeting to expect a crowd like this since tonight was not only the Tap Room's regular $24.99 Lobster Special, it was also the Grand Opening of their new Karaoke stage. Steve looked insanely thrilled at the near capacity response. He kept checking the line out the door and grinning like a demon. Sarah had to slap the bar top repeatedly to get his attention. "Steve! I need two G&Ts, extra lime, and another bucket of beer."

"Sorry, kiddo. Didn't see you standing there." He planted six long-necked bottles in a galvanized bucket and rattled it full of ice. "How you holding up?"

"Is it always going to be like this?"

"Let's hope so!" he laughed, centering two gin and tonics on her tray. He added a wad of fresh cocktail napkins with a flourish. "Head back out. Keep everything in play. You're doing great."

"Thanks!" Sarah wormed back into the crowd. The truth was she had never felt so unsure and exhilarated in her life. Juggling multiple orders from multiple tables was proving to be a very scary sort of fun. Most surprising of all, she felt calm, competent, in control. Before Steve had unlocked the front door, she had been as nervous as a teenaged girl on her first car date, but now that she was in the game she felt fine plus Steve, her new boss, thought she was doing great. That was good enough for her. Leslie had been nice enough to warn her to keep the banquette open since Tony Garza and his crew were expected at seven. Sarah had learned that Leslie, a six-year Tap Room veteran, was Steve's official right hand. Leslie had hosted her own little pow-wow with the wait staff after Steve's meeting.

"So? Are you a virgin?" Leslie had asked.

"Excuse me?" Sarah said.

"Have you ever worked the floor before?" Leslie had shifted her mass of ginger hair off her shoulder. She was a forty-something divorced mother of three young girls, petite, and tough as nails. "How do you want to split up the tables?"

"I'm game with whatever you think will work best," Anna-Marie said. A-M was a sloe-eyed brunette with a waistless body that was solid muscle. Her short skirt revealed legs as ripped as cabled hawsers. Her calf muscles looked like Popeye's arms.

"Smart answer. My suggestion is that I take the six tables by the bar plus the stud rail by the shuffleboard table-"

"Hold on!" Alien protested. "How come you get six tables?"

"Hear me out." Leslie raised her hand. "That leaves you the five tables by the windows, including the big double. The tourists will want those tables because of the view, plus it's romantic. They usually tip pretty good. Sarah will get the four center tables plus the banquette. A-M can cover the five tables in the back, and I'll take any hammerheads who come in to play shuffleboard. They only stop in for beer, so I'll need to pick up the extra table to make up for volume."

Sarah laughed. "Hammerheads? What are they, the house band?"

"Cute." Leslie smirked. "They're the construction guys, honey. Construction's a nice, steady paycheck on the island but like I said, it's a tip on a beer, not a dinner."

Still worried about the Stafford loan hanging over her head, Sarah quickly calculated the numbers. "Tell me again why I only get four tables?"

"Hey, I'm doing you a favor. Those four tables make you special because that means you get the banquette, and that means you get Tony Garza. Tony's one of the last commercial scallopers. Whenever he's in port, he provides the local color the tourists eat with a spoon. Tony also brings in his four huge sons, and they all order steak dinners. Same dinner, every time. You'll get used to it, but that's why you have to keep the banquette open because Tony will flip out if his table isn't ready when he arrives. Oh, kid, don't look so worried. I didn't mean to scare you. Tony's wife always calls ahead to warn us whenever he's in port. It all works out. Just remember though, whatever else you do, don't make Tony mad."

And so, on Leslie's untested advice, Sarah had ignored the longing gazes of several larger parties at the door. She had kept the big banquette open even though the clock was moving past seven and there was still no sign of the Garza party of five. She was beginning to worry. How much longer should she wait? Dropping the bucket of beer off at her table full of rowdy college buddies, she returned to the middle-aged couple at table three.

Evidently, while she had been filling their drink order, he had presented his wife with the single long-stemmed pink rose that now lay beside her elbow. Sarah felt warmed by his old-school romantic gesture. Giving a woman flowers was such a simple thing to do that she wondered why more men didn't do it. The couple was so intent on each other that they were startled when Sarah returned with their drinks. "Two gin and tonics, extra lime. Would you like to see a menu?"

"Magnus?" The wife brightened hopefully. "What do you think, dear? Could we stay for dinner? Watching the karaoke might be fun."

"No, Diana, we cannot." Magnus adjusted his glasses. His clipped New England tone grated against his wife's prettier English accent. "You know my feelings about eating a meal outside of our home. Don't protest, please. You agreed that going out for one cocktail would be enough of a treat to celebrate our anniversary. I'm going to hold you to your promise." Magnus pulled out his wallet. "How much do I owe you, young woman? I'd like to cover our check now, so that we can leave once we're ready."

Sarah watched Diana shrink back like a snail touched by rock salt. Happy anniversary, you poor thing. She could read what was going at this table like a book. Magnus was the kind of man who did everything for outward show, but nothing he did had any real heart or feeling in it. "It's nine dollars."

"Here's a ten. Keep the change."

"Thank you. Let me know if you change your mind." Like that's going to happen, Sarah noted grimly. Tucking the ten spot in her ticket book, she tried to ignore the fresh worry that started to gnaw at her tender confidence. She began to wonder again about her meager four table assignment. Had Leslie played her for a sucker? Folding her tray under one arm, she turned and walked straight into a wall of men wearing identical yellow slickers.

"I hope you saved my table, little lady," an amazingly deep bass voice rumbled.

Involuntarily, Sarah stepped back. The speaker was short and muscular, as fully wide as he was tall with a thatch of black hair that crowned a pair of eyes as tawny as a lion's. He also possessed the most ruggedly weathered face Sarah had ever seen in her life. His skin was so deeply furrowed that it looked like it had been plowed and then someone had used a ruler and a knife to square it off into inches.

"Tony ... Garza," she stammered.

"The only, the only." Shrugging off his slicker, Tony hung it on a peg. He gestured toward the four other men still struggling out of theirs. "And sons." He smiled, and his amazing topaz eyes disappeared into a nest of wrinkles. "I'm sure they warned you we was coming. Ed, Joey, slide in there, boys. You know the drill." Tony seated himself in the center of his sons, looking kingly as they settled in. "And what is your name, little lady?"

"Oh! I'm sorry. I'm Sarah, and I'll be your server this evening."

"Nice to meetcha, Sarah. I hope you'll be our server every evening. I'm Captain Tony Garza, and these are my boys: Paul, Tony Junior, Joey, and Ed." He folded his hands. "We like to keep it simple. We'll need a bucket of beer to start, five cups of chowder, five steak and bakes, steaks medium rare, potatoes with all the fixins, five salads with oil and vinegar dressing." His golden eyes twinkled. "Think you can remember that?"

"Sounds easy enough." She closed her ticket book. "No dessert tonight? We have hot apple cobbler with cinnamon ice cream."

"We don't eat sweets." Tony declared. "Bad for your teeth."

"Bad for your figure." Ed leered.

Tony reached around Joey to slap Ed's head. "Keep it clean or go sit in the truck. It should be easy enough. You pick."

"Ow, Dad! That hurt!"

"Excuse my son, missy. He'll be polite. I know his mother raised him better."

Sarah gave Tony a warm smile. As intimidating as he seemed to be at first, there was something innately trustworthy about him. "I'll be right back with your beer and the chowder."

"Crissakes!" Ed muttered. "She's just as easy to watch walking away!"

Sarah caught the sound of the second smack as she turned for the kitchen.

"Excuse me, miss? Miss?"

Sarah spun on her heel. Evidently, the anniversary couple had finished their one drink and already moved on, and a single man had taken their table. He fulfilled the minimal Tap Room dress code by wearing a corduroy blazer over his Pink Floyd T-shirt with black jeans. He also had a wispy braid hanging down his back. Bussing the dirty glasses to her tray, she gave the table a swipe while offering an apology. "I'm sorry, sir. I didn't see you sitting here. What can I get you?"

Mr. Braid stared, his mouth hanging open in an unattractive gape. His Adam's apple bobbed as he swallowed hard. Maybe he had already been over-served somewhere else? He looked plenty pale, plus beads of sweat were popping out across his forehead. Reaching out, Sarah touched his forearm. "Sir? Are you okay?"

Mr. Braid snatched his arm away. He scrambled up so quickly that his chair clattered backward before it hit the floor with a bang. Sarah jumped. Her heart started racing. *What had she done wrong now?* All of the other diners had stopped eating their meals to watch the disturbance like it was some kind of dinner theater. They might think this was entertaining, but Sarah felt terrified. Her pulse was pounding painfully in her throat. Mr. Braid was staring at her so hard, he was reminding her of Mason at his worst whenever Mason fell into one of his moods and he started to get all possessive about her body. *What is up with that?* I've never seen this guy before in my life!

"Katie?" Mr. Braid tottered. He leaned against the table for support. "Is that you?"

Katie? Obviously, he had confused her with someone else. Sarah struggled to stay calm. Mr. Braid still looked a little wild-eyed, but surely nothing bad could happen in a room full of people, right? "No, sir. My name is Sarah."

"Sarah?" Kneeling slowly, Mr. Braid righted his chair without ever shifting his eyes. His face had contracted tight with doubt. "Your name is Sarah. How long have you worked here?"

"Tonight's my first night."

He blinked repeatedly. "Where are you from?"

"Vermont."

"Sarah." Mr. Braid sat down and smoothed his hair, looking calmer. "Sorry if I startled you. You really do look like someone I used to know. I wasn't expecting it." He cleared his throat. "Could you bring me a draft beer, dark if you have it? Whatever's on tap is fine."

"Would you like to see a menu?"

"No. Just the beer for now, thanks."

She tightened the grip on her smile and felt her blood pressure rise. Great, just great. A lone nut-job beer drinker sitting at one of her four-count tables, and another solid strike against her cash flow kitty. Her financial future was starting to look bleak. Mr. Braid seemed to read her mind.

"I'm expecting friends. I'm sure they'll order something more."

"I'll keep an eye out for them." And keep an eye on you, too, Sarah decided as she headed for the kitchen. The Tap Room customers were certainly turning out to be a mixed bag. Adding the Garza steak order to the overhead spinner, she rang the tinny bell. "Order up!" Returning to the waitress station, she discovered that Steve had disappeared. She found him hunkered down behind the bar, stuffing a thick wad of twenties into a zippered bag. Looking up, Steve caught her eye and winked.

"You know it's going to be a good night when the cash won't fit in the register." Locking the bag in a drawer, he pocketed the key. "What can I get you?"

"I need another bucket and one tall dark draft." Leaning into the bar, Sarah took a breather. "Steve? What do you know about the guy sitting at table three?"

He peered into the milling mob. "Billy Bear? Good enough guy. Don't see him in town much anymore. Why? Is there a problem?"

"No. He thought I looked familiar."

"Got you confused with some movie star, maybe?"

"Charmer," Sarah laughed. So, Mr. Braid's name was Billy Bear. She filed it away for future reference. She was determined to learn everything she could about the bar trade, and Leslie had said that one good trick was to memorize the customers since they tipped you better when you remembered them by name. Alien suddenly slipped in beside her, jostling her elbow.

"Steve? I need another bucket. The animals are thirsty tonight. What a zoo!"

"Next one is yours." He thumped a fresh bucket on the bar and slid the foamy dark draft onto Sarah's tray. "Back at it, kiddo. Don't forget to breathe."

Using the bucket like a wedge, Sarah nudged aside clumps of customers as she made her way back to the banquette. She found Tony Garza holding court. He was declaiming loudly to anyone who would listen.

"Are you kidding me? I don't trust the Feds to know anything! The scallops will adjust—what the hell do the Feds know about scallops? That whole harbor breach project was retarded! Supposed to flush the inner harbor—I say, what's wrong with keeping the harbor the way it was? Hasn't silted up in over a century. No, you can't fool me! What they're really doing is lining their pork-belly pockets with our hard-earned tax dollars and upsettin' the fish patterns for no good reason!"

Sarah planted the bucket in the center of the table. Rubbing his calloused hands, Tony reached for an icy bottle.

"Ah, missy, that looks great. I wonder, though. Did you remember to bring us a church key?"

"I did." She pulled a bottle opener from her apron pocket. "I'll be right back with your chowder. Before I go, though, do you need extras? Some folks like hot sauce, lemon, extra pepper, more butter?"

"Absolutely not! That recipe is wicked good the way it is," Tony growled. Popping the caps, he handed the cold beers around to his sons. "We'll let you know if we change our minds."

"Be right back." She squeezed through the crowd to check on her other tables. This barmaid gig was tougher than it looked. It wasn't so much about handling the food as it was about handling the customers. As she drew near to table three, Sarah almost dumped her tray. A second customer had joined Billy Bear. She instantly recognized the newcomer as Kurt, the artist from the boat. He noted her arrival, too. Leaning back, Kurt hooked an arm around his chair and stared at her in stunned amazement.

"I warned you," Billy said.

"Here's your dark draft. Good evening, sir. Can I get you something?"

"What is this?" Kurt narrowed his eyes to slits. "Some kind of setup?"

"I'm sorry?" Sarah leaned forward. Kurt's voice was so low, it was difficult to hear him over the raucous crowd noise.

Kurt turned toward Billy although his eyes never left Sarah's face. "Her voice is wrong, Billy. That should have been your first clue. It's too high-pitched, but I agree the resemblance is remarkable." He waggled his fingers. "Billy tells me your name is Sarah. Well, Sarah, you certainly do have a rare beauty, but you must have heard that before. What color are your eyes? It's too dark in here to tell."

Seriously? Sarah chuckled. Was he really trying to use that lame pickup line on her? "They're hazel."

"They're not gray?" Kurt persisted. "I've been searching for a girl with gray eyes."

Even though she knew Kurt was a married man and a bit of a sleeze, she could see now why women fell for him. He had a magnetic sort of bad boy charm and a smoldering charisma. She had to admit that it was a powerful, sexy combination. "They're hazel, I promise. I inherited them from my mother. What can I get you to drink?"

Kurt leaned forward on his elbows, dissatisfied somehow with her answer. "Bring me a bourbon and soda, with rocks. Little soda, less ice."

"Be right back." Sarah turned for the kitchen. She knew she should focus on her tables, but she was finding it strangely difficult to switch her focus off Kurt at table three. What was it about the guy that made him so compellingly attractive? Was it because she knew he was an artist? Was there some natural empathy there? Was it his obvious self-confidence, his latent sense of power that came so close to arrogance that it simply radiated off him? She gave herself a shake. What on earth was she doing? She was supposed to be working, dammit! This wasn't a cocktail party. She wasn't going to make any money daydreaming like this! She dropped her tray loudly on the steel countertop. "Cook? Got my chowder?"

"Ready when you are." He ladled out five steaming bowls. "Steaks are under the broiler. Eleven minutes more, no less."

"I'll be back." Lifting her tray with both hands, Sarah cruised to the bar to place her fresh drink order. She knew that carrying an over-loaded tray was risky, but if she was successful, it would save her a round trip. Leslie had also said that another trick of the bar trade was to maximize your efficiency by trimming off the service time between your tables whenever you could. Sarah had discovered that finding new efficiencies kept the game interesting. She rested the tray on the lip of the bar. "Steve? I need a bourbon, double with rocks, soda splash."

He ignored her. Steve continued to stare into the dining room, his mouth slack, his eyes glazed.

"Steve!" Sarah shouted. "My soup's getting cold here!"

He remained oblivious to her call. Sarah turned to see what was causing this type of reaction and that's when she saw her.

CHAPTER SEVEN

A woman had joined the two men sitting at table three. She was a blonde, one of those fatal blondes, six foot tall or near enough with hair the color of clover honey. Her stylish haircut proved what a New York salon could do when handed a blank check. She was slim without being skinny, and her curves only underscored the strength of her slender lines. Against the veritable sea of sports coats and simple linen frocks, this woman wore a body-hugging black cat suit with ankle boots that played up her long, long legs. Holy cow! Sarah thought. Her legs are as long as my whole body! The woman laughed at something Kurt said. She looked toward the bar and Sarah felt an electric snap of recognition. I know her! It's Sally, that woman from the boat. Looking down, she also recognized that it was decision time about the Garzas' chowder since it was beginning to curdle. She needed to either serve it up or send it back to the kitchen. "Steve!" Sarah shouted again, her shrill tone finally snapping him out of his trance. "Drinks, please!"

"I'm sorry. What did you say?"

"Bourbon and soda, double, little soda, less ice. What's wrong with you?"

"It's not his fault," an equally dazed man leaning against the bar stammered. "Poor bastard's been stupified. My God, Sally Poldridge, the witch of Wauwinet, in the house tonight." He rattled the ice in his glass. "Better make my next one a double if Sally's back in town. I'm gonna need it."

Steve splashed some well bourbon into a short glass. He gave it two cubes of ice and a hiss of soda before sliding the poorly made cocktail across the bar. "Here, Sarah. Go see what Sally wants."

"O-kay." She made room for the drink on her tray, feeling oddly like a sacrificial lamb. Weaving through the crowd, Sarah returned to the banquette, noting that even Tony Garza had fallen silent. He was staring sullenly at Sally with a beetled brow and a look of outright hostility. All four

Garza sons were carefully keeping their heads down. They continued to stare at the tabletop as Sarah set out their chowder.

"I don't know what she's doing in here," Tony muttered. "That bitch has no business in my restaurant. I should run her skinny ass out! Look how she's putting herself on display. It's not decent."

Joey calmly folded his hands. "Sally's entitled to come in here if she wants to."

"What are you, her fuckin' lawyer?" Tony dropped his spoon, splattering his chowder across the table. "Having her here is putting me off my food." His amber eyes blazed. "How are the steaks?"

"A few more minutes," Sarah quavered. She couldn't help it. Her knees trembled at his fury. "Cook's fixing your potatoes now."

"You make sure they're hot! If they're over-baked, I'll send them back to the kitchen. Don't think I won't!"

"Lighten up, Dad," Joey remonstrated. "It's not this girl's fault Sally's here. She had nothing to do with it."

Tony blinked slowly like a tortoise. "You know what, Joey? Damn if you're not smarter than your old man. Apologies for my manners, missy. You're doing a fine job."

"I'll go get your steaks." Sarah ran the bourbon cocktail over to table three. She was beginning to feel like a circus juggler trying to keep all of her tables in play. Billy had obviously been thirsty since he'd already drained off the top half of his beer. The good news was that at least he'd stopped staring. He was focused now on Sally instead, and picking his cuticle to pieces.

"What do I tell them the next time?" Billy said.

"You should have told them the truth," Sally snapped. "Getting a tattoo isn't a crime. Now they're going to wonder what you're trying to hide."

"You should have answered your phone!"

"I was busy." Shrugging her slim shoulders, Sally looked up. "Is this our little doppelgänger? I can certainly see a resemblance, although I do believe this one is taller. In any case, Kurt, she is so your type."

"Leave the girl out of this." Kurt swept his shredded cocktail napkin to the floor. "She doesn't need to be a part of your game."

"Yet," Sally laughed. "She doesn't need to be a part of my game yet, but I live in hope."

Sarah noticed that Kurt's hand shook when he reached for his drink. She felt saddened. Alcoholic artists were such a dreadful stereotype. Having the shakes must make it tough to control the paint on your brush. Raising the glass to his lips, Kurt closed his eyes. He took a reverential sip of the bourbon and then carefully wiped his mouth with his fingertips.

"Ma'am? Would you like to order something?"

"Please! Don't insult me!" Sally tilted her chin. "I'm not nearly old enough to be called *ma'am.*" Placing her elbows on the table, she framed her breasts with her forearms. "And what is your name, pretty lady?"

Sarah's blush grew so hot that even her earlobes got warm. She had been the focus of this kind of frank appraisal from plenty of men, but she had never seen such a look of raw sexual hunger coming from a woman before. Leslie certainly hadn't offered her any advice on how to handle this situation! Since she wasn't sure how to respond, she fell back on what she already knew by heart. "I'm Sarah, and I'll be your server this evening."

"Very good, Sarah. Fetch me a Stoli rocks with a lemon twist." Sally leaned forward and enhanced her cleavage. "What I'd really like to know, though, is do you like to party?"

Sarah felt trapped. Flirting harmlessly with male customers was an accepted part of a barmaid's job description, but how on earth was she supposed to deflect this aggressively pushy woman? She suddenly felt queasy. She knew she was powerless, and she needed to hang onto this job. She had no home to go home to, and no bankroll to fall back on. All it would take was one serious customer complaint and she would be back out on the street with no place to live. Sarah felt locked by indecision. What should she do? Fighting a tide of rising panic, she decided to add a polite layer of frost to her reply and to try and joke it off. She prayed that Sally would be kind enough to take the hint. "Not when I'm working, actually."

"How about later, hummm?" Sally persisted. Raising one eyebrow, she leaned back in her chair and smiled lewdly. Her cap sleeve rode up to reveal an intricate black tattoo inked across her upper arm.

"Dammit, Sally!" Billy reached over to tug on her sleeve. "I told you to keep that covered up!"

"You don't get to touch me until I say so." Sally hissed. Wrenching her arm away, she tugged her sleeve even higher. "Let's ask Sarah how she likes my tattoo. Billy here did it. He's quite talented in the tattoo department. I bet he'd just love to do you."

"Are we through here?" Kurt drained his glass. Standing up, he opened his wallet and threw a twenty on the table. "I've told you before, Sally. I'm through playing your games."

Sally smirked. "You'll be back. You need me. Who else can you trust?"

Kurt turned unsteadily for the door. His involuntary stagger told Sarah that the double bourbon she'd served him hadn't been his first drink of the night. She placed the twenty in her ticket book. "What about his change?"

"Keep it," Billy remarked sadly.

"He's right," Sally sneered. "Kurt won't be coming back for it tonight, and he won't remember what he did with it tomorrow -"

There was the sudden explosive pop of a shattered wine stem near the door.

"Sorry!" Kurt apologized. Backing away, he bowed courteously to Alien as she struggled to control the remaining glasses on her tray. "Sorry! Didn't see you comin'."

"I rest my case, your honor," Sally laughed again. She stretched her arms high overhead and her cat suit grew thin. "In any case, Kurt's right. It is getting late. Time to get my own little party started."

As Sarah headed for the kitchen to collect the Garzas' steak order, she watched Sally stroll toward the karaoke stage. She noted that Sally's passage drew the attention of every man and woman in the room. Sally knew the effect she was having. She kept glancing over her shoulder to make sure of her audience as she threaded a path through the tables. Malcolm, the new karaoke master, also noted her approach. He adjusted his headphones nervously before handing Sally the portable mic.

She switched it on, and purred into the amplifier. "Good evening, everyone. This looks like fun. What have we here?"

"Karaoke, madam," Malcolm explained. "Would you care to sing for us? You'd be the first."

Sally lithely hopped on stage. She scanned the audience, and lowered her voice to a husky contralto. "I'd love to be the first. I love popping cherries." The crowd gasped. Sally snapped her fingers at Malcolm to regain his shocked attention. "Do you have a song list handy?"

He proffered a binder filled with plastic sleeves. "Lady, we got ten thousand songs. You name the tune, I bet we got it."

Sally flipped through the pages and sauntered closer to center stage. "Let's wake these people up. Do you have any Pepper Anderson? Let's try 'Call Me Home.'"

"We got that one." Malcolm pressed a sequence into his karaoke deck. He glanced at his friend on the bongo. "D-Buzz? Give me the beat. And a one, a two, and a tree."

As the instrumental soundtrack began to warm up, D-Buzz tapped out a playful initial rhythm. Sally dropped the folder and partnered in, snapping her fingers to create a jazzy, underlying beat. "That's right." She pointed at Malcolm. "Got any light?"

"You know I do."

Malcolm flipped a switch and a spotlight split the darkened stage. As soon as Sally entered the column of light her cat suit turned transparent. Another startled gasp rustled through the room when it became apparent that Sally wasn't wearing a bra. A hammerhead by the shuffleboard table forgot to hold onto his beer. He dropped his bottle and it thudded off his steel-toed boots. He began to jump in place, cursing the bottle as it spun in a circle, spouting foam.

"Yes, sir!" Sally laughed, delighted. "That's what I was looking for!" The song began and Sally began to sing:

Everyone feels a little lost, sometimes
Everyone feels alone.
Don't you worry about a thing though, baby,
'Cuz you know I'll take you home.
Lay your troubles down on me, baby,
'Cuz you know I'll get you home.

A tourist in a regretable Hawaiian shirt gave Sally a wolf whistle. Dropping her hips into a swivel, she pointed him out across the room while sharing a knowing wink. Sarah caught the man's obviously appalled girlfriend hiss. "Really? Are you serious? That cougar's a total skank!"

"Shut up! She's the bomb!" he replied, rudely waving her to silence as Sally continued.

I'll keep you snug 'til morning,
Call me again around suppertime.
Call me anytime you need me, baby,
As long as you remember to call me fine; that's right.
I need a real man to call me home tonight.
Won't you call me home—tonight?

The song ended on a lingering note and Sally spun the lyrics down to a throaty whisper as the room fell silent. Still standing center stage, she scanned the audience looking for a reaction. The crowd maintained its stunned silence. Shrugging slowly, Sally handed Malcolm the mic.

A gentleman diner in a patchwork jacket began to clap. "Goddamn!" he roared, ignoring the furious, reproving look from his wife. "Goddamn! That's the best thing I ever saw!"

Sally quickly retrieved the mic. "Thank you very much. I'll be here next Monday night, too, to sing more of your favorites."

"And I'll be right here!" he shouted. "Steve? You've got my card. Save me this table. I want a permanent reservation!"

"Stop it, Harrison!" His livid wife pinched his arm. "You're making a complete ass out of yourself! Like hell you will!"

"You just try and stop me!" Harrison replied, fending her off.

Captain Tony's face had flushed a dangerous purple, and the veins were standing out in knotted cords along his neck. Setting her tray on the edge of the table, Sarah slid the first of the platters in front of him. She was relieved to see that his focus wasn't on her or on his incoming dinner anymore. He was staring intently over her shoulder instead. She turned to follow his sightline in time to see Sally hop off the stage. Sally slowly sauntered toward the hammerhead who had dropped his beer. Clearly apprehensive, he straightened at her approach.

Sally flicked her fingers up the buttons of his jacket. "So? Like what you see?"

"Yes, ma'am." He swallowed heavily. "You know I do."

"You're cute, handsome. What's your name?"

"Charlie, uhm, Erskine."

"Well, Charlie Uhm Erskine, got any plans for this evening?"

"No, ma'am." Charlie cleared his throat. "Never too busy for you."

"That's the right answer, Charlie Uhm Erskine." The crowd parted as Sally strolled toward the door. Pausing, she turned and looked back over her shoulder. "Coming?"

Charlie grabbed his keys and abandoned his friends. The room fell silent again as he followed Sally into the night. A collective sigh rustled through the room as the door closed.

"Someone needs to strangle that bitch," Tony breathed, "before somebody gets hurt."

Sarah slipped the second platter off her tray. She felt sorry for karaoke performer number two. How on earth could you beat Sally's performance? She had held the room in the palm of her hand. Trying to be helpful, Joey slid the steak platter toward Ed. As she shifted the next platter off the tray, Sarah heard a car alarm begin its rising three-note sequence from the street. The alarm was quickly joined by a second, and then a third. A chair scraped the floor as an older man stood up to peer out the window.

"What the hell?"

"Todd?" A second diner stood up. "What's going on out there?"

His wife laid her hand on his arm. "Robert, it's the Porsche."

There was a sudden chorus of wooden squeals as more and more chairs were pushed away from the tables as diners began to rise. Dropping their napkins, they abandoned their half-eaten meals. Reaching for jackets and purses, patrons began to scurry for the door. A scrum developed. Sarah felt a shove as one couple hurried by. A man by the window stood up and bolted for the door. He stepped on the arch of her left foot. She heard a crunch through the sudden haze of pain as he ran on without offering an apology. Sarah struggled to grip her still-laden tray while blinking through a veil of tears. What was going on? The cacophony of car alarms suddenly doubled as they were joined by the brassy clanging of an old-fashioned firebell. She felt a ripple of pure terror. Was The Tap Room on fire? She saw Steve vault over the bar. He began to shove his way through the crowd to the bottleneck of customers swarming the door.

"Everyone stay calm!" Steve yelled. "There's nothing at all wrong here!"

Sarah staggered as a second panicky couple shoved her aside. With a slow dawning realization of horror, she felt the tray begin to slip from her fingers. "No! No, no, no!" She cried as one china platter lipped over the tray. It smashed to shards against the hardwood floor. Sarah scrambled to save the last platter, but she slipped on the oily salad now squelching beneath her shoes. With nothing to grab onto, she lost her balance and fell to her knees in the center of the stampede.

Clutching the edge of the table, Sarah struggled to rise. Men were shouting in fear and women were screaming as the mob pressed for the door. Joey reached out to snatch her arm. He tried to pull her into the safety of the banquette but she slipped from his grasp. Sarah was helpless to resist this shrieking tide of humanity. She was jostled, and her arms were pinned to her sides. Her toes barely touched the floor. Pummeled and pressed, she became a part of the panicking melee that squeezed through the front door and spilled outside.

The mob fell apart in the street. Tripping over a curb, Sarah washed up in an alley. Panic had such a knobby grip on her mind that she finally had to shriek to make it let go. Her crushed left foot throbbed. Her ribs were bruised where someone had ground an elbow into her side. She tasted blood and realized that she had unknowingly bitten her lip. Sarah spat the coppery taste from her mouth and noticed that the grimy alley glittered with glass. Someone had used a brick to smash the windows of all the illegally parked cars. That explained the car alarms, but who would do such a thing? She wiped her sweaty palms on her apron and carefully stepped out of the alley, still on the lookout for the mob. The street looked safe enough, and she began to navigate the edge of the queue of agitated people pouring out of the neighboring restaurants and bars.

"What's going on?" she asked a man shambling by. "What is this?"

He stopped tapping his smartphone long enough to look up. "Someone's gone berserk! He's smashing all the shop windows in town."

A running man pulled up short. "Sonofabitch! Look at my car!" He glanced over his shoulder. "I wonder if I saw the guy? Heading for Old South Wharf?"

Sarah struggled to make sense of what she was seeing. Her mind was still in free fall from the downpour of drenching fear. Security strobe lights tripped by the damage stippled the night into alternating bands of half-shadow like some freakish discotheque. The strobes were blinding. She raised one hand against them and then had trouble believing her eyes. Some maniac had smashed all the plate glass windows of the shops on Easy Street. Powdered glass blanketed the cobblestones like drifts of fresh snow. This level of vandalism was more than angrily slashing a tire or keying the paint on somebody's car. This level of deliberate destruction was inconceivable. Who would do such a thing?

"Was it The Whistler?" she asked.

A woman in a red business suit stopped talking into her cell phone. "You saw The Whistler? Jeanne, a girl here said she saw The Whistler!"

"No, I didn't say that. Lady, I never said that."

"Did you hear me, Jeanne? The Whistler's in town! Let me call you back. I need to call 911. Where the hell are the cops?"

CHAPTER EIGHT

John sipped the sour well of coffee stewing in his mug, and sent the event summary he knew the chief would want to the printer. He felt sleep-deprived and over-caffeinated to the point of painful clarity. Speculating about the Easy Street vandal was pointless until the team completed their witness interviews and they had solid information to work from. Collecting critical details would have to wait until later in the morning, once their witnesses began to wake up from their big night. He could already imagine the tsunami of virulent gossip that would be unleashed on the town over the next few hours.

Tapping his fingers, he searched for something useful to do. What he really wanted to do was to read Paul's autopsy report on the Satan's Tub victim. Paul had promised to get the report to them first thing in the morning, but *first thing* to Paul probably meant sometime closer to ten o'clock. He needed to do something to fill the dead time. Dreading the chore, John reached for the beach permit file.

Each year, island residents rushed to get their annual beach permits. He had heard, from his mother, of all people, that displaying a single digit beach permit on your vehicle was the latest low-profile insider status symbol. Using a No. 2 pencil, John propped the manila envelope open and peered inside. The envelope was stuffed fat with scraps of paper and post-dated checks from locals over-eager to get their names on the beach permit list. Jenny had divulged this latest fad over Sunday dinner, remarking how this ridiculous new phenomenon had been the sole topic of interesting conversation at her last Island Girls Garden Club meeting, and wasn't it a shame that normally sensible people went to such ridiculous lengths to separate themselves from the common tourist herd? John found his mother's check on top of the stack. He tossed the pencil.

"What are you doing over there?" CJ said.

"Nothing." He crammed the envelope into his top drawer. He would deal with the beach permits later.

"You look played out. Did you get any sleep last night?"

"A couple of hours. I'm fine."

The keypad beeped its sequence. John straightened as Chief Brock pushed through the Plexiglas door. He was trailed by Toby Talbot, the young diver from the bog. From the dark look on the chief's face, John knew that he had heard about the vandalism. John had emailed the chief a preliminary status report at 21:23, and followed up with a voicemail, but the chief had never returned his call. For the life of him, John couldn't fathom what Toby was doing there. Did the Salty Dogs bring even more disturbing news to share?

"What the hell happened on Easy Street last night, Lieutenant?" the chief blustered. "I just came through the basin. It looks like Hurricane Eduoard blew through there."

"Criminal vandalism, sir." John indicated the printer. "I've prepared bullet points for your review." He couldn't control himself and added: "Since I couldn't reach you last night."

"Damn technology! I never got your call. What's the skinny? Was it The Whistler?"

"No, we don't believe so, sir. Witnesses report an adult white male running toward Old South Wharf, but we found no evidence of The Whistler at the site."

The chief tugged his lower lip. "An adult male? At least it wasn't those hooligan kids again. That'll satisfy the parents. Damnation! I can remember when this duty was dull. Be sure to keep me posted, Lieutenant Jarad. In the meantime, I'm here to share some good news with you. We've been looking for a Community Service Officer, and I believe we've found him." He slapped Toby heartily on the back. "Toby presented a stellar report, simply steller. He passed his background check and his physical with flying colors. I stopped by his house this morning to deliver the good news myself, in person."

John suddenly developed a splintering headache behind his left eye. From what he knew of Toby, he liked the kid just fine, and yes, the chief had every right to make the CSO decision on his own, but John felt betrayed. Yet again, the chief had ignored established departmental protocol to make a personnel decision without consulting him first. Sure, the chief had the authority to do so, but he was the one who had to deal with any fallout.

CJ applauded. "Nice work, Toby! I know you've been working really hard on this."

"Thank you, ma'am. This is the best day of my life."

"I'm not so sure," Ted groused. "I know CSO is mostly bike patrol, but it bothers me the kid won't be packing a sidearm. That's not right. If he's wearing a uniform, he should be allowed to carry a weapon. I know he's got a carry permit because we issued him one. What if he needs to stop the action? What's he gonna do? Pull out his tire chalk?"

The chief's face turned brick red. John quickly interrupted. "We didn't make the regs, Ted, we only follow them. CSO's are not allowed to carry arms of any kind. In that capacity, they do not have the same legal powers as a sworn officer."

"I know what the regs are, Lieutenant," Ted countered. "What I'm saying is I don't like them. Can't we at least give the kid a Taser? Can we get him that much?"

"I'm just happy I get a shot at independent housing," Toby said. "My mom's so excited that I'm moving out of her basement she's throwing me a *bon voyage* party. Of course, you're all invited."

The chief chuckled. "You tell Mercy we'll be there with bells on. Lieutenant Jarad? Let's get this CSO his new duty belt."

Throttling his frustration, John decided to put the best face on things. He pulled a cardboard box off the top of a filing cabinet. "Got one right here, sir. Here you go, rookie! Catch!"

Toby handily caught the box. "Thank you, Lieutenant Jarad. This really means a lot to me."

John watched Toby remove the duty belt from its protective sleeve. He recalled his own excitement when he learned he had been promoted to Lieutenant-Commander. The thrill of that acceptance letter had hit him so hard that his hands had trembled. That acceptance had been a vote of confidence and trust from the community that was looking to the force to make difficult choices, and to do the right thing for the good of all. The added bonus was that he no longer needed to constantly wear the full duty belt with its fifteen pounds of assorted gear. He also knew that he was one of the lucky ones, because he still felt thrilled to report for duty each day. Most folks he knew weren't nearly so lucky with their jobs.

"Excuse me, Chief?" Tina pointed out the window. "Looks like a squall's approaching."

"Holy hell." The chief peered through the blinds. "That does look like a delegation. Better let them in, Tina."

She pressed a buzzer and the plexiglass door sprang open. John stood as two women and a man filed in. All three were wearing suits and looks of patent outrage. John recognized Stephanie Humphries, the town manager, in her trademark red suit and Magnus Wolfe, the high school principal. He guessed that Valerie Stanhope was there to represent the various neighborhood associations and the Board of Realtors. John took a deep breath and steeled himself because none of them looked happy.

"Chief Brock?" Stephanie said. "Lieutenant Jarad? We need to talk."

"Madame Moderator." The chief clasped his hands. His face assumed a look of rapt attention. "Ms. Stanhope, Magnus? What can we do for you today?"

"Are you serious, Charles?" Magnus slapped the newspaper in his hand. "The Whistler was seen in town last night."

"Excuse me, Mr. Wolfe," John said. "If you're referring to the Easy Street vandalism, there's no evidence that The Whistler was responsible for it, whatever the newspaper says. We believe The Whistler suggestion was a rumor."

"Then who did it?" Valerie piped up. "Was it those hooligan kids from East Quammock again?"

"Preliminary evidence indicates that a single adult male was responsible. We'll be interviewing witnesses today, and we will pursue an active investigation."

"I don't really care who did it!" Valerie shrilled. "What I want to know is what you are doing to catch these people! Summer rentals are down twenty-three percent! Cancellations are pouring in! No one wants to bring their kids to an island with a serial killer on it!"

John's head throbbed. "No one has suggested that The Whistler is a serial killer. There's no evidence yet that he's even connected to the victim we found in Satan's Tub."

"What about the other ponds?" Crossing his arms, Magnus huffed, "Say, Gibbs, or Long Pond? Have you investigated them? What if The Whistler has been using them all as his dumping ground, too?"

"That's a very constructive suggestion, Mr. Wolfe," John said. He made a mental note to commend CJ for making that very suggestion yesterday morning, which had given the Salty Dogs enough time to continue their search. "We have investigated the other ponds, sir. So far, we've found no evidence of any other victims."

"So far! So far!" Valerie wailed. "My God! We don't even know what we're dealing with here!"

Chief Brock cleared his throat with a rumble. "To be fair, Valerie, we've only uncovered the victim forty-eight hours ago. We haven't even seen the autopsy report yet, right, Lieutenant Jarad? You need to give us the time to do to the job properly."

Magnus rattled his newspaper before tossing it onto the nearest desk. "Maybe forty-eight hours for that victim, but you've known about The Whistler for years, Charles, for years! I want to know what you're doing to catch *him*. I've been feeling a lot of heat lately, a lot of heat from the parents and from the School Board over this situation. They have every right to be worried. I need to know what you're doing about it."

John stepped in. "You make another very good point, Mr. Wolfe. I'm sure we're in complete agreement. As a matter of fact, we're glad you stopped in this morning, because we'd like to share the plan we've developed to catch The Whistler." He pulled a folded map from a brass bucket, spread it out across a table, and circled the center of the island with his finger. "I believe we should concentrate our investigative efforts around the Altar Rock and Satan's Tub area. I suggest that we pull a report within a two-mile radius. We can collect the names off the public tax records -"

"You won't get the names of any renters that way," Valerie objected.

"True, but that's where we work with local realtors to pool the rental information."

"Why focus on Altar Rock?" Magnus asked. His forehead contracted into a nest of wrinkles. "The Whistler's attacks have all been south of town. Altar Rock is a perfectly respectable neighborhood. Why, I live in Harbour Post myself, just down the road."

"Because," John explained, "having The Whistler show up at Satan's Tub on Sunday was the first change he's made in his behavior. That leads us to believe that Altar Rock, or somewhere nearby, is his home turf. I think that when The Whistler found Ms. Kane at Satan's Tub, it was a lucky break for him—an opportunity too good to miss. I don't believe The Whistler planned that attack, and if he made a mistake on Sunday, then we should capitalize on it by focusing our attention there. Consider this: We've had forty-three attacks by The Whistler over the past three summers between mid-May and the second week of September. There hasn't been a single reported attack before or after the season. That suggests to me that The Whistler isn't local, or not a full-time local anyway. I think we should canvass the Altar Rock and Satan's Tub area, looking for any repeat seasonal residents. That detail might lead us to our actor."

Comprehension slowly dawned across Magnus' face. "You think The Whistler's a coof?"

"I think it's a very good possibility that The Whistler is from off-island, yes, or that he's a temporary summer resident."

Stephanie tapped her lips. "I'm not so sure. Magnus? What do you think?"

"It certainly sounds plausible, Stephanie. At least it's something I can take back to the parents and the Board when I try to reassure them."

"Val? How about you? Are you comfortable with this new approach?"

"I suppose I'll have to be, right?" Valerie cut her eyes at Chief Brock. "I have to say it's nice to see that we're at least trying to be proactive about this, this year, since that hasn't always been the case."

"Very well." Stephanie cocked her head. "Chief Brock, Lieutenant Jarad. Let me reiterate our position so that we're absolutely clear on it. The Nantucket Police need to catch The Whistler before he strikes again. The public is expecting to see a show of strength to stop this persistent menace. They need to be reassured that Nantucket is a perfectly safe place to bring their families to enjoy the many wonderful things our island has to offer. It's not too late to save the season, but we need to stop The Whistler now.

If there's another attack of any kind, I can promise you that the Board of Selectmen and I are prepared to make immediate and sweeping changes in response to public demand. Additionally, we expect daily updates until the vandalism issue is resolved. Is that clear?"

"Perfectly clear, perfectly clear, Madame Manager." Stretching his arms wide, Chief Brock shepherded the delegation toward the door. "Now let's move on and let these people get back to work." The Plexiglas door began to close, but Chief Brock blocked it with his hand. He looked back into the room, and his bushy eyebrows waggled as he frowned. "Nice save with that proposal, Lieutenant Jarad. Very nice save. Next time, though, maybe you could run things by me first? We are playing for the same team, you know." And with that, the chief was gone.

CHAPTER NINE

Ted reached into a desk drawer. "Let me show you guys something. Package came for me yesterday. You won't believe what I got."

John squinted. Ted was slipping his head into some kind of olive drab webbing. When Ted looked back up, his gray hair was sticking through the crisscrossed elastic straps in bristling tufts. He also had what appeared to be a pair of binoculars strapped across his eyes.

"Ted? What are you wearing?"

"SuperView NightVision goggles, sir. My latest gear. You really do need full dark to appreciate these beauties, but they come with a thermal tube, an IR illuminator good to one hundred and fifty meters, independent eye focus with diopter adjustment, and a thirty-degree FOV. I wish we'd had a few of these sets in Kuwait City. It would've changed the whole ballgame."

John felt a ripple of competitive curiosity. Of course he had heard of SuperView goggles before, but he had never actually field tested a pair. They were Black Ops, and impossible to come by on the open market. "Where did you find those?"

Ted pushed the goggles to his forehead. "Bought 'em off a guy on eBay, sir. Cost me three-twenty-five plus eighteen bucks shipping but I'll tell you what, these babies are worth every dime."

"Three hundred and fifty bucks? That's a lot of money for one new piece of gear."

"You spent more than that on your new Sigma, sir."

"That was different. It was time to upgrade my sidearm. Once Smith and Wesson built their new accessory side rails for the laser sight, it ended that discussion."

"My old dad used to say that just because you buy a piano doesn't mean you can play one, sir. We've all heard you say that you want to put your thirty years in and never have to pull your piece." Ted looked around the room for a consensus. "Crissakes! Half the time, you're not even packing anymore."

John felt ruffled by Ted's challenge. His sidearm had spent a lot of time locked in a gun safe lately, but that was because his new role as Commander carried a more administrative feel with it. John Q. Public didn't need to know about the backup piece John still carried in his ankle holster. "I carry my Sigma on all calls, Sergeant, not to mention I schedule more time at the practice range than you do. Don't forget, I see the reports."

"I exceed the regs every month, sir, plus, I got all the real practice I needed to get–in the field."

"Excuse me, ladies?" CJ said. "If you two are through comparing sizes, then I need to ask a question. Ted, what did you get those goggles for?"

Ted stared at her with surprise. "To catch The Whistler, of course! Think about it, CJ. Sucker runs through the graveyard, and only works at night. I say we stake out the cemetery, and use these goggles to spotlight the motherfucker. Then, ten to one, next time, we take him out."

"Not a bad Plan B," John noted.

Pulling the goggles over his eyes, Ted swept his hand over the light switch. The room was plunged into a milky darkness. He stood, and he began to step between the desks, his arms outstretched like Frankenstein's monster. "I can't tell you guys how much this rocks!"

"Look, everyone!" Tina giggled. "Ted's gone Borg!"

The security keypad beeped its sequence again and Paul Jenkins stood in the doorway, framed in a halo of warm daylight. Paul paused. He looked uncertain. "Why are you people sitting in the dark?"

John flipped the lights back on. "Ted's demonstrating his new toy. He spent his last paycheck on a pair of night-vision goggles."

"To catch The Whistler? Ted, my friend, that's pure brilliance. You are underestimated by senior members of this department."

"That's what I keep saying, but nobody listens." Ted held the goggles loosely in his hand. "Underappreciated Ted Parsons, that's me."

Paul pulled an accordion folder from his briefcase. Moving toward the central table, he fanned manila folders over the outspread chart. "I know you're going to want to see this. I have the preliminary findings on our bog victim." He pushed his glasses back up his nose. "This one was tricky, a real challenge. I found a couple of surprises, but in the end I believe I got it right. The victim was female–"

"No shit, Sherlock," Ted chortled. "I should get your paycheck."

"Don't mind him," John said. "It's my fault; I got him stirred up. Please, Paul, continue."

"Thank you. The victim was between approximately eighteen and twenty-five years of age. I can tell you that she never had a child because of her pelvic structure." Paul pulled out an x-ray. "At some point in her youth, she broke her right forearm pretty severely. You can see the bone scarring along the radius and ulna, but it healed quite nicely, without any sign of infection." He retrieved a second x-ray from the file. "She also had an exceptional set of teeth. Nice and even without a single cavity or filling, although I did note some unusual wear patterns."

CJ probed her molars with her tongue. "That is exceptional."

"It is, and I believe that it indicates that our victim originally came from a dairy culture."

"Excuse me, sir?" Toby piped up. "What's a dairy culture?"

"Good question. It means that our victim's childhood was spent somewhere that offered a high proportion of dairy products on a daily basis. Going off her bone density, and the condition of her teeth, I'd say our victim had a more than adequate supply of dairy calcium in her early diet."

"Where do you find dairy cultures, sir?" Hank asked.

"Another good question. The U.S., Britain, Scandinavia, parts of northern Europe and Western Africa, and Central Mongolia."

John folded his arms. "I suppose that narrows the search down a bit."

"But wait, there's more." Paul fanned a set of color photographs across the chart. "Here's the first surprise: strangulation was not the cause of death."

"Then how do you explain the bruises on her neck?" John asked.

"Yes, they were present, but the bruising was old, and there's evidence of tissue recovery." Paul tapped the photograph. "However, I believe the bruising does serve as evidence of chronic and repeated tissue abuse."

"Tissue abuse?" Ted guffawed. "What the hell does that mean?"

Paul looked up over the rim of his glasses. "Has anyone ever heard of erotic asphyxiation?"

Hank blinked. "Erotic what?"

"Oh, shit," CJ said. "You're talking about the choking game."

"I am." Paul grimaced. "It's extremely risky behavior that can lead to permanent brain damage, stroke, or death. Technically, erotic asphyxiation is the induction of cerebral anoxia–intentionally reducing the flow of oxygen to the brain during sex to heighten the pleasure of orgasm. The adult technique usually involves using a rope or a belt. According to practitioners, the lack of oxygen produces an exhilaration that intensifies the overall physical sensation."

"Take it easy, Doc, will you?" Ted muttered. "You're getting weird on us."

Paul flipped open his report and smoothed the pages. "It's an easily addictive behavior like gambling or porn. Recovery can take years. Some devotees even create elaborate sexual rituals. Others have been known to construct mechanical devices to bring about the asphyxiation."

"Mechanical devices?" CJ whispered. "Shit. Now I've heard everything."

"Sadly, CJ, it's a hidden tragedy that we don't usually discover until we come across an accidental death by hanging. The death toll–according to the FBI–is between five hundred and a thousand deaths a year." Paul shook his head. "I find it hard to believe that number, but it's a learned behavior that seems to sweep through our schools, especially among the adolescent male population. Some communities have even raised it to epidemic status. It has a lot of nicknames: Airplaning, Space Monkey, Space Cowboy, Suffocation Roulette." Paul tapped the report. "The average participant is between nine and fourteen years old, and males outnumber females two to one. What makes this case unique is that we've found evidence of erotic asphyxiation in a twenty-something female. What makes it even more bizarre is that she wasn't playing the choking game alone."

"She had a partner," John stated.

"Or partners." Paul corrected. "In either case, I believe the repetitive tissue damage around her neck is thumbprint bruising. Someone deliberately and repeatedly pressed on her carotid arteries to shut off the flow of oxygen to her brain during sex."

"Did you find any non-related DNA during the autopsy?" John asked, hoping for an easy break.

"No such luck. I swabbed, but the acidic bog water erased any obvious DNA evidence. But here's what makes me think we're on the right track." Paul splayed yet another set of photographs across the table, a set of graphic close-ups of the victim's neck, forehead, cheekbones, and hennaed eyes. "See these reddish-purple dots on the sclera? Here and here? Those are petechia. They're caused by minor hemorrhages whenever excessive repeated pressure is applied to tissue. Petechia are considered classic signs of the practice of erotic asphyxiation."

"Okay, you've convinced me." John crossed his arms. "So, we know our victim liked to play dirty, but let me get this straight. You're saying that's not what killed her?"

Paul removed his glasses and rubbed his eyes. "No, that's not what killed her."

"She drowned in the bog then?"

"No, I found no evidence of water in her lungs."

"Crissakes, Paul, cough it up!" John lost patience. "How did she die?"

Paul shared a gruesome autopsy photograph. "Blunt force trauma to the temple region of her skull. I should also mention that it was the left temple region, which may indicate your proverbial right-handed killer. I found an interesting bruise forming under the skin during the autopsy. It had an ovoid shape, which indicates the weapon had a rounded or curved edged on it, almost like a scythe, but without a sharpened blade on it, because it didn't break the skin. Additionally, and here's the second surprise: she was being poisoned. I found evidence of persistent liver damage and signs of dilutional hyponatremia. Whether the poisoning was intentional or not remains an outstanding question."

"How could a poisoning be unintentional?" CJ asked.

"Street drugs are cut with all kinds of nasty chemicals. If our victim found a toxic street source, she more than likely poisoned herself with each dose. I sent a liver sample to Nelson Labs to confirm my suspicion, but it'll be weeks before we see the results." Paul smiled ruefully. "Sadly, CJ, as you know, CSI is nowhere near as fast as they portray on TV."

"Was the street drug heroin?" John asked.

"I don't think so. I found no evidence of needle or nasal scarring. I did, however, find significant evidence of acid reflux disease, which is rare in a person this young. I think our victim liked to pop pills, and right now I think the pill of choice, given from what I can surmise about her lifestyle and the unusual wear patterns on her teeth, was ecstasy."

"There you go with the tooth thing again," CJ noted.

"It's a fact. Habitual ecstasy and cocaine users grind their teeth. It's one of the few physical symptoms of prolonged abuse, besides the brain and liver damage, of course. I ruled out cocaine use because of the lack of nasal or sinus irritation." Paul reshuffled his files together neatly. "My report is still preliminary, pending the lab results, but I've signed off on it. I believe you can proceed along my line of reasoning."

John considered this new information. A habitual ecstasy user? He was surprised by that finding. Cocaine, marijuana, and even crystal meth had washed ashore, but ecstasy was mainland club scene junk from bigger cities like Boston, Providence, or New York. What was a club drug like ecstasy doing on Nantucket? "Anything more, Paul? What about that tattoo?"

"There's nothing special about that, I'm afraid. It involved standard, commercially available ink."

"Tina?" John turned. "You were researching the Internet for that design. Did you find anything?"

"I found a ton of images out there, Lieutenant, but I didn't find a perfect match." Tina tapped her monitor. "Most of the images seem to center on Celtic culture, though. The three interlocking circles are supposed to represent the three planes of existence: the physical, the mental, and the spiritual side of human nature. The interlocking circle represents eternity."

"Wait a second," Ted said. "Doesn't Celtic usually mean Irish?"

"We get a lot of summer help from Ireland," CJ said. "Girls who come over to work in the shops or act as mother's helpers."

"Ireland, or the British Isles to be more exact, would be one of those dairy cultures that I mentioned earlier," Paul noted.

John felt the blood tingling in his veins. The familiar premonition meant he was standing on the lip of the precipice, and the investigation was beginning to take shape. Any minute now, he would see the lead and know where to begin. It felt exactly like the slight momentary hesitation a ship makes on the crest of a wave, that heart-stopping second before the rushing unstoppable downward swoop. He pressed on. "Let's consider, then, the suggestion that the victim might be an Irish woman who came over to find work. Where does that take us? How would we check on that?"

"She'd need to register for a visa, right?" CJ drummed her pen against her blotter. "She'd need some kind of federal documentation. They don't let you just hop on a plane and cross the pond anymore."

"Actually." Hank cleared his throat. "She'd need a visa and a temporary labor certificate, an H-2B if she was here to work a seasonal, non-agricultural job. She'd also need a local employer for a sponsor, or a close family member to use as a reference."

John swiveled his chair. "Hank? How do you know that?"

Hank shuffled shyly. "My family's originally from the Azores, sir. Sometimes, when the work in Pico dries up, my cousins come over to find jobs. The younger ones love coming to Nantucket, because their parents, let me tell you, those Portuguese are strict."

"Who would we contact for a list of the, what did you call it? An H2-B? U.S. Immigration or the State Department?" John massaged his temples. "Asking the Feds to do anything is going to take months."

"Actually, Lieutenant, you don't need to ask the Feds for anything." Hank reached for the discarded newspaper, and flipped it open. He tapped a quarter-page classified ad. "It's all right here, sir. Lack of available help must get published in a local paper before you can even apply for an H2-B. The easiest way to get that information would be to go ask these folks: Hussey, Howe & Company, the 'seasonal employment specialists'."

"I'll be damned. It's classic." John felt washed by a wave of pure respect for his junior officer. "If you want to find out how someone died, then first find out how they lived. Nice work, Hank. You just developed our first solid lead."

"Thanks, Lieutenant," Hank stammered. "Hussey-Howe are the folks my family uses, anyway. They're pretty much the only ones on the island who do this type of work."

John checked his watch: 10:32. The agency staffers should have settled in by now. Fanning through the autopsy photographs, he selected some relatively benign close-ups and reached for his keys. "I'm going to go see if they can help." He felt the thrill of pursuit surging through his veins. He wanted to bolt out of the door in his eagerness to follow the lead, but pulled up short instead. This investigation wasn't only about him. Every person in that room had contributed something critical to the end result, and he needed to acknowledge that fact. "Nice work on this one, team. I think we can all be proud of this, if it pans out."

He was rewarded by a roomful of delighted smiles. He even earned a grudging grin of respect from Ted. Damn! John realized. I've finally done something right. He vowed to make use of the team more freely next time. With a start, John realized that this was the perfect time to put that new vow into practice. "Hank? Are you coming with me to interview Hussey-Howe? It was your lead."

"Me, Lieutenant?" Hank scrambled to comply. "Yes, sir!"

CHAPTER TEN

John pulled the cruiser out of the lot. Hank had said something earlier, and his irrepressible curiosity itched. "You said you were from the Azores, Hank? What brought you to Nantucket?"

Hank straightened the folds in his crisply pressed uniform. "I said my family was originally from the Azores, sir. That was three generations ago. We're Americans now."

John shifted uncomfortably. He hadn't meant to offend Hank, but he really didn't know that much about the guy since he had been another Chief Brock pick. Hank had barely squeaked by the force's height requirement, but there was no denying that Hank kept himself trim. He didn't have an ounce of fat on him. His straight black hair held a military part, and his brown eyes radiated injured pride.

"Apologies, Hank. I didn't mean to imply otherwise. Maybe I phrased the question wrong, but naturally, I'm curious. I've heard about the Azores all my life."

Hank flicked a nervous sideways glance. "It wasn't because of the fishing, if that's what you were thinking, sir. We were dirt farmers. My grandfather Eleuterio still talks about growing oranges on the side of the volcano on Pico. That's the island my family was from, originally."

"Your family farmed a volcano?"

"Yeah," Hank laughed. "And now we live on a sandbar. Go figure." He began to pick at his cuticle. "Most folks don't realize the Azores are a thousand miles to sea – not the thirty miles from the mainland like we are here. That's what makes the Portuguese the best sailors in the world. We had to be. Some historians say we even discovered America before Columbus did. Have you ever heard of Miguel Corte Real or Dighton Rock?"

"Can't say that I have."

"That's no surprise." Hank dropped his hands in his lap. "American history is funny that way. If it's not mainstream, it doesn't get mentioned. I just wish people would learn that Portuguese means more than sourdough bread."

John parked in front of a two-story brick storefront. Hank had brought up a valid point, but life was all about balancing your perspective. A too narrow view did no one any good. "True, true, but the bread's not bad, either."

"You're right, sir." Hank opened the door and stepped out. "I guess that's something."

John tucked the folder of morgue photos under his arm. They crossed the sidewalk and stood before a door splashed with dappled sunlight. John stooped to read the names engraved on a brass plate next to a row of black rubber buttons. He identified the button for Hussey, Howe & Co. and mashed it with his thumb. The built-in speaker connected with a crackling hum.

"Yes?" A quavering female voice answered. "May I help you?"

"Lieutenant Jarad, Nantucket Police. I'd like to speak with someone about the foreign worker situation?"

"Do you have an appointment?"

The woman's voice carried the fluting upper-crust overtone that John knew was ingrained and not simply imitated. "No. I was hoping to keep this informal."

"One moment, please. I'll check."

The speaker disconnected with an alarming electronic crackle. John straightened. "Rudely left standing on the sidewalk," he noted. "Have you ever run across a roadblock using these people before, Hank?"

"No, sir." Hank scratched his jaw. "But then, we always had an appointment."

The speaker clicked repeatedly. "Lieutenant Jarad? Ms. Howe is available to see you now. Our office is located at the head of the stairs, second floor, on the right. Please come straight up."

The street door buzzed and he started up the narrow staircase. The stairs were so old, their central tread was worn hollow, and so narrow that John kicked the riser with each step. The hallway smelled of shellac and lemon polish. It made a heady perfume. The varnish on the walls had crackled into a pattern like a sea turtle's shell. At the top of the stairs, an opaque glass door and the transom above it were lit from within. The glass panel displayed the words Hussey, Howe & Co., Employment Specialists in two crescents of gilded script in a typestyle left over from the Roaring Twenties of the last millennium.

John opened the door and uncovered an office the exact opposite of the inherited antiquity in the outer hall. Plush maroon carpeting underscored a pair of tufted leather chairs, and a series of maritime prints hung on the paneled walls. As they entered, an elderly woman rose from behind a desk.

Adjusting her glasses, she tottered forward to greet them.

"Hank Viera, what a delight! I didn't know you were at the door. How's Filomena?"

"Grandmother's fine, Mrs. Vickery." Hank gently took her outstretched hand. "She's home now, recuperating. Thanks for asking."

"Please mention that I asked after her, won't you? We've missed seeing her in church. Dear me, a broken hip is nothing to fool around with. Sad to say, I've seen it happen to far too many of my friends lately."

She next turned her shrewd eyes on John. He noted that although the delicate skin under Mrs. Vickery's eyes overlapped in several crepey layers, her blue eyes sparkled with a nimble intelligence.

"And you, Lieutenant Jarad? Aren't you one of Jenny's boys?"

John smiled, amused to still be defined in this manner. He was a commissioned police Lieutenant and almost thirty years old, and that was always the first thing people mentioned. Nantucket was such a small world. No matter how independently you lived, you dragged your family history behind you like a second shadow. "Yes, I'm her son, John."

"Ayeh, I thought so. You're the spitting image of your brother, Micah. He was often over at our house, playing with my sons Ethan and Nick." Mrs. Vickery cocked her head like an alert sparrow. "I'll see if Clarissa is available." She tottered away on surprisingly high heels before tapping a half-opened inner door with her knuckle. "Clarissa? Are you free?"

"I am now, Mrs. Vickery, and I'm not moving my car if that's what this is about. That parking space was guaranteed when I bought the building. The police should know that-"

"I don't believe that's why the officers are here, dear. Lieutenant Jarad mentioned that he wanted to discuss the foreign worker situation."

"Oh? Very well. Send them in."

Mrs. Vickery escorted them to an inner sanctum even more luxuriously appointed than the reception room. Casement windows framed the million-dollar view down Main Street toward the yacht basin. The carpeting in this room was hunter green, and the atmosphere vibrated from an array of PC monitors and fax machines mounted on a sideboard table. As they entered, a woman looked up from a binder opened on her desk. Her eyes narrowed and she frowned.

John was surprised to see that Clarissa Howe was mixed race. He hadn't anticipated that. Her skin was the color of polished teak. Her dark hair was cut in a bob to just below her ears. Clarissa had plenty of curves that she made no attempt to camouflage with her choice of apparel. She toyed with a beaded string that held a pair of reading glasses around her neck. Was the gesture an unconscious nervous tell?

"My dear, you remember Hank Viera? And this officer is Lieutenant Jarad."

"Hank, of course. Delighted to see you again. I hope you've brought us more business." Clarissa waved them toward a semi-circle of chairs. "Take a seat. I don't mean to sound rude, but we are extremely busy right now. Our season has already begun. What can we do for the Nantucket police?"

John took the chair on the far right of the row, keeping Hank on his left. Surprisingly, Mrs. Vickery made no move to leave. Instead, she settled into the partner's chair at Clarissa's right hand and looked like she planned on staying. Instinct warned him to proceed cautiously until he knew where he stood. John placed the autopsy folder on the floor next to his foot. "We'd like some information about foreign workers. Hank? What was the name of that form, again?"

"An H2-B, sir."

"Ah." Clarissa steepled her fingers. "Our temporary seasonal workers. We facilitate a lot of them. It's one of the reasons we're so busy at the moment. What is it that you need to know? I can tell you that Hussey-Howe is required to register as the employer of record with the U.S. Department of Labor, and that all H2-B employees must register directly through us. Isn't that right, Mrs. V?" Clarissa toyed with her glasses. "We also need to file a blanket I-129 Petition for Non-Immigrant Workers with the Bureau of U.S. Citizenship and Immigration Services for our alien worker visas." She pointed to a stack of forms in a bin. "That's the reason for the mountain of paperwork you see on on my desk."

John sat up. An idea was beginning to take shape. "Let me get this straight. These seasonal workers are actually Hussey-Howe employees?"

"Yes, they are, but my point was that H2-B employees are legal immigrant workers. There is nothing illegal about any part of our process. Everything we do is fully documented with the federal government." She checked her watch. "That covers our general business practice. Have I answered all of your questions?"

With a flash of inspiration, the investigation opened up. It was so simple. If these foreign workers were Hussey-Howe employees, then surely they could pull some kind of report on them? And if they did pull a report, what were the odds that the bog victim was one of the names on that list? "All but one," John said. "Are any Hussey-Howe employees missing?"

Clarissa blinked. She stood and slowly walked to the window, crossing her arms. "That question puts me in an awkward position, Lieutenant. Of course, we do occasionally lose a seasonal worker—every agency does. It can't be helped. Some foreign workers come to the U.S. with no intention of returning home. They hop a mainland ferry, and that's the last we ever see of them."

John began to feel the warning heat of rising frustration. If Hussey-Howe had a history of missing employees, then why weren't these people being reported to the *local* authorities? "Working with the Feds is all well and good, but if these people are MIA, then why didn't you report them to us?"

Mrs. Vickery coughed softly. "I can answer that question, Lieutenant. It's because we're not regulated to do so. I'm sure that may seem short-sighted, but that's been our standing policy. We've never had the staff to cover any voluntary notifications. We're a small business operation. It's difficult enough to manage as it is." Her trembling hands smoothed her collar flat. "Besides, it's never been a large number, at most one or two employees a year. We do report any runners to Immigration within the federally mandated forty-eight hours. We've never been out of compliance on it, not once, in all of our many years in business."

John felt appalled. One or two missing people a year? Twenty people in a decade who fell through the cracks, and their loss was simply dismissed? Someone, somewhere, simply drew a line through their name in a ledger, and that's as far as it went?

Clarissa turned away from the window. "What are these questions really about, Lieutenant? Who is it that you're looking for?"

He leaned forward. "I'm sure you've read about the victim we found in Satan's Tub. We have good reason to believe she may have been a foreign worker."

"And how did you come to that stunning conclusion?" Clarissa asked.

"The autopsy report points that way, not to mention that no one else has been reported as missing: no residents, none of the tourists, no day-trippers coming from the mainland. The only people missing are these foreign workers that no one cares enough about to report on, whenever one of them goes missing." His voice cracked as his anger broke through. "I can promise you, though, that someone, somewhere is missing this woman, and we're going to find out what happened to her, and return her to her family."

Clarissa looked alarmed. "What is it that you expect from us?"

"I want you to give me a list of those missing employees, for a start."

"Impossible." Clarissa lifted her chin. "Employee data is strictly confidential. Families on both sides of the client relationship put their trust in us. I'd like to help you, Lieutenant, but I will not give that up. To do so would undermine the integrity of our business. That is a line I will not cross."

The blood began to pound in John's ears. He had enough probable cause to ask Judge Coffin for a warrant and to force her to give him that report, but was that the best course of action? He stared at the carpet and saw the packet of autopsy photographs at his feet as another idea came to mind. "Would you be willing to look at a photograph, to see if we can identify her that way?"

"Let me see what you've brought." Clarissa stretched out a hand. She returned to her desk, and centered the folder on her blotter before opening it slowly. Using her fingernails like tweezers, she separated the photos before sharing each one with Mrs. Vickery. Once her methodical review was complete, Clarissa sighed. Her shoulders slumped in relief. "I want to help you, Lieutenant, but I've never seen this woman before."

"I have," Mrs. Vickery stated. "I know her." Removing her glasses, she drew the photograph even closer to her eyes. "She was before your time, my dear, when your father was still with us. Lemuel Howe passed away two years ago, Lieutenant, and Clarissa came in to continue the business." She angled the photograph toward the window to capture better light. "I can't recall her name, but her file would still be in the archive. We're very thorough about record retention, Lieutenant. We have to be. We never throw anything away."

John's heart leapt. "Could you search this archive to find her name?"

"That sounds reasonable enough to me." Mrs. Vickery re-stacked the photographs neatly like a deck of cards. "Clarissa, I believe that's what your father would have done."

Clarissa tapped her lips. "The archive is still paper, so that will take some time. I'm willing to help with one caveat: if we do find her file, and if we determine that the family who hired her is still on the island, then I insist that we be allowed to contact the family first, to let them know what to expect. I am not willing to spring this on anyone, Lieutenant, and that is not negotiable. As I said, client trust is the foundation of our business. Can you work with that?"

That was a compromise he could live with. "How long will it take you to sift through your archive?"

Clarissa's laugh was deep and throaty and honest. "Take it easy on us, Lieutenant! Hussey-Howe has been in business since 1827. You're asking for a lot of research, on top of our regular workload."

"And to forestall your next question," Mrs. Vickery coughed delicately, "I was not an original founding member of the firm." She smiled at her own wit. "Clarissa, why don't I ask Molly Widdoes in to help us? This type of detail work sounds right up her alley."

"That's a great suggestion, Mrs. V." Clarissa closed and returned the folder. "We should have some news for you, Lieutenant, either later today or first thing tomorrow. How does that sound?"

"That sounds great-"

John flinched as his beeper vibrated. He checked the message: CD 4-17. Code four, vehicular accident. Anything code four demanded his immediate attention. He stood. "We appreciate your cooperation. We've got another call. Hank? Let's roll."

Hank followed him down the steep steps at a trot. "What's up, Lieutenant?"

"A four-seventeen." Sliding behind the wheel, John dialed up the handset before hitting the overhead lights. He refrained from turning the siren on until they were out of the town limits because local residents objected to the noise. "Dispatch? Tina? What've we got?"

"Four-seventeen on Milestone Road, sir. Firefighters and EMTs are in route. Just past the turn for Nobadeer Farm Road. Sounds like a real mess, sir. I've fielded three nine-one-ones on it so far."

"On our way." John peeled left on Orange Street. Rapidly and repeatedly, he scanned the side streets and back alleys for incoming traffic. Forget looking for random kids on bikes; today's modern hazard was oblivious joggers wearing headsets. "Where's Ted?"

"Ted just checked in, sir. He's on site."

"Good. ETA four minutes."

The tires squealed as they raced around the rotary. Reaching Milestone Road, John pushed the unit even harder. The driver of a delivery truck noticed the flashing strobes in his rearview mirror and pulled over into the sand. As they blew past, John gave him a two-finger salute. It was nice to see that someone still obeyed the traffic laws. Up ahead, an EMS van was already parked behind a fire truck on the shoulder of the road. John pulled in sharply behind it and parked. Ted had already set out a line of sputtering red flares, and he was directing the traffic around the site to keep things moving. John was pleased to see that Ted had taken the initiative on this. It was proactive, and the correct response. Leaning down, he popped the trunk. "Hank? Refresh those flares and relieve Ted on traffic detail."

"Yes, sir."

"Glad to see you, Lieutenant." Ted cocked his thumb. "Looks like pure accident, sir. A big doe jumped out right in front of the car. The driver – that hot-looking MILF with the EMTs over there – wasn't speeding but then, it doesn't take much to wipe out one of these little foreign jobs. Good thing the kid was strapped in the backseat because that doe leveled the windshield." All of this reporting was leaving Ted breathless. "Blondie's pretty shook up. The airbag deployed, and it broke her nose. She wasn't making much sense when I got here. The girl EMT says she's in shock."

John surveyed the site. A sporty red Audi A4 was slewed diagonally across both lanes of Milestone Road. The right fender, grill, hood, and the windshield were smashed. The accident path was littered with bits of metal, shards of tinted glass, and tufts of tan fur. A crimson puddle of blood was leeching off the asphalt into the sand, turning the pale sand pink. The bright puddle had already drawn a feeding line of bottle-nosed flies. Stepping carefully, John scanned the line of limping tracks that staggered off onto Conservancy land. "Any witnesses?"

"Just Eddie there, sir." Ted pointed to a weedy-looking man who was leaning against a rusting red pickup truck. "Says he saw it happen. Swears no one was speeding, it just happened so quick, no one had time to react."

"I'll talk with Eddie in a minute, but it sounds right." John evaluated the road's surface. "No skid marks, no attempt to avoid collision." He walked toward the EMS van where a tanned, well-toned blonde woman with a big diamond ring and earrings to match was holding a blue ice pack to her face. A pretty little girl of six or seven years old sat next to her. She kept repeatedly patting her mother's leg.

"Don't cry, Mommy. You're going to be okay."

John knelt. "Ma'am? Is there someone we can call for you?"

The woman lowered the blue ice pack and John's stomach heaved. Her nose was clearly broken, and she was already developing a spectacular set of black eyes. John hated seeing bruises on women and children, no matter the reason behind them.

"I'm sorry, Officer." She wiped the tears from her eyes, and flinched. "I don't know where that deer came from. I didn't see her at all. I swear I was paying attention. Mommy was paying attention, wasn't she, sweetheart? She wasn't talking on her cell phone this time, was she? You'll tell Daddy that, won't you?" Her shoulders shook as she began to weep. "How can they walk on legs so thin? I am so, so sorry! I didn't mean to hit her!"

The EMT in the neon yellow vest folded a thermal blanket across the woman's shoulders. "That's the shock talking, Lieutenant. We've already notified her husband. He's flying in on the next shuttle."

John studied the daughter. He smiled when she met his eyes. "You're being very brave, miss. I'm sure you're a good help for your mother."

"Thank you, policeman." She smiled shyly.

John stood. Mother and child were in capable hands. There was nothing more he could do for them at the moment. He nodded to the EMT. "We'll follow up with you later." Returning to the site, he stood next to an oddly silent Ted, who had tucked his thumbs into his duty belt. Ted looked obviously uncomfortable.

"No way that doe survives the hit, Lieutenant." He grimaced. "Not with losing that much blood."

"You got that right, Teddy-boy," Eddie crowed. "I seen her limp off. She looked all busted up. Barely limped away on the three good legs she had left. She'll bleed out, eventually."

John fingered the snap on his holster. He hated thinking of the animal staggering through the brush, suffering a lingering death in helpless pain. "What do you think, Sergeant? Could we track her down and finish this?"

Ted looked doubtful. He scanned the horizon.

"I suppose we could try, sir. We're gonna have some trouble tracking her through all the scrub. My bet is she's halfway to Eel Point by now."

Eddie hawked and spat into the sand. "You'll find that doe soon enough, warm as it. Sooner or later, some hiker's gonna smell it."

CHAPTER ELEVEN

Anxiety twisted Sarah's stomach into a knot. Steve Barnett looked haggard. His skin held the smudgy gray undertones of a February Pittsburgh sky. He had such dark circles under his eyes he looked like a raccoon. The sable stubble on his cheeks and chin didn't help matters any, either.

Steve had called them down to an emergency staff meeting. He was pacing the dining room floor with his hands clasped behind his back. In spite of the double ibuprofen Sarah had taken for her sprains, she still flinched when Alien nudged her sore ribs.

"Get a load of him," Alien whispered. "He thinks he's Captain Bligh."

Steve stopped his restless pacing. "Okay, folks, listen up." He nervously eyed his staff. "I've got news. Not all of it's bad. True, it's not what I hoped for, but I think that if we stick together, we should be alright."

We'll be alright? What did Steve mean by that?

"First, and most importantly, I'm glad to report that no one was seriously injured because of the trouble last night. We were lucky. It could've been worse, a lot worse. Yes, there were some complaints, and if you hear of any, pass them along and I'll send them to the attorneys. They're handling that part of this now." He dragged his fingers through his hair. "Here's the thing. The Fire Marshall has closed The Tap Room." He waved down the sudden uproar. "It's not permanent, but we do need to add a second emergency exit before we can reopen. The owner has already talked to the insurance company and the architect, and demolition will begin as soon as we get the permit. We've asked for an accelerated review and then, once we pass inspection again, we'll re-open The Tap Room as soon as possible, hopefully by the end of next week."

"Woo-hoo! Free vay-kay!" A line cook pumped his arms in the air. "Par-tee! Surfside beach here we come."

Steve pinched the bridge of his nose. "I suppose you could look at it like that, but here's the rub. We've all been furloughed. I've tried talking the owner out of it, but he won't budge, rat bastid that he is. He did agree that you can stay in The Dorm and that we will keep the kitchen open for employees only, but he won't cover anyone's salary – including mine – until we reopen, however long that takes." His shoulders slumped. "I'm sorry. That's the best I could do."

Panic needled Sarah's heart. She quickly calculated her cash on hand plus the eighty-three dollars from last night's tips. Somehow, she would have to stretch ninety-three bucks to last a week, but with free food and housing, she knew she could do it. She would just have to be careful, that's all. She smiled grimly. Even though the United Bank of Sarah was now officially closed, being a university student had taught her nothing if not how to keep to a tight budget. She gave a lame passing thought to the safety net her old credit card had provided, and rejected the thought as unworthy of her new life. She was braver than that. She didn't need Mason's backup credit any more. She had been right to cut the card into pieces and bury it in the cow barn back in Vermont. Her escape lay in not leaving any trail markers that Mason might follow to find her, and that included having the bank mail Mason a blank billing statement each month until he finally got tired of it and closed the account.

Steve lowered his chin to his chest. Sarah felt a bloom of sympathy for the guy. He looked so tired, so defeated, so beaten.

He crossed his arms. "I can't blame you if you decide to bail on me, but this wasn't my decision to make. Yes, it will scuttle our chances to compete during Restaurant Week if you go because I won't have time to hire another great staff, but we'll muddle through somehow. We always do. Right now, you need to do what's best for you." He brightened. "I can promise that I'll do everything I can to make up for the lost wages -"

"Screw you, man!" The skinny line cook jumped up. "No pay? Is that what you're saying? I'm outta here! I'll have me another job lined up in an hour."

Steve looked about ready to collapse. The line cook strutted toward the door and then fell back as the door slammed open and Leslie rushed in. She stepped aside to let the line cook out before blocking the door with her body.

"Sorry, I'm late!" She pushed her hair back off her face. "Listen! I've talked to some of the other restaurant and bar owners, and they're willing to take on anyone who needs part-time work until The Tap Room re-opens. I know this isn't the greatest solution, but it's one that will work, and it will keep our crew together." She crossed the room and stood by Steve's side. "What do you say? Are you guys willing to stick it out for one week? I know I am."

A chair squeaked. Cook, the head chef, stood up. He laced his hands together and cracked his knuckles. "You caught a bad bounce with this one, Steve. I don't know about the rest of you mugs, but I signed on to work at

The Tap Room. Count me in. I'm staying."

"Count me in, too!" Alien scrambled up. She laughed. "Besides, I've got no place else to go."

Sarah shivered as the truth in Alien's words struck home. Alien was right; she didn't have a choice either. She was stuck. She needed to keep the housing that came with this job or else she would be living out on the street. Returning to Pittsburgh was not an option either, because that meant running into Mason. Until she could make a change in her life for the better, she would just have to take whatever came at her and like it because she was trapped by circumstance. She wanted to rage at the helplessness of her situation, but she knew that it would do no good because no one cared enough about her to help out. She was truly on her own. It was up to her to help herself. She would just have to keep her eyes open for any opportunity to make her situation better and until that time, she would have to tough it out.

Thankfully, the situation wasn't permanent. She had survived worse. This was only a temporary setback, a delay. She would be back on her feet by the end of the summer, and on her way again, as planned. Not to mention she had already made this decision the minute she had stepped on the boat. Sarah stood. "Count on me, too. I'm staying."

There was a scraping of many chairs as the rest of The Tap Room staff joined her. The dining room echoed with a bellowing chorus of shouted agreement. Steve wiped his eyes and surveyed the room. Other than the line cook who had left earlier, the entire Tap Room staff proved loyal.

"Thanks, guys. This really means a lot to me." Steve turned. "And thank you, Leslie, for what you did just now. That was very thoughtful of you."

"Hell with that." Leslie beamed. "I saved your bacon."

"Yes, yes, you did."

Steve reached for Leslie's arm. Wrapping his arm around her waist, he pulled her close and kissed her hard on the lips. Sarah knew it was probably inappropriate behavior coming from a manager, but it was funny as hell because Leslie went as stiff as if she'd received an electric shock. When Steve released her, her eyes were wide with surprise.

"Thank you, too, I guess!" she sputtered.

"So what do we do now?" Alien asked. "Want to go looking for a part-time job?"

Sarah was surprised by Alien's questions. She hadn't realized before that Alien considered her to be half of a team. She had drawn the line at being involuntary roommates, but when Sarah considered the idea of hanging out with Alien, she thought, Why not? It might be fun to hang out with someone. True, Alien wasn't her first choice for a permanent new best friend, but the pickings were slim. She shouldn't turn her nose up at Alien's offer. She briefly considered going back to bed and curling up to nurse her sore foot and ribs but then she thought, To hell with that! She couldn't remember the last time she'd had a full week off, and she wasn't going to waste it lying in bed. Maybe it was time to explore what Nantucket had to offer. "What's there to do if we're not working?"

"Girlfriend, that's the right answer." Alien smiled warmly. "Daytime, or nighttime?"

Sarah felt ashamed when she saw how Alien lit up once she agreed to her suggestion. Maybe Alien had been feeling a little lonely and friendless, too? "Let's start with daytime."

"Great!" Alien ticked the points off on her fingers. "We have two options: We can explore the town and go shopping, or we can rent bikes and ride to the beach."

Shopping was always on Sarah's top list of favorite things to do but today it sounded risky, knowing that she could blow her entire budget on one solid purchase. Riding bikes to the beach sounded slightly more affordable but still, Sarah found a reason to worry. "How much will renting bikes cost?"

"Won't be much. I know the Bike Man personally. He'll cut us a deal."

"Then let's do that."

The bike rental shop was one block over from Steamboat Wharf on Easy Street. Most of the shops on the street catered to the tourists by offering cheap T-shirt deals, hand-dipped ice cream, and homemade fudge. Every other sunburn victim sported some new item of clothing with the acronym ACK on it. Alien had explained that ACK stood for Nantucket's airport, Ackerman Field. Even scarier were the old guys strolling through town wearing T-shirts with the phrase 'I AM the Man from Nantucket' stretched across their beer bellies. Really? Did these guys even look in a mirror before they went out in public dressed like that?

The Hit The Road Bike Shop proved to be a Quonset hut leftover from the Second World War. Sarah followed Alien warily as she stepped across the threshold into the dim warehouse. Dozens of bikes were arranged in a row against the back wall. The workbench on Sarah's right was littered with a mound of cycling debris including a socket wrench snarled in twisted wire, an uncapped glue tube next to a square deck of rubber patches, and a handful of chrome whistles scattered around a lethal-looking teepee of loose spokes.

"Hell-o, ladies." The proprietor stepped out of the dim back room. He was rangy, at least six feet tall and dirty blonde. Even though he looked to be entering solid middle-age, he was holding onto his youth by sporting a hipster soul patch on his chin. He stubbed his cigarette out in an overflowing ashtray before clapping his hands and rubbing them together. "I sure hope I have what you two fine ladies are looking for today."

"Down, boy," Alien stated. "Dave, this is my friend, Sarah. We need bikes. We want to ride out to 'Sconset."

"'Sconset's a great ride. I just came from there. Sarah, nice to meet you." He scratched his goatee. "Let me set you up with the Fliers. They're oldies but goodies, just like me." Rolling two bikes from the lineup, Dave began to paw through the debris on the worktable before pulling two looped steel cables free. "Here we go. Don't forget, all my locks are preset at 0-0-7." He snickered. "Makes it easier to remember."

Sarah felt compelled to mention the flaw in his logic. "Haven't the bike thieves figured that out by now?"

Dave winked. "That's the beauty of my system, babe-o-licious. We're on an island thirty miles to sea. Where they gonna go? Besides, the ferry dudes know to keep an eye out for my bikes. We do a little import/export business on the side, if you know what I mean. You two want helmets?"

"None for me, thanks." Sarah loved the freedom of feeling the wind in her hair. "I'm good."

"I'll bet you are."

"What's the damage, Dave?" Alien said. "We gonna need these for a couple of hours."

"How about ten bucks, each?" He rolled a side door open. "I'll cut you a deal since you introduced me to your pretty new friend. You can pay me when you bring them back. I know where you live. Carpe diem, ladies. Enjoy your day."

Sarah hopped on her bike and pedaled away. It was a good thing that riding a bike was one of those skills you never forgot because she couldn't remember the last time she'd ridden a bike, plus she wanted to put some distance between herself and Dave. She hadn't liked the way he had studied her every move in the bike shop, and her creeper sixth sense was tingling, and that was one feeling she never ignored. Alien quickly caught up with her. They wobbled gleefully down the paved street.

"This way, Sarah! I'll show you the bike path. Follow me."

She followed Alien easily enough. The afternoon sun had warmed the vegetation and the pine trees lining the road added their spicy cedar scent to the air. The path proved to be an effortless series of dips with gentle curves and rises. It was so pleasant to be out in the sunshine that Sarah knew she had made the right choice. She could hear Alien singing up ahead but since Alien couldn't carry a tune, Sarah had no idea which song it was, and that was okay, too, since it didn't matter. She was just grateful that Alien had suggested that they go the beach. She had made the right decision.

The pine trees began to thin out. They were replaced by low, twiggy bushes covered in white blossoms that looked exactly like popcorn. The landscape began to change, too. It became a rolling moor crisscrossed by many sandy lanes and snaking footpaths. The bike path unexpectedly crossed the road, and after checking both ways for non-existent traffic,

Alien followed it. The path began to run beside a section of split-rail fencing festooned with magenta roses. Alien coasted to a stop and leaned against the fence.

She pointed uphill, to the right. "I thought you should see this. That's the path to Altar Rock."

"I don't know what Altar Rock is," Sarah admitted.

"It's the highest point of land on Nantucket, although that's not saying much. You can see a whole panorama of the island from up there."

A panorama? Sarah felt intrigued. "How far is it?"

"About a mile, mile and a half. Do you want to see it? We'd have to leave our bikes here. It's sand all the way in, but that is why we brought locks."

"Do you mind? I would like to go see it."

"Let's do it." Alien pulled a lock from the wicker basket strapped to her handlebars. She locked the bikes together and began to march uphill.

As the sweat popped out along her hairline and across her shoulders, Sarah realized that Nantucket was so flat that it didn't take much of a rise to create the sensation of mastering a decent climb. She struggled for footing in the gravelly soil, but she had always enjoyed the feeling of healthy exercise, and carrying a loaded tray across a barroom floor couldn't compare to this. Pumping her arms, she topped the first rise. The path angled sharply up and the wind began to catch her hair. She stopped to take a look around and was delighted to see what a change in perspective made. When seen from above, the nondescript scrubland of the moor became a nubby blanket of dulcet greens and slaty grays. The pines on Milestone Road framed the view. Puffy clouds scudded along the horizon, competing with incoming breakers in lines of crisp Bristol white. Right then and there, Sarah decided that Altar Rock was a prime contender for the first of her Nantucket paintings.

"Why have you stopped?" Alien called. "Is something wrong?"

"No!" Sarah laughed. "Something's right." She continued up the path. "I was looking at your panorama, and thinking about doing a painting."

"I didn't know you were an artist," Alien puffed. Reaching the top of the hill, she pointed to an anvil-shaped boulder surrounded by a ring of lesser stones and crushed beer cans. "Okay, Michelangelo, here you go. Take a look at this."

Sarah joined her. She was searching for a rock that fit her idea of what an altar should look like when she noticed that the anvil-shaped boulder was resting on the crest of the hill. "Get outta town! That's Altar Rock? I'm so disappointed. I was expecting something, well, bigger."

"I'll bet you say that to all the boys," Alien guffawed. "Okay, I admit it's a little over-sold, but get a load of the view."

Sarah turned. Alien was right. The view alone was worth the hike. She had spent the last month in such a spinning whirl that she hadn't even stopped to breathe, but when she stared off into the distance, Sarah felt her spirit brighten. She could see the town church steeples pointing to the barrier beach at Coatue. She turned and faced south. The land on this side dropped steeply to meet the distant cranberry bogs where two perfectly round ponds reflected the brilliant silvery sunshine back into her eyes like polished mirrors. She inhaled deeply and relaxed all the way down to her toes, captured by a feeling of pure spellbound rapture. Her soul bubbled up and overflowed with bliss. Sarah felt as if she had finally found the one true place, the sanctuary she had been searching for all these long and lonely months without ever really believing that such a place existed. She refused to analyze the feeling because she feared that if she started to pick at it she would lose the delicious sensation that she was finally and wonderfully free.

"That big pond there is Gibbs'." Alien pointed with her cigarette. "The smaller one is Satan's Tub. Damn, but these Puritans had a sick sense of humor." She took one last drag on the cigarette and stubbed it out against Altar Rock. "I'll bet you don't get a view like this in Pittsburgh."

"Actually, we do," Sarah admitted. She was terrified by the thought, but if she was going to trust Alien enough to be her friend, then she would need to share some information about her past. "I shared a condo on Mount Washington with my fiancé. The view was spectacular. You could see The Point and all the way across the three rivers to the North Shore."

"You have a fiancé?" Alien cocked her head. "Where is he now?"

"I should have said ex-fiancé." Sarah blinked away sudden tears. "It was a horrible relationship. Mason was nuts. I had to leave him. He killed my dog. He said it was an accident, but I know that's a lie, because I saw him do it. He did it on purpose, too, to punish me. To prove that he was in control of me."

"Did you just say he killed your dog?"

"Um-hum." Sarah dried her face. She hated to be seen crying in front of other people. It left her feeling vulnerable, and weak. "I saw Mason's face when he did it. It was no accident. He got mad at me, so he bounced the ball off our balcony for revenge, and Murphy went after it. Okay, so maybe Murphy wasn't the smartest dog on the planet, but that's why I left. Mason thought it was funny. I could put up with all the shit he put me through, but what kind of man hurts a dog?"

"That is sick." Alien looked outraged. "But you're safe now, right? That prick doesn't know where you are?"

"That's what I'm praying for." Sarah faced the hard truth. "The only way I could get free of Mason was to leave Pittsburgh. He doesn't know I'm here. If he did, he'd come after me." She hugged herself tight. She wasn't cold, but she couldn't stop shivering.

"Let's get you out of this wind. It's too breezy up here." Alien started down a path. "This trail is steeper, but it looks like a shortcut. You'll feel better once we get to the beach."

The new trail was steeper. As Sarah followed Alien into a sandy ravine, she worried about Alien's reaction to her tale of woe. What would Alien think of her now? Had she come off sounding like a complete nut job? Had she revealed too much, too soon? Alien seemed sympathetic, but their friendship was so new that Sarah wasn't sure. Should she have mentioned that Mason was the first man she had ever truly loved with her whole heart? Did that explain any part of this? But then, what did it say about her that she could even fall for a guy like that? It was all too confusing. She couldn't begin to untangle it. That was a big part of the problem. There didn't seem to be a good place to start.

The gorse lining the path began to tickle Sarah's legs. She stopped to brush them off.

"We'll have a tick check when we get back." Alien jumped across a pebbly wash. She landed awkwardly and flailed both arms to keep her balance. "Sorry about this trail. It's rougher than I expected."

"I hate ticks," Sarah admitted. "I hate them even worse than slugs. Actually, I'm not partial to any insects. Thanks for bringing it up."

"Don't mention it." Alien laughed. She hopped over an eroded gully before following a twisting path into a protected sandy hollow. "The good news is that if you get a tick on you, I can burn it off using one of my cigarettes."

"You're a true friend." Sarah searched the dirt for her next foothold. "I appreciate your thoughtfulness, but let's try to avoid that scenario for today if we can, okay?"

Alien stopped so quickly that Sarah bumped right into her.

"Hey! What's up?"

"I don't think we should go this way anymore. What's that clinking sound? Do you hear that? What's making that noise?"

"I don't hear anything." Sarah stepped toward a flatter wedge of sand. Looking to her right, she froze in horror. Someone had severed a deer's head and planted it on a stick. Her brain ticked in involuntary slow motion as her eyes absorbed the gruesome details. It wasn't just any stick, but a substantial pole stripped of its bark and planted with intent in the gritty soil. The bloody, matted head faced Satan's Tub. From the location, and the placement, it was obvious that the object had been given some kind of ritual meaning. A bloodstained whistle dangled from a cord strung through the animal's black nose, and the clinking sound was the noise the whistle made whenever the breeze batted it against the pole. The whistle's pendulum swing continuously disturbed the cluster of iridescent flies that were feeding off the deer's emptied eye sockets and distended purple tongue.

Sarah flinched. Her movement dislodged a pebble avalanche that gathered speed as it rolled down into the hollow, disturbing the flies at their horrible feast. The buzzing, thrumming sound shifted as the flies abandoned the pole and flew to meet the intruders. Within seconds, Sarah was enveloped in a cloud of swarming insects.

"Ohmigod!" she shrieked. "Get them off me! They're in my hair!"

"Run!" Alien shouted. "Run, Sarah, run this way! Follow me."

They struck off the path running in a blind panic. Racing downhill toward the road, they tore through the gorse and brambles. Thorns shredded Sarah's legs. Alien tripped over an exposed root system and went flying. She landed hard on her palms and her knees.

"Keep going!" She rocked in pain. "I'll catch up!"

"I'm not leaving." Sarah tugged her arm. "Not without you."

They limped back to their bikes. Once Sarah realized that she was free of the clinging flies, she released Alien's arm and bent over. Her stomach heaved and she threw up.

"That's okay," Alien wheezed. Clutching her chest, she waved weakly. "Do whatever you have to do to feel better."

Sarah spat the sour taste off her tongue. "What was that thing?"

"I don't know." Alien howled in frustration as she fumbled with the lock. "I don't know!"

The back of Sarah's neck and scalp began to prickle, and the space between her shoulder blades felt strangely exposed. Her heart was beating like a trip hammer. Was someone still up on Altar Rock, watching them? Through a scope or binoculars, maybe? Alien pitched the lock into her basket and Sarah yanked her bike free. Alien didn't hesitate. She hopped on her bike and took off. Sarah stood on her pedals, racing to catch up.

"We need to find the cops," Sarah shouted. "Tell them what we found."

In spite of her bloodied knee, Alien reached Milestone Road first. She rode pell-mell straight into the middle of the road and dropped the bike, waving her arms like mad at the only vehicle on the road, a white pickup truck loaded with fishing tackle.

"Stop! Stop!" Alien shrieked. "We need help!"

The truck pulled to the side of the road with squealing brakes, and the driver stepped out. Sarah was surprised to see he was a uniformed police officer.

"What's the trouble?" he asked.

"We found this thing, this horrible thing," Alien reported, "on Altar Rock. A deer's head, all covered with flies."

"Yes." Sarah found her voice. "Stuck on a pole. There was a whistle, too, on a cord through the deer's nose."

Alien turned. "You saw a whistle? The Whistler did this?"

The cop looked uneasy. He glanced around. "Let's take care of you two first." He wheeled Alien's bike off the road before lowering the tailgate of his truck so they could both sit. "Let's start with names. I'm Lieutenant Jarad, and you are?"

"Eileen Lippman, and she's Sarah Hawthorne."

He pointed at Alien's bloodied knee. "Do either of you feel the need for a paramedic?"

"No, I'm fine. It's only a scrape. But I'm worried about her. Sarah? How are you feeling now?"

How was she feeling now? Sarah felt confused and vague and yet at the same time the world seemed to offer a singular clarity as if she was moving at a slower pace slightly out of sync with everything else. The only thing that really bothered her was that she couldn't seem to stop trembling. She lifted her hands to her face. They were quivering like silver maple leaves before a summer storm. She flexed her fingers to make them stop, but still, they quivered. Why couldn't she control that? "I'm okay." Her voice sounded hollow to her ears. She tried to joke, "But I'm not going back up there again anytime soon." Her laughter came out sounding like a croak. What was going on?

"Take my jacket." The cop unzipped his windbreaker. He draped it over her shoulders. "You're in shock. You two stay put. I'm calling for backup."

Sarah was instantly enveloped in a layer of protective warmth. She smelled key lime, and assumed it came from the aftershave the cop had rubbed off on his collar. It was a warm, masculine scent, and it reminded Sarah of home, and of her father. She clung to the sudden feeling of comfort, but it was all too fleeting. It simply melted away. Her throat began to tighten involuntarily, and without being able to stop herself Sarah began to sob. She covered her face with her hands. She didn't want Alien to see her fall apart like this again, but she couldn't help it. She was so geared up to be on the defensive all of the time that this simple act of thoughtful kindness from a stranger breached her defenses, and all of her heartache came pouring out.

Alien patted her shoulder. "It's alright, Sarah. We're safe now. We'll be alright."

"No, it's not alright, Alien!" She wept. "I'm a mess, a hot mess! But I can't help myself. He's being too nice."

"I noticed he's not wearing a ring, either," Alien chuckled. "Straighten up, girlfriend. He's coming back."

Sarah stifled her sobs with the back of her hand. As she did, she realized with amazement that sharing her fears with Alien had somehow lessened their talon grip on her. She no longer felt so shrouded by doubt. She dared to think that maybe she might be getting past some of the shit in her life, and that things might actually be changing for the better. Her persistent depression darkened this bright thought. Maybe she was one of those pathetically sad loners who never found true love. Was she already too damaged, and blindly hoping for too much? She thought not, and decided to insist on it. She was sick of running away from her life. Enough was enough! She wanted her future to be filled with happiness and contentment and hope and, she dared to think it, maybe even love? Real, true love? The kind of love the poets and singers wrote about so much that you know it must be true, but the question was, how to find it. She heard the crunch of boots on gravel as the lieutenant returned, and quickly dried her eyes.

"My team is on the way." He checked his watch. "Processing this site is going to take a couple of hours. Are you both on the island for awhile?"

Sarah winced when Alien nudged her sore ribs.

"We're here the whole summer," Alien said. "We're waitressing at The Tap Room."

"Great. Then I'd like to suggest that I have Sergeant Parsons take you back to town in my truck. We can load your bikes in the back. But that means you'll need to come into the station tomorrow to make your statements."

He caught Sarah's eye. His eyes were the warm chocolate brown of cinnamon and coffee. Her heart flipped like a pancake. Sarah even heard the sizzle.

"Can I trust you to do that?"

Sarah considered the idea of sitting through another police interview. She was ashamed to admit that it wouldn't be her first. She cringed when she thought of the last time. Mason had picked a street fight with a Cleveland Browns fan during a mortifying Steelers loss, and he had been tagged for D&D. The cops had picked Sarah up in the general witness sweep, and she had lied to cover for him. She had sworn that the Brownie fan had thrown the first punch. The cops had released Mason with a warning.

Sarah had never forgiven herself for that incident, but when she considered this new interview, she felt the conviction rise up within her that this time things would be different, because what had happened to that deer at Altar Rock was wrong, and that whoever had done that needed to be stopped. This cop—this kind, thoughtful policeman intended to stop that kind of stupid, evil behavior, and she needed to step up to the plate and help him get the job done.

For the second time that day, Sarah decided to hold the line but this time, it felt even better because this time she was through being a victim, too. It was time to take a stand. She shrugged and dumped the memory of Mason's sicko behavior and his whole line of quaking misery into the dust where it belonged.

"Count on me," Sarah repeated. "I'm staying."

CHAPTER TWELVE

CJ checked her watch as she entered the station. She was a little early for her shift, but she had a sneaking suspicion, and she saw that it was true. John was still hunched over his desk, jotting notes across three separate legal pads.

"You're going to fry your brain to crispy bacon if you keep at it like this," she said.

John nodded, without looking up. "I wanted to sort things out, and I had a couple of new ideas I wanted to share with you, in person."

"Sort what out?" CJ crossed the room. He had titled each notepad with a heading: Satan's Tub, Easy Street Vandalism, and Altar Rock Display. She pulled up a chair.

"I've identified the actors for each event," he said, "and it helps to keep things straight. There were four actors at Satan's Tub: The Whistler we knew about, plus Actor X, the second man who attacked Candy. Then, Candy herself, plus the victim in the bog, whose name may be Katie." He tapped a pad with his pen. "We only saw one actor at Easy Street, who I'm calling Actor Y, and then, The Whistler again, at Altar Rock."

"That does help," CJ admitted. "But here's the thing: the animal mutilation at Altar Rock takes The Whistler's pathology to a new level. He's getting bolder, more aggressive. Did you make a note of that?"

"I did. It's classic sociopathic behavior. I think chasing Candy into Satan's Tub on Sunday provoked a higher level of excitement for him, and that's what triggered the Altar Rock display. Notice the timing, CJ. There's been a smaller window between each event. He's feeling more confident, more willing to take on risk."

"You mean he's getting cocky. Okay, I'll play devil's advocate. What else have you got scribbled there?" She angled a notepad for a better view. "Represents the end of a successful chase, or hunt?" She pushed the tablet back. "Artemis was the Greek goddess of the hunt, and so was Diana, for the Romans, but that's pretty much all I've got."

"You think The Whistler is up on his mythology?"

"You're the one who always says to question everything."

"True. Let's consider the end of a chase then, since that's been his historic pattern. I think The Whistler built the Altar Rock trophy stand to memorialize what happened on Sunday. Chasing Candy into the bog thrilled him to a whole new level. That emotional elevation was bad enough, but what happened at Altar Rock made it even worse because I think The Whistler experienced a revelation when he slaughtered that deer. Killing that deer may have been the first time he's ever killed anything with his own hands. He's discovered a new range of power now – the power over life and death."

She shuddered. "He's not going to be satisfied with chasing anymore."

"It's worse than that. He's not going to be satisfied with killing an animal anymore. Once one of these monsters get triggered, they don't back it down."

"So who is this prick? We never seem to get any closer."

"But we are getting closer. We've narrowed the field of suspects. Let's think this through. The trophy stand turned out to be a whittled down walking stick. What does that tell us?"

CJ settled in. Logic Tree was one of her favorite exercises because it wasn't just theory. It was practical, and it actually made sense. "The walking stick tells us that The Whistler was out for a hike when he found the deer, and he was willing to use what he had on hand to make the trophy. Plus, he must also be carrying a knife, because he used the knife to kill the deer and to whittle the stick."

"Or, he found the deer and went home again to get supplies, which means he lives nearby. Say, within a mile of Altar Rock. Plus, if he had to run home to get supplies, he would have known the clock was ticking before someone else found the animal. Racing against the clock plus the fear of exposure would have heightened his excitement." John drew a connecting arrow. "Let's call this Scenario One. If The Whistler was out and about, and he didn't need to go home to get supplies, then how would he have concealed the knife? He could explain the walking stick easily enough, but a knife would be too public. I can't see him displaying a knife on his belt. He's too clever to be that obvious."

"A kit." CJ felt her pulse skip a beat. "He's got a kit or a case, or some kind of backpack, maybe. Something so normal that no one would comment on it."

"I like the backpack idea. It would also explain the stain we found in the sand. He's carrying a water bottle, too. After he slaughtered that deer, he'd be covered with splatter. He used the water to wash himself, afterwards, when he was done."

"That would also explain the fibers we found. John, here's an idea. He took his shirt off so it wouldn't get bloody, and used it later to dry off. Maybe we should look for someone with sunburn. Yesterday was bright out. He wouldn't have used any sunscreen under his shirt."

"Good thinking." John looked pleased. "We've already surmised he's carrying a kit with a water bottle and a knife. What else will he want to carry from now on?"

Fear flicked CJ's stomach. "Restraints. He's going to start packing some type of human restraint. Zip ties, handcuffs, even duct tape would be next on his list. I really don't like where this is going. And don't forget, according to Candy, he's already carrying cigarettes, and either a lighter or matches."

"Cigarettes, lighter, or matches." He added the items to the list. "He's going to enjoy adding to his kit. It's going to become his new favorite toy, the secret hobby he's hiding from the world. He'll enjoy shopping for his new gear."

"Okay, I give. You win. You have fully creeped me out."

"I know one thing. When we do catch The Whistler, he won't look like the monster he is. He'll be the perfect husband, brother, colleague, and boss, because that's what these types are. He'll be a regional bank manager, or a Sunday school teacher since sociopaths naturally gravitate to positions of authority. They actively seek out ways to manipulate people. It's the only way they ever feel alive."

"What's our next step?"

"Here's my idea." John crossed his arms. "I want you to move to day shift, effective immediately. I can't cover this by myself. Hank will do a fine job supervising the lobster shift from now on. He's certainly ready for the promotion. What do you say?"

"You want me working days?" CJ was surprised by the suggestion. Her mind raced down the new path. What would it mean to start living life like a normal person? With a little effort, she could reconnect with her network of cousins and friends. She wouldn't be caught dozing at their kids' little league games or backyard barbeques anymore, stressed out from working nights and trying to fit her vampire schedule into their normal lives.

But wouldn't she miss working nights? True, sometimes she felt like an alien outsider when she patrolled the island alone at 3:00 a.m., but there was a peaceful kind of contentment in it, too, when all of Nantucket was hers. She knew where the deer herd liked to bed down, and which pin oaks the owls preferred, but if John needed her to work day shift, so be it. She only knew one thing. She would do whatever it took to see that The Whistler investigation got done. "I'm in."

"Good." John stood. "Straight up nine o'clock. Here's my next idea. We should stake out Altar Rock, tonight. Forty percent of all criminals return to the crime scene once paranoia convinces them they've missed a critical detail. I'm hoping The Whistler is one of them."

"I'm not so sure, John. Altar Rock seems more like a one off." She hooked her arm on the back of the chair. "It might be a better use of resources to deploy the team around the Lobster Pot vicinity. We know The Whistler likes to stalk there."

He stood, and locked his desk. "I'm not using the team. I'm going to Altar Rock alone, unless you're coming with me."

"You're not using the team. Why not?"

"Because I don't know who I can trust." He shrugged on his tactical vest. "I trust you, but that's it. Are you coming with me?"

"My vest is in my locker." CJ stood. "Let me get it. I already said I was in."

* * * * * * *

John drummed the steering wheel with his thumbs. He was anxious to get to Altar Rock to test his theory. "We'll drive in as far as the transponder. That should provide enough cover, and it's right on the main trail. We can walk in from there."

"Sounds like a plan." CJ fingered the snap on her holster. "With everything else that went down today, did you review the blotter? Did you see we recorded another vandalism at 203 Wauwinet Trail last night?"

"I did see that. Sally Poldridge's place. That's nothing new. We've had trouble at that address for years."

"Yes, but this time we're not talking about tipped over patio chairs or cement planters. At approximately 1:17 a.m., someone pitched a cobblestone through Sally's rumpus room window. She was entertaining a new friend at the time, when the stone shattered the glass."

"And, what? You think the two vandalism incidents are connected? One in the center of town, the other out in Wauwinet?"

"It just seems odd that we've seen so much broken glass lately. In any case, I have to give Charlie Erskine credit. He jumped up naked out of the hot tub and gave chase, but he cut his feet on some of the glass and it slowed him down. Sixteen stitches in both heels. He'll be hobbling for awhile. The actor got away."

"Sounds like a disgruntled ex-boyfriend. There'd be a long list of them. Sally has quite a history."

"How about this? How about a disgruntled ex-girlfriend?"

"Who has Charlie been dating?"

"Not Charlie's girlfriend, you idjit. *Hers.*"

"I didn't know Sally played for that team."

"From the scuttlebutt I've heard lately, Sally pinch hits for both teams, as needed."

"I suppose the actor could have been a woman." The cruiser bounced as he turned right onto Altar Rock Lane. "Forgive me. I'm showing my natural bias."

"Whoever it was stood watching them for a good long while, because I found the hydrangea he or she was hiding behind. The grass was smashed flat, but here's the kicker: when I interviewed Mrs. Adrienne Barlow of 201 Wauwinet Trail, she swears that not a single car drove down their cul-de-sac anytime after eleven p.m."

"What was Mrs. Barlow doing awake at 1:17 a.m.?"

"She claims the new spillway lights are keeping her up. I've seen them. They are bright. She swears that she sat at her kitchen window drinking chamomile tea until dawn. If she's right, then the actor was either someone local, or he came in on foot."

"How about by boat? The Wauwinet shoreline is that close."

"I thought of by boat, but if the actor used a boat then the security detail at the spillway should've picked the boat up on their radar. They've been pretty vigilant lately because of the Greenie threats. From what they said, they don't have much else to do but to stare at their monitors all night long. One guy said he was so bored he was going to start weaving Nantucket baskets."

"How far from the spillway is 203 Wauwinet Trail?"

"About a mile, mile and a quarter, maybe. Why? You think one of the security guys might be the actor?"

"You just said the actor was local, plus we know that they're bored. Some of those guys are ex-Navy SEAL. They could easily slip past Mrs. Barlow, without even trying."

"How about smashing that window though? That sounds personal to me. Okay, so maybe a couple of those guys are emotionally retarded enough to spy on Sally's antics, but they'd never deliberately cause property damage. No way. Besides, the timing is wrong. Like you said, we've had trouble at 203 Wauwinet Trail ever since the house was built. The Haulover spillway is only two years' old."

John pulled the cruiser next to the transponder, and parked. Pale sand dust drifted in front of the headlights, obscuring the white cone that protruded from the squat square of concrete directly in front of the car. The cone was surrounded on all sides by FEDERAL PROPERTY—NO TRESPASSING signs and an eight-foot tall fence of maximum security razor wire. CJ shivered.

"I hate that fucker," she said. "It's so big brother. Why would anyone put an ugly thing like that right next to a historic landmark like Altar Rock?"

"Maybe because it's an airplane beacon, and this is the highest point of land that we have on the island."

She hurrumphed. "Just because you're right doesn't mean I have to like it."

John stepped from the cruiser and softly closed the door. The thrill of the hunt already sparkled through his veins. The stake out idea was a long shot, but what if he was right? He popped the trunk, and handed CJ a halogen flashlight. "Follow standard protocol. Only use this if you need to. It's a dead giveaway."

"Got it. I know the drill."

"Just checking. Let's go."

He led the way, moving single file up the footpath. With each step, the gravelly soil crunched a gritty two-beat beneath his boots. The moon cast enough light to see by, even when slightly obscured by streaming lines of wispy cloud. The trophy stand site was slightly to the left, overlooking the main road. He altered their course.

"We should have brought Ted's goggles," CJ whispered. "They might've helped."

"Good luck borrowing any of Ted's gear. He probably sleeps with it -"

"Shit!" CJ dropped into a crouch. "There's a light. Someone's coming."

"Stay low." John unsnapped his holster and drew his Sigma, his heartbeat in his throat. His mind raced over the topographical maps he had memorized earlier that day. "CJ, follow the path to the right, to the top of the hill. I'll go left, and get below. Once you get to the top, turn the flashlight on, and head downhill. Make a lot of noise. That will flush whoever that is right at me."

"Got it." She touched his arm. "You be careful."

"I will. Give me a minute to set up, and get going."

CJ vanished into the gloom. John started to work his way along the hill, keeping his finger off the trigger and his eye on the circle of yellow light bouncing down the narrow path. There could be no doubt about it. Whoever held that light was walking straight to the crime site.

He crouched behind a thicket of Scotch broom. It was eerie how silent the night was. There wasn't a bird or a cricket stirring. His palms felt sweaty, so John gripped the Sigma with both hands. It was tough judging distance in the dark, but he figured he had less than a hundred yards until contact. Time seemed to tick by in milliseconds. He started to count each breath as the unknown walked even closer.

The hair on his arms stood straight up when he heard the toothy whistle.

It took a few notes, but he recognized the theme song from *The Bridge over the River Kwai*, his brother Micah's favorite movie. There was a sudden unexpected rustling in the scrub to his left. John stood as a dog exploded out of the bushes into the moonlight. The spaniel planted itself on the small sandy plain and assumed a silent and perfect point right at him.

"Sheba, heel!" A male voice shouted. "Dammit, dog, don't make me chase you."

The halogen spotlight began racing downhill. CJ was on her way, but John still hadn't identified the target. A vague shape materialized in the darkness. He raised the Sigma level with his eyes. "Hands in the air! Let me see them. Now!"

The silhouette emerged from the shadows. A man was holding the dog's leash loosely in one hand. "What is this? What's going on?"

"Hands in the air," John repeated.

"Lieutenant Jarad?" The man raised both hands. "Do you want to explain the meaning of this?"

John peered across the top of his gun. He felt the tension drain out of him like water. The interloper was the high school principal, Magnus Wolfe. CJ raced up and assumed a secondary position, holding her gun steady and spotlighting Magnus with the flashlight.

"Tell us what you're doing here, sir," John said.

"What do you mean, what an I doing here?" Magnus turned. "Would you put that light down? It's hurting my eyes."

"I said, sir, tell us what you're doing here."

"Are you insane? What does it look like? I'm taking my dog for a walk."

The flashlight bobbled as CJ adjusted her grip.

"You've walked into a restricted crime scene, sir," John said, as doubts began to crowd his mind. Magnus was a respected member of the community, and a year-round resident. He was only carrying a leash, not the backpack or the kit they had expected The Whistler to carry. It wasn't a crime to go for a walk, or to whistle a show tune, either. Had he just put his foot in it? John slowly lowered his weapon.

"This is outrageous!" Magnus sputtered. "I take a stroll through a quiet residential neighborhood, and I encounter an armed police response. Chief Brock and the Council will certainly hear about this!"

CHAPTER THIRTEEN

CJ's eyes felt gummy, and her brain unfocused. Evidently, five hours' sleep was not enough time to reset her internal clock. She craved sleep the way she had craved nicotine back in the day when she had first weaned off cigarettes. She felt the need for more sleep slipping through her veins like sand. She poured a cup of coffee, and tried to blink the mental fog away.

"It's nice to see you working days, Detective Allamand," Tina said.

"If you say so, Tina. This is going to take some getting used to."

She checked on John. He sat at his desk, peering at his laptop. John looked even worse than she felt. CJ doubted that John had gotten any sleep at all. Knowing him, he would have taken last night's Magnus Wolfe fiasco personally. He was wired that way.

The security system trilled, and Ted entered the station. CJ was surprised to see Ted since he wasn't due to report for his shift until eleven. He stepped aside, and held the door open for Candy Kane. Candy's hands were still bandaged, and she was hiding her eyes behind black designer sunglasses, but considering what she had been through, Candy looked good.

"Thanks, Ted," Candy said. "You are truly a prince among men."

"We can stop by the store on the way home," he said, "whenever you're ready."

"Ted Parsons, where have you been hiding all of my life? It's nice to finally meet a gentleman, for a change."

John stood up. "Miss Kane? What can we do for you today?"

"You told me to come in if I remembered anything more," she said, "and I have. Ted thought I should mention it. He kindly offered to drive me in."

Ted pulled out a chair next to his desk. He motioned to her to sit. "I said we could amend her statement, Lieutenant. It's easy enough to do."

"What did you remember?" John asked.

"The second man." Candy sat. She raised her bandaged hands. "The one who did this to me. When we were fighting, we got close. I saw The Whistler smoke a cigarette, but this guy didn't smell like a smoker. He reeked. Like a distillery."

"Tell him about those other details you mentioned," Ted said.

Candy settled her hands carefully in her lap. "I really don't know how tall The Whistler was, but he looked stocky. He kept up with me, though, so I know he can run. The second guy, the prick I fought, was as tall as me, but he was wiry, and like I said, he reeked of booze. He wasn't wearing gloves, though, so I probably marked up his hands pretty well." She wheezed a laugh. "Sure I did. I kept blocking his punches with my face."

Ted stopped typing. He reached across the desk and touched her wrist. "All that's over now. We're going to catch him, and make him pay."

"I know you will." She glanced around the station. "I'm sorry. Is there a ladies' room I could use?"

"Yes." Ted pointed. "Down the hall, second door on the left. It's marked."

"I'll be right back." Candy stood. She held up her hands. "I've learned this takes more time than it used to."

CJ waited for Candy to leave the room, but her irrepressible curiosity itched. Ted and Candy seemed to be on pretty friendly terms. She leaned forward. "Ted? What does this mean? Are you two dating?"

Ted scratched his jaw. "I wouldn't call it dating, exactly, but I do have hopes. Candy's still pretty beat up, and she's afraid to be alone in her house. I've been staying up nights, parked outside, on my own time, so she can get some rest."

"I'm impressed," CJ said. Ted was a decent guy, but she hadn't expected to see this level of consideration come from him. "How did you meet her?"

"Candy was coming out of the Safeway, having trouble with the cart. Beat all to hell, and still independent. You gotta respect that. I figure once she's healed up, we can start dating regular, but I'm taking it slow. Candy's something special. I don't want to fuck it up."

"Not to put too fine a point on it," John said, "but aren't you old enough to be her dad?"

"I am." Ted appeared genuinely pleased. "And I say bully for me."

"I have to question the wisdom in dating a witness to an active investigation."

"What is that supposed to mean, Lieutenant?"

"I mean that I'm not sure that dating Ms. Kane is the wisest thing you could do. It might reflect badly on the force. Some members of the public might suggest that you're taking advantage of a woman in a fragile emotional state."

"Fragile emotional state? Are you kidding me? Candy's tough as nails. Not even The Whistler could put her down."

"I'm just saying that dating her now might not be the best ethical choice you could make."

Ted glowered. "But there's no actual rule against it, is there, sir?"

"No, there's no actual regulation against it, Sergeant Parsons. I just think that it might be best to hold off on dating Ms. Kane until after The Whistler investigation is complete."

"Any idea of when that might actually be, sir?"

"We're making progress. We've narrowed the field of suspects."

"Yeah, we all heard how well that went over last night." Ted stood. He leaned on his knuckles. "If I'm not breaking any regulation, then I don't see one goddamned reason why I should stop dating Candy. She's a terrific girl, sir. Any woman that good-looking won't stay single for long. Crissakes! This might be my only chance-"

"I'm sorry." Candy stood at the end of the hallway. "Is there a problem?"

"No. Of course not." Ted slapped his laptop shut. His face and neck were lobster red. "Come on, Candy. We're done here. I'll give you a ride home. We can discuss this later."

Ted stormed off. It was a good thing the security door was automatic because CJ wasn't convinced that Ted would have stopped long enough to open it. He looked that furious. John stood frozen behind his desk.

"By God." He whispered. "We will discuss this later."

CJ's heart sank. What on earth was going on between these two guys? Didn't they have enough on their plates already? Working days was going to suck if this kind of pissing contest was always going on.

She heard a hesitant knock, and looked up. Eileen Lippman and Sarah Hawthorne, their two Altar Rock witnesses, were standing at the door.

"Buzz them in, Tina," CJ prayed the caffeine would kick in. "We're not done yet."

* * * * * * *

John was so frustrated he couldn't speak. This ongoing feud with Ted was driving him nuts. How did Ted manage to flip his switch every single time he tried to exercise his authority? He didn't have a squabble with any other members of the team. He hated getting into wrangling arguments like this one, because it stole the wind from his sails. Now he was going to feel hesitant and uncertain for the rest of the day.

"Lieutenant?" CJ said. "Are you ready, sir?"

"Coming." He reached for his jacket. John noted that although Eileen Lippman looked merely curious, Sarah Hawthorne kept drying her palms against her skirt. Was that an unconscious, nervous tell? "Ms. Hawthorne? How are you feeling today? Better?"

"Yes, thank you."

She had purplish half-moons under her eyes. Had she lost sleep over yesterday's event? That would be natural enough, but she was also clutching her elbows against her ribcage, a classic tension indicator. Was all of this a reaction to what she had seen at Altar Rock? Or was Sarah Hawthorne afraid of something more?

"Thinking about this still gives me the yips," she said. "And please, call me Sarah."

"Call me Eileen, too. Let's get rid of the formal if we can. It makes me nervous."

"There's absolutely no reason to feel nervous. This is simply a preliminary interview. Before we get started, though, I wanted to thank you for what you did yesterday. It took real courage to report that abomination. Some folks might have left it for someone else to find. You two did the right thing. Thank you."

He was off to a good start. Eileen smiled warmly, and Sarah visibly brightened.

She crossed her arms. "Can we do this together?"

"No, I'm afraid not. Protocol dictates that we interview you separately."

"Sarah, are you okay with that?" Eileen asked.

"I guess so. I was just asking."

John picked up his clipboard. "Let's get started. Detective Allamand and Eileen will use Interview Room A. Sarah, we'll take Room B. Once we get settled, we'll ask you to sign a waiver allowing us to tape the interviews. It's a standard request."

"You really don't want to see my notes," CJ said, lightly.

He led them downstairs into the sub-basement. The girls' flip-flops sounded incongruous compared to the leather slap of his police issue boots. The layout was simple enough: Interview Room A was on the left, Room B on the right with a unisex bathroom in between. The hallway had been freshly painted, and the scent of naphtha hung in the air. Each interview room was furnished with two folding chairs and a steel table bolted to the concrete floor.

John opened the door to Room B, and waited for Sarah to enter. He took the chair closest to the door before passing her the clipboard. She scrawled *Sarah Hawthorne* across the signature line. He noted that she was left-handed before reaching forward to switch the intercom recorder on.

"Lieutenant-Commander John Jarad, witness interview Sarah Hawthorne, Whistler investigation, Altar Rock event. Wednesday, June first, 2011." He checked his watch. "Nine-thirty-three A.M. This conversation is being recorded. Sarah, is it being recorded with your permission?"

"Yes." She rubbed her bare arms briskly.

"Is it too cold in here for you?"

"No, it's not that." She smiled, gamely. "I'm nervous. There's a lot of authority in here. Not to mention the only thing human in this room besides you and me is that box of tissues."

She was right. The atmosphere was deliberately kept sterile since interviews worked more efficiently that way. "Let me know if we need to adjust the temperature, or if you need to take a break. Please state your address, age, occupation or employment."

Although it wasn't necessary, she leaned forward to speak directly at the mic. John noticed that her cheeks were flushed with color, and her eyes held a nervous intelligence. She had an oval face with a pointed chin and generous lips, and her hair was such a deep walnut that it was almost black. That color emphasized the golden flecks in her hazel eyes.

"My address is The Dorm on Straight Wharf. I'm twenty-three, and I'm a waitress at The Tap Room." She laughed, nervously. "I've only been on Nantucket four days. That's kinda hard to believe, with all that's happened."

He had noticed an odd accent at Altar Rock, and here it was again. "Where are you originally from?"

"Pittsburgh, Pennsylvania." She shared a tremendous smile. "Home of the Steeler Nation."

"Pittsburgh? That's a bit of a hike. What brought you to Nantucket?"

She blinked. "I came looking for work. I heard they were always looking for good help on Nantucket."

"That's certainly true." John folded his hands on the table. He was getting a feel for this interview, and settled back in the chair. "You're here by yourself?"

"Yes. My mom died last year, and my sister's in Germany, studying beer, so I'm pretty much on my own."

"I'm sorry to hear that about your mother." John took a closer look. In spite of her bluff manner, Sarah Hawthorne was very young. "Your sister is studying beer? How's that going?"

"Joanie's doing well. Once she gets her certificate, she's coming home to open her own craft microbrewery."

"That's ambitious. It was bold of you, too, to strike out on your own like this."

Her face suddenly closed up like a fist. "Sometimes, there's not much choice, is there?"

"No, I suppose not." John felt intrigued. He could sense more to Sarah's life story, but it was time to get this interview back on track. "Let's get started. What took you to Altar Rock yesterday?"

"That's just it. We weren't going to Altar Rock. We were going to the beach, but Alien wanted to show Altar Rock to me because of the panorama."

"I'm sorry. Alien?"

"Oh! I meant Eileen." She stammered. "Her name's Eileen. Alien is kind of a nickname."

"I see. How long have you known Eileen?"

"Only the four days, too. She's my new roommate."

"How's that working out?"

Sarah shrugged. "About as well as it ever does."

"No problems?"

"Nothing major. Alien smokes, but I'm dealing with it."

"Alright. So you rode your bikes and hiked to Altar Rock. When did you notice that something was wrong?"

"We had no idea." She shuddered. "It was turning out to be a perfect day, until we found that poor deer."

"You didn't see anyone else while you were at Altar Rock?"

"No, not a soul." She splayed her hands across the table. "It was only Alien and me. Then she suggested that we take the shortcut, and we found that terrible thing."

John sat back as a cruel suggestion reared its ugly head. Maybe The Whistler had actually slaughtered the deer, but how innocent was Eileen Lippman's suggestion that they follow the shortcut? Sarah Hawthorne wouldn't be the first coof to get hazed for being an island newcomer. "Let's take a step back. I want to make sure I understand the event. Eileen suggesed that you follow the shortcut?"

"Yes, it was all her idea." Sarah looked puzzled. "Why do you ask?"

"How did Eileen react to finding the deer?"

"She was as freaked out as I was. We both ran like crazy until we ran into, well, you."

"And you didn't notice anyone or anything else while you were at Altar Rock?"

"No, like I said. Plus, it all happened so fast. I don't know what Alien is going to say."

She started sweeping her focus from one high corner of the room to another, a classic distraction signal. Sarah was hiding something, and he decided to call her on it. "Sarah, I need you to tell me the truth. I'm trying to help. Is there something you're not telling me?"

She flushed under his gaze, and twisted her fingers into a knot.

"This really doesn't have anything to do with what happened, but I was wondering, you know, how public does this have to be? I mean, can we keep this on the down low? Does my name have to be in the papers?"

This was an angle he hadn't anticipated. "Why? Is there a problem?"

"God! This is so embarrassing." She wiped away sudden tears. "There's this guy I know back home, and I really don't want him to know that I'm here. If Mason finds out where I am, he'll come after me. He already did, once before."

John felt sucker punched in the gut. He hadn't expected this new wrinkle. "Have you filed a restraining order against Mason?"

"No." Her voice grew even softer. "I never did."

"Why not?"

"I guess I hoped he would go away and leave me alone, or stop."

In any case, he had a solid answer for her. He could keep her Altar Rock testimony confidential. The Commonwealth had recently enacted witness protection legislation. If Sarah needed him to be her shield, so be it.

John looked at her and saw Sarah as a real person for the first time. It was the strangest thing, as if her outline had suddenly snapped into place. She had a single chicken-pox scar high on her left cheek like a beauty mark, her only flaw. During their discussion, she had firmed her lips into a bloodless line. Sarah looked frightened, angry, determined, and brave, and John liked what he saw. "What's Mason's last name?"

"Hollister. Mason Hollister." She covered her left hand with the fingers of her right. "We were engaged, but I broke it off. He's wacko."

"Does Hollister have a felony record?"

"No," Sarah sniffled wetly. "But he has a couple of misdemeanors. One time for pot, and once for public intoxication." She snatched up a handful of tissues and blotted her eyes. "I'm sorry, but this is really upsetting me."

"Take your time. We're not in any hurry."

"Thank you." She wiped her nose. "Making me afraid was part of Mason's game. He used to break into my house, and watch me while I was sleeping. One time he jumped me in the ladies' room at Macy's. Mason thought it was funny, like some kind of joke. If he sees my name in the paper, he'll track me down. I'm so sick of running! I don't have anyplace else to go."

Her desolate cry touched John's heart. Jarads had called Nantucket home for thirteen generations. He couldn't imagine leaving the island permanently for any reason. If he didn't live on Nantucket, he feared that he wouldn't know who he was anymore. John felt a sudden welling respect for Sarah Hawthorne, and an interest in what she was trying to do. Here she was facing all of this radical change, and trying to build a new life from scratch. When he thought about leaving all of his friends and family behind, he wasn't sure he could do it.

"We can keep your testimony confidential," he said. "We'll simply list you as a CI, a confidential informant. It's perfectly legal to do so. We'll do everything we can to protect your privacy going forward."

"Really?" She smiled. "That's almost too good to believe. I'm sorry to be such a pain, but I just want to move on with my life, you know?" Her voice quavered. "I keep trying to get past this part of my life, but it's like it won't let go."

He considered his own recent break-up with Ava. All of that was over and done with, and he had absolutely no interest in mending that particular net, but if what Sarah was telling him was true, his experience was a cake walk compared to her blistered history.

"Would you believe me," he said gently, "if I understood a little of what you've been going through?"

She studied him thoughtfully. "You know, I might."

John felt time stop. His heart began to thud against his chest. He didn't know if it was from excitement, or from fear. A sudden reckless wave of fresh possibility rippled over his soul like the wind over the surface of a still pond. Between one breath and the next, his interest in Sarah gelled into something solid, something *real*. Sarah possessed something key and vital, and he suddenly wanted to add that rare spark of vitality to his own life.

"Is something wrong?" she asked.

"No, everything's fine." He grappled to turn his focus back to their interview, but he couldn't take his eyes off of her. He didn't even want to try. His integrity shrieked: Maintain some distance! She's a witness! But John felt the irrepressible pull of interested curiosity, followed by the warm blush of hypocrisy. What was he doing? This behavior was completely unprofessional, not to mention he had just reamed Ted out for doing the exact same thing.

He leaned against the table for support, ashamed that he needed it. "Here's the plan. We will do our best to protect your privacy during the investigation. If you remember anything more, give us a call, and we'll schedule a follow-up session. If anything more develops on our side, we'll be in touch. How does that sound?"

"Sounds good to me. Thank you." She twined her hands together again. "I really appreciate your help with this. Sorry to be such a bother."

"It's no bother," John said, and he meant it. "This concludes the recorded conversation with Sarah Hawthorne."

He switched the recorder off, amazed that his voice hadn't betrayed him. It had remained perfectly steady and clear, so no harm done. His professionalism was still intact. He opened the door and followed Sarah out into the hall. The door to Interview Room A stood open. CJ had already finished her interview. He found her waiting upstairs, sitting at his desk with Eileen.

CJ scrambled up. "All done?"

"I believe so, for now. Eileen, we've been asked to keep these interviews confidential. It is within our power to do so. This means you cannot discuss any details of your interview with anyone until the case is resolved. Will that be an issue?"

She cut her eyes at Sarah. "No, I don't think so. Okay."

John reached for a pen. He felt raw, as if all of his nerves were exposed. He couldn't meet Sarah's eyes. He was afraid she might read of his new interest and need in them. "Sarah, thank you again. We'll be in touch."

"Glad I could help."

He sat down heavily as CJ escorted the two women to the security door. Maybe this lapse in professionalism was simply a fluke, caused by sleep deprivation. How else could he explain this sudden magnetic attraction to someone he'd barely even met?

CJ returned. She sat in the spare chair and rested her elbows on the edge of his blotter. "Everything okay, John? You look strange."

"I'm fine. I want to see the transcript of your interview, as soon as it's ready."

"I'll download it to the printer." She cocked her head. "That Sarah seems like a nice girl. You two were in there for quite awhile."

"She's an interesting person. I mean, she has an interesting history."

"Did I detect a little attraction between you two? Is it possible that the tide has turned, and that John Jarad is finally on the mend?"

"Can it, CJ. I'm not that kind of hypocrite. She's a witness."

"O-kay." CJ sat back. "So? We're keeping witness' identity confidential now? News to me. Want to clue me in why we're doing that?"

John rubbed his eyes. "There's more to this than The Whistler now. We have something new, something more, to add to our list."

"You can't be serious. What more? What now?"

"Sarah brought a stalker history with her. It sounds like *Bestealcian* or some other form of erotomania, to me."

CJ's jaw dropped open. "That does it! I want back on nights!"

Chapter Fourteen

Bestealcian. John recalled the Old English word for stalking. *Bestealcian*, an invasion of privacy specifically designed to cause fear in the object of desire. Aberrant human behavior had been his favorite subject at the university. What was it that compelled a person to move from common interest into obsession and psychosis? How did anyone migrate from day-to-day rationality into an increasingly aberrant and compulsive pattern of behavior? Were human monsters born that way, or were they created?

His thesis topic had included the study of serial killers like John Wayne Gacy, Jr., the monster who tortured, raped, and murdered thirty-three young men in Chicago. At the same time Gacy was luring these young men to their deaths, he was dressing up like a clown to entertain the neighborhood children at their birthday parties. Of course, with Gacy, there was evidence of early childhood head trauma, plus years of alcohol and drug abuse. Was chemical imbalance a part of the equation? How on earth had Chicago law enforcement missed what was going on right under their very noses?

And, more importantly, was this the behavior type Sarah Hawthorne was running away from?

John heard the security door open. He looked up to see Chief Brock enter the station.

"Lieutenant Jarad? I need to speak with you. Let's take it into a conference room."

The chief wanted to keep it private? That couldn't be good. "Yes, sir."

"Have a seat, son." The chief lowered his bulk into a chair. "John, I've fielded a dozen phone calls already this morning. Folks are upset by that cowboy stunt you pulled on Altar Rock last night."

"We had good reason to believe The Whistler would return to the scene, sir-"

"But he didn't. And no matter how good your reasoning was, the truth of the matter is that The Whistler wasn't there, and now you've upset the citizenry. Hell, John, I know what you were trying to do. I was thirty years old once myself, but if we don't resolve this soon, they're going to demand that we bring in the Staties or the Feds, and I don't want to do that any more than you do." The chief ran his hand over his bald head. "But that's not the only reason I'm here. I can handle the ruffled feathers. That's my job to do. I'm here because of the way you went about it. I need to know why you didn't involve the whole team in the stake out last night."

"I didn't involve the whole team, sir, because it occurred to me that The Whistler has been able to guess our every move. I'm not sure who I can trust."

"That's an ugly statement. You think The Whistler is a member of the force?"

"Or, he's getting information from a member of the force, sir. Directly or indirectly, he's getting information from somewhere."

"That would explain why we've had such limited success with the capture so far. What do you suggest that we do?"

"Detective Allamand suggested that we stake out The Lobster Pot vicinity, sir. That's a solid idea. My suggestion is to that we take the whole team there, next."

"And how will doing that fix this leak, if there is one?"

"If we manage to trap The Whistler in that situation, and he escapes us again, the way he escapes might point us to the leak. Honestly, sir, I thought we were this close last night. I was wrong. But with each step we are narrowing the field."

"You're putting me in a tough spot. If The Whistler does elude us again, I'm going to have an impossible sell with the Council. They'll demand our heads."

"They're already doing that, sir, but they have to understand that we're trying. We have made progress. The Council has to give us the leeway to keep making these attempts, or we cash in, and call in the Feds."

"Alright. You've sold me on the idea." The chief tapped the table. "But you need to use the whole team on the stake out idea, and no more of these lone star cowboy stunts. And we need to see real results because I need something to give to the Council. I don't know how much more of this they—and the community—will stand."

"Understood, sir." John followed the Chief into the hall.

Ted had returned for his shift. He was sitting behind his desk, thumbing through a report. Here was another unfinished piece of business. John wasn't looking forward to their discussion, but he might as well tackle it now. It wasn't going to get any easier. "Ted? Got a minute?"

"Sure thing, Lieutenant."

"Let's go into a conference room." No need to make this a public performance. John pulled out a chair, and waited for the door to close.

"Sit down, Ted. We need to talk about what's been going on around here lately. We seem to have a problem communicating."

"Tell me about it," Ted muttered.

"What I'm trying to figure out is why? I've never asked you to do anything outside of your standard range of duties. Why do we keep tripping into this issue?"

"Permission to speak candidly, sir?"

"By God, I wish that you would."

"Alright." Ted leaned his elbows on the table. "I've been taking orders for a lot of years, sir, a lot of years. I've paid my dues, civilian and military, or at least I thought I had, until Chief Brock had that accident, and then the Council went and hired you to take his place. What were they thinking? Crissakes! I've got a coffee mug that's older than you are, Lieutenant."

"The Council promoted you to Senior Officer at the same time they promoted me."

"Sure they did, but I should have been made chief. It wasn't fair, what they did. It was my turn."

So that was it. It was so simple. Ted was jealous. "We've talked about this before. You're a terrific field officer, Ted, but you'd need to get recertified to move beyond being our defensive tactic officer. That decision isn't up to the Council. It came straight from the Commonwealth."

"I know that, sir, but I'm not going back to school. I'd look like an idiot, sitting in a damn classroom full of rookies. They'd call me grandpa."

John felt bracketed by the stalemate. Ted was too proud to go back to get the education he needed for a promotion, and he couldn't promote Ted without it. Was there another answer?

"How about this?" he asked. "How about becoming the Homeland Security Liaison for the Nantucket force? We've been asked to nominate someone. You're the perfect candidate. You've got the background for the job."

"Homeland Security?" Ted perked up. "What would I need to do?"

"You'd work with the Department of Homeland Security online. There would be some travel involved, and you'd get reimbursed for expenses. Plus, you'd be the new mentor contact for the community outreach program that needs to be developed, but it would be your baby. You'd get to design the program from the ground up, any way that you think is best."

"Now that sounds more like it," Ted mused. "I think I'd like that."

"Consider it done. It's a great opportunity, Ted, and a great fit."

"Since we're talking so candid now, Lieutenant, I've got some advice for you. Don't take this wrong, sir, but I think you have too many rules going on inside your head lately. And when you don't have a rule, you make one up. Like this thing with Candy, sir. There's no regulation against dating a witness, and you know it, but you're making it out like there is. No man in his right mind could follow all these made-up rules you have, but somehow, you expect me to. It's not fair, Lieutenant. I don't have a crystal ball. I can't guess what you're thinking, sir, and that kind of thing is going to get you into real trouble someday." Ted cleared his throat. "If you want my advice, sir, you need to learn how to trust yourself, pronto. You'd do a fine job if you'd only loosen up. Regs are great, sure they are, but sometimes you need to go with your gut. Sometimes that's a mistake too, but nine times out of ten, it'll be the right thing to do."

Was Ted right? Was he too rigid in his thinking? Instead of being authoritative, was he coming off as puritanical? John saw a compromise. "Fair enough. Let's try this. I'll be more consistent following the regs as they're written, and we'll sit down again in a month to check on our progress. I know we can fix this, Ted. This might be a good place to start. What do you say?"

Ted stretched out a hand. "I'd say that sounds fair enough to me, Lieutenant."

John clasped Ted's hand. With Ted on his side, he felt his anxiety ease. Ted was true blue, and he needed to remember that. He stood and opened the conference room door, and followed Ted out in time to hear two high-pitched female voices talking rapidly. John was delighted to see CJ talking with Mrs. Vickery.

"I wondered where you'd got to." CJ's eyes were bright with fresh news. "You're going to like hearing what Mrs. Vickery has to say."

Mrs. Vickery clutched an old school index card against her ruffled blouse. "Before I share this information, Lieutenant Jarad, I wanted to thank you for asking us to collect it. Researching your request was surprisingly informative from a business perspective. We hadn't thought to research our missing employees independently before. Doing so caused us to rethink part of our standard practice, which should reduce our risk going forward."

"You're welcome, Mrs. Vickery. Glad to help." John's palms itched as he reached for the index card. Were they this close to learning the identity of the bog victim? He turned the card over and read the name aloud. "Katherine Mary Roark of Ennis, County Clare, Republic of Ireland."

"She preferred to be called Katie. She's the girl I remembered from your photograph." Mrs. Vickery clasped her wizened hands. "According to our records, Katie went missing around the nineteenth of August, 1999." She *tsked* against her teeth. "The date should have clued us in that something was terribly wrong. Every other runner has waited until after Labor Day to depart, I believe, since the completion of their contract involves the payout of a substantial bonus." She pointed a finger at one line on the card. "Charles and Lila Stanton were Katie's host family that year. The Stantons are very reliable people. I believe they still live in Wauwinet."

"I know Lila does." CJ gaped. "She's my cousin."

John snapped the card with his finger. "And you never saw this Katie Roark out there?"

"Can't say that I did." CJ shrugged apologetically. "Lila hires a new au pair every summer. She's a single mom with four kids, now that Frank split. She needs all the help she can get."

John felt a rush as the pace of the investigation accelerated with the identification. "Give Lila a call. Ask her for some time today. We want to talk with her, but don't let her know what it's about. Mention it's part of an investigation, but leave it at that."

"Got it." CJ stretched for a phone.

"This is thrilling!" Mrs. Vickery gushed. "It's exactly like what I would see on TV."

He turned. "Thank you again for your help, Mrs. Vickery. Please pass our thanks along to Ms. Howe, too. You've both been extremely helpful."

"You're so like your father. So polite," Mrs. Vickery cooed. "You will keep us posted?"

"Of course, we will." John escorted her to the door. "We'll share whatever news we can, when we can."

"We'll wait to hear from you then, Lieutenant Jarad. Good day."

He turned to see CJ replacing her handset. She was frowning.

"No answer. I left her a voicemail. Lila's usually pretty good about getting back to me."

Instinct tempted John to jump in a cruiser and race to Wauwinet, but he held himself in check. Sometimes he chafed at the human politics his job required, but he knew his constituency too well. No one appreciated having a police cruiser come roaring up their driveway unannounced. He checked his watch. "Give her fifteen minutes and try again."

"Roger that." CJ stared at Katie Roark's morgue portrait pinned to the corkboard. "You know, it takes real guts for these au pairs to do what they do. These are young women, too, not young men. They're exposed to every creep and predator out there: employers, landlords, pimps. Not to mention a culture that doesn't know what to do with a single woman. I know all about it."

"Don't get soft." Ted splashed some coffee into a mug. "These girls know what they're getting into. Besides, it's only their job. They can always go home if they want to."

"Can they?" John said, as he recalled Sarah's wailing cry: *I don't have anyplace left to go!* "What if they have no home to go back to?"

"Then they do their best to make a new one." Ted shrugged. "There's nothing new going on here, folks. We all came from somewhere else, at one time or another."

"Give us your tired, your poor, your huddled masses?" CJ said. "Is that what you mean?"

"Why not?" Ted risked a sip of his coffee. "Unless I woke up in Kuwait City again this morning, this is still the land of opportunity, right?"

The security door trilled, and Paul Jenkins pushed through. Paul looked tired and grim. He gripped a manila folder in his hand.

"Of course it's nothing new," CJ snapped. "I'm just saying I admire these girls, that's all."

"Admire which girls?" Paul asked.

"All these au pairs. I was just saying how much I admire them."

"I admire everything about them." Ted chortled. "There's nothing at all wrong with a hot, sassy, nineteen-year old girl."

"Crissakes, Ted!" CJ sputtered. "Put a cork in it for once, will you?"

"Why? What did I say wrong this time?"

"There was something wrong with what happened to this one." Paul settled his glasses on his nose and flipped the folder open. "This is the final tox report from Nelson Labs. I wish I I could say I caught this with my preliminary results, but that is why they're called preliminary. I was right about the cause of death. She died of a skull fracture, not drowning."

"She has a name, you know," CJ said. "It's Katherine Mary Roark, Katie Roark, from Ireland."

"I didn't know that," Paul said. "You've made an identification? Excellent work." He traced a bar chart with his finger. "There were also signs of persistent liver damage from active MDMA use, which makes these additional findings even more disturbing, but her hormones were right in line for it. She was only eight weeks along, though, which is why I missed it during the autopsy."

"Oh no, Paul, don't tell me this." CJ paled. "You're going to break my heart."

"Yes, I'm afraid so. Katie Roark was pregnant."

Chapter Fifteen

Needles of bright sunlight telegraphed off the waves of the inner harbor on John's left. He reached for his sunglasses and, in spite of the fundamentally dark reason for their visit, felt his spirits rise simply because they were actively pursuing the investigation. Sometimes, just moving around made him feel better. It was human and perverse, but true. CJ was keeping strangely silent as she studied the landscape.

"Did you have any luck contacting the Irish An Garda?" he asked.

"I did. It was easier than I thought it would be, but I forgot about the time difference. I caught them all at tea. Did you know that tea actually means they were eating their supper?"

"I did know that. My mother still has English cousins."

"Humph. I talked to Chief Superintendent Connall Dermody. He asked us to email them everything we have. He also said he appreciated the call, but he wasn't surprised to hear about the investigation. Evidently, these Roarks are a rough bunch. He didn't come right out and call them criminals, but he sure implied it. He thinks one brother, Kevin Roark, might still be local. They'll try to run him down, but he left a false forwarding address."

"Nice."

The first of the spillway's NO TRESPASSING signs flashed by. The bullet holes punched through the enameled sign were already bleeding rust. The tripod base was being swallowed up by twining bayberry. CJ pointed to the flat marine landscape.

"Remember when they bulldozed the crap out of this place? Look at it now. Mother Nature has taken it all back. You'd think they'd learn. You can't even tell where the bulldozers were anymore."

Score one for him. John awarded himself a mental point. He had been willing to bet that bringing CJ to Wauwinet would trigger another one of her tree-hugger rants. In spite of her law-enforcement calling, CJ was secretly a hippie. He had suspected it before because of her politics, but now he had the proof. He had been tracking the all-natural organic food CJ brought each day for lunch. John shuddered. What the hell was tofurky? He didn't want to know.

The asphalt road suddenly bloomed high-tech as it expanded from two lanes to four at a wide access juncture. John immediately slowed the cruiser to crawl across a steel grid that ran the full width of the Haulover from the inner harbor on his left to the Atlantic Ocean on his right. CJ plugged her ears with her fingers.

"Speed up, please. This thing sets my teeth on edge."

He sped up, but he knew it wouldn't help. The monstrous spillway grid stretched ahead of them for solid tenth of a mile. John discarded his sunglasses and blinked rapidly to adjust his eyes. The steel road grid was bookcased on either side by concrete seawalls that rose straight up out of the sand to a towering height of eighteen feet. The salt-stained seawalls created a dim, reverberating channel that only amplified the mosquito-like whining of the high-speed turbines spinning in their bunkers beneath the steel grid. These turbines produced the island's electricity with each rise and fall of the tide, and their high-pitched hum sounded exactly like an overheated teakettle that never ceased.

One, two, three, four. John started counting the halogen lights that arched over the spillway every fifty feet. These security lights were mounted on aluminum poles that looked like some kind of weird alien space pods. This was the source of the light pollution that so irritated the local neighborhood.

A blockhouse stood at the end of the spillway. The square, squat, two-story building housed all of the permanently stationed security and any on-site technical personnel. The blockhouse stared at the Atlantic through narrow, orange-mirrored slit windows. There was a tangled collection of radar, wireless communication, and satellite dish technology clustered on its roof. His mother had dragged John to enough art galleries so that he had picked up some appreciation for sculpture, and, if you looked at that collection with an open mind, the rooftop did look like some form of modern art with a capital A.

"I hate driving over this abomination." CJ shuddered. "Not to mention what it's doing to the harbor ecosystem. Federal bastards! Whoever signed that zoning ordinance should be taken out and shot."

"The courts decided in favor of the spillway, CJ. It wasn't one person's decision to make."

"Don't even go there; you know what I meant. Riding roughshod over the local ordinances, not to mention the protests of residents. You saw the protest marches, John, you were there. How would you like driving over this godforsaken *machine* every time you went into town for your groceries?"

CJ had a point, but it wasn't that simple. Major changes never were.

John hoped that once some of the newness rubbed off, maybe folks might see some of the advantages the spillway brought to Nantucket, like having an independent local energy source. Not everything new was automatically bad. "It generates enough clean wave energy every day to power every home and business on the island. That has to count for something. What would you rather do? Host a nuclear power plant? Besides, it's supposed to ease our coastal erosion."

"Ha! That's a nice way of saying the Feds needed to reassure everyone living out here that the spillway wouldn't wash their homes out from under them. Crissakes! We live on a sandbar. I know I wouldn't be reassured by having the Feds say they fixed anything. Especially when they had to come in twice over the winter to drop more breakwaters in. That tells me their design was fundamentally flawed from the get-go."

"You can't expect them to get it right out of the box, CJ, they're dealing with tidal sand. That was a normal adjustment, something to be expected."

She refused to listen. "I'm not the only one who's upset by this. We never did catch the actor who kept moving those surveyor's stakes around, or whoever it was that put the sugar in the site manager's gas tank."

"Rabble." He drove over a speed bump at the end of the grate and sped up. "Greenie rabble."

CJ turned to face him. "Don't dismiss these people, John. Greenies are passionate, intelligent people deeply committed to their beliefs. They'd love nothing more than to restore the Haulover to its natural habitat." She surveyed the baby dunes with their struggling tufts of poverty grass. "Don't count the greenies out. If we gave them a decent enough chance, they might just pull it off."

He turned left on Wauwinet Trail and the cruiser began to bump down the private shell lane.

She pointed to a modest saltbox house on the left. "Mrs. Adrianne Barlow, 201 Wauwinet Trail. The lady with insomnia. See how her kitchen window overlooks the road?"

"I see her point." John craned his neck. "It would be hard to get past her without being seen. The pines might block the moonlight, but you could still see a moving silhouette against all this water."

"Not to mention the shadows from those spillway lights." CJ settled back. "Lila's house is the one on the right, 202 Wauwinet Trail, temporary home of Katie Roark. 203 is that big *Architectural Review* house in the back, right on the dunes. That one belongs to Sally Poldridge."

"That is some house." He leaned over the wheel. "I've never seen it up close before. Who lives in the house harbor side?"

"204? Some artist. Kurt Stockton. But he's only a summer resident."

"I've met Stockton before. I tagged him for a DUI six years ago. Judge Coffin let him off with a ninety-day restricted license, daytime use only. The judge knew Stockton's dad. They were old college buddies. You know the drill."

"I do know the drill. That doesn't mean I have to like it."

The lane ahead split into a W. John followed the right hand split toward the Stanton house. Rugged sea pines gave way to cultivated hydrangeas mixed with exotic zebra grass. The driveway led to a garage stuffed with bicycles, lacrosse sticks, surf-casting tackle, and body boogie boards. He parked. The house had been angled so that the windows framed the best ocean views. The grass in the yard had been pounded flat to form a path that led from the garage around the east side of the house down to a pebbly cut in the bluff to the beach.

CJ headed for the front door. She had the envelope of morgue photographs tucked under her arm. "How do you want to play this? Lila is my cousin. Do you want me to take the lead?"

"Let's do that, and start with easy. Refresh my memory. What do we know about her?"

"Lila Stanton, single mother of four kids plus one big-ass dog. Her husband Frank split right after Morgan was born. Turns out Frank was gay, but he didn't know it. Took him four kids to figure it out. I'm godmother to their son, Wills." She thumbed the doorbell. "Oh, and don't mind Lurch. He's a peach. Just don't let him knock you down. He'll take you off at the knees if you let him."

"Lurch?"

"Lila's big-ass dog."

John swallowed hard. He didn't particularly like strange big-ass dogs.

The door opened to reveal Lila's friendly, inquiring face. John could see the Allamand family resemblance in Lila's widely spaced eyes. She was using both hands to actively restrain a black and tan Burmese mountain dog. Lurch was so glad to see new people, his tail was thumping against the door like a baton. He was also drooling thick strands of saliva like spaghetti noodles.

"Come on in. Just give me a minute, I'll put Lurch in his kennel. Heel, Lurch, heel! Dammit, dog! I said heel!"

They listened to the drawn-out scuffle before Lila returned, dusting her hands. "Sorry about that. I know Lurch is a pain the ass, but he's great with the kids. Come on back to the kitchen. I need to give a pot a stir."

The hallway was lined with wainscoting below a set of beachy seascape watercolors. Scrawled children's artwork had been scotch-taped haphazardly all up and down the wallpaper. John watched his step since large, toe-catching holes had been chewed into the oriental runners that carpeted the scratched hardwood floor.

Lila lifted a lid and gave the contents of a cast iron pot a good stir. She turned down the heat. "That's better. CJ said it was Lieutenant Jarad? Any relation to Annie Jarad? We play doubles tennis whenever I get the chance."

"Yes, Anne's my sister-in-law. She's married to my brother, Pete."

"Nantucket is such a small world. Pull up a stool. You had some questions? What can I do for you?"

He sat. "We'd like to ask about an au pair you employed in 1999. Katherine Mary Roark?"

"Katie? Wow, that is going back." Lila blew her sweaty bangs off her forehead. "First au pair I ever hired but boy, did I need her help. Morgan was just a newborn. That gave me four kids under the age of seven, although I mostly took care of Morgan myself. Katie was a great girl, a little rough around the edges, but really terrific. She was fabulous with the kids. Stevie was really hurt when she left without saying goodbye. He had trouble sleeping for months after she left. Kept having terrible nightmares. I finally had to take him to a holistic shaman to sort it out." She shrugged. "But Katie was young. I guess taking care of three kids was too much for her to handle, so she split. Can't really blame her. Wills was a handful, even as a toddler. You know this, CJ. He still is."

CJ leaned on the counter. "We believe Katie went missing around August nineteenth? Is that right?"

"That sounds about right. I remember it being sometime around the middle of August. Not really convenient, but there it was. Luckily, Hussey-Howe sent me a replacement girl right away. Joramae, from the Philippines. She was terrific in her way, too."

"Why didn't you call us when Katie went missing?"

Lila had the grace to appear uncomfortable. "I did tell those people at Hussey-Howe. They said they'd take care of it since Katie was their employee. Besides, I didn't want to get Katie into any trouble. You know me, I'm a live-and-let-live kind of girl. At least Katie left a nice note."

This was news. John piped up. "Do you still have it?"

"Her note?" Lila laughed. "Take a look at this place, Lieutenant. Even if I had kept it, I wouldn't begin to know where to look for it."

"Do you recall what her note said?" John asked.

"I might. Let me think." Lila tapped her chin. "She was going off to live with some friends in D.C. She was sorry to give me such short notice, but the chance was too good to miss. Honestly, I think that the gist of it, as far as I can remember. It wasn't a letter."

"Did Katie leave any personal effects? Anything we could look at?"

"No, not a thing. She stripped her room bare. Took all of her clothes and her duffel bag. She even emptied the wastebasket." Lila snorted. "Not that she had much to begin with. You've never seen such a ragamuffin, when Katie first got here."

John felt a sudden thrill. They were getting closer to the truth. Katie Roark had either packed her own things or her killer had done so to bolster the idea that she was leaving Nantucket to cover the crime. It was time to try for an identification. He gave CJ the nod.

CJ cleared her throat. "Lila? Did Katie have any tattoos?"

"She most certainly did. Dragged her sorry butt home one Sunday morning with this black tattoo inked all over her arm." Lila circled the area around her left shoulder. "Made things difficult since she needed to stay out of the sun and the water for a couple of weeks until it healed, but what the hell? We were all kids once, right?" She eyed the envelope. "Are you going to tell me what this is about?"

"Lila." CJ slid the envelope across the countertop. "We have bad news about Katie."

"Bad news?" Lila's freckles suddenly stood out as her face paled. "How bad?"

"You read about the woman we found in Satan's Tub? She had a tattoo like the one you've described." CJ tapped the envelope. "We brought photos. Could you take a look?"

"No, not here." Lila shot to her feet. She plucked the envelope off the counter and parted the curtain to check on her kids. "Let's go into the den. I don't want the kids to hear about any of this until I've had a chance to talk with them first. We can't go through that again. Stevie was a wreck. This way. Follow me."

She led them through a butler's pantry into a sitting room filled with worn slip-covered chairs. One entire wall of the den was a built-in bookcase stuffed with paperback novels held in place by pickle jars filled with scallop shells. A painting in a gilded frame held pride of place over the mantle piece. It featured a group of children building a sandcastle near the base of the Brant Point lighthouse. John didn't know much about art with a capital A, but the painting looked masterful and direct. He did notice one odd thing: the faces of all of the people in the painting were hidden from view. The children either wore sunhats or they had their sunburned shoulders turned. The face of the young woman in the painting was hidden behind a fall of her dark salt-tangled hair as she bent down to pick a handful of shells off the sand.

Lila collapsed into an armchair. She stared at the envelope in her lap with horror. "Ohmigod. I so don't want any of this to be true."

"Take your time." CJ dragged a wooden chair closer. "But we need to know."

Lila sighed. Popping the flap open, she removed the photos and slowly turned them over in her hands. A sob escaped her. She began to shake. "Oh, it's Katie. What's wrong with her face? Why is she so red?"

CJ reached forward and touched her arm. "The bog dyed her skin that color after she was dead."

"I can't believe this is happening." Lila struggled to frame her next words. "How did she die?"

"If it helps any, she probably didn't feel a thing."

"Don't coddle me, Cynthia Jane." Lila's eyes sparked angrily. "Answer the question."

"Blunt force trauma. Something fractured her skull."

"And then whoever did that put Katie in the bog?"

"That's what it looks like."

"Christ!" Lila snatched a tissue. "And I thought she was off living her happy new life!"

"Mrs. Stanton, did Katie have any enemies? Anyone we should know about?"

"Enemies? What are you talking about, enemies? Katie was nineteen! Of course she didn't have enemies." She fell back against the cushions. "Thank God, at least I heard about this before the kids did. Oh, shit! Now they're going to hear about this everywhere they go this summer, aren't they?"

"For awhile," CJ said. "Then it will fade, like everything does. We'll need to get through the hard part but we're here, your family and your friends, to help."

Lila gamely tried to smile. She twisted the tissue through her fingers. "I know this is going to sound selfish, but I was really hoping to have a quiet summer this year. Stevie really needs to stay focused on prepping for college. You know how difficult it's always been for him. He hates any kind of transition. Everything is always such a struggle." She flung her arms wide and thumped the pillows. "Oh, hell! There goes that idea."

"Mrs. Stanton, we need to ask you for something more." John shifted uncomfortably. Asking people for help during a crisis was one of the toughest aspects of his job. "We need someone to come to the morgue, to formally identify the body."

"It has to be me?" Lila flushed crimson. "I'm sorry. That came out wrong. Of course, I'll do what I can. Poor Katie. I don't suppose you had any luck reaching that lame brother of hers in Ireland?"

"Kevin? The authorities are still trying to find him. He's moved a couple of times over the last decade."

"Good luck with that! From what Katie said, he sounded like a real squid. Do you know he made her send him part of her wages every month to keep her room back home open? He said if Katie didn't send him the money, he would box up her things and put them out on the curb with the rest of the trash. Who does that to a young woman starting out?" Lila pitched the tissue into a wastebasket. She looked up at the painting over the mantle piece. "Strange to think, isn't it? That's Katie up there in that picture. She's the girl with the long hair."

John felt gooseflesh crawl up his arms. He should have guessed. The truth had been staring him right in the face. He stood and moved closer to the painting. Seen up close, it was a remarkably gifted piece of work. "This girl? This girl is Katie Roark?"

"Yes." Lila sniffled. "The artist lives next door. You might have heard of him? Kurt Stockton? He's pretty famous. He adored painting Katie and the children together. They're in almost every painting he did that summer."

CHAPTER SIXTEEN

"I'll drive." John tossed his jacket into the backseat. He slid behind the wheel.

"Can't we walk over? It would reduce our carbon footprint."

"Don't get soft," he quoted Ted. "If it's warm enough for shirtsleeves, it's warm enough for deer ticks. Did you want to catch a dose of Lyme disease today?"

"Fine." CJ slid in. "What do you know about this Stockton other than the DUI?"

"I know his grandfather built their place in the forties, after the war." John executed a neat three-point turn and headed back toward the W junction. "My dad used to come over to play poker. Stockton didn't grow up on the island, though. They sent him to some posh prep school. He lives on the mainland now with his wife Melissa, during the winters. Somewhere in Connecticut, maybe? That sounds right. She's an artist, but we never see her. She hates Nantucket. Spends her summers in Europe."

"Tough life."

He pulled in next to a battered Volvo convertible parked at a strange angle. The house appeared deserted. All of the shades in the windows were drawn.

CJ pointed to the dented car. "Looks to me like Stockton's pretty good at hitting things."

"And even better at getting away with it." He closed the door. "Nothing like having a family lawyer on permanent retainer to smooth the rough spots out."

"I get the picture. Tough life, part two."

They walked to the door. John tried the bell and he heard it chime, but there was no response. CJ knocked loudly and peered through the sidelights.

"I don't see any movement. Looks like no one is home."

They trudged across the pea gravel driveway toward an outbuilding that might have been mistaken for a garage except for a line of skylights set into the angled roof. Two cross-barred carriage doors hung open on heavy industrial steel tracks. John paused on the threshold, and rapped his knuckles against a rough wooden panel.

"Mr. Stockton? Hello? Anyone home?"

The only sound was the wasping murmur of a speedboat buzzing the shoreline.

They stepped into what was obviously a working artists' studio. A crate was stacked with unopened quart-sized cans of commercial paint. Even with both doors wide open, John could taste the linseed oil that hung in the air. It coated his tongue. Empty canvasses were stacked next to a filthy sink propped up on cinderblocks. A lumpy mattress strewn with tangled sheets was pushed against a wall and set directly on the concrete floor. Next to the mattress, a finely carved Moroccan side table held an emptied wine bottle, a circle of guttered pillar candles, and a cluster of pills. The triangular blue pills had the pharmaceutical stamp VGR50 on them. The round white pills were unstamped. John heart a gasp and he looked up. CJ was staring open-mouthed at a painting displayed on an easel in the center of the room.

"John? Take a look at this."

The painting was huge, at least six feet long by four feet high. It featured a naked and supremely confident young woman reclining on a tufted leather couch. Her right arm stretched up over her head to toy with a strand of her long, dark hair as she relaxed against an assortment of silk-embroidered and tasseled pillows. Her left arm rested diagonally across her stomach with her curled fingers modestly covering her pudenda. A strand of small shells formed a choker around her neck, with a second, longer strand draped between her breasts. Her nipples, lips, and toenails were painted the exact same shade of vibrant pink as the lips of the shells. Her shoulder tipped into the frame just enough to hint at the circular black tattoo on her left arm.

John cleared his throat, twice. "I think we've found a portrait of Katherine Mary Roark."

"Posed as Aphrodite, the goddess of love."

John flinched. Kurt Stockton was leaning in the doorway, studying their reaction with wry amusement. Stockton was wearing a maroon cashmere sweater with fitted jeans. His hair was still damp. He looked tanned and trim, solidly built and in obviously great shape. He pushed off the doorway and entered the studio.

"Best thing I've ever done. The problem is, I can't seem to finish it." He rubbed his hands together drily. "Excuse me for not greeting you when you arrived, but I was taking a shower. I'm meeting with clients in a few. As you can see, this is my studio. I'd invite you in, but oh, that's right. You're already here."

"Lieutenant Jarad, Mr. Stockton." John scrambled to recover his poise. "This is Detective Allamand."

"I remember you, Jarad. So? What can I do for the local constabulary today?"

"We'd like to ask you a few questions," John said.

"Ask away." Stockton sat in a sagging director's chair and crossed his legs. "I've got nothing to hide."

"Wasn't Aphrodite blonde?"

Stockton smiled brilliantly, delighted by the question.

"You must be thinking of Botticelli's Venus, Lieutenant. Il Botticelli had his preferences, I have mine. Personally, I prefer brunettes. Blondes aren't as resilient. They simply don't hold up. Nothing personal meant, Sergeant, if in your case the carpet matches the drapes."

CJ bristled. "It's Detective."

"We'd also like some answers about the woman in this painting, Katharine Mary Roark."

"Also known as Katie Roark," CJ added.

"May I ask why you're asking questions about Katie?"

Time to go fishing. John carefully selected his lure. "We're talking to anyone who might have seen Katie Roark the summer she was on the island, in 1999. She's been reported as missing."

"Please, Sergeant, take a seat. Having you standing over me is making me nervous." Stockton waved CJ toward a nearby short stool. "Granted, it is primitive, but I do try to maintain a modicum of civilized behavior in here."

"Thank you." CJ sat. She opened her notebook across her knees and pointed her pen. "It's pretty obvious that you knew her."

Stockton raised his eyebrows and smiled without showing his teeth. "Did you intend to mean that biblically? I can assure you that I did. I'm delighted to report it was probably the most erotic summer of my life, and I've seen a few. But Katie? She was something special. I've never met anyone with such an appetite for life. Katie wanted everything, and she wanted it now. She overflowed with a rapacious form of *joie de vivre*. That means the enjoyment of life, Sergeant."

"I knew that," CJ said shortly.

"Katie wasn't afraid to try new things but she wasn't reckless either – it wasn't that. It was more like she wanted to live each day with the sole intent of finding something new and different to try. She had this insatiable need that was almost animalistic. You could see the hunger staring from her eyes. It was one of the truly remarkable features of her face. I certainly didn't have any trouble painting it, as you can see." He studied the canvas. "The paint simply flowed out of the end of my brush. I don't even recall mixing the colors on my palette. It was as if the colors were already there, waiting

125

to be used. I'm not sure if that makes any sense if you're not an artist, but I've never felt such a sense of pure ease when painting before. With Aphrodite, it's like I found some new and rare kind of magic."

"We've seen another example of your work, sir. You didn't paint anyone's face in that one."

"I don't paint anyone's face in any of them, Lieutenant. Capturing expression has always been difficult for me, so I don't put it in my work. Sergeant, you look confused. I'll try to explain it, and I'll use small words. It's like a singer knowing his range. You avoid the notes you know you can't hit. It's the same thing with art." Stockton shrugged. "Aphrodite, though, Aphrodite is the exception that proves the rule. Every artist has one or two oddities in their *oeuvre*. Aphrodite is mine. I don't pretend to understand how it happened, I'm only delighted that it did. I leave the reason of why it happened to God. I only wish I could finish it, and exhibit it to the world."

"That's nice." CJ flipped a page. "So, it's safe to assume you two had an affair?"

"Yes, Sergeant, we most certainly did. I'm not going to apologize for it. Katie was over the age of consent. Personally, I think she knew exactly what she was doing. We enjoyed a mutual exchange of pleasure." He chuckled. "She was insatiable, and quite the *mondaine*. Like I said, Katie loved to experiment, to try new things."

"Including ecstasy?"

"You're being judgmental." Stockton stood, and started pacing. "Have you ever tried ecstasy, Sergeant? Personally, I think that you should. It would loosen you up. Colors are more vibrant, people are warmer, and more loving. This harsh world of ours is a kinder place. I'm sorry, the short answer is yes, Katie loved taking ecstasy. She had an unforgiving childhood. Catholic guilt, abusive nuns, and a suspiciously tender uncle, if I read things right. Ecstasy helped Katie purge all that shit out of her head. It also helped her blur the line between fantasy and reality so that she could more fully explore her sexuality." He combed his fingers through his hair. "And to guess your next question, no, I don't know where Katie got her supply of it."

John stirred. "When was the last time you spoke with Katie Roark, sir?"

Stockton tapped his lips. "You said Katie was on Nantucket in 1999? I started working on Aphrodite as soon as I met her, so that would have been sometime that August?" He snapped and then splayed his fingers. "She was here one day and gone the next, like smoke."

"Do you remember which day it was?"

Stockton laughed. "You want me to remember a specific day? That's not going to happen. I've never kept a journal, and my aging brain is fading fast. Sometime during the middle of August is probably the best I can do." He tapped his temple. "I do recall that I hadn't started packing my paint kit yet for the mainland move, so it couldn't have been that close to Labor Day."

"And it didn't bother you that Katie disappeared so suddenly?"

"No, Sergeant, no, it did not. Katie was always talking about moving on to greener pastures. Like I said, she was always on the prowl, looking for the next big, best thing. She did mention some friends who lived near the Beltway once. I assumed she left to be with them." He picked up and thumbed a dry brush. "Earlier, you said Katie was missing. Where did she end up?"

It was time to share some truth. "Katie Roark was the victim we found in Satan's Tub," John said.

Stockton returned the brush to the tabletop with a snap. "I was afraid of that."

CJ clicked her pen. "You don't seem surprised to hear the news, Mr. Stockton."

"Well, I wouldn't be, would I? I'm not stupid, Sergeant. When I read the description of the woman in the bog, I wondered if it might be our Katie. She left so hurriedly, so unannounced. It wasn't much of a stretch to guess that's why you two are here today, asking me questions about her. I can only assure you that I know nothing about the way Katie died, or how she ended up in that bog. I'll take a polygraph test to prove it, if one is needed."

"We may ask you to volunteer for one eventually, sir."

"Fine by me. Like I said, Lieutenant, I've got nothing to hide." Stockton crossed his arms. "May I ask how Katie died? Can you tell me that much? You said you found her Satan's Tub. Did she drown?"

Stockton would know soon enough. It was public information. "She died of blunt force trauma."

He blinked. "You're sure of that?"

"Why do you say that, sir?"

"Because, Sergeant, it wouldn't surprise me to hear that Katie'd been strangled." Stockton returned to his chair and sat, steepling his fingers. "Don't look at me like that, Lieutenant. I assure you the sex was consensual, but Katie did like to practice risky behavior. You don't already know this? She liked to be choked almost unconscious during sex. Losing control helped Katie reach orgasm. I'm sorry, Sergeant, is this topic too graphic for you?"

CJ was turning pink.

"Not at all."

"Good. Katie also liked to fuck women. I know personally that she hosted three-ways on more than one occasion. Once Katie got going, she could put on quite a show."

"Mr. Stockton?" John interrupted. CJ was turning purple. "Would you be willing to look at some photographs, to help with an identification?"

"Of course. Let me see what you've brought." Stockton reached out a hand. "I'll do whatever I can do to aid the police effort." He shook the morgue photographs out of their sleeve. "Oh my, yes, how tragic. Yes, that is Katie Roark. I have to say I've seen her looking better."

John was shocked by the insensitivity of the comment, but CJ looked ready to explode. The stool squeaked as she stood.

"Sir? She was responsible for taking care of three small children that summer. If all of this happened like you say, then how did she find the time?"

"Katie managed it beautifully, Sergeant. She was quite inventive that way. She spent every morning wearing those little brats out, and then she slipped them Benadryl in their lunchtime milk." He chuckled. "Half an hour later they'd be zonked out like a light, and Katie'd run across the yard to meet me. Worked like a charm. We met almost every afternoon."

"What did you say? She doped the kids with Benadryl?"

"No harm done, Sergeant, I can assure you. Parents do it all the time." Stockton leaned back and clasped one knee with both hands. "It only meant the kids took a more convenient naptime each day."

"Are you serious?" CJ was shaking. "My God! What dose did she use?" She ticked the months off on her fingers. "May, June, July, and part of August? Stevie had nightmares for months after she left. Holy hell! Of course he did. The poor kid was addicted to Benadryl, and we didn't know it!"

"You are seriously overreacting to the suggestion, Sergeant."

"The hell I am! Wills is still struggling with ADD. Crissakes! We thought it was genetic. How old was he when she was dosing him, like two?"

"I think we're through here." Stockton checked his watch and rose. "I really do need to get to town to meet my client. I can't afford to be tardy in these difficult economic times. Unless you had something more?"

"You're not going anywhere," CJ said. "I'm not through with you."

John had never seen CJ this furious before. He gripped her arm. "Back it down, Detective."

She wrenched her arm free.

"I said stand down, Detective. That's an order. Go stand by the cruiser, and wait for me."

Stockton smoothed his hair as CJ stomped off. "You really should learn to control your bitch, Lieutenant. I don't think she's stable. Should I be concerned?"

"Don't worry about her," John kept an even keel. He was not going to let Stockton win this round. "I'll take care of my direct reports, thank you, sir. You let us know of any plans you make to leave the island."

"As I said, Jarad, my summer plans are fixed in stone the same way they are every year. I'll be on Nantucket through Labor Day, barring an unforeseen emergency, of course. Now, if you'll excuse me, I really do need to keep that appointment. Corporate clients with deep pockets wait for no man."

Stockton made a great show of sliding the carriage doors shut before fastening them with a Yale lock. He carefully skirted a still glowering CJ before climbing into his convertible. As he pulled away, once he was sure he was in the clear, Stockton gave her a jaunty wave.

"Prick!" CJ spat. She slammed her fist into the cruiser. "Did you see that guy's face when he looked at those photos? It was clinical. You could see him detach. He's a total sociopath."

CJ was right, but the prognosis didn't make Stockton an exception. Twenty percent of the general population exhibited sociopathic tendencies. It was hard-wired into the species. Whether learned behavior or inherited traits, sociopaths were simply incapable of making emotional connections. CJ was still so angry he was going to have to talk her down. "I think so, too."

She released her breath so hard, she puffed out her cheeks.

"Sorry I lost my focus. That guy pushed all of my buttons."

John relaxed. She was coming down off of high boil. He had know that she would. "I could see that."

"Do you think he killed her?"

"I'm not sure. His curiosity about how she died seemed genuine enough."

"I noticed you didn't mention her pregnancy."

"Let's keep that detail to ourselves, for now. Don't worry, CJ, we'll be back. Plus, I'm going to ask Paul to DNA test the baby to determine paternity."

"That'll be expensive," she warned.

"Don't I know it. Everything is expensive. Somehow I'll have to convince the Council that it's worth it."

She glanced worriedly at the house next door. "How the hell am I supposed to tell Lila that she was dosing those kids? That developmental addiction might be what's been wrong with them?" CJ ran her fingers through her cropped hair until it stood on end. "I know Lila. She trusted those au pairs to help out. When she finds out this was going on, she's going to find some way to blame herself. Lila doesn't need any more guilt. She's barely hanging on as it is."

"We'll go tell her together. We'll explain what we've learned. It's all we can do, CJ. She has to know the truth."

"I know she does. You're right. I just don't want to deal with it." CJ briskly rubbed her arms. "If we have to do this, let's get it done. I want to get out of here." She shivered. "I hate Wauwinet. I've been jumpy as a cat ever since we crossed that goddamned spillway."

CHAPTER SEVENTEEN

"Did that dishy Lieutenant Jarad ever call you back?" Alien asked.

Sarah stopped folding her clothes. It was a fair question. John hadn't called her back, and she had wondered why not. She thought they had shared some mutual interest during the interview, but maybe her guydar was off. Maybe he didn't want to come near her now that he knew about Mason because he thought she was damaged goods? That was a depressing thought. Sarah dropped her crimson hoodie on top of the stack, and felt a return of that sickish feeling in the pit of her stomach that always seemed to hint that everything she did was somehow wrong. Maybe John was already dating someone else? That thought wasn't much better. "Nope. He never did."

"Men. Go figure." Alien lolled on her bed. "He sure seemed interested to me."

"I thought so, too." She picked up the hoodie again. "He's the first really interesting guy I've met in long time. There was something, I don't know, kind about him. I thought I felt a connection, but I've been wrong before."

"Screw him." Alien reached for her bag. "Hey, listen. A bunch of us are going to the Bug House tomorrow night to listen to live music. Cheese for Dinner is playing, and cover is only five bucks. Why don't you join us?"

"I don't think so, Alien. It would feel awkward. I won't know anybody."

"Screw that! Come on, Sarah. What do I have to do to shake you up? You need to get out of this room. Besides, that band is so loud, you won't be able to talk to anyone anyway, and Friday night really kicks off the weekend. We're just going to dance, drink some beers, you know, hang out. It'll be fun."

Sarah considered the suggestion. It did sound like fun, and she loved to dance. Her stressed out budget wouldn't take that big of a hit if she only nursed one beer. Besides, what else was she going to do for her big Friday night? Go sit in the Atheneum and read more free books? She hated being constrained by her budget all the time. This penurious waiting game was driving her nuts. She needed more life in her life! "Alright. Count me in. Thanks for asking."

"Rock on. We're planning to head over around nine, nine-thirty." Alien swung her bag over her shoulder. "Catch you later."

The room felt twice as empty without Alien in it.

Sarah wandered over to the window and rested her forehead against the glass. Going out dancing was all well and good, but that was still twenty-four hours away. She needed to find something to do to fill all of this lifeless, empty time. A breeze stirred the curtains and cooled her face. She heard the repetitive scraping of a skateboard as an unseen teenager tried to master a complicated new maneuver with his deck. Looking into the alley, she watched a pair of lovers strolling along, holding hands. His voice was too low to catch what he said, but the girl tossed her head and laughed at whatever it was that he whispered in her ear. Sarah sighed. People–happy, gregarious people–were out there living their lives, while she felt stalled in an endless abyss, feeling disconnected and alone. Only one thing offered a glimmer of hope, and she blessed Alien for asking her to go out dancing. Maybe she would meet someone new and exciting at The Bug House, someone who would add some color to her drab life. In the meantime, she needed to do *something*. Maybe she should visit the art galleries on Old South Wharf? That would be interesting, and it wouldn't cost her a dime. Besides, looking at art always made her feel better whenever she felt this low.

"Screw this." She stole Alien's line and reached for her keys. Locking the flimsy door, she ran down the steps into the kitchen and on through to the bar. An ice-cold Dr. Brown's cream soda would be the perfect thing to sip on as she navigated the crowded streets. She pushed the swinging double doors open and her flip-flops squeaked as she pulled up short.

"Watch where you're walking!" Steve shouted from the storeroom. "For God's sake, don't kick anything over."

The Tap Room floor was covered with cardboard boxes lined up neatly under clear plastic tarps. The empty space between the rows was filled in with half-emptied bottles culled from the well.

"Steve? What the hell is this?"

"I'm running an inventory." He carried another case of bourbon from the storeroom. Puffing with effort, he set the case on the floor with the others and dusted his hands. "The demo crew is coming today to breach the outside wall for our new door. I want to make sure I know exactly what I have on hand before I let those hammerheads in here. Things might start to evaporate." He reached for a clipboard. "This is how I tally my booze. I factor in a drink count per bottle, then match the receipts against the till. It's the only way I can keep everyone honest."

Sarah's head was spinning. Fractional math had always been a weakness. "Why not just subtract the cost of the inventory against the take, and call it profit?"

"Ha!" Laughing made Steve look ten years younger. "I can see you've never worked retail before. There are a lot of crooks and cheaters out there, and not all of them are the customers. I hired one real operator last year, a bartender. He almost gutted me before I figured out what he was up to. Firing him was the highlight of my year."

"Why? What did he do?"

"Each night he'd sneak his own private bottle of hootch into the well, work it through my customers, and pocket the difference."

"I'm not following you. What did he do?"

"It was pretty clever." He leaned against the bar. "He'd buy a bottle of cheap booze on sale, let's say gin. He'd bring the gin in, and set his bottle in the well. Then, every time someone ordered a gin drink, he'd pour the drink from his bottle and hold back enough cash to cover a drink count in his head. You figure twenty drinks per bottle at five bucks a pop, and he gets to pocket an extra hundred bucks cash. Then, when his bottle was empty, he'd go back to using house booze and ringing up full totals. That way my inventory always matched the till, but our nightly totals were down, and he was doing this using bottles of gin, vodka, and rum. We were down three, four hundred dollars a night. I couldn't figure out what was going on. The place always looked packed, but the nightly totals were down. Then I realized it only happened on nights when he was working, and I found the empty crap liquor bottles in our recycle bin. It was the only mistake he made. Now, I run an inventory before every big event, or for special spot checks like this one. It's the only way I can sleep at night."

Sarah was amazed by the effort, but if you were looking for a way to take total control of a product, it did make sense. "Do you need any help doing this?"

"Really?" Steve looked surprised and delighted. "No one has ever offered before. If we doubled up, we could be done by noon."

She reached for an apron. "What do I need to do?"

"It's simple enough." Steve was all eagerness as he demonstrated his system. "I'll go through the boxes to confirm the bottle count, and then call out the tracking number printed on the bar code on each label. You check that number off my inventory list. That's it."

"Sounds easy enough."

"It is. Here's the trick: premium brand codes begin with a P. That's self-evident, right? Well brands begin with a G for generic, and special purchase begin with a W for wholesale case lot." He caught her curious glance. "Wholesale case lots come direct from the distillery. They're usually batch overruns or some end-of-the-year inventory that they're trying to get rid of.

Wholesale case lots can only be sold to restaurants or bars according to state law. They're not allowed to pass through into the retail sales channel."

"Kind of like with cigarettes?"

"Exactly like with cigarettes. I buy wholesale case lots whenever I can for two reasons: one, because booze never goes bad and two, the special pricing makes them a deal. Got it?"

"Got it." Sarah tapped the list. "P for premium, G for generic, W for wholesale case lot."

"Excellent. Let's get started."

Running the inventory turned out to be a surprisingly arduous job. It took most of the morning to get everything tallied to Steve's complete satisfaction, but when they were done even Sarah had to admit it was a job well done. The inventory list was complete and back to hanging on its nail behind the storeroom door next to Steve's new riot police whistle. The display bottles had been dusted and returned to the mirrored shelves behind the freshly polished bar. Steve had his hands on his hips as he surveyed his kingdom with pride.

"Now I call that a good day's work." He rang up a No Sale on the register and pulled a twenty dollar bill out of the till. "Here, Sarah, take this. Seriously, take it. This would have taken me another couple of hours without your help. Treat yourself to some lunch. Buy yourself a five-dollar watermelon frappe."

Sarah felt flush with the unexpected cash. Buy a frappe? Was he kidding? Nuts to that! Now she could treat Alien and her friends to a round of beers as a nice way to say thanks for asking her along to the bar. Things were starting to look up. "Thanks, Steve. I never say no to cash."

"Sound business practice as far as it goes. Now, go do something fun. It's a beautiful day out. All work and no play makes Sarah a dull girl, although, in your case, I sincerely doubt it."

She pushed the front door open and stood blinking in the sunlight. It was a beautiful day, with puffy white clouds sailing across a cerulean sky. Sarah reached into her purse for her shades and ducked down an alley, heading for the Old South Wharf. The wharf ran out from the pebbly end of the harbor, and it supported a row of cute studios that opened on both sides for shopping convenience. A brick courtyard held seasonal plantings with benches for any shoppers with weary feet. The courtyard also separated the studios from a grand two-story retail gallery planted on the landside. This gallery had a sign in its window advertising luxury condominiums for sale above. Sarah tilted her head back and looked up. The harbor view would be magnificent. Someday, when she was rich, should would own a condo just like that. As she strolled onto the wharf, she felt her spirit rise. She should have remembered this trick. Being surrounded by art always made her feel better.

One of the cute studios had a signboard shaped like a giant quill. Sarah ducked inside to admire examples of the artist's free-flowing calligraphy. The next studio offered delicate dolphins and mermaids made out of hand-blown spun glass. These exquisite tchotchkes had disproportionately monstrous price tags. She quickly noted the *you break it, you buy it* sign posted on the register and ducked back out, fearing a costly sneeze. Stepping around a Jaguar convertible, Sarah entered the grand retail gallery. This place was designed to impress. The maple floor looked as glossy as a basketball court, and it reflected the shining canister lights back into her eyes. As huge as it was, the studio was empty, and Sarah relaxed. This was more like it. She could take her time, and appreciate the art in peace.

She stepped up to the first painting, a seascape in a gilded frame. A woman in a billowy white dress stood on top of a hill, staring out to sea. She had her back turned to the viewer, and she was clutching a straw bonnet in her hand. The stiff breeze was suggested by the sweeping lines of her dress, and by the streaming pink ribbons on the hat. The composition and brushwork were handled competently enough, but in the end, the painting felt lifeless. Sarah moved on.

The next painting showed a group of small children building a sandcastle on a beach. Sarah snorted. This composition was a no-brainer, but whoever the artist was, he or she wasn't stupid. They understood their market. Kids building sandcastles would be an easy sell to any coastal buyer, although ultimately this painting was a cheat, too. Like the first one, none of the subjects faced the viewer. Even the babysitter's face was hidden as she crouched to retie the toddler's daisy chain sunbonnet. Although masterfully executed, not painting faces or trying to capture human expression equaled easy, cheap art in her book, because it was fundamentally soulless. Sarah stooped to read the artist's signature: *Kurt Stockton, 1999.*

The signature hit her like a revelation. This big fancy gallery belonged to that artist from the boat, the man who had started the ruckus in the bar. Sarah reread the signature to be sure, and she knew she was right. What a hoot! Nantucket was turning out to be just like Pittsburgh, where everyone and everything was related. She was about to shout a hello and make her presence known when a woman's voice carried down the open staircase from the condo unit above. The woman's contemptuous tone stopped Sarah in her tracks.

"Why were the police were at your house this morning?"

"You tell me. And by the way, where are my paintings that you sold for her? Wait! Don't tell me. Don't even bother. Every word that comes out of your mouth is a lie."

"I've still got them. I've been keeping them safe. Safe from you. You owe me that much, Kurt. I saved your ass, and don't you forget it. That little bitch was going to bleed you white. You were screwed, and once again I was left behind to clean up your mess. You need to remember that, and be more grateful."

"Sally? What really happened that night?"

"Nothing! Nothing happened. Forget about it. Forget about her. What's done is done. I'll handle this like I always do. There's no reason to worry about Katie anymore. Just keep your mouth shut, and we'll be fine. The only thing left to worry about now is Billy."

"Billy? Why Billy? What does he have to do with anything?"

"Crissakes! You're pathetic. Who do you think helped me clean that up? I had to call Billy. You were useless–passed out drunk as usual. God forbid I ever have to count on you for anything."

"Calm down. You're overreacting, as usual. You don't have to worry about Billy. You've still got him on a leash. He'll behave. Throw the dog a boner."

"God! I hate it when you're crude."

"You used to like it. Besides, you worry too much. Have you looked in a mirror lately? All this stress is making you look old."

"Fuck you."

A door slammed. Sarah caught the clack of high-heeled sandals descending the outer stairs. She ducked behind a beam as Sally Poldridge flashed by the window in a blaze of aquamarine silk and tawny hair. Turning toward the exit, Sarah hoped to make a silent getaway, but as she turned her flip-flops stuck to the polyurethaned floor and squeaked a protest.

"Hello? I'll be right with you."

Kurt Stockton bounded down the inner staircase, ducking low to avoid the ceiling while tucking his pale blue Oxford cloth shirt back into the waistband of his chinos. His eyes lit up when he saw her.

"Hello! What brings you to my humble abode?"

"I'm Sarah Hawthorne, from the Tap Room?"

"I know perfectly well who you are, Sarah Hawthorne from the Tap Room. My question was what brings you here?"

"I had some free time. I thought I'd come see some art. You know, see what the competition is doing."

Sarah hated that statement the minute it left her lips. She sounded like a complete jagoff, but Kurt seemed to ignore the impertinence of it. He moved lithely down the stairs to take up a position next to the sandcastle painting. "You're an artist, too? What do you think of this one? I just sold it to a hedge fund manager looking to diversify his portfolio. He overpaid for it, but who am I to say no?"

Sarah struggled to come up with something nice to say. "It's well executed."

"You think so?" He raised one eyebrow. "I thought some of the colors were a little too primary, myself."

"Not at all." She was beginning to feel at ease with the topic, and starting to hit her stride. "Actually, the work reminds me of Boucher. The sky is that luminous."

"You admire the French court painters, do you? I prefer Fragonard. I like his subject matter better."

Now Sarah knew she was being teased. Fragonard's subjects were notoriously sensual and indelicate. "His subject matter was certainly more mature." She quoted her favorite art teacher, "More sophisticated, or more debauched, depending on your view."

Kurt laughed easily. "Sarah Hawthorne, you interest me strangely. You're not the innocent you make yourself out to be. Let me ask you this. Who's your favorite painter?"

"Living or dead?"

He placed a hand on his heart. "Let us honor the dead, first."

Her answer took no thought at all. "John Singer Sargent. I love the way he used color to express personality. It's subtle, but it's there. No one did it better."

"Really? I couldn't agree more. I sometimes wonder if Sargent's sitters knew he was making fun of them. There's a portrait of one of the Vanderbilt brothers that borders on pure parody. I adore Sargent's work. I'd love to talk with you more about him, someday, if you have the time."

Was he still kidding her? Or had she finally found someone who shared the same passion for art that she did? "I don't want to take up your time. I know you're busy."

"Don't be ridiculous! That's the advantage to being self-employed. I get to decide on my own hours." He reached into a wicker basket. "Listen. Here's what we'll do. This is an invitation to our gala opening on Saturday night. Why don't you plan on coming, as my date? That way, if things get too stuffy, we can duck out, find a good bottle of wine, and discuss great art. How does that sound?"

Was he serious? It sounded like heaven. Sarah suddenly felt as gauche as a schoolgirl, all elbows and knees. "Are you sure?"

"As sure as I've ever been about anything in my life." He took her hand. Folding her fingers around the thick cream paper, Kurt turned her hand over and kissed the inside of her wrist.

Sarah gasped as his prickly whiskers tickled her skin.

He looked up, and studied her with playful eyes. "I can feel your pulse, Sarah Hawthorne. When two hearts race, both win."

CHAPTER EIGHTEEN

"Hi, Lieutenant." Toby jumped up from behind the console. "Tina asked me to watch the phone while she ran out for a sandwich. She'll be right back."

"That's fine." John paused to take a second look. Toby's curls had vanished. His scalp was now as sleek as an otter. "What happened to your hair?"

"I know. It's a big change." Toby sheepishly ran a hand over his new buzz cut. "My mom cried when she saw it, but I thought, you know, I should start to look more professional."

"It certainly does that. You look like a Marine."

"Sergeant Parsons said so, too. He stopped by this morning. He left a present on your desk."

"Ted left me a present? What is it?"

"He didn't volunteer any details, sir."

John warily approached Ted's mysterious gift. The object was flat and roughly eighteen inches square, wrapped in brown paper and held together by loops of frayed twine. John contemplated the array of risks associated with opening anything left for him by his difficult subordinate officer and decided that a combination of pluck, desk scissors, and his old wooden ruler should do the trick.

He carefully snipped the twine. When nothing exploded, John unwrapped the paper and uncovered a topographical map of Nantucket executed in intricate detail. Ted had sectioned the island into five different Whistler surveillance sites, with each site marked to correspond to a different color and capture team. Because of the island's level terrain, it was almost impossible to mount a completely unseen surveillance operation, but Ted had apparently done it, using his combat experience to advantage. Ted had marked an X on every point that might offer sufficient cover, and the five sites overlapped one another to ensure that there were no gaps in coverage, all the way from ground zero, the old South Cemetery, to the very edge of town. It was a masterful piece of deductive reasoning, and John stood in awe of it. He couldn't wait to share this with the team at this afternoon's staff meeting.

Of course, that meant he would have to give Ted credit for doing the work, and that might come off sounding a bit stiff and artificial, but he would just have to push through that. Ted had done the work; he deserved the credit. John recalled his initial reaction when he saw the package. He felt washed by a wave of embarrassment. Why was it always so easy to fall back into thinking the absolute worst of people? Recently, Ted had shown nothing but a willingness to change. If they still had a problem, then the crux of the issue must lie with him. He hoped his revised perception of Ted became a new habit, pronto. He didn't want to get a reputation as a head case.

And speaking of head cases, he had a new one to add to his list: Kurt Stockton. But at least with Stockton, John felt forewarned. He already knew that alcohol and prescription drug abuse were involved. It was a shame CJ had lost control of her temper so badly yesterday since there was definitely more information to fish for from that particular stream, but having CJ on the case going forward would only escalate Stockton's resistance. If he wanted to follow up on the Stockton lead, he'd best do it alone.

No time like the present. "Toby? I'm going to Wauwinet. Tell Tina to call me if anything urgent comes up."

"Will do, Lieutenant."

As John headed northeast on Polpis Road, he realized that he had overlooked the advent of Spring. After the dull winter months, the island had returned to life. The beach rose canes held tight clusters of buds, and there was a haze of new green growth on the trees. John lowered the window and filled the cruiser with crisp air as a pair of spandex-clad cyclists flashed by on the bike path on his right. He overheard them share a laugh as they receded in the rearview mirror. He relaxed against the seat. It was a beautiful day. How had he missed noticing this?

The cruiser's tires hit the spillway grid with a hum, startling John from his reverie. The road grid reminded him that for all of the seasonal changes, Nantucket had seen some major human-inspired changes as well. New developments were springing up like mushrooms after a summer rain, and these homes weren't modest family cottages, either, but huge McMansions built without regard for neighborhood propriety or old-time Quaker modesty. One new mansion near Sankaty Head was so outrageously overbuilt that it reduced the seventy-foot tall lighthouse to the status of a fancy lawn ornament. John shook his head. What these new coof owners didn't seem to realize was that there was a reason Nantucket homes were built to be easily lifted and shifted. Nantucket natives understood that their homes were built on a sand base that could erode away in the course of one severe winter's storm. Even Sankaty Light had been moved inland in an attempt to save it from the eroding bluff and the scouring tide. He didn't want to know how much that effort cost. Of course, all it took was a big pile of money to save a landmark like Sankaty Light. We can save or build anything we want. Look what the federal government did with this spillway.

The cruiser bucked over the speed bump and the road smoothed out again. John put his foot down and picked up some speed. Wauwinet was certainly rugged, with its forest of wild cedar trees. The landscape looked vaguely oriental, like some of the Japanese woodblock prints he had seen at a travelling art show his mother had dragged him to once. Wauwinet homes were more than a little isolated. Was that why Stockton liked living way out here? Because it kept him away from prying eyes?

John slowed the cruiser to spare the shell topcoat driveway. He knew the artist was home because both carriage doors were wide open.

He parked and crossed the driveway to find Stockton standing in the middle of the studio, staring at a fresh canvas. Stockton was holding a can of paint in one hand and a fat, dripping brush in the other. The canvas held a sketch of a couple sharing a bottle of wine at a café table by the sea. John really didn't know that much about art, but the composition looked promising enough. The Aphrodite portrait had been shifted to another easel against the wall.

He was surprised to see that Stockton could work on a new painting with the unfinished one staring down over his shoulder. Having those hungry eyes always on his back would have given him a case of the yips. He rapped a knuckle against the door. "Mr. Stockton? Don't let me startle you."

Stockton flinched, and his brush flicked a spray of crimson droplets across the floor. "What? I didn't hear you-"

Stockton looked dreadful. His eyes were bloodshot, and his face was a pasty blue-white that didn't look healthy. He staggered sideways, and the brush splattered a line of crimson paint across the knees of his khaki pants. "What do you want?"

John felt a ripple of concern. His conscience prickled at speaking to anyone in this condition. Stockton was on his own property. He could do whatever he liked, even if it meant getting stoned. Maybe he should excuse himself, and ask Stockton to come to the station once he had sobered up, but the man was squinting at him.

"Jarad? Come in, come in! I could use some company. This fucker isn't going anywhere." Stockton tossed the dripping brush into the sink, and swept his fingers across the back of the chair, leaving a smear of sticky red fingerprints. "What can I do for you today, Lieutenant Jarad? See? I should get a gold star. I remembered your name. That doesn't always happen."

"Maybe I should come back later?"

"Don't be ridiculous." Stockton sniggered, and tapped the side of his nose with a finger. "Let me ask you something, Jarad. This island's quite a nice fishing hole for fresh pussy, don't you think so? Fresh fish every season, imported at no cost. Crissakes! Who wouldn't want to summer here? It's a pussy paradise. The good news is that I found my new piece this morning, fresh off the boat. My new *belle du jour*. Got her baited, hooked, and set. All I need to do now is to reel her in." He mimed the action to his words. "Brrrr! Don't look so disapproving. This can't be news to you; you've lived here all your life! Besides, we should be friends. I've already told you everything I know about Katie. What she did was her business, not mine."

"You're not upset by what happened to her?"

"No, I'm not. I've already said I thought she went to live with friends."

"But we both know she didn't go live with friends. We both know she's the victim we found in Satan's Tub."

"You've already told me that." Stockton reached for a bottle of bourbon and took a swig. He sloppily wiped his mouth with the back of his hand. "And I've already said I don't know how Katie got there. Give me a lie detector test if you don't believe me. I'd pass it."

"How about a DNA test? Would you pass one of those, too?"

"What do you mean DNA test?" Stockton blinked blearily. "Enough of the riddles, Jarad. What's that supposed to mean?"

"Did you know that Katie Roark was pregnant?"

"What?" Stockton rocked forward and whispered, "Katie was pregnant?"

"Yes. It's been confirmed."

"Ohhhh. So that's what Sally meant. I didn't know that. Katie told me she was using birth control."

"An Irish Catholic girl from County Clare, and you fell for that?"

"I swear, Jarad, I didn't know Katie was pregnant." He shook his head. "Not that it matters. And then she went away."

"But we both know she didn't go away, someone put her away. And whoever killed Katie Roark killed her baby, too. Doesn't that bother you?"

"Does that bother me?" Stockton walked over to the sink. He turned the tap on, and splashed water on his face, toweling it off on his sleeve. He slowly turned the tap off. "Does that bother me?"

The man's shoulders were shaking. John thought Stockton was crying until he turned and John realized with a shock that Stockton was laughing instead, a silent, heaving, uncontrollable laugh so gripping that the man was forced to hang onto the lip of the sink for support.

"No, that doesn't bother me, Jarad. Katie Roark was a cheap little whore, a dime a dozen au pair, for Crissakes! You can rent girls like her by the hour. Look at this! Look at my work! I got everything I needed from her right there on that canvas. What I didn't need was a mewling, puking infant crawling across my studio floor, so my final answer is no, it doesn't bother me."

"But it might have been your child!"

"Might is the operative word." Stockton dragged his hands across his face. "Christ! But you're naïve. It might have been my child, but here's a news flash, Jarad: I had a vasectomy when I turned thirty to prevent that sort of thing. Procreation was never a part of my big picture."

John was thunderstruck. He felt outgunned and outplayed. He didn't know what to say next.

Stockton looked sly. "Don't look so shocked, Jarad. It's not common knowledge. Not even my wife knows about it. Melissa wanted a family, but like I said, it was never a part of the program." He climbed into the director's chair. "I think there's something wrong with your perception about people, Jarad. You only see what you want to see. Why is that? I've said it before, but I'll try again. Katie Roark was a cheap little whore who fucked everyone. There! That was simple enough. Did you manage to grasp it this time?"

"Yes. That's perfectly clear."

"Good! You really do need to learn that the Katie Roarks of this world don't matter a damn in the greater scheme of things. They're cheap labor. They're the hired help, the disposable tools. You really need to let this go." Stockton blinked blearily. "Let me ask you this: have you heard from anyone else about the importance of this investigation? Any single other person? No? Can't you guess why that is? Because nobody else gives a shit about that little tramp. She's not even a blip on their radar. You're the only dumb fuck who thinks that this is worth spending any time on. Everyone else has already checked out on it, and you should, too, because the truth is nobody else cares."

Was Stockton right? Was he the only one who really cared enough to find out what had happened to this one lost girl? John plumbed the depths of his heart for an answer, and found it resolute. "But I won't let it go, Stockton. I'll never let it go, until I know who killed her, and I see that justice is done."

"More fool, you," Stockton snorted. "But go peddle it elsewhere, because whatever happened to Katie, it wasn't me that did it." He reached for the bottle and took another swig before slumping in the chair. Raising his arm, Stockton leveled his focus along his outstretched index finger. "And unless you're going to charge me with something, I suggest that you leave."

"I suggest that he leave, too."

John jumped. He hadn't heard anyone sneak up behind him. Sally Poldridge stood in the doorway, and her face was flushed with fury.

"I'm appalled by what I see going on here, Lieutenant. You should be ashamed of yourself, interrogating him in this condition." She quickly moved to Kurt's side and put a hand on his arm. "He's in no shape to answer your questions and you damn well know it. He doesn't have a lawyer present, and he won't remember one word of this if you ask him about it tomorrow."

"It wasn't an interrogation. We were simply holding a conversation."

"Semantics? You're arguing semantics with me? Perhaps it was legal, but where do you stand on it ethically?"

Kurt stood up unsteadily. He tottered toward the mattress. "Sally? Make him go away."

"I will, darling," she murmured, guiding him to the rumpled bed. "Lie down now and close your eyes. That's right. Let it go. I'll take care of things, like I always do." She smoothed his forehead and rocked back on her heels, pointing toward the door. "Wait for me outside, Lieutenant, I'm as serious as a train wreck. If you don't leave this instant, I'll file a formal complaint. Hell, I might do it anyway."

John held his ground. "I'd like to talk about your role in all of this, if you have a minute."

"Fine, but go wait by the car. I'll need a lift. You can drive me home."

CHAPTER NINETEEN

It was easy enough to see how he'd been spotted. Sally's elevated jewel case of a house was built on top of a dune, the highest point of land for miles around. All she'd had to do was to look out one of her many windows to see the cruiser parked next door, and curiosity had done the rest.

John pushed off the fender as Sally stormed out of the studio. She paused to adjust her sunglasses against the glare. Even under the afternoon sun's harsh focus, John had to admit that Sally looked magnificent. Her lean runner's body was bronzed, her bare arms were sculpted and her toned thighs peeked out from her wrap-around skirt whenever it was snatched by the breeze. Even at forty-plus, Sally looked fit enough to walk around without wearing a bra which was what he could see she was doing now. He knew that every bit of her outfit had been picked for deliberate and provocative effect, but he had to admire her skill in pulling it off.

"You." She marched over, still pointing a finger at him, still furious. "What you did in there was unconscionable. Kurt's in no shape to talk to anyone."

"In my defense, he was more lucid when I first arrived. Does he usually drink like that during the day?"

Sally swept her fingers through her hair. "It's complicated. Kurt's a complicated man. Life is difficult for him."

"Life is difficult for all of us. That's no excuse."

"I know that." She toed out her espadrilles. "These shoes aren't made for hiking. I'll need a ride home."

It meant bending the regulations slightly, but there was no better way to open an inquiry than with having the witness feel they owed you a favor. "I can do that."

Sally opened the passenger door and slid in. "Why were you talking to him? What did Kurt say? You do know that he's a complete liar ninety-nine percent of the time, right?"

John decided to stall. Sally was known to be clever, and he didn't want to reveal too much. "You were very kind to him back there. Have you known Stockton long?"

She waved his question away. "We knew each other back in college. Boston University, Class of Eighty-six. I was an art major, Kurt was an artist. We ran in the same circles, hung out in the same dive bars."

"And thirty years later you both ended up as neighbors in Wauwinet? That's some coincidence."

"I know it seems odd, but it was pure chance. I only moved to Wauwinet after I married Seth. This was his family home, not mine."

Without warning, Sally reached down and raised her skirt, running her hands quickly down her shins, around her ankles, and back up her calves. "Sorry. I felt a tickle. I worry about ticks."

John felt a pulse of raw heat. Just how pathetic was he? He had completely failed to keep his eyes on the road, where they needed to be. Worst of all, Sally had caught him looking.

"That's better." She smoothed her skirt demurely over her knees. "Every time I feel an itch, I need to scratch it. Know what I mean?"

"Lyme disease is nothing to monkey around with." His voice sounded odd to his ears. As he parked, John told himself to get a grip. Sally was famous for this type of seductive behavior. He wasn't going to fall for it. He was stronger than that.

"Come inside, Lieutenant." The breeze molded Sally's clothing to her figure as she stepped from the car. "There's something I want to show you." She laughed and waved him in. "Abandon hope, all ye who enter here."

John shivered as the refrigerated air chilled his skin. He wasn't used to air conditioning this early in June. He followed Sally into an expansive living room. It was hard to keep from gaping at the plate glass windows that rose from the floor to the coffered ceiling that arched thirty feet over his head. Growing up as he had in the rabbit warren of the ancestral Jarad homestead, he felt transported in the presence of this much open space. It was incredible to think that this cathedral of light could actually be called *home*.

Sally had moved behind a padded leather bar. She selected a highball glass and reached into a bucket for some ice. "I keep losing you, Lieutenant. Do you mind if I call you John? Lieutenant Jarad seems so formal, when it's only the two of us."

"That's fine."

"It's five o'clock somewhere, John. Can I fix you a drink?"

"Nothing for me, no. Thank you."

"Are you sure? It's important to stay hydrated." Sally sliced a lime in half and gestured with the serrated knife. "How do you like the digs? Grand enough for you?"

"I saw this house featured in *Architectural Review* once. It's even more impressive in person."

"Some men say that about me." She laughed. "That was all Seth's doing. He loved the notoriety of it." Dangling the frosted glass between her fingers and her thumb, Sally sauntered down a paneled hallway. "This room is fine, but I prefer a more intimate space, a room with more … discretion? Follow me, John. Do keep up."

Taking a sudden right, Sally disappeared.

Against the thundering protest of his better judgment, John followed Sally down the hall. This was exactly the type of cowboy stunt the chief had warned him against, but she had the information he needed. He trotted down a springy set of carpeted steps into a two-story room shaped like half a drum. The room featured even more immense glass windows, and a party-sized hot tub with a flat screen TV mounted on the wall. A built-in bookcase was filled with DVDs. John read some of the titles: *Intercourse with a Vampire*, *Behind the Red Door*, *Pulp Friction*. Sally had a porno collection. No surprise there.

"How do you like my playpen?" she called. "It's my second favorite room in the house."

John gazed at the hexagon of plate glass. "Is this the window that was vandalized?"

"Yes, but I don't want to talk about that now."

"Why did Stockton break it?"

"My! Aren't you clever! How on earth did you ever guess that?"

The surmise had been obvious. The motive, however, was not. "Aren't you going to tell me why he did it?"

"Why does a drunk do anything? Kurt gets that way sometimes. He has deep anger issues." Her voice carried a faint echo. "You really should come in here with me, John. I want to show you something. I think you're going to find this very interesting."

John stirred, unsure of his next move. It was obvious that Sally was willing him on, but it was also obvious that she had no limits when it came to inappropriate behavior. Evidently, Sally did whatever she damn well pleased, whenever she pleased. He wanted to get more answers from her, but Sally's list of conquests was notorious, and he did not want to become a statistic.

He stepped across the threshold into her bedroom, and discovered the heart of that truly amazing house. Sally had added a master bedroom suite to the lowest level, with even more floor-to-ceiling windows. The windows trimmed off the view of the dunes, so that all you saw was a solid expanse of plush aqua carpeting that met the vision of the restless sea. The smooth stretch of cool blue ran from the floor to infinity, and it encompassed the silk coverlet on Sally's king-sized bed. She was sitting on the edge of the bed, relaxing back on her elbows, and dangling an espadrille off her toes.

"Like the view?"

"I can't take my eyes off it."

She patted the mattress. "Come sit by me, John."

"Thanks. I'd prefer to stand."

"I'm not as obvious as you think." She laughed, amused. "I meant turn around, and take a look."

John turned, and the sight that met his eyes staggered his senses so completely that he stepped back, bumping his calves against the mattress and groping for a seat as he sat. The entire inside wall was plastered with magnificent paintings, their gilt frames bumped up right next to each other. It was obvious that they had all been painted by the same master hand. The portraits varied in size and composition, but it was their content that staggered his imagination. Every one of them was painted with such a vivid intensity, it was as if the artist had captured the subject's very soul. An elderly line fisherman stared from one frame. The toothless old man was worn out and weary unto death, his knuckles scarred from a lifetime of merciless toil. A woman in a white dress stood poised as she sheltered the three small children huddled at her feet. She had raised one hand to scan the horizon for a long-lost ship, with the fear of their perilously dark future shining from her deeply troubled eyes.

"My God," John breathed. "Where did you get these?"

"They're Kurt's work, his real work, I mean. I never get tired of looking at them." Sally adjusted her position, and the mattress jounced in response. "This is Kurt Stockton, the real Kurt Stockton, the best of the best. When you see these paintings, you realize how incredibly talented Kurt really is. He's the real deal, and we mere mortals need to make some concession for this level of talent. I know Kurt has a dreadful reputation, but his gift is so pure, it's like Picasso. True, he's a bastard in real life, but his gift is like seeing the hand of God."

"I can't believe Stockton painted these."

"I know, especially when you see the commercial dreck he sells in his shop. But every once in awhile, like a piece of a dream, Kurt produces one of these amazing beauties. That's the real reason I still live in Wauwinet, to be near Kurt in case he paints one more. Whatever else he does, whatever else I do, doesn't matter. This work is immortal, and I'm the one who found it first."

John couldn't tear his eyes off the paintings. An older husband with his trophy wife, the man examining his glass of blood-red wine, oblivious to the salacious look his wife was sharing with another man half-hidden in the shadows. A girl, a young girl, vibrant and brimming with life, riding her bicycle down the center of a country lane, demonstrating her balancing prowess by stretching both arms high overhead, her eyes closed in self-evident joy of living bliss.

"How did you end up with them?"

Sally dropped her shoe. She rolled onto her hip and rested on an elbow. "Some I bought, some were gifts, some I saved from him. Kurt has a horrible self-destructive streak. He gets frustrated that he can't paint at this level all of the time. It's the strangest thing. His talent comes and goes, off and on, like a switch. I've seen it happen. I've tried to suggest that it's because of his drinking, but Kurt won't hear of it. In the meantime, he still needs to produce something to sell. Keeping Melissa and all of his little chippies happy is an expensive habit. That's why he paints the dreck in his shop. These paintings, though, these are real. Can you feel it?"

"I can. There's a real power at work here."

"It's such a shame that Kurt's talent is so unpredictable. Of course, he doesn't think it is, but I've caught him lying about it before."

"Lying about it, how?"

"He says he didn't paint some of these, even when I've stood over him and watched him do it. Kurt has this insane idea that some outside force is channeling through his body when he paints at this level. Take the one of the girl riding the bike, for instance. I had to wrestle it away from him. I caught Kurt down on the beach, trying to burn it. It's a miracle I saw the bonfire in time. If you look close, you can still see sand stuck in the paint. I found it, still wet, lying face down on a dune. I had to blow Kurt, right then and there, to make him forget what he was trying to do, or it would have been toast, but in the end, I think my effort was worth it, don't you?"

John shifted uncomfortably. "You and Stockton have a strange relationship."

"Men are strange animals." Sally sat up. "I've given up trying to figure Kurt out. Now, I only manage him. We're like an old married couple, friends at best. I keep an eye on Kurt's books, and manage the commission side of things and he, I'm afraid to say, likes them younger each year. Still, I stick around because he needs me, and because I make sure the best part of him, these paintings, survive."

"You knew of his affair then, with Katie Roark?"

"I knew of his affairs with all of his little chippies, I live next door. It's hard to miss what he's got going on over there every summer. And, at the end of every summer, I cleaned them up, paid them off, and kept a painting or two for my commission. It seemed like a fair exchange to me."

"Stockton implied that you might have enjoyed a more active role in those relationships more than once or twice, yourself."

"He said that?" Sally laughed. "I'll admit I've enjoyed the fruits of Kurt's labors more than a few times. Don't look so shocked. We're all adults. Kurt knows that I'm here if he needs me, and so should you."

Her direct gaze was making him squirm. John folded his hands in his lap. "You said that you managed Stockton's business. Did he ask you for help managing Katie Roark's disappearance, too?"

He caught the involuntary widening of her irises, a fear reaction, before she blinked.

"I don't know what you're talking about. Katie's missing? I know she took the money Kurt gave her. Where did she end up?"

"She's the victim we found in Satan's Tub."

"No!" Sally clutched a pillow. "How thrilling! The bog victim was our little Katie? Such a tragedy for a young girl. What happened? Can you tell me that much?"

"It was a deliberate act, if that's what you're asking."

"Murder? Murder on quaint little Nantucket isle? Oh, my! How the society matrons will be shocked."

"You're taking this news rather lightly."

"Of course I am, John. I'm not a hypocrite. It's not like Katie meant anything to me. Would you prefer that I lied about her?"

"No. Let's stick with the truth when we're doing so well with it, but I have to ask: if Katie Roark meant so little to you, then why do you have her tattoo on your shoulder?"

Sally straightened her sleeve. "You're not playing fair with me, John. I'm not sure I should share anything more with you. Whatever will you think?"

"You can share more with me. I can handle it."

"Oh, there was never any doubt in my mind that you couldn't handle it." She inched closer. "You see, like so many things, Katie brought a few new games to the party. At first, it started out like a little harmless fun. The first time Katie invited me to Kurt's, it was supposed to be a surprise three-way for his birthday, but I have to say things definitely took off from there."

"So you did have a relationship with Katie Roark."

"I wouldn't call it a relationship. It was more like a partnership. Kurt was always the focus." She rubbed the tattoo with her thumb. "These tattoos were Katie's idea. Mine is on my right arm, hers was on the left, Kurt was tattooed over his heart. It was supposed to represent some kind of Irish symbol, the three of us moving together as one, get it?"

"I do get it. But I think that's some form of blasphemy."

"Don't turn prudish on me now, John. Blasphemy is just another empty word. The world is so full of them." Sally drew her legs up on the bed and leaned forward, emphasizing her cleavage. "Three ways wasn't the only thing Katie brought to the party. She also introduced me to a new parlor trick that I didn't know about, and that takes some doing."

"Why don't you tell me about Katie Roark's new parlor trick?"

"It's called the choking game." Sally pressed her breasts against his arm. "It would be easier for me to show you."

148

He felt her heat through his sleeve and swallowed, hard. How far did he really want this to go? Sally was right about one thing. He was an adult. Was it time to finally live without all the made up rules in his head? *No more cowboy stunts, son.* He recalled Chief Brock's warning, and stood up quickly.

"Where are you going?" Sally asked, surprised.

"This is wrong. I should get out of here. I took this too far."

"Don't be ashamed, John." She laughed, and rolled off the bed. Strolling to a dresser, Sally picked up a brush and began smoothing her hair. "Sometimes I forget how young you really are. Let me clue you in. Shame is another one of those words they use to control us, like guilt, or responsibility. Essentially, it's meaningless."

"I don't think anyone or anything could ever control you."

"Good God! I hope not." Sally adjusted her diamond rings. "I learned early on you have to take what you want from this world. No one is going to give it to you. Like my first husband, Stevie. He never could think things through properly. I kept waiting for him to make something of himself, but he never did. Then I met Marty. Marty taught me the truth about power, economic power. '*He who holds the gold makes the rules.*' That was Marty's lesson, and Marty was right, because once you have enough money, no one gets to tell you what to do."

She moved to the window. "After Marty died, I married Seth. Seth was my favorite husband, because he left me this house, and his stock portfolio. I'm free now, and I live the way a man would, if he had the money." Sally turned. "That's what pisses everyone off, because I don't live the way they think I should, like a decent woman, whatever that's supposed to mean. It's ridiculous. Self-righteous fuckers. '*Judge not lest ye be judged*' and boy! Do they sit in judgment on me. At least I'm honest about what I want, and how I get it. They're the hypocrites about the way they live, not me."

John felt sickened and swamped. Was Sally right? Was following a modest personal morality a sham meant only for self-deluded fools? He held to his integrity, and struggled to right his thinking. He had always relied on clear-eyed honesty to anchor his own moral compass. He couldn't imagine living any other way.

"I can see by your face you're still hung up on guilt," she said. "What is with you cops? You always take things so personally. You never can let them go."

"What do you mean by *you cops*?"

"Chief Brock was exactly the same way. So afraid of what people might say. I kept asking him, who are these people and why do you care what they think? But no, he had to go home to sleep in his wife's bed, not mine. I warned Brock it wasn't safe, that he'd had too much to drink. He should have stayed with me, but no, he drove home instead, and look what happened. Such a tragedy. Such a disgrace."

"That's why the chief was on Polpis Road that night. He was coming back from seeing you."

"Yes." Sally crossed her arms. "You're like Brock in a lot of ways. So narrow-minded, so provincial, so prudish. Is that an island type? Are cops born so parochial? Or is it learned?"

He needed to get away, to find somewhere quiet to think all of this through. "That's it. I'm going."

"Use that door." Sally pointed. "It's a shortcut to the patio. I never lock it. It amuses me to see who will come through it next."

"There won't be a next time for me, I can promise you that."

"We'll see. You're not the first man to say that, John. They all return, eventually." Sally smoothed the rumpled silk bedspread. "My money says you will, too. At least now it should be easier, since the horse knows the way."

He pulled the door shut and ran up the dune toward the car, trying to process all that he had learned. Chief Brock had been with Sally the night of his accident. What a shocker! He had never suspected that, and how much of what had been going on over at Stockton's had the chief known about? Was it possible that the chief had covered up a murder, to protect his illicit affair? This new line of reasoning made John question everything, but it all boiled down to one thing: *What had the chief known?*

Cranking the ignition, he peeled away from that damned and wicked house. He checked the time on the dashboard clock. Two-fifteen. He had been in Wauwinet for almost two hours, and what had he learned? Yes, he now knew that Stockton and Katie Roark and Sally were linked, but he was no closer to proving anything. He was supposed to brief the team about his plan to trap The Whistler in less than thirty minutes, and instead of focusing on his duty, he'd spent the majority of the afternoon focused on the tent in his pants.

The cruiser hit the spillway speed bump hard. John felt the jolt all the way up his spine, and he glanced up barely in time to avoid a head-on collision with a sinuous line of competitive cyclists weaving across the long steel grid. John snatched the wheel hard right, and caught the look of apprehensive fear in the pack leader's eyes. He pulled over into the breakdown lane, and parked. He seriously needed to refocus, before he got someone killed.

Rolling down the window, he let the hyper-oxygenated air pour across his overheated face. The air felt so good, he needed more of it, so he opened the door and left the cruiser, breaking into a run to the spillway's side.

He grasped the cool railing with both hands, and stared into the streaming green water. The tide had turned, and the rolling seawater was pouring back into the inner harbor, spinning the turbines in their concrete bunkers twenty feet below his feet. He could feel the turbine hum in his knees, and the prickly static electricity they produced raised the hairs on his arms. The rushing water turned into mini-Niagaras when it smashed into the new underwater barriers. The sound of the roaring water was so overpowering that it soothed his senses, and his brain began to clear.

John glanced back up the road. Rules or no rules, there was a right way to behave, and that was not it. *What the hell is wrong with me? What was I playing with back there?*

CHAPTER TWENTY

"Cheese for Dinner did a tour of college campuses last year," Mona said. "Did you ever get to see them?"

"No." Sarah hunched her shoulders and kept her hands tucked in her hoodie pocket. The night was chilly and the side streets of town were dark. "They never made it to CMU."

"CMU?" Cynthia asked. "What's that?"

"Carnegie Mellon University. In Pittsburgh? I swear, some of these East Coast bands think if they have to travel west of Philadelphia, they'll fall off the map."

"Can't blame them for thinking that when it's so true," Cynthia giggled.

Cynthia was a strawberry blonde. Sarah was already beginning to not like her.

Alien pushed open an iron gate. "Let's take the shortcut. I'm getting thirsty."

Sarah stopped. "Get outta town! Have you lost your mind? Alien, that's the cemetery."

"It'll trim five minutes off the walk, plus these folks won't mind; they're dead. What's the worst that could happen?"

"The Whistler could happen." She held her ground. "You have heard of him, right? He might be in there right now, waiting for a group of really stupid girls to come walking through."

"Hey! Who you calling stupid?" Mona asked. "Eileen, I'm not so sure I like your new friend."

"Don't be such a squid." Alien stepped through. "He only chases single women. He won't bother a bunch of us." She snapped her fingers. "Go with the flow."

Mona pushed past. "And you can follow me, because the flow is going this way."

Sarah tripped on Alien's heels. "I still think this is a bad idea. I swear, this is like running into a bear. I don't need to outrun the bear, I only need to outrun you, and if anything jumps out at us right now, I am so out of here, you won't even see me, because I'll be a blur, and don't expect me to wait around for you because you are on your own, and you'll never catch me anyway, not with your smoker's lungs."

"Would you please stop being such a nelly?" Alien raised a hand. "Hold up. Did you hear something?"

"Ha-ha, very funny. I know this game. It's called Let's Scare the Baby. Great! Now I'm going to pee my pants before we even get there."

"No, seriously. I thought I heard something."

A female giggle rolled in from the darkness, and an inebriated couple stumbled out of the shadows. She was leaning heavily on her boyfriend with her arm around his neck, and her unbuttoned blouse gaped open. She gave them all a silly, drunken grin and waggled her fingers. "Whoooo! Did we scare you? Did you think it was The Whistler?"

"We knew you were there," Mona said. "You made enough noise."

"That was Betsy." He nuzzled her neck. "Bets likes making noise. Dontcha, babe?"

"Knock it off, Cal." She pushed him away and buttoned her blouse. "Let's get back to the bar. It's almost time for shotski."

"Yeah, like you need more." He bowed gallantly. "Right this way, ladies. The party is over here."

They scrambled through a twiggy gap in a boxwood hedge and stepped directly into a busy parking lot. Cars, SUVs, and open Jeeps were parked every which way without apparent rhyme or reason. An insistent bass beat spilled from car speakers to mesh with the beat coming from the band inside the bar. The powerful thumping rhythm merged into something primeval, as fresh and real as a hot pulse. Sarah felt her interest quicken. A column of warm yellow light spilled into the lot every time the bar's front door opened, and it highlighted the couples hidden between the parked cars. A sweet herby mix of cheeb and clove perfumed the air. A bulky bouncer was perched on a stool under the single spotlight over the door. He snapped his fingers for her ID.

"Sarah Hawthorne from Pittsburgh, Pennsylvania. Damn, that's wicked strange. You look like someone I used to know." He handed the ID back. "Word of warning, ladies. I noticed you came in through the graveyard tonight. Don't go home that way. It's a full moon so The Whistler will be out. He's always on the prowl this time of year. Make sure you don't go home that way, straight up." He folded their cash into his pocket and pushed the door open. "Enjoy the show."

The Bug House was crammed with people. Sarah couldn't even see the stage.

"What'll you have?" Alien bawled in her ear over the roar of the crowd.

"Let's start with a bucket of beer." She pulled her twenty out of her pocket. "My treat."

"Great! Hey, that table behind that post looks open. Grab it. I'll get the beer."

Mona and Cynthia waved to some friends and disappeared in the crush of people. Turning her back on the bar, Sarah got her first good look at the place. The Bug House wasn't anything special, just a boxy room with a beat-to-hell dance floor, a stage at one end, and a couple of battered pool tables at the other, but the place swarmed with rowdy partiers. She claimed the open table and accidentally nudged the guy standing to her right. He turned and, seeing her, smiled.

"Sorry! It sure is packed in here," she said.

"Definitely the place to be. I'm Duncan Pratt. What's your name?"

"Sarah Hawthorne." Duncan was sandy blonde and classically handsome with chiseled features and a dimpled chin. Sarah guessed that he had picked out his salmon-colored polo shirt to complement his early tan. She shamed herself for being so critical, so fast. He was only trying to be nice.

"Nice to meet you, Sarah. I see you're on empty. Can I get you a drink?"

"My friend is getting us some beer. Here she comes. Alien, this is Duncan."

Alien set the bucket down in the middle of the table. She had also already captured a new friend of her own. "Nice to meet you, Duncan. Everyone, this is Pedro."

"She made that up. It's really Pete." He knocked his free fist with Duncan. "Sorry, dude. Didn't know this was a party. I only brought two."

Sarah took a hard pull on her beer. It was icy cold and hit the spot. "What is that?"

"Cuervo Especiale. They were out of Patron, but this should do the trick."

"Alien? You're drinking shots?"

"You bet! Jose Cuervo is a good friend of mine. I love tequila. Your brain turns off but your body keeps going. Looks like I've got some catching up to do." She grasped the proffered shot glass between her fingers and her thumb and tossed it back. She coughed, and waved her hand over her mouth. "Oh, my. That was delicious!" She pointed to the shot glass Pete was still holding. "Are you going to drink that or just admire it?"

He looked confused. "I was."

Alien took the shot glass from his hand and tossed it back, too. "Catch me later, gator."

"I think I'm in love." Pete pointed. "The band's coming back. Are you ladies ready to dance?"

"Sarah?" Duncan said. "How about it? Care for a spin?"

"Yes, I'd love to."

Duncan's fingers tickled her ribs as he guided Sarah to the dance floor. Cheese for Dinner slid into a classic reggae song as more dancers joined in. The temperature under the stage lights hovered around ninety, and the beer was starting to make her sweat, but Sarah didn't care. This was all about dancing and having fun. She concentrated on keeping to the beat, of enjoying the physical sensation of stretching and spinning within the time, of losing herself in the moving mass of anonymous dancers. She began to feel like someone who fit in, like someone who really had it going on, like someone who didn't have to worry about past mistakes or any future worries. This was all about the now. She knew that some of this feeling was from the beer, but she didn't really care, because it was such a relief to turn her persistent worries off.

The song ended and the crowd began to chant: "Shotski! Shotski!"

"What's that about?" Sarah asked.

Duncan took her hand. His fingers were sticky, and she flinched.

"Come back to the table and I'll show you. See what that waitress is carrying? It's four shot glasses glued to a waterski. They fill the glasses and everyone lines up to do a shot. That's a shotski."

"I've never heard of such a thing. What are they drinking?"

"Jagermeister, lemonheads, tequila, whatever you want. Want to try it?"

"No way. Not me. I don't do shots."

Alien gave her a nudge. "Come on, Sarah, live a little. You can dance it off later."

"No thanks. You don't want to see me on hard liquor, and maybe you should slow down a little, too? That'll be your third shot in less than fifteen minutes."

Alien laughed. Her face was flushed, but she looked vibrant and full of life. "Don't rain on my parade, roomie. If you're not willing to play, then get out of my way."

As the boisterous crowd chanted its approval, her new friends found a willing fourth and they lined up for the next loaded shotski. On the count of three, they raised the waterski and tipped it back. The crowd whooped and hollered and cheered them on. Alien shouted, 'Yes!' And she raised her arms in triumph. Duncan coughed and swiped his mouth on the back of his hand. Then he turned and swatted Sarah's butt.

"I need to go drain the monster. Don't get lost in the crowd. The next dance is mine."

What was wrong with her? Sarah felt hollow and disconnected. She didn't want to be a stick in the mud, but this wasn't her idea of fun. This seemed so ridiculous, so juvenile, so pointless. She didn't know any of these people, and she wasn't even sure she wanted to. Not to mention that Alien had broken into a heavy sweat and suddenly turned a sickening shade of chartreuse. "I don't want to stop your fun, but maybe you should switch to water for awhile?"

"Actually, I'm not feeling all that great."

"Are you going to puke?"

Alien swallowed thickly. "No, I don't think so. Well, okay, maybe."

"Let's get you some air." Sarah grabbed Alien's arm as Pete returned. He was carrying another fully loaded tray. "Thanks, but we've had enough."

He smiled toothily. "Don't worry if you need to get going. You can leave her with me. I'll make sure she gets home okay."

"No, thanks. We came in together, we'll go home together."

He took a step forward and blocked their access to the door. "I said you can leave her with me."

"And I said we were leaving. Come on, Alien. I'll call us a cab."

"Wait a second, bitch! I paid for her drinks! I should get something out of it." He leered. "If she can't take care of me, then maybe you can. A blowjob will be fine. We can step out to my SUV right now."

"On what fucking planet?" Sarah shouted. She was shaking with fury. The fact that Pete would take advantage of someone who was drunk and his obvious sense of entitlement enraged her. She emptied her pockets and threw all her money on the table. "Keep the change, jackass! Alien? We are leaving, now!"

Compelled by the grip on her arm, Alien stumbled toward the door. She tripped over a power cord duct-taped to the floor and earned a mocking fit of hooting giggles from the crowd.

"Been there!"

"Done that!"

"But I wasn't doing anything wrong!" Alien wailed.

"You weren't doing anything right, either." Sarah shoved her way through the crowd, searching for Mona and Cynthia, but they had vanished. Putting her shoulder to the door, she pushed it open and stepped into the cooler night air. Maybe they were in the parking lot, and she could get some help? She glanced down the rows, but they were nowhere to be found. "Alien, I swear to God tomorrow we are going to discuss your idea of fun, but right now, I need to find a cab."

"Sorry, ladies." The bouncer stepped back into the light. He was smoking a sweet blunt. "You just missed the last one. It'll be twenty minutes before they circle back. Feel free to hang out with me, though, if you like."

"Shit!" Checking her pockets, Sarah was shocked to find they were empty. "I threw everything I had at that jackass at the bar. Alien? Do you have any money left in your wallet?"

Slowly, Alien began to paw through her bag. "I left my wallet?"

"No! Money! Do have any money left?"

"Nope. Sorry. It's all gone."

The bouncer tried to be helpful. "There's an ATM machine inside."

Sarah didn't have a bank card, and even if they got more money, she didn't think they could wait the twenty minutes for a cab. She had dealt with drunks before, and Alien's naptime clock was ticking. She studied the dark road back to town. "I guess that means we're walking. I don't know. Maybe the fresh air will do you good."

"Be sure to stick to the side of the road, ladies. It's getting late, and people have been drinking. If you see car lights coming at you, move well off onto the shoulder. Make sure they see that you're there."

"Thank you. We'll be careful." Sarah shivered. The temperature was at least thirty degrees cooler than it had been on the dance floor. The chill raised goose bumps on her arms. The only warmth she felt came from her right hand as she tugged Alien forward.

"I'm sorry." Alien tripped on the gravel. "Sarah, I know you're mad, but could you at least slow down a little? I can't see where I'm going."

"Just keep walking. It'll get easier once we get away from the lights."

An overloaded Jeep blaring hip-hop music roared by. Once the driver saw them he leaned on his horn, and the boys in the back seat howled and shouted obscenities. Startled by the unexpected noise, Alien ambled off the asphalt into the sand. She giggled and staggered right, overcompensating for the shift and drifting directly into the traffic lane.

Sarah grabbed her arm. "For the love of God, Alien! Can't you walk a straight line?"

Alien giggled again. "Sorry! That doesn't seem to be working. Don't know what got into me."

"Three shots of tequila in less than twenty minutes is what got into you."

Alien stopped. She drew herself up stiffly. "I take full responsibility for my actions. I drank all the tequila." She slumped and continued to shuffle toward town like a zombie. "Bed, bed, bed. I really want my bed."

"Keep putting one foot in front of the other. We'll get there eventually."

"Damn, I'm tired. Could we siddown a minute? I needa rest."

"No, no, don't sit down." Sarah tugged her arm. "Sitting down is a bad idea."

"I know." Alien pushed on a gate. "Lesh take the shortcut home."

"No, we've already discussed that. We are not taking the shortcut tonight. We'll just keep walking along the road. This way. Follow me."

"But that way takes too long!" Alien wailed.

"But it's safer. And it's what I'm going to do."

"Fine. Then you do that. But I'm goin' this way." She pointed at the graveyard. "Find your own way home, bitch."

Sarah felt ready to pull her hair out. Dealing with Alien drunk was like dealing with Mason whenever he got stoned. There had been no arguing any sense into him, either. She couldn't physically drag Alien along the road back to town. She started praying for a taxi, a police car, for any kind of ride. At this point she was even willing to risk asking for a hitch, but the dark road was deserted.

Alien stumbled through the gate. Sarah hesitated. Her common sense was screaming, but what else could she do? She couldn't let Alien walk home by herself. She wouldn't be able to rest until she knew that Alien was also safely home in bed, too. At least with the moon the cemetery was well lit enough to see, and because it was mostly full of dead Quakers, there weren't any gravestones to trip over. It actually looked like a peaceful meadow of gently rolling hills. Sarah pretended that was enough, as Alien shuffled down the shell path.

"Don't you think it's weird they don't have tombstones?" Alien asked. "We could be walking on their graves right now, and not even know it."

"Try not to think about it." Sarah hurried her along. "Focus on getting home."

"I just think s'weird, that's all." Alien stopped. She cocked her head. "Did you hear something?"

"Seriously, Alien. Keep walking. You're doing fine. We're almost there. I can see the lights from town."

"No, I swear I heard something buzzing, like electricity. Did you hear that?"

SIZZZZZZZZLE-ZAP.

"There it is again! Did you hear it that time?"

The moon shifted from behind a streamer cloud. A man stepped out from behind a bushy cedar. He was wearing a dark raincoat, and he had a black ski mask over his face. Sarah felt her legs turn to water. "Alien, we really need to get out of here, and I mean like now."

SIZZLEZZZZZZZZZZZZZZZZZZ-SNAP.

"What the hell was that?" Alien stumbled. "Ball lightening or something?" She broke into a shambling trot. "What was that back there?"

"I don't know! I don't know." Sarah pulled Alien close. "Follow me. Hurry up. You're going to have to keep up with me."

The silhouette rose from the mound directly in front of them. Sarah felt all of her breath leave her body in one great whoosh as The Whistler raised his arm. *Did he have a gun?* She braced for impact as a stream of electric blue sparks spilled from his fingertips. The bright sparks dulled to orange as they arced toward the ground. She felt paralyzed by fear. *Holy shit! He's got a tazer!*

The Whistler laughed hoarsely. SIZZZZZLE-SNAP. "Want to play with my new toy? Who wants to feel a million volts first?"

"Run, Alien! Run for town! Move!"

She pushed Alien up the nearest mound. The steep angle forced them to drop to all fours. Alien made it to the top first and then somersaulted down the back slope in a tumbling, bruising free fall. Sarah scooped her up and they continued to run along a lane between two parallel burial mounds.

"Run, run!" Sarah yelled. "Keep going!"

"Where are you going, girls?" The Whistler ran along the ridge of the mound on their left. "Don't you want to play?"

"Leave us alone!" Sarah grabbed Alien's arm. She swung around and they ran in the opposite direction. Alien was sobbing now, and barely able to keep to her feet. Sarah felt lost, horribly lost, without any sense of direction anymore. She couldn't see the lights of town, or the edge of the graveyard where they had come in. She didn't know which way to go or which path to take. She only knew that they needed to stay ahead of the lunatic who pursued them so easily. She could hear The Whistler laughing at their pathetic attempt to escape.

"Don't run away, girls! I won't hurt you—much!"

Their frantic footsteps suddenly rang hollow as they crossed a decorative wooden bridge. Alien's sandal caught the lip of one of the uneven boards, and she went flying. She raised her arms in time to protect her head, but she hit the ground with a thud hard enough to knock her breathless.

"Get up!" Sarah shrieked, dragging her up by her arm. "Get up! Can't you get up?"

"I can't, I can't." Alien moaned, rocking in pain. "I'm done. I'm so done."

The Whistler strolled down the mound, one mocking martial step at a time. "Well, well, well. What have we here?" SIZZZZZZZZZLE-SNAP. "Are you girls ready to play my game?"

"Fuck off!" Sarah screamed. Her heart was thudding in her chest so hard she couldn't breathe. Straightening up, she planted both feet and cocked her fists. It was all she had left, but this fucker was going to have to go through her to get to Alien. "Leave us alone!"

"He-he-he." The Whistler laughed breathlessly and raised the tazer. "So you're going to dance with me first?"

There was a metallic shuffling sound, and an echoing muffled curse as another man clambered from the storm drain beneath the bridge. Freed from the constriction of the steel pipe, he straightened and stood. It was the gray-haired cop from the station, and he had some weird kind of goggle contraption strapped over his eyes.

"Gotcha, motherfucker," Ted said. "How 'bout dancing with me?"

* * * * * * *

The Whistler took off running. Ted watched the actor heading west along the ridge of one of the longer burial mounds. He paused for the briefest of seconds to direct the two terrified girls, "Stay here. Hank will be right with you." He took off in pursuit.

The goggles bathed the landscape with an eerie green glow, but Ted was delighted at their effectiveness. Finally! Some new technology that wasn't a complete pain in the ass. Pumping his arms, he gained on the target. The Whistler chanced a backward glance as he ran up one of the burial mounds, and he began to empty his pockets.

"Hank!" Ted shouted, pointing to the spot as he raced past. "Mark this site! Fucker threw something down."

Redoubling his effort, Ted clipped the distance to The Whistler in half. The blood was roaring in his ears. His lungs were burning like liquid flame. Ignoring the pain, Ted sped up another slope. His thigh muscles shrieked in agony and he berated himself for the oversight. *Gotta stop training only on the flats*, he noted grimly. *These hills are killing me.* He kicked it up another notch.

There was a tinny drumming sound and CJ rolled off the tool shed roof on his right. Dropping to all fours, she rose and directed a halogen beam so bright it illuminated The Whistler from that side. The Whistler raised an arm to shield his eyes and altered his trajectory left, dipping down below the ridge of a mound to avoid the powerful beam.

Fucker knows his ground, Ted admitted grudgingly. *He's done his homework.*

"West gate," CJ reported into her handset. "Actor is heading for the west gate."

Ted saw The Whistler toss something else aside as he struggled out of his coat. He had one arm free and was working to free the other one when a second moving silhouette appeared from the right. Toby took The Whistler out with a stunning flying tackle that pitched both men off the summit and ended the pursuit in a tangled, rolling heap at the base of the burial mound.

Ted pulled his service piece and ran up, panting. His heart was pounding ready to burst. "Hands in the air! Let me see your hands."

"Get off me! You're hurting!"

"Keep still." Toby pressed a knee into The Whistler's back as he cuffed the man's flailing arms. "Settle down. We've got you now. You're under arrest."

Ted stripped the goggles off his eyes. The blood of the pursuit was still pounding in his veins. This was the best feeling ever, an incredible feeling, a magnum high. The lieutenant ran up out of the dark to join the ring of pursuers around the capture. Ted smiled in broad triumph. "A good night's work, this!"

The lieutenant knelt. "Let's see who we have here." He rolled The Whistler over. Clutching the man's arm, he raised The Whistler to a sitting position, and stripped off the ski mask.

CJ shone her flashlight. The Whistler squinted into the glare.

"Holy hell!" Toby gasped. "I know this guy. He's the principal at the high school."

"He certainly is." The lieutenant dusted his hands. "Hello, Magnus."

"We own you, motherfucker!" Ted crowed. "We own you."

Hank walked up, escorting a bedraggled pair of party girls. The girls were clutching each other, and the shorter girl was sobbing with fright. Hank handed the lieutenant some evidence bags, and CJ shone her light again. One bag held a chrome police whistle. The other held a lethal skinning knife. Ted felt the truth crystalize around him. It had been a near miss. This night could easily have turned out to be a whole different affair, but the lieutenant–John–had managed it just right. Ted bent over his knees and gulped more air. "There's a tazer out there, too. Saw him toss it. Shouldn't be that hard to find."

"I don't know what you're talking about." Magnus raised his chin. "You're trying to frame me. None of that material is mine."

Ted froze. For one heart-stopping moment, he worried that somehow this prick was going to get off because of the lack of credible evidence, but then he saw John smile. Ted was glad that the smile wasn't directed at him. It didn't look at all friendly.

"Tell that to Judge Coffin," John said. "If none of this material is yours, then you're going to have a hard time explaining how your fingerprints are all over it."

Magnus stopped struggling. Looking down, Ted noted that his hands were bare.

"Tazers are tough to work with wearing gloves." John resettled his holster. "You didn't have time to polish everything clean this time, Magnus."

"Bam!" Ted hooted. Triumph soared in his soul like a geyser. "Stick a fork in him. He's done."

CHAPTER TWENTY ONE

John tipped back his chair and cocked his head to listen. He heard a growing roar of approval with individual voices shouting praise: "Way to go, Talbot!" and "Good man, good man."

"Get ready," John warned. "Here he comes."

The applause built to an even higher pitch as Toby entered the station. Toby stopped, stunned to see the room filled with a sea of standard blue uniforms. Every member of the Nantucket force had turned out to offer their congratulations, and to share in this gloriously memorable day. The buzz about The Whistler's capture was palpable, and the camaraderie was a sight to see. Everyone was grinning. The room was filled with nudges, raucous friendly laughter, and delighted backslapping. The force exploded into a heartfelt round of applause and shrill whistles.

Toby turned scarlet with embarrassment. Even the tips of his ears were pink. "Thank you all, but this was completely unnecessary."

"Get used to it, Toe," CJ laughed. "You deserved every bit of it. You nailed The Whistler."

"How did the news get out so quickly?" He hung his jacket neatly on the back of a chair. "There were reporters waiting outside my mother's house this morning. I had to run this gauntlet all the way through town."

"Island grapevine." Ted raised his coffee mug in salute. "Folks heard about the capture before it hit the papers. You should have heard the calls I fielded last night. My phone was ringing off the hook until dawn."

"Oh! And the *Inky Mirror* wants an interview," Tina said. "They'd like to run a special edition."

"For the love of Mike, sir!" Toby collapsed into the chair. "Can't you do something about this? I hate being the focus of so much attention."

"Give it time, Toby. This too shall pass," John said. "It will die down eventually."

"Is it too late to call in sick, and go fishing instead?"

"Yes, I'm afraid so." John smiled. Glancing out the window, he noticed

Chief Brock striding through the crowd. He felt a ripple of unease. The chief was glad-handing friends and waving to cheering supporters, and he entered the station grinning from ear to ear. A path opened up for the chief as the force parted like the Red Sea.

"Where is he? Where is our man of the hour? Nice work, Toby, nice work!" He slapped Toby heartily on the back. "This is just the sort of news we needed to start our season off right. There's nothing like a firm display of police competency to encourage visitors to our fair isle this summer. This news will do wonders for local business, my boy, wonders! I can't tell you how delighted the Chamber of Commerce is with us right now."

"Thank you, sir. It truly was a team effort, following Sergeant Parsons' plan."

"I'm sure it was, I'm sure it was. I didn't mean to denigrate Ted's effort. This reminds me of why I chose law enforcement as a career in the first place. Thank you all, team, for executing our strategy so brilliantly. I'm delighted to see that our capture plan worked so well." He chortled. "I didn't know Ted could still move that fast. Kidding, Ted, just kidding."

"No worries, sir. I will admit I needed some ibuprofen to get moving this morning."

"Don't we all? Ibuprofen, the breakfast of champions." The chief turned. "Has Magnus said anything further this morning, Lieutenant?"

"No, sir. But his lawyer is upset that he's waived legal representation." John slid a legal pad across his desk. "I've outlined a plan for the interrogation. Would you like to review the notes, before we get started?"

"No need, Lieutenant, no need." The chief slid the notes back across the desk. "I trust you to be thorough. Here's an idea: Why don't you and Detective Allamand cover the interrogation, and I'll tackle the media? Divide and conquer? What do you say?"

John bit back his retort. Yet again, the chief had passed the buck. John couldn't help but wonder why. Questions about the chief's motivations still clouded his mind. He had spent the very early morning wrestling with dark doubt and deep suspicion. "That sounds fine, sir, but could we talk in private for a moment?"

Worry lines creased the chief's forehead as he led the way to the conference room. He waited for the door to close before he spoke. "What's this about, John? You sound serious."

"It is serious, sir." He pulled out a chair and sat. "I don't know how to say this other than to come right out with it, but I need to know, before we interrogate Magnus Wolfe, if everything about The Whistler investigation is solid. Should I expect any surprises?"

"Surprises?" The chief blinked rapidly. "Like what?"

"I don't know like what, sir. I only know I came into this case cold, and there weren't any case notes for me to review. Two years' worth of this investigation happened before I came on board. We've got Magnus Wolfe dead to rights, sir, unless there's something about the investigation I don't already know. Is there anything else I need to know, before I go in there?"

"I was afraid of this." Chief Brock ran his hand over his dimpled scar. "This is all my fault. I've been negligent. I never kept notes. Before the accident, I never needed them. It was never my practice. I kept everything organized in my head." He massaged his temples. "The truth is, John, I'm a fraud, a complete faker. Everything I knew about this case, or any other case for that matter, is gone." The chief looked up, haunted. "I can remember names and faces, but that's about it. I've tried to remember what I've done, or what I needed to do, but it's blank, all blank, like a clean slate. The doctors say I may never get that part of my memory back." He leaned his fists on the table. "Let's be honest here, John. The truth is that I need to hang onto this job for eleven more months to collect my pension. That's the least I can do for my wife. And so I go on, coming in every day, faking what it is that I need to do. I'm sorry, son. If it's any consolation," he pulled a small spiral bound notebook from his pocket, "I keep notes now. I have to. It's the only way I can remember my day to day."

John felt thunderstruck by the chief's confession. It had never occurred to him that the chief might be faking his responses, because he had camouflaged everything so well. His answer explained so much. What John had thought was a deliberate attempt to hang him out to dry had in fact been the chief's desperate attempt at self-preservation. In spite of the fundamental deception, he had to admire the chief's courage in successfully navigating what must be a daily living hell. What would it feel like to be unsure of your next action, every time you opened your eyes to a new day?

"There's something more I needed to tell you too, sir." John swallowed. He needed to be honest in return. The chief deserved that much. "I interviewed Sally Poldridge yesterday over the Satan's Tub investigation. She said the reason you were in Wauwinet the night of your accident was because you were coming back from seeing her. No one will hear about it from me, sir, but word of it may get out."

"Sally's been known to lie." The chief hooded his eyes like a tortoise. Clasping his hands, he stood and started pacing. "It's a terrible thing not to remember what you did, John. I know my wife suspects me of something. I can see it in Mary's eyes whenever she looks at me, but I don't remember if I did anything to justify her suspicion. If there was a lapse, I can only pray that she'll forgive me. The damning part is that I don't know if I need to forgive myself."

John felt a surge of compassion as he listened to the chief's pleading words. He knew all too well how easy it would be to fall for Sally's insistent seduction. He couldn't blame the man for not keeping effective case notes, either. No one believes that they could be suddenly struck down without warning until it happened. This persistent disbelief was one of the fundamental truths of the human condition. We all think we're immortal. It comes as a shock to find out we are not. John studied the mortal man who stood before him and realized: There but for the grace of God, go I. Yes, the chief had failed in the performance of his duty, but the chief knew it, and he would have to live with that failure until his dying day.

"Are we okay with this, Lieutenant? You'll keep our conversation confidential?"

"Of course I will, sir. Thank you for being so candid."

The chief shuffled over. He rested a broad hand on John's shoulder.

"I've never said this before, John, and perhaps I should have. You've done a fine job with this investigation, better than I ever could. Remember that I said that, son, when the dark nights take hold of your soul, because they will. They are always out there, waiting." Dropping his hand to his side, the chief assumed a look of hearty hopefulness and reached for the door. "Now let's go take care of business, shall we?"

CHAPTER TWENTY TWO

John found the team clustered around Tina's console as she reverently replaced the handset.

"Oh-mi-god," she said. "Toby? That was a producer for *The Ellen Show*. They want you to fly to LA for a taping."

"Lieutenant!" Toby wailed. "Help me, sir!"

The chief rapidly snapped his fingers. "I'll field that one. They're circling like sharks, my boy, like sharks! There's nothing like good exposure to get your career started right. But before we get started, come give me a hand with this crowd. You're the one they came to see, but let's move them along. They're creating a hazard."

"Yes, sir."

Toby did not look enthusiastic, but he picked up his jacket and obeyed.

John took a steadying breath and felt for the cuffs on his belt. He didn't have all the answers he needed, but it was time to tackle the preliminary Whistler interrogation. He gave a passing thought to his surprise when he discovered that Sarah had been one of the two party girl victims at last night's Whistler event. He needed to schedule a follow-up interview with her since her statement had been almost incoherent. She had obviously been drinking, and her focus kept straying to the welfare of her even drunker friend, Eileen. In spite of that, he still felt that pull of interest in Sarah. He needed to keep his focus on the task at hand, but what was that about?

CJ reached for a pen. "How do you want to play this?"

"I have an idea, since all of his victims were women." John felt his pulse quicken. "I think we're dealing with a misogynistic personality disorder. If Magnus thinks you're just another dumb woman, it might trip him up."

CJ considered the suggestion for a moment. "Alright. You want me to play dumb. I'll take one for the team. What's the strategy?"

"I'm going to work to become his new best friend." John headed for the stairs. "We know Magnus is used to being an authority figure, so I'll keep asking him for advice. We also know that he's used to correcting inappropriate behavior in others and yet here he is, charged with doing the very same thing. I'm hoping that discrepancy will shake him up. And one more thing: We already know that Magnus is the physical type, so watch him carefully. If he starts to fidget, we'll know we're getting uncomfortably close to a truth he doesn't want to reveal."

He trotted down the stairs. The hallway had recently been painted institutional green, and the air still smelled like paint. The holding cells had retained their original tan color, since current theory held that neutral colors helped to keep prisoners calm. Their shop wasn't as elaborate as the facility at Barnstable, where Magnus would eventually be going, but it would do.

There were five holding cells in the basement. Three were on the right, with two more on the left. Four of these cells had never been used. Each cell was a state-mandated ten by ten square feet fronted by cold-cast steel bars. Each cell held two bunks, a steel sink, and an open toilet. Magnus Wolfe was in the last holding cell on the left. He was sitting on the lower bunk, his hands resting limply on his knees. His breakfast tray lay untouched on the floor next to his feet.

He raised his head. "I heard you coming."

As John unlocked the cell, he was shocked to see the change six hours had made on the man. Magnus's skin hung in baggy folds off his skull. He had purplish shadows under his eyes. Magnus seemed to recognize his rough condition. Reaching up, he did his best to smooth his hair using his fingers.

"How did you pass the night, sir?"

"I hardly slept." He swallowed repeatedly. "I can't imagine how I'm going to explain this to Diana."

John removed the handcuffs from his belt. "We're ready to speak with you now, sir."

"My calendar appears to be free." Magnus laughed drily. He shook his head at the cuffs. "You won't need those. I'm not going anywhere."

"It's protocol, sir. I can't remove you from the cell without restraint."

"Very well then." Magnus held out his wrists. "We must follow protocol, mustn't we?"

John cuffed him quickly. Taking Magnus by the arm, he led him down the hallway, CJ following one step behind. "Thank you for making this easy for us, sir. We appreciate your cooperation."

"Let's get this over with." Magnus shuffled around the table and collapsed into a chair. "Have you heard from my wife yet?"

"Yes, sir. She's on her way, with your lawyer, now."

"I told you I didn't want a lawyer!"

"She insisted on it. She wouldn't take *no* for an answer."

"I'll have to speak to Diana about that," Magnus snorted. "Strange time to start exercising her independence."

"Mr. Wolfe, I'd like to tape our interview, sir, instead of taking notes, but I need your permission to do so. It makes things easier."

"By all means, let's make things easier. That is the modern way."

"Thank you again, sir." John flipped the switch to start the digital recording. "Lieutenant John Jarad, Nantucket Police, County and Town of Nantucket, Commonwealth of Massachusetts. Interviewing Magnus Wolfe, Detective CJ Allamand present. Mr. Wolfe is aware of and has given his permission to record this conversation. Mr. Wolfe is charged with eleven counts of reckless endangerment plus stalking violations of Section 43."

"Eleven?" Magnus straightened his shoulders. "Our tallies don't match. I think you may have missed a few."

"As stated, sir, we have eleven formal charges on record. Were there more?"

"He-he-he. You're the detective. You tell me."

"Let's start with the eleven charges we know of, and go from there. First off, Mr. Wolfe, may I call you Magnus?"

"Of course. Be my guest."

"Thank you. Alright then, Magnus, I'm hoping you can help me understand what was going on out there. I'm still a little confused by it. Can you explain to me how all of this got started?"

Magnus raised his cuffed hands. He scratched his jaw. "It's a little hard to explain. In a way, it feels like a dream."

"It was no dream," CJ stated.

"I know that." Magnus snarled before dancing his fingertips lightly along the edge of the table. "You have to understand that the game is an amazing creation. It's brilliant, in its way." He leaned forward on the table. "It all started the year Diana left the island. Diana despises the rabble, you see, so she goes to visit her sister in the Adirondacks for July and August while I stayed home. I stayed home because I despise her sister."

"Sisters-in-laws are tough," John said. "I've got two of them."

"Then you know what I mean. But I started having trouble falling asleep whenever Diana was gone. The house was too quiet without her in it. You know how you toss and turn and can't ever get comfortable? I even bought an expensive new mattress, but that didn't help. I tried drinking a glass of wine with dinner, too, but that didn't help, either. I was restless, wound too tight. It got so bad that I started dreading dusk because I knew that I'd have to face another set of long empty hours that came with it."

"You couldn't just watch some TV?" CJ asked.

"Have you seen the programming they have on TV these days?" Magnus snapped. "There's a reason they call it an idiot box. I refuse to waste my time on it." He rested his hands on the table. "I even asked my PCP for advice. He wanted to prescribe Solifan, but I refused to take any drug that interferes with proper brain function. These doctors don't know what they're playing around with."

"I agree with you there," John said.

"The insomnia got so vicious that one night, I simply couldn't take it one minute more. I got up to take a walk. I was hoping physical exercise might tire me out, but you know Polpis Harbor. It's so distinctly residential. I worried the neighbors might think it strange I was walking so late at night, and I needed to protect my reputation. Then I had an inspiration, and I drove into town. Town was so much better. At least in town, I could walk among the crowds. No one would think that was particularly strange."

"Makes sense to me, sir. But if you started out walking in town, then how did you end up at The Bug House?"

"That's a no-brainer. I heard their music one night when the wind was right, and I strolled over to see what was going on. When I looked through the hedgerow, I saw all these young people in the lot. They were so exuberent, so filled with life, but I couldn't horn in on their action. They'd laugh at an older guy like me. So I only watched them. That's all I did. It was entertaining, something to do. Then, one night, I saw this girl, this lone girl stagger out of the bar. She was three sheets to the wind, and she started to walk back to town, alone. I don't have to tell you how dangerous that was. She could barely stand. I was afraid she was going to get herself killed, so I followed her, to make sure she got home safely. That's all I did, I swear. I followed her home to make sure she got home safely."

"Sounds plausible to me," John said.

CJ squinted. "When did this become a chase?"

Magnus squirmed. "That first year, it was only a game, that's all it was, a game like Hide and Seek. Those girls needed me. I was their secret savoir, their white knight. I only followed them to make sure they got home. And then the second year, the game started to shift. I wanted to see how far I could push it, how close could I get before they even realized I was there? That was still relatively easy to do. Most of them were too drunk to notice I was following them, but it added nice spice to the game. Once or twice, I even did your job for you."

"What do you mean?" CJ leaned forward.

"Remember the night Lauren Whipple was accosted by that gang of ruffians? And a good Samaritan stepped in to save her? I did that. But it served as a warning, because she might have recognized me from the Board. That's when I decided to add the ski mask to the game." He tapped the table. "That mask was a smart idea, and it was the first enhancement."

CJ crossed her arms. "Helping Miss Whipple once doesn't make up for terrorizing all those other girls later."

"But I never touched them! And, as the game developed, I always followed my rules. That was the imperative. I never broke a single rule."

John settled back. It was insane, but he was starting to grasp the framework of The Whistler's demented game. "Let's talk about these rules, Magnus. Can you explain them to me?"

Magnus nodded eagerly. "They started off easy enough. Rule number one: There was absolutely no touching allowed. I could look all I wanted, but I could not touch. I know that sounds ridiculously old-fashioned, but it was very important that I stay faithful to my marriage vow to Diana. Looking at other women is only natural, and it doesn't break my vow."

"But you did more than look at them, sir," CJ said. "You chased them. You chased Candy Kane into Satan's Tub."

"No, I did not! She tripped into that bog by herself! You can't blame that one on me!"

"Let's step back." John drummed his fingers on the table. He wanted to get the sequence of events clear in his mind. What had actually happened at Satan's Tub was still muddled. He was beginning to get a glimmer of an idea, but he wanted to make sure. He pulled Katie Roark's photograph from between the pages of his legal pad. "Did you ever follow this woman?"

Magnus craned his neck and gazed at the photo carefully. "She doesn't look familiar and I have an excellent memory for faces. Did she say that I did?"

"No, sir. She's the other victim we found in the bog."

"He-he-he." Magnus uttered his strange whistling laugh. "Then you've got a pretty puzzle on your hands because whoever she is, that was not my work." His eyes gleamed with a strange righteousness. "The newspaper said that girl disappeared in 1999. I was in England then, developing a research grant with Magdalen College. That's where I met Diana, my wife. If you have any doubts about my veracity, my passport and a call to the State Department will prove it."

John felt another puzzle piece fall into place as the threads of this tangled case were slowly starting to unravel. If Magnus Wolfe was overseas when Katie Roark was murdered, then he needed to look elsewhere for her killer. Plus, if Magnus was telling the truth when he said he never touched any of his stalking victims, who had beaten Candy Kane so brutally that night at Satan's Tub? Candy had reported that the actor was a stranger to her, and she had maintained her story ever since. Her testimony let Skip Pedders off the hook. If the second man at Satan's Tub wasn't Skip Pedders, who was he?

Every instinct pointed John toward Kurt Stockton and Wauwinet for that answer.

He made a mental note to query the State Department to confirm Magnus's passport history. That confirmation would button down the suggestion that Katie Roark's murder and The Whistler investigation were unrelated except in the circumstance of their overlapping crime scene location. John felt a glow of satisfaction. They were making solid progress. "Let's get back to what happened on Sunday morning with Ms. Kane. Why did you pick her?"

"It was pure luck. She was a random gift from the game." Magnus hunched forward. "I never expected to find anyone in Polpis Harbor. When I did, it was too good an opportunity to miss. You have to understand how much thought goes into the game. Very little about it is random. I map everything out before each chase, and I'm very, very careful. Preparation is ninety percent of the challenge. Most of the fun is in the anticipation, but good things do come to those who wait." Magnus rubbed his hands together. "I've discovered that the more work I put into the game, the better the game becomes. After awhile, the game even took on a life of its own. It developed its own power. Then, every time I added a new rule or enhancement, like the whistle or the mask, the game got even better."

"I meant to ask you about the whistle," John said. "Where did that idea come from?"

"I took a real chance with that one. I'm surprised you police never tumbled onto it. Now that you know who I am, do you care to guess?"

"Magnus Wolfe, whistle, wolf whistle. I get it now."

"You are a clever boy."

"How about that knife?" CJ asked. "Where did that fit into your game?"

"The knife was a prop, only meant for show. I never meant to use it. I ran into a couple of hoodlums last year who needed a stern warning, that's all. The knife was an enhancement of the last resort."

CJ crossed her arms. "You used the knife at Altar Rock."

Magnus turned to face her. "That doe was a mercy killing! You should have seen her when I found her. She was crushed! Crushed! I did her a favor putting her out of her misery."

"Wicked mercy," CJ scoffed. "You stabbed the animal thirty-six times, and then you cut off her head and stuck it on a pole. Shit!" She pushed back from the table and stood. "Let's at least be honest about this stupid game thing. It was more than a game to you, wasn't it? Look where it landed you. That game was your life."

Magnus rattled the cuffs. "You don't seem to realize how much effort this took! I memorized maps. I visited the gym every day throughout the winter to stay in tip-top shape, but it was worth it because every time I added a new enhancement to the game, it got better." He scowled. "I don't expect you to grasp the complexity of the game. Women aren't logical thinkers."

"That's it for me. I need some air." CJ turned for the door. "I'll be outside if you need me."

Her timing was perfect. CJ was giving him the one-on-one space he needed to push for a complete confession. "Let's get back to the game, Magnus. I'm fascinated by it. This year's enhancement was adding the tazer. Have I got that right?"

"He-he-he. I gave that addition a lot of thought. All through November I pondered: What new enhancement could I add to make the game even more thrilling? It's not as easy as you might think, because of the no touching rule that had to be strictly followed. And then one day, I heard Dr. Sharnez mention the uses of a tazer in his science class, and I knew it was the perfect choice. Perfect! Once I made the decision, I had to add one. Not adding it would have spoiled the game. Once an answer comes to you, you don't get to pick and choose. You have to adapt. That's the second rule."

"So you already knew you were going to repeat this behavior again this year?"

"You're not listening to me, either!" Magnus thundered. "I have to play the game every year. It's the only thing keeping me sane." He flattened his hands against the table. "Can you imagine the tedium of the school year, and of my existence? How much of my day is spent managing mindless, endless minutia? How many hours I have to endure listening to the constant whining parade of dissatisfied parents when they come to see me—to see me!—to complain about their lackluster children? Any rational man would go insane, and I've been doing this for twenty-seven years! This game is all I have to keep me going." He shook the tears from his eyes. "This year Diana offered to stay home and I panicked. Panicked! I need to play the game. It's the only thing keeping me alive."

Magnus leaned forward. "You're beginning to feel it now, too, aren't you? You were always such a good lad, always doing exactly what you were told, always following their rules. But let me ask you this: Are you any happier following their rules than I am following mine?" He wheezed. "It's those girls who did this to you, isn't it? I've been watching them for years, for years! So innocent, so pure. Then they leave my school and they harden into whores. Whores! I know that's a harsh word, but it's what they become. They lose their personal respect. You can see it in their eyes, in the way they walk, the way they dress. Their voices get shrill, they get fat, sloppy. I've seen them on the street wearing pajamas! But it's not their fault. It's what our society tells them to value. Listen to their music! Sure, some of them stumble into decent jobs or a solid marriage, but most of them end up lost. Lost! They start in on a string of broken marriages, and they produce a pack of brats from different fathers, and it's endless. Endless! They're all out there waiting for someone to come fix their sorry lives, but they're waiting in vain for the someone who never comes."

His impassioned words conjured up the grim morgue photograph of Katie Roark, the lost girl from Satan's Tub. She had been a friendless immigrant abused for her youth, and then cast aside to finish her fate at the bottom of a muddy bog. How much of her life had been free choice? Which set of rules had she felt compelled to follow? Sarah Hawthorne next sprang into John's mind. She was also fleeing a brutish situation back home. Where did all of these young women come from? Where were their families? Shouldn't someone care?

He stood. "This concludes the recorded conversation with Magnus Wolfe. Thank you, Magnus. Let's get you back to your cell." John reached forward and switched the digital recorder off.

As he escorted the deeply troubled man down the hall, John considered his own recent challenges in following his own set of self-imposed rules. I'm not happy where I am. How did I get here? Have I walled myself into a cell of my own making? I don't want to live with this hollow emptiness inside of me anymore. I need to make a big change. How do I break free? Casting his memory back, John recalled CJ's advice about finding a girl, the right girl, the one who was less structured, not more, and he knew exactly what he needed to do.

CHAPTER TWENTY THREE

"Sarah?" Leslie shouted down the hallway. "Phone's for you!"

"Got it!" Sarah rolled off the bed.

"Watch the dress!" Alien swept a swath of tissue paper aside. "Your toes are still wet."

Sarah crabbed down the hallway toward the phone on her heels, carefully keeping her toes upright so as to not ruin the fresh crimson polish. Alien was helping her get ready for tonight's art opening gala event, and she was grateful for her help. Being all girly had never been one of Sarah's priorities, but tonight was going to be something special. She had curled her hair, and she wanted to put her best foot forward. After the Bug House disaster, if Alien wanted to mend some fence by helping her get dressed, she was all for it. There was no sense in holding onto hard feelings. It was best to let things go.

Leslie had balanced the receiver on top of the vintage wall-mount phone. Sarah lifted it carefully using both hands, knowing that the frayed cord was finicky, and she could lose the connection with one careless jiggle. "Hello?"

"Sarah? Hi. It's John Jarad. I was calling to see how you were doing."

Sarah blushed. Her memory of what she was now calling 'Fright Night' and her statement to the police was spotty. While she clearly remembered walking to The Bug House, the stumbling run through the graveyard carried with it the descriptive clarity of a fevered hangover. "I'm a little banged up, but it's nothing a couple of Tylenol won't fix."

"That's good to hear."

"Why? Was something wrong with my statement?"

"No, we have what we need. I would like you to come in and add some clarifying detail, at your convenience, of course." He cleared his throat. "Actually, this is a social call. I was wondering if you had any plans for this evening?"

"Tonight?"

"Yes, that's generally what 'this evening' means." He coughed. "Sorry. That sounded patronizing. That's not the way it was meant."

She clutched the phone in her hand. What should she do? It was flattering to get asked out by the dishy lieutenant, and she had certainly felt an interested pull in his direction, but Kurt had asked her to the art gala first. Her mother had always said 'Stick to the original plan,' not to mention that Kurt had certainly raised the stakes by sending over the fabulous dress. "I'm sorry, John, I can't. I've made other plans."

"Oh! Of course. Short notice. Perhaps some other time, then?"

"Sure. Thanks for asking."

She replaced the receiver. While it was thrilling to be desired by two separate men, maybe she needed to be more practical about her future. Honestly, what did a police lieutenant have to offer? She couldn't imagine living her life as a policeman's wife, whereas Kurt was an established artist. They shared a common interest in art, and Kurt could introduce her to the international artistic community. His client list included attorneys, hedge fund managers, and real estate moguls. Their wives managed successful public relations careers or they were busily developing private fashion lines. These were the kind of people who appreciated Art, and Art was hardwired into Sarah's soul. She wanted to spend her life exploring the art world, and exploring it with another artist was her dream. True, Kurt was married, but he might be able to introduce her to someone else from that world who shared her vision. It made more sense to follow this path.

She trotted down the hall to find Alien still enthralled with the dress.

"Tissue paper?" Alien held up a great handful. "Who wraps a dress in tissue paper?"

Sarah clasped her hands. "They didn't want it to wrinkle."

"I've never seen a real Toshiro Geta dress in person before." Alien raised the silk-padded hanger and the dress slithered across the bed. "I think this dress cost more than my parent's house. Let's get you in it."

Sarah raised her arms and leaned forward. The dress slid over her body like a second skin.

Alien straightened the thin spaghetti straps and stepped back. "Girl! If you wear that dress outside, you're going to kill someone. Are your toes dry yet?"

"They should be, by now."

"I'm not sure about these shoes. Platform stilettos and cobblestones don't mix. But I do have to say this neutral patent leather is fabulous." Alien tapped her chin. "We'll need to call you a cab, Cinderella. You'll never make it to Old South Wharf on foot."

"These shoes do feel a little big."

"Kick them off. I know a quick fix. Stuff tissue paper in the toes likes this. There. How does that feel?"

"Perfect. Alien, I can't thank you enough. I'm so excited! This feels like a dream."

"Have some fun tonight hanging out with the hoi polloi. Better you than me." She handed over the beaded purse. "Sarah, you look amazing. I'm really happy for you. Our little Sarah is all grown up. Right. I'll go find you a cab."

Sarah lifted the mermaid skirt and inched along the hall, careful not to snag the hem on a splinter as she descended the outside steps. When she had first opened the dress box, the beauty of the fabric had stolen her breath away. In the sunlight, the fabric sparkled like tiny diamonds. The dress was clingy and light and had some kind of reptilian pattern burned into it. Kurt's handwritten notes had simply stated: *Wear this.*

She stepped through the kitchen into the bar. Steve was tapping the end of his nose with a pencil while he reviewed the bill for the final Tap Room renovation. He tottered, pulled up a chair, and sat down.

"Holy hell. Sarah, you look fantastic!" Concern clouded his eyes. "You will be careful tonight, won't you?"

"What do you mean, careful? It's a gallery gala. What could happen?"

"You do know that Stockton is married, right? I don't want to say anything negative about the guy, but I don't want to see you getting hurt."

"Yes, I do know that Kurt is married. Thanks for worrying about me, Steve. That's sweet."

"Okay. 'Nuf said." He shook the pencil playfully. "Because it's official. We need you. We're re-opening the Tap Room on Monday. Brace yourself for Karaoke Night, part two."

"What? You didn't learn from your mistake the first time?" She laughed.

"Ha-ha. Very funny. This time, we'll be prepared for it."

"Count me in. I wouldn't want to miss out on all the fun."

The front door cracked open. A wedge of light spilled into the room. "Sarah? Your cab's here."

"Thanks, Alien." She walked out into the sunshine. It felt odd to be so well-dressed at that time of day since everyone else on the street was wearing T-shirts, shorts, and flip-flops. This must be how a movie star feels on the red carpet. Where are my RayBans? Sarah pulled them from her beaded bag and immediately felt better, more in control. A man passing by took a good hard look. He stumbled as he tripped over the curb.

"Have a ton of fun tonight." Alien handed her into the cab. "Good luck."

And she was off, rolling through the cobbled streets. It was only a half a mile to the Old South Wharf, but because the streets were one-way, the length of the trip doubled. Sarah relaxed against the seat and took stock of the moment. Her heart was racing with excitement. How things had changed in only one day! Tonight was hers. Anything was possible. She stared at the monumental homes that lined the street, and imagined living in one of them. She felt like a queen returning in triumph to her throne. Sarah had never felt this absolutely splendid before. If this was the way she was going to feel from now on, she was all for it.

The cab slipped down an alley and pulled up in front of Kurt's studio. Kurt stood in the doorway, looking sleek and oh-so-successful in pressed khaki pants and a pink Oxford cloth shirt. She gave a nod of approval. It took a real man to wear pink. Kurt opened the cab door and reached for her hand.

"Sarah, my dear. You look radiant. That dress is fantastic. How are your feet? Are they tired?"

"No, these shoes are phenomenal. Why?"

"Because you've been running through my mind all day." He barked a laugh and kissed her cheek before tucking her hand into the crook of his arm. He leaned in to direct the cabbie, "Put this on my charge. Make sure to include a good tip."

The cabbie touched his cap. "Will do. Thank you, sir."

"I don't have to tell you I'm nervous about this," Sarah said.

"No need to be nervous. We're going to knock 'em dead. Between appreciating my artwork and admiring your beauty, we've got this night sewn up." He waved a waiter over and handed her a flute of bubbling champagne. "Drink up. It's not meant to be all work. I want you to enjoy yourself. The widow Clicquot bottles terrific compensation."

"What do I need to do?"

"You, my dear, are here solely to entertain my guests." Kurt waggled his eyebrows. "I will be talking to clients and convincing them to invest their hard-earned dollars in my overpriced artwork. Your job is to charm them into buying it."

Sarah sipped the champagne. It was delicious. "I can handle that."

"I'm sure you can." He turned. "Before we open the doors, though, there's something more I needed to say. This is going to be hard for me, but I'll do my best." Kurt grasped his crystal flute with both hands. "Sarah, I want you to know that I'm starting to have complex feelings for you, but I wanted to be open about it. You do know that I'm married, right?"

"Yes, I do know that." Where was he going with this?

"Good. Here's the thing. My wife and I have separated. Melissa seems to be living her own life in Europe these days. I never even really see her anymore. Occasionally, we run into each other at an opening somewhere, but that's about as far as it goes. We haven't lived together as man and wife for years. In a way, yes, I suppose I do still love her, but it's more like the love I have for a sister now, not a wife." He took a deep breath. "Jesus, this is tough. Help me out. Can't you see where I'm going? What I'm trying to say is, I need to know how you feel about me."

Sarah stared at the bubbles rising in her champagne. "I don't know how I feel about you, Kurt. It's too early. I hardly know you."

His eyes twinkled. "But you're not actively repelled? I know there's an age difference and we'll have to overcome some of the social bullshit, but do you think you could ever share the same level of feeling that I have for you? Because, if you think you can, I'd like to take our friendship to the next level."

Sarah's breath caught in her chest. What was he saying? "Lovers? You want us to be lovers?"

"Yes, love, lovers." Kurt reached for her hand. "And I mean that in the best possible way because I really do think that I'm falling in love with you. I don't know why these things happen so quickly sometimes, I only know that they do. So, what do you say? Could you ever feel the same way about me?"

A unfamiliar confidence surrounded Sarah like a cocoon. A grown man was declaring his love for her and asking for her love in return. It would be easiest to just say no, and she fought the impulse to turn around and run. Somehow, she needed to find the courage to fight her fear and to not let it spook her into making another hasty decision she might later regret. To her surprise, she found a strand of courage that she didn't know that she had. Sarah clung to it like a lifeline. It reminded her that she was an adult. It was time to stop acting like an irrational child. It was time to start trusting her instinct again, and to stop being so terrified that she was going to make another disastrous mistake like she had with Mason. Kurt was being open and honest with her. That's what adults did. He deserved her honesty in return. How did she feel about him? Was building a future with him a possibility? And even more frightening, why not?

As Sarah considered her answer, the world suddenly became a brighter and scarier place simply because she was going to trust something new and completely unknown again. She knew next to nothing about Kurt Stockton. There was no magic GPS pointing her in the right direction. Should she follow this uncharted path? It led to the life she wanted, right? Why was she so afraid of success? "I think I could feel something special for you, Kurt, if you gave me some time."

"Bless you for that." He kissed her fingers. "You have no idea what your trust means to me. Sarah, I'm going to make sure that you're very, very happy." He dropped her hand and reached for his glass. "I'm delighted to see that dress is such a success. I thought it would be. You look like a rock star. Every woman in here tonight is going to wish that she looked like you." He tapped his watch. "Six o'clock on the dot. It's show time. Ready?"

He unlocked the door and threw it wide open. "Welcome! Welcome, friends! I hope you brought your checkbooks!"

Sarah hugged an interior partition as the first of the guests swept in.

Everyone looked drop-dead elegant. This was definitely not the scruffy crowd from the street. The men were wearing blazers with crisp buttoned-down shirts and heavy gold watches. The women were in real pearls and pashminas. The waiter stepped forward to offer champagne as they entered, and they graciously accepted their crystal flutes before moving into the studio to preview the show.

"That's a good sign," Kurt whispered as he danced past. "The first ones in are the Spensers with some of the Whipples. Do your best, my girl. Mingle. Mingle."

Sarah moved to a corner that featured more paintings of bonneted children building sandcastles, striped lighthouses, and women with flowing ribbons and white dresses. Kurt's commercial artwork held no real interest for her, but the people watching was fantastic. She knew enough about shabby chic to know that really rich people with really old money weren't always the best dressed. Some of the elderly men wore Bermuda plaid jackets with frayed cuffs. Their wives had skin like tanned leather, a by-product of a lifetime spent near salted wind and tropical Caribbean sun.

"See anything you like?"

She heard a familiar voice in her ear and turned–and almost dropped her glass. John was standing at her elbow. For a split second, Sarah had trouble placing him, because he was out of uniform and out of context. John was wearing red pants with a navy sportscoat and a perfectly knotted silk bow tie. A petite woman with coiffed white hair was on his arm. She cocked her head like a curious sparrow.

"Good evening, Sarah. Mom? Let me introduce Sarah Hawthorne. Sarah was a key witness during The Whistler investigation. She was tremendously helpful. She's originally from Pittsburgh."

"How do you do? It's very nice to meet you, Sarah. Please, call me Jenny. Everyone does."

"Nice to meet you, too." Sarah was floored. Of all things, she had never expected to see John at an art exhibition. Apparently, he read her mind.

"My mother loves everything artistic. I get drafted whenever she needs an escort."

"It doesn't hurt you to broaden your perspective too, son." Jenny patted his arm. "My dear, that dress is to die for. Is it Toshiro Geta?"

"Yes, it is." Sarah smoothed the dress over her stomach. She couldn't begin to imagine why her palms were suddenly sweaty, or why she felt that her cleavage and her bare shoulder blades were overexposed.

"Toshiro is a textile genius. I love his haute couture."

John cocked a thumb toward the paintings. "What do you think of this work?"

Time to get busy. Who knew? Maybe the Jarads had some money, and they were looking for a new acquisition. "Kurt Stockton is a genius with composition. You can see it in every one of his paintings. It's no wonder there is such a strong demand for his work. Paintings at Kurt's level are an investment. They will only appreciate in value over time."

John blinked. A look of dark concern flitted across his face. "That sounds suspiciously like a sales pitch. Are you working for Stockton now?"

"Yes, part-time. Kurt needed some help tonight. There's no denying his talent."

"I agree with you, there. I've seen some of his other paintings. Have you?"

"No. Only what's represented in this gallery. All of his other paintings are in private or corporate collections."

"That's certainly true. You should ask Stockton about them. It's quite a story." John studied his hands. "Sarah, I can only ask you to be careful. Stockton may not be all that he seems."

She overheard a loud guffaw. Kurt was huddled in a corner with three businessmen in slim-fitting suits. They looked like a pod of investment bankers. Kurt delivered his punch line and solidly downed his champagne. He snapped his fingers at a passing waiter and replaced his flute.

"We won't keep you, my dear. We can see you're busy," Jenny said. "I hope we see you again soon. John seems quite smitten."

"Mother!"

"I hope so, too," Sarah said. "Thank you for coming. Enjoy the show."

There was a scrum of commotion near the door. Sally Poldridge entered on the arm of an older man with silvered hair and a deep tan. He looked like a model for Ralph Lauren. Sally was wearing low-rider gold lamé harem pants with a cropped turquoise silk top that showed off her trim midriff and some chunky, big gold jewelry. For a forty-plus cougar, she looked amazing.

Kurt broke away from his city buddies and hurried over. He swept Sarah up.

"Come with me, please. I need your support. We're going to go beard the dragon."

"Why? What's going on?"

"Just follow my lead."

Sally pointed her escort toward the bar and drifted over in a cloud of heady gardenia perfume. "Good evening, Kurt. Lovely show. How's it going?"

He rubbed his hands together. "Evidently, the economy is improving. We're already seeing solid sales."

"Splendid! That's always good to hear." Sally stared over the rim of her glass. "Aren't you going to introduce me to your new little friend?"

"We've met," Sarah said.

"Have we? Oh, that's right. You're that little waitress from the dive bar.

Let me think. Karaoke night, right?"

"Yes, that's right." Sarah started to simmer. She smiled graciously, and fought it down. "We're reopening on Monday. You should stop by. Everyone so enjoyed your performance."

"Oh, look! She's using three syllable words! Why, Kurt, she's charming. I heard you had a new playmate lined up for this year. My! You do have a penchant for brunettes, don't you?"

"Ignore her, Sarah, like I do." Kurt cleared his throat. "Actually, Sally, I'm glad you came. I have something I needed to say to you, and now is as good a time as any." He smoothed the buttons on his shirtfront. "I've decided it's time to make some changes in my life."

"Bravo, Sarah! Well played. This must be your influence. Kurt's never exhibited any signs of independence before."

"She had nothing to do with it." Kurt gulped his champagne. "I've got a new business plan. I've decided that from now on, my paintings will only be sold directly through me."

Sally narrowed her eyes. "But darling, you know that I work on pre-sale commission. I already have a corporate buyer lined up for most of this show."

"That's over." Kurt avoided her eyes. "There aren't going to be any more pre-sale commissions. The market is better, but my margin is still too small. This makes better business sense." He rotated his glass between his palms. "I'm cutting you loose. From now on, Sally, I'll be acting as my own agent, and not using you."

"Do you think that's wise?" Sally asked.

"Yes, I do." Kurt finished his champagne and set his glass on a table. "Whatever partnership we had is over. Closed. Finished. *Finito*. Done. From now on, you are on your own."

"Darling, I don't want to be argumentative, but this strange decision of yours could make things unpleasant. Are you sure you've thought this through? We've had our private agreement for decades. I'd hate to have to bring in the … attorneys."

"I've already talked with my attorney. You don't have a thing on me. We never signed a binding contract."

"Yes, I suppose that's true." Her voice turned dangerously brittle. "But like I said, we did share our private understanding."

"And like I said, that's over. It's time to clear the field, and move on."

"But what if I don't want to move on?"

Sarah jumped as Kurt's fist hit the table. His champagne flute bounced off the tabletop and shattered against the hardwood floor.

"I just said that's not up to you!" he roared. "I'm not paying you one more dime—not another nickel! We are through, and if you decide to fight me on this, then fine! You're in this as deeply as I am."

"For God's sake! Lower your voice. You're causing a scene." Sally smiled at the room. "You realize this changes everything, don't you, Kurt? And I do mean everything? Are you prepared for that? Is that your final answer?"

"Yes, it's my goddamned final answer," he snarled. "I'm not going to change my mind."

"Then there's nothing more to say, is there?" She resettled her gold watch on her wrist. "This has been a treat, but I'm afraid I have to run. Sven and I have an early reservation to catch. Sarah? A word of caution, from one girl to another. Don't let Kurt run your life. You can see how well he manages his own."

"Bitch," Kurt spat.

Sally gathered her escort up and swept out of the gallery. The other patrons stopped staring and slowly returned to their drinks. Kurt walked the perimeter of the studio, counting the red sale dots next to each one of his paintings. Circling back, he took Sarah roughly by the arm.

"Let's get out of here. I want to go home. I'm through being the sideshow monkey. I've sold enough paintings. Can you drive a stick?"

"Of course I can." Sarah tried to keep up with him in her heels as her heart sank. This ugly scene was not the pleasant evening she had imagined. Where was the glamour? Where had the romance gone? Had she only imagined it? Kurt had so suddenly turned his warmth off that she felt like the hired help. "My dad made sure we all knew how. It was one of the things he insisted that we learn."

"Too much information." Kurt dug into his pocket and tossed her his keys. "The car's parked out front. Have at it."

CHAPTER TWENTY FOUR

Anger was a powerful form of energy. Sarah had kicked off her shoes and hiked the trailing hem to her knees. She had some trouble working the unfamiliar clutch whenever she needed to downshift to meet a curve, but the real issue was that she was so boiling mad at Kurt's jackass behavior that she could barely focus her eyes to see.

He had settled into the passenger seat and was humming contentedly. Feeling the heat of her anger, he turned.

"What? Is something wrong?"

"I'm so pissed at you right now I can hardly breathe. You were really rude to me back there."

"I was? Why? When? What did I do?"

"Kurt, you treated me like a servant. Is that what I am to you? What about everything you said?"

"Sarah, no." He reached for her hand. "I've told you what you mean to me. We've covered all of that. I'm sorry if I hurt your feelings. I didn't mean to." He pushed his fingers through his hair. "It's that Sally. She makes me crazy. She always has. She knows how to push my buttons. Please don't let her come between us. That means Sally wins. That's what she wants."

Her anger cooled. Kurt was making sense. Sally was a troublemaker. She had seen it before, firsthand, during Karaoke Night. Sure, Kurt wasn't perfect, but at least he was trying to be honest with her. To expect him to be perfect was unrealistic. He was a grown man. He carried a lot of baggage. She blushed. For that matter, so did she. If this relationship was going to work, she needed to at least give Kurt a decent shot at it. She simmered down and softened her tone. "This is a nice car. Nicer than I'm used to."

His spidery fingers tickled her bare knee. "Stick with me, kid. I'll introduce you to a lot of things you're going to learn to like."

He leered, and flicked his fingers at the coming crossroad. "That's our turn, up ahead."

Sarah dropped the car into second. "We take a left, right?"

"Righhhhht," he slurred.

Evidently all the champagne he had guzzled at the gala was kicking in.

As they entered the intersection, Kurt reached over and gripped the wheel, giving it a hard shove. "Left! I said left! Left!"

Sarah dropped the car into neutral and stood on the brake as the acrid smell of burnt rubber seared her nose. The convertible fishtailed sideways, blocking the road. She gave Kurt a shove. "Let go of the wheel! You said right."

"Right! Right!" He roared with laughter. "The other right. I meant left."

"You fuckin' jagoff." Sarah elbowed him rudely and popped the clutch, feeling frantically for first gear, desperately trying to get the car straightened out before they faced any oncoming traffic. "You're going to get us killed."

Kurt covered his face with both hands and peeked through his spread fingers. "Look around you, babe. Who you gonna hit? There's no one out here but you and me. Relax! Quit acting like such a child."

Anxiety gripped the pit of her stomach as doubts about their relationship flared up again. After this drive to Wauwinet, the blinders were off. She saw Kurt for what he really was: a middle-aged train wreck. She had already dealt with one addictive personality, Mason. Did she really want to hitch herself to another? Or did the problem lie with her? Where did this problem stand?

Straightening the car out, Sarah turned down a private driveway. The gnarled forest thinned out to expose acres of moonlit meadow and the rolling sea. In spite of her confusion and aching disappointment, the beauty of the landscape caught her imagination. It all looked so tranquil, so calm, so peaceful.

"Stop the car!" Kurt ordered abruptly. "Stop the car now!"

She planted her foot on the brake again, afraid he was going to puke.

"Shhhhhhh!" He pointed toward the trees. "Shut off the engine. Do you hear that?"

What did he mean? Sarah turned the engine off and stilled her ears to listen. At first, she only heard the breeze, but as she continued to listen, Sarah heard an inconsistent and oddly steady plopping sound. It reminded her exactly of her mom's old coffee percolator on the electric stove back home. "What is that?"

"It's the trees." Kurt draped an arm over her shoulders. "They're weeping pines. The ground water is saline, so the trees weep the salt to get rid of it. It's the only way they can survive."

Sarah felt enchanted. "I've never heard of such a thing. Pittsburgh trees don't weep."

His fingernails traced a design on her thigh. "There are a lot of things I could clue you in on, if you'd only let me try."

She removed his hand from her leg. "Let's not go there. I'm still mad at you."

"Fine." He sat back and scowled. "There's nothing worse than a prick tease." He pointed to a house that was completely dark except for a yellow lantern hanging over a carriage door. "Head for the light. That's my house."

She restarted the car and waited for further instruction that never came. Kurt had crossed his arms and dropped his chin to his chest, apparently asleep. Great! So now she was his chauffeur, too. She let the car roll to a stop in front of the dark house. The driveway circled back in a big loop to the main road. A footpath meandered through a rough garden before heading down the slope toward a boathouse perched on the shoreline of the property's harbor side.

Kurt snorted. He opened his eyes and struggled to rise. "Leave the car where it is. It's perfectly fine." He opened his door and headed unsteadily for the house. "Come on in. I'll make us a pizza. They always leave me some in the freezer."

Sarah studied the keys in her hand. The evening had definitely not turned out the way she had hoped. Should she take the car back to town now, and return it in the morning? She winced at the idea of taking the car without Kurt's permission. He might call the cops on her, and report it as stolen. Then where would she be? Who would the cops believe, an island resident or a barmaid, fresh off the boat? Plus, if her name made the papers, Mason might be able to track her down again. She was trapped, and she knew it.

Lights began to flick on throughout the house. Sarah watched Kurt stumble into the kitchen, flicking on even more lights as he went. Pretty soon, the whole house was lit up like the sinking Titanic. He pulled a pizza box from the freezer, and her stomach growled so hard that she saw stars. She hadn't eaten anything since breakfast because she wanted to look good in the dress. Hunger finally decided her. She would eat some pizza, and take it from there.

Sarah stepped carefully across the driveway in bare feet and entered a hall. Closing the front door, she dropped the car keys in a Chinese porcelain bowl on a table. Kurt was whistling in the kitchen, so she headed that way. She passed a masculine study on the left that held a huge leather sofa and the biggest flat screen TV she had ever seen. A polished wooden staircase on the right led up to what she assumed were the bedrooms on the second floor. After Kurt's boorish behavior earlier this evening, she would not be spending the night up there.

The frost-covered pizza disk was laying forgotten on the counter. Kurt was clutching a bottle of wine in one hand as he pawed through a drawer with the other.

"There you are. Help me find a corkscrew. There's one in here somewhere."

She crossed her arms. "Don't open that for me. I don't want any more wine."

"Really?" He set the bottle down and caught her arm. "I was opening it especially for you." Pushing her back roughly against the dishwasher, he ground his hips into hers and nuzzled her neck. "Don't be like that. Don't you want to have a good time?"

"Stop it, Kurt." Sarah pushed him off and rolled away, repelled by his drunken obviousness. "I'm sorry if anything I did made you think this is what I wanted. I should leave. Coming here was a mistake."

He made a snatch at her, and when he missed, his shoulders slumped like a sad clown. "Don't leave me. I'm sorry. This is all my fault. I should have had dinner. This always happens whenever I skip dinner."

"I'm sorry, too. Look, can I borrow your car? I'll return it first thing in the morning."

"Of course you can borrow my car." Wearily, he closed his eyes. "But before you go, I want to show you something." He stumbled back down the hall toward the front door. "You'll have to follow me to see it."

"What is it, Kurt? Where are you going now?"

"Trust me," he called. "Come this way." Opening the door, he vanished into the night.

Sarah stepped outside, lifting her hem and looking for the drunken lunatic among the shadows. Kurt had already crossed the driveway. He was hunched now under the lantern, unlocking the carriage doors to the garage. He put his full weight behind one of the doors, slid it open, and disappeared inside. Maybe he had a second car she could use? He flipped on more lights and Sarah felt her pulse quicken. She stepped nearer. What she thought was a garage was a fully functioning studio.

She caught the familiar rubbery scent of fresh paint even before she saw the dozens of quart cans lined up against the wall. Her eyes skipped over the studio, and her mind delighted in an unconscious inventory of rolled brushes, fresh canvas, and art supplies. A six-foot-long roll of un-stretched canvas lay furled in one corner like a spare sail. Sarah paused, standing on the threshold, halfway in and halfway out, and breathed in the rich chemical perfume of a working painter's studio. The familiar acrid metallic aroma burned her nose. She teased out the individual scents of canvas flashing, tart framing lumber, linseed oil, and snappy turpentine. The edge of these chemicals filled Sarah's lungs, and she breathed deeply. She had missed this heated sensation. This was the perfume of her true world.

Kurt pulled a tarp down off a painting on an easel and dropped the tarp to the floor. "Tell me what you think of this."

It was a masterpiece, an unfinished masterpiece. A female nude reclined on the same leather couch Sarah had seen in the den. The composition immediately keyed into her mind Goya's *Naked Maja,* but Kurt had played off that iconographic classic and then risen light years above it. This was no flat, impersonal third-person portrait. This living girl had breathed. Her eyes sparkled and teased. Kurt had done the impossible. He had captured her living wit in transparent oil. "Sweet Lord Jesus," Sarah whispered. Would she ever be able to paint anything this good in her whole life?

Kurt cocked one hand on his hip. "What do you think of her?"

"It's perfect." She stepped even closer to study Kurt's detailing. She was also struck by how much the girl in the painting looked like her. The resemblance was even closer than sisters. They could have been twins.

"Yes, it is," Kurt crowed. "This is for all the critics who called me a hack. Fuckers! This one is as good as anything out there. Ever. In the history of the world."

"No one could ever criticize this work." Sarah continued to scan the portrait, awestruck. "But it's unfinished."

"I know that. Sarah," Kurt picked up a brush. He separated the bristles with his thumbnail, "that's why I need you. This model left me, and now I'm afraid if I touch the painting, I'll destroy the little I have. I'm terrified that if I touch it again, I'll ruin it. That I'll make a mistake." His eyes pleaded for understanding. "I'm afraid to even try. This has been going on for years. I'm stalled. I'm trapped. But I think you can help."

"What can I do?"

"Be my new model. Sarah, you look just like her. You have to see that. If I had a live model, I might be able to finish this work. Please, Sarah, please, help me. I need to finish this painting and break free of it. I can't seem to do anything new, until this one gets done."

Kurt's desperation touched Sarah's heart. She knew what it felt like to be trapped, and there was nothing in it to like. Toxic anxiety bloomed in a trapped space, and who wants to live with that? She could see that Kurt genuinely needed her help, and wasn't that what life was all about? Helping each other out of fixes? That was especially difficult because painting was such a solitary pursuit. Artists spent hours alone with their creativity, thinking only of their work. When it was finished, the world applauded politely and quickly moved on to the next big thing. Creative artists only had each other, because no outsider really understood what was involved in completing their creative work. If she could help Kurt finish this painting and break free of it, then shouldn't she do that? If she was in the same fix, wouldn't she be asking him for the very same thing?

"I can see where you're coming from. Yes, Kurt, I'll do what I can."

"Thank God! We finally agree on something."

He tossed the brush in the sink and reached for her, pulling her close. His fingers danced up her spine.

"What do you say we go drink that wine now? We can get started first thing in the morning."

"No, Kurt. Not tonight." She pushed him away. Although Sarah stood in awe of his amazing talent and found some part of him compelling, she was still way too leery of his mood swings to make that kind of commitment. "You've got what you wanted, but seriously, can I borrow your car? I'll come back first thing. We can talk about it more in the morning."

"If that's what you really want." He pinched his eyes shut. "Let's go back to the house. I'll get the keys."

Kurt stepped out into the night. Sarah followed him slowly, flicking the lights off as she went. She slid the carriage door shut, and stood in the darkness for a moment, waiting for her eyes to adjust. Kurt had gone on ahead without her. He continued to shuffle across the driveway, and when he opened the front door, he turned.

"Coming?"

Sarah crept across the driveway to protect her bare toes and found Kurt waiting in the hallway. He was clutching the newel post and looking sly. She scooped her fingers through the Chinese bowl. The car keys were gone.

"Stop it, Kurt. You're only going to piss me off again. Where did you put the keys?"

"Keys? What keys? I don't have no stinkin' keys." He laughed. "I guess that means you'll have to stay with me now."

"You're such an ass." She started to steam again, but knew that any effort in arguing with a drunk was a waste of time. "That doesn't mean I'm going to sleep with you. I'll sleep downstairs, on the couch."

"Really?" His shoulders slumped. "Alright. Do whatever you have to do. Will you help me upstairs to bed first?"

"I've already said that's not going to happen."

"This isn't about sex, I swear. I really do need your help getting up these stairs. I've got a bad knee."

"I'm trusting you on this one, Kurt." She took his arm and shouldered half his weight. They started up. "So help me God, if you try anything, I will seriously kick your ass and walk home."

"You don't want to walk home tonight. Look how dark it is out there. Brrrrr! Too spooky."

Kurt misjudged the height of a step and toe-tripped into the wall. A mermaid print bounced off its nail and continued to bounce down the stairs, catching each step by the corners of its frame until it finally shattered into glass shards against the hallway floor.

"Oops!" Kurt leaned dangerously backward to survey the damage. "I never liked that print anyway. Came with the house." He turned and continued to slog up the staircase. "Don't worry about it. The maids will clean it up in the morning."

Releasing her arm, Kurt staggered through a doorway on the right. Sarah heard a thud and stepped inside to make sure he was okay. Kurt was spread-eagled across a four-poster bed and blinking blindly at the ceiling fan. Raising his head, he saw her standing in the doorway. He patted the mattress by his side.

"This feels great. Why don't you stretch out with me for a moment?"

She leaned in the doorway. "Go to sleep, Kurt. We'll talk about it in the morning."

"You win." He sighed. "I'll behave myself, but where's the fun in that? Promise me, Sarah, you won't leave me? You'll be here when I wake up? I'm so tired of being alone."

Unless she found where Kurt had hidden the keys that would be an easy promise to keep. "Yes, I'll be here in the morning when you wake up. Now, go to sleep."

"Thank you. You're a gem. A peach, a real peach."

Sarah snatched a T-shirt off the dresser to sleep in as she passed it and noted with satisfaction that Kurt was snoring even before she got to the head of the stairs. Drifting back down, she carefully sidestepped the broken glass on the floor. The last thing she wanted to do was to cut her bare feet and then try to find a first aid kit in this huge house, even if Kurt had one. She looked at the shattered frame and paused. Maybe she should sweep it up? But where would the broom closet be? It was probably best to take Kurt's advice and leave it for the maids in the morning. Evidently, cleaning up after Kurt Stockton was a job best left to the professionals.

Slipping into the den Sarah slipped out of the dress, folding it neatly over a ladder backed chair. The wind rattled the windows and she jumped and peered out the window, but saw nothing but the moon and all the dark trees. Being in a strange house had spooked her into imagining things. There was no one out there. Pulling the T-shirt on, Sarah swaddled herself in a wooly afghan that immediately enveloped her in a cocoon of downy warmth. This was the ticket. She would be plenty comfortable enough now for the night.

The lime-green LED clock on the DVD player glowed 10:47 p.m. Sarah picked up the remote. She was so wired from the evening she wasn't sure she could sleep. Maybe she could find a decent movie? It was hard to believe she hadn't watched any TV since she left Pittsburgh a month ago. If she found something good on TV, then at least the night wouldn't be a total waste.

She pointed the clicker at the screen and started pushing random buttons, hoping for the best. The unit began to whirr, but instead of offering an options menu, the screen sprang suddenly to life. The girl from the painting shook a playful finger at the camera before unhooking her bra and stepping out of her lacy red thong. Sarah was shocked to see just how much the living girl looked like her. She even recognized the way the girl kept flipping her hair over her shoulder. They shared the same gesture. It was uncanny.

Kurt began to give off-screen direction. "Okay, Katie, lie back. Move that pillow with the fringe a touch more to the right. Yes, that's it, okay, perfect. Now tuck your left shoulder in a bit, no, not that one, the other left. Yes, that's good, good, better, better, best. Let's move this light a tiny bit more, there. Perfect. Okay, now raise your right arm over your head and point your tits right at me. Can you arch your back a bit more? A tiny bit more? Perfect! Hold that pose. That's just what I needed."

The onscreen girl shared a cynical smile. The camera got jostled and she dipped from the frame. Returning to central focus, she maintained the strained pose as Kurt continued to mutter his strangely disembodied instructions.

"You know, Katie, it wouldn't hurt to trim the bushes every once in awhile."

"I thought you liked me hairy." She ticked the hair growing from her left armpit. Giggling, she rolled onto her stomach and slapped her ass. "And firm. Let's not forget you said you liked me firm."

"Goddammit!" Kurt shouldered his way into the frame, and roughly shoved her back into position. Sarah saw a flare of genuine fear light up the girl's eyes. "Don't get me started or we'll never get this done!"

"Sorry, luv." She bit her lips, contrite. "Kurt? Luv?"

"What?"

Sarah heard the scrape of bristles on canvas as Kurt started painting.

"Are you going to make me famous?"

"Is that really what you want?"

"More than anything! I want to be a famous American movie star, dripping in pink diamonds. The toast of the known world!"

"It's not impossible." He chortled. "Every man in America would pay good money to see you the way I see you now. Be a good girl, and hold that pose while we have this light, and I'll give you everything you want when we're through."

"I bet you will, you randy old goat." She laughed, carefully maintaining her pose. "Kurt?"

"Yes, love?"

"Do you really love me?"

"You know I do, Katie. I've told you that repeatedly."

"Do you love me more than you love your wife?"

"Katie, we've been through all of this. Melissa and I are separated. She seems to be living her own life lately. Yes, occasionally, we run into each other at an opening or an exhibition, but that's as far as it goes. We haven't lived together as man and wife for years. I suppose I do still love her, but it's more like the love I have for a sister, not a wife. The feelings I have for you are real. I know we'll have to deal with some of the social bullshit -"

"AAARRGH!" Sarah threw the clicker at the wall, and the DVD image stuttered and died. That prick! That total prick! Kurt had told this girl the very same thing he had said to her, almost word for word. The phrasing was so similar that it had sounded like a script. Holy shit! That's exactly what he had done. Kurt had used a script on her! He had probably delivered those very same lines to dozens of women over the years. He had played on her trust, and she had swallowed his self-serving bullshit hook, line, and sinker.

Sarah was so furious at her gullibility that she stood up, shaking, and the afghan slid to the floor. After everything she had learned from that idiotic relationship with Mason, she had stepped right in it again! She wanted to march upstairs right this minute and confront Kurt about his lies, but she wouldn't be able to wake him, and even if she did, he wouldn't remember their argument in the morning. It was so frustrating, but she had dealt with drunks before.

She began to pace the floor. She needed to do *something*. The jagged edge of rage was coursing through her blood. It would serve Kurt right if he woke up in the morning and she was gone. She couldn't take his car, but she could call for a cab. Grabbing her beaded bag, Sarah checked it for fare. Empty. All she had was her room key and a lipstick. She hated the idea of searching Kurt's house looking for money. She would feel like a thief. If she searched though, and found practical shoes and some pants, she could hike back to town, even though it was getting close to midnight and Wauwinet was at least eight miles from the Dorm. It did look spooky out there, with the wind and all the scary trees. Did she really have the nerve to walk home alone, eight miles in the dark?

Picking up the afghan, Sarah sat down to consider her options. She could call Alien and ask for a ride, but then Alien would need to borrow Steve's car to come fetch her. That meant the news of her latest escapade would flood the gossip mill in town since Steve was gossip central. Sarah was already getting a reputation for trouble that she didn't particularly want. She didn't want to add any more fuel to that particular fire.

Faced with this wall of indecision, she decided to stay in the den and sleep on the couch. She suddenly felt drained. She would leave the rest of it for the morning. There was only so much she could do. Kurt was upstairs, snoring away. She had nothing more to worry about from his direction. Wrapping the afghan around her shoulders, Sarah rolled up like a pill bug and made a comfortable nest on the couch as the wind rattled the windows. She reached up to turn out the light. This was a sensible decision. It was not a good night to be out and about.

The staircase creaked. Sarah raised her head to listen. The sound wasn't repeated, so she snuggled back down. She wasn't used to sleeping in this big of a house. Surely, it had some settling-in-for-the-night noises of its own. Rolling on her side, Sarah tried to preserve her bubble of warmth as she got even more comfortable. She heard the rattle of a car's ignition in the distance. Knowing that Kurt had hidden his keys, and that at least his car was safe, she closed her eyes and dove for oblivion.

CHAPTER TWENTY FIVE

Toby tapped the cardboard box of donuts sitting on his lap. The lid popped open and the scent of warm vanilla filled the truck. He laughed and handed John a paper sack. "Martha clued me in, Lieutenant. She says the extra one's for you. She called it a Jarad dozen. Twelve for the rest of us, plus one for you to eat on your way to the station."

"That Martha's wicked smart. Knows me all too well." John bit into a deliciousness so sugary, it immediately coated his teeth. "If we're going to keep carpooling together, she'll need to start sending out fourteen."

"No, thank you. None for me, sir. I've had my breakfast. I eat oatmeal everyday. It's good for my heart."

"Keep it up, Toe." John licked the glaze off his fingertips. "You're going to live forever."

Carpooling had started off like a mentoring chore, but to his surprise John enjoyed the time spent with the CSO every morning. Toby was a very personable guy. He was bright, easy to work with, eager to please. Sure, he was a little formal, but that would rub off in time. With CJ and Toby both working dayshift, John found himself looking forward to tackling his workload each day, and that hadn't happened in a good long while. Of course, he had known CJ forever, but getting to know Toby better was like discovering a slightly goofy kid brother that he didn't know he had.

And John was surprised that Toby had turned out to be so even-keeled, knowing his blighted family history. Toby's only sibling, Bess, had been killed in a cold case hit and run years ago, and his dad, Frank, had died in a ghastly trawler mishap.

John recalled the story that Paul had shared with him once over a pitcher of beer. Paul had been called to the cargo hold of the *Mercy/Me* the day the trawler put back into port, the crew strangely subdued and silent. True, they had missed seeing Frank Talbot on the dock the day they had left, but everyone, including the Captain, had been busy getting ready. They had assumed that Frank had been too ill to make inspection again. No surprise, there. Frank was getting on in years, and he was known to take a nip or two, no harm in a man doing that.

When no one at the Talbot household had answered the phone, the Captain, worried that he would lose the flush of the tide, had instructed the crew to load the eleven tons of block ice needed to keep the fish fresh into the hold. The crew had loaded the ice, and the *Mercy/Me* had steamed for the Grand Bank. Seventeen days later, when they unloaded their catch, the crew found what remained of Frank Talbot. Evidently, no one had heard Frank's screams as they had loaded the ice, and no one had suspected that Frank was onboard, inspecting the hold. The strange thing was that Paxton's Mortuary didn't even have to embalm Frank Talbot, because between the weight of the ice and the weight of the fish, Frank had freeze-dried out about as effectively as any dead pharaoh king of Egypt.

Paul had wanted to write an article outlining the details of the bizarre case for one of his professional journals, but for the life of him he couldn't think of a decent way to ask either Mercy Talbot or Frank's family for permission.

The dashboard radio emitted a static fart. John reached over to adjust the volume. "Dispatch? That was garbled. Copy back, please."

"Lieutenant Jarad? Confirm."

"We're here, Tina. What've you got?"

"A four-eight-zero, sir. Near the six mile marker on Milestone Road."

John felt light-headed as his blood pressure plummeted. A 480 meant a felony Hit and Run with grave bodily harm. He had started the day off with a 480 once before, as a rookie. It had been the call for Bess Talbot. He glanced at Toby. Had Toby realized what a 480 call meant? Was this too close, too personal, too soon? Should he redirect Toby away from this particular investigation? Or would shielding him be such an obvious ploy that in the end, it would do Toby more harm than good? John quickly made his decision. Toby would stay. He was a sworn officer of the law. Toby was strong enough to handle this, and no one got to pick and choose. "On our way. Status?"

"Allamand and Parsons are on site. Cottage Hospital has dispatched a first response unit. The M.E. is riding in with them. Officer Ketchem is on his way."

"So are we."

John slid the blue flash onto the roof of his truck, but refrained from engaging the siren. Even with an emergency call like this one, he recognized the close correlation of the siren to several nearby homes of some very vocal Council members. 8:17 a.m. on a Sunday morning was way too early to rouse this particular neighborhood. Luckily, traffic looked to be minimal.

He pulled a U-turn and raced down Milestone Road. The open meadowland on the south side of the road was acreage so featureless that it skewed the perspective so that scrubby bushes took on the appearance of individual trees dotting an African savannah. Pranksters had been playing off this optical illusion all winter long by propping plywood animal cutouts scaled to size across the grassy plain. He found the accident site easily enough. Ted had fired up a row of spitting red flares directly in front of the cutout of a mother elephant with her baby in tow.

Gawkers had already converged on the site. They were illegally parked in the opposite meadow, and they leaned negligently against their cars. Putting the unit in park, John ignored this peanut gallery for the moment, knowing all too well that listening in on a police scanner and then beating the authorities to the scene constituted a perfectly respectable island hobby and form of local entertainment.

"Toby, renew those flares." He pointed to a parked cruiser. "You'll find more in the trunk."

"Yes, sir."

His shoes began to crunch on broken glass. John circumscribed a wider arc as he headed toward a crumpled Volvo convertible. The car sat, skewed and abandoned, on the grassy verge between Milestone Road and the bike path. Both front tires had flattened on their rims. The honeyed sweet scent of spilled antifreeze filled John's nose. He crouched, and saw a Schwinn bicycle wedged beneath the car. Straightening up, John noted that some prankster had recently introduced the cutout of a large chimpanzee into the crook of a nearby tree. When he realized what he was really seeing, John's heart dropped to his knees. Oh no. Poor Oz.

CJ trotted over, cradling her forensic camera in her arms. She looked composed, but her face was so pale that her lips were blue. "Glad you're here. I can't believe this happened."

"Any witnesses?"

"Not to the accident, no, but Father Duffy called it in. He's over there. He's been asking for you."

"Let's get you started first. You know the drill. I want photographs of everything. Use that milestone as your Cartesian coordinate. NSEW, I want it all. Pull Toby in to help when he's done with the flares. I'll be back to help you measure."

Her eyes narrowed. "You sure you want Toby in on this?"

"Why? Because of what happened to Bess?"

"It did cross my mind."

"I know. Crossed mine, too. But Toby has to take this on, CJ. We can't shield him from it."

"I knew that. I just wanted to put it out there." She *tsked*. "Tough way to start his career."

Squealing brakes announced Sam's arrival from Madaket. His battered Jeep slid to a halt and Sam's usually stoic face, framed by the driver's side window, collapsed with shock as he registered the body in the tree.

"Sonofabitch. Is that really Billy Bear up there?"

"We believe it is. Steady on, Sam. Come with me. I'll need your help with witnesses."

They headed for an elderly man standing next to a tan four-door sedan. Father Duffy was wearing an old-school clerical collar, and he clasped his thin hands at their approach.

"Father Duffy, sir? You called this in?"

"I did, John. What a fearsome accident." He winced at the broken figure hanging from the tree. "I have to believe I was the first one to actually notice him up there. There was a bit of fog this morning. I can't believe that no one else thought this important enough to stop to render assistance. What would that say about modern humanity?"

"You did the right thing, sir. Did you notice anyone else around when you first arrived?"

"No, not a soul. The road was completely deserted, both ways. Originally, I stopped because of the glass. That's what I noticed on the roadway first. Then I saw the wreck, and I got out of my car to see if there was anything I could do to assist. At first, I was relieved because there was no one in the car." He started to tremble. "Then I noticed the tree. I thought it was another cutout, you know? They way they've been hanging them from the trees all winter?"

"I know this is difficult, sir. We appreciate your help. Officer Ketchem can escort you home when you're ready, if you need assistance."

"I'm fine, thank you. I just wasn't expecting to see this." Father Duffy dragged a hand across his brow. "I was on my way to St. Paul's to officiate a christening. '*In the midst of life, we are in death.*' What a terrible reminder."

"Sam? See to the Reverend, will you?"

"Yes, Lieutenant."

John moved briskly to check on the traffic situation, which was starting to pile up because of the impacted lane. Ted was doing a fine job, directing the line of impatient airport commuters snaking toward Ackerman Field.

"Whoa, whoa, whoa!" Ted shouted as a motorist in a BMW tried to bypass the line of redirected traffic by driving directly through the accident scene. Ted planted himself solidly in front of the offending vehicle, and leaned both hands on its hood. "Excuse me? Where do you think you're going?"

The driver stuck his head out the window. "You people can't block the road like this! I'm going to miss my plane."

"Excuse me, sir." John stepped in. "You'll need to move back into line. We're investigating a fatality."

"That's not really my problem, is it?"

"I could make it your problem, sir, if that's really how you want your day to go."

"Fascist," the driver snarled. He did, however, put his car in gear and reverse to the end of the line.

Ted looked flummoxed. He dropped his hands to his sides. "I swear I don't know what people are doing anymore. What kind of moron drives through an evidence field?"

"The usual kind," John said. "Keep the line moving, Ted. You're doing a great job."

"Thanks, Lieutenant." Ted looked troubled. "This wasn't pure accident, was it, sir?"

"We're still working that out, but it's not looking that way."

Paul was standing alone in an area of patchy grass, staring at a single docksider moccasin lying on its side in the gritty dirt. "SOB got hit so hard, it knocked him out of his shoes."

"That is Billy Bear up there, isn't it, Paul?"

"Afraid so." Paul resettled his glasses. "If it's any consolation, he didn't suffer. When you get hit that hard, the aorta blows out on impact. Sorry to say, I've seen this before."

"With Bess Talbot?"

"Yep. Only she ended up in a ditch, not a tree. The end result was the same." Bending down, Paul opened a forensic evidence case and offered up a box of nitrile gloves. "Put these on. I know this one is going to court. I've called the death, but the paramedics are waiting for your word to bring him down."

John rolled the gloves on. "Let's get him down as quickly as possible. No need for the kids to see this horror on their way to the Kiddie Beach this morning."

"Confirmed," Paul agreed.

CJ returned. She had traded in her camera for a tape measure. John handed her a pair of gloves, and they moved toward a stain scraped into the road's tarry surface. They crouched, and she pointed.

"It's safe to assume this was the point of impact," CJ said. "The stain is paint off Billy's bike, but I sampled it to make sure." She stood and had him hold the end of the tape measure as she paced the distance to the tree. "Fifty-three and a half feet from the point of impact." The tape rolled up automatically as CJ walked back. "We should assume this was a deliberate act, John, vehicular homicide as opposed to manslaughter."

"Why? Because of the lack of rubber on the road?"

"That's what I'm thinking. There was no attempt to either reduce the vehicle's speed or redirect it from the point of impact. It's clear as day."

He gazed up at the tree. Thankfully, he couldn't see Billy's face from this angle. John wasn't sure that was something he ever wanted to see. Sometimes, his imagination provided more than enough visual imagery.

"Bring him down, Paul. Make sure they bag his hands. CJ? Come with me."

They returned to the crushed car. "What do you think of this?" John asked. "I've noticed two different kinds of glass."

CJ nodded. "I like seeing broken glass, because it tells me a lot. The thicker glass came from the windshield, the thinner came from the broken headlight. I once found broken glass in a burglar's hoodie. Put him at the site of the break-in. We nailed him because of it." She flicked on her flashlight and stooped to peer under the car. "I can see the bike crushed between the rear tires. There are scratches all down the drive train." She stood and dusted her hands. "The bike continued to work its way under the car as the actor accelerated after impact. Billy rolled up the bumper and then slid backwards along the hood. His body mass shattered the windshield, and acceleration after impact multiplied by body mass is what propelled him into the tree."

John noticed the ignition keys were missing, and although the dashboard sparkled with crushed glass, very little of it had settled into the channeled upholstery. Had the actor anticipated the result of this crime, and protected himself somehow?

"There's a bonus," CJ said. "There's blood on some of the glass. If it's not Billy's blood, then once we identify a person of interest, we can request a DNA sample and try for a match." She noted the license plate number. "It should be easy enough to run this registration."

"No need," John said. "I know who owns this car. Kurt Stockton, from Wauwinet. I should know; I've stopped him in it often enough. Let's cover all the bases, CJ. Call in an BOLO on Stockton. Notify Port Authority to lock it down. ID all departing passengers, both ferry and plane."

"They're going to hate doing that."

"It's not an option. Tell them to do it anyway."

John turned, distracted by the blatting sound of an overworked motorcycle. A rider on a dirt bike was racing across the meadow. Sliding to a stop, the rider dropped the bike, and ran toward the paramedics, who were hefting a body bag onto a gurney. John started over, but he felt his heart sink. He would never reach Ozzie in time. He was too far away, and on the wrong side of the road. Luckily, Ted grasped the situation. He intercepted Ozzie, and wrapped him in an efficient bear hug.

"Let me go! He's my dad!"

"Don't go over there, Oz," Ted said. "Trust me on this one, son. You don't want to see him like this."

"Goddamn you! I said turn me loose."

"Oz! No! Listen to me! He wouldn't want it, either."

Ozzie broke free. He stood rigid, and rubbed his eyes with his fists. "Shit! What happened to him?"

"It was a hit and run, Oz. He didn't feel a thing."

"Fuck! I told him not to go. I knew something bad was going to happen!"

"Why do you say that, Oz?" John said.

"Because Dad got a call last night, late. He never goes out late anymore. Not since he sold the car. I told him it was too dangerous to ride his bike to 'Sconset, but he wouldn't listen."

"Do you know who he was meeting in 'Sconset?"

"He didn't say. He just said he was meeting a friend at Le Coc d'Or for a drink."

John pulled out his keys. "Ted? Put Oz's bike in my truck and take him home. I'll take the unit back to the station."

"Come on, Oz. That makes sense. We'll go see your dad tomorrow, together." Ted slung an arm across Ozzie's shoulders as they headed for the truck.

CJ rejoined John again. She looked worried. "Port authority has security code orange in effect. They weren't happy, but they complied." She glanced at Oz. "So what's going to happen to him now? His dad was all he had in the world. How old is he, anyway? Seventeen?"

"Ted will keep an eye on him. He's good like that."

"I heard Oz say Billy got a call. We could ask Judge Coffin for a subpoena, and check the phone records."

"Let's do that. But first, come with me." He headed toward the parked car. "I want to check Wauwinet, to see if Stockton made it home last night."

"Wauwinet? So, like what? Stockton ran Billy down and then left his car and walked home? Wauwinet has to be ten miles from here."

"Not if he crossed the moor. Going cross-country would trim the distance in half. Plus, with the moon last night, he'd have plenty of light."

John pulled a U-turn and put the pedal down as CJ buckled her seatbelt. The cruiser roared back down Milestone Road. Hooking a hard right, John caught his favorite Polpis shortcut. CJ gripped the door and cast her eyes at him when the cruiser bucked over the spillway speed bump, but she didn't say one word. Spewing gravel, they pulled to a stop in front of Stockton's house. The house looked deserted, with half of its curtains drawn. CJ opened her door and left the unit first. Drawing her weapon, she swiftly crossed the yard as John covered her from the opened door of the car. Peering into a side window, she waved him in.

"Sounds quiet," she whispered. "Do you think he's already bolted for the mainland?"

"If he did, we'll catch him on the other side." He leaned on the doorbell and rapped his knuckles against the door. "Nantucket police. Open up."

"That worked. Someone's moving."

He heard the scuffling sound, too, and readied his weapon as the unknown inside fumbled with the lock. The heavy door swung open to reveal a woman with sleep-tousled hair. She had an afghan thrown over one shoulder like a Roman toga, and underneath she was wearing a T-shirt and not much else.

It was Sarah Hawthorne.

John glanced at her bare legs and felt his idea of a rosy future with Sarah evaporate. It had been a nice daydream, but he had hesitated too long, and now his chance was gone. He flinched as Stockton stumbled down the staircase, dressed only in boxer shorts. Stockton blearily clung to the bannister.

"Sweetheart? Who is it?"

"It's the police," Sarah said.

Stockton raised his hands and offered them a jaunty wave. "Morning, officers. Is there a problem? Don't know what I've done this time, but I'm sure we can work it out. That's why we hire lawyers, right?"

John closed his teeth so hard he heard his molars crunch.

CJ slowly lowered her weapon. "Mr. Stockton, sir? Did you know that you're bleeding?"

Stockton looked surprised. He studied his upper arm. "Another war wound, I suppose. Things did get a bit wild last night. Sarah, don't step in the broken glass, you silly goose. You're in bare feet."

She frowned. "I don't remember you getting cut last night, Kurt. When did that happen?"

"It's no big deal. A band-aid will take care of it." Stockton clapped his hands, and rubbed them together briskly. "Alrighty then, officers. Care to come in for some coffee?"

CHAPTER TWENTY SIX

"You can't hide in this room forever." Alien stood in the doorway. "I still don't get what you were thinking. Of course you could have called me for a ride. We were really worried. We couldn't imagine where you went."

"Please don't yell, Alien." Sarah slumped on the edge of her bed. "I feel stupid enough as it is."

"You should feel stupid. Steve was ready to call the police."

"He didn't need to." She fell back on the mattress. "They found me anyway."

"This isn't funny! I don't think you realize how much trouble you're in. People are saying you were Stockton's accomplice, his alibi. That you're covering for him."

"But that doesn't make sense! If the police think Kurt killed Billy Bear, then why did they let him go?"

"Because maybe they're still building their case against him. Did you ever think of that?"

"No, I didn't." She hadn't thought of that. The suggestion dropped Sarah to an even lower level of gloom. Raising her arm, she checked her watch: 5:52 p.m. It was a good thing Hawthorne girls were tough, because she seriously needed to rally. It had been a rough thirty-six hours, and tonight was The Tap Room's Grand Karaoke Night Reopening. She was due to cover her tables in eight minutes. Rolling off the bed, Sarah tied her apron on. "I only hope the police are through with me. They grilled me for almost three hours yesterday. I never want to see the inside of a police station again."

"You only got what you deserved. Just swear to me the next time you'll let us know where you're going before you disappear. It's not that hard. Pin a note to the fucking door."

"I will. I promise."

They clattered down the staircase and crossed the rancid alley.

"So what did you tell them?" Alien asked.

"The police? I told them the truth. That Kurt had too much to drink, and I drove him home. That we talked about painting for awhile, and then I put him to bed–alone–and I went downstairs to sleep on the couch. I swear, that's all we did."

"It sounds innocent enough." Alien held the screened door open.

"That's what I'm telling you! It was innocent. Completely innocent. Only no one believes me." Sarah shook the tears from her eyes as they skirted the manic kitchen staff. No one was going to catch her crying. People could think whatever they liked, but she hadn't done anything wrong.

She heard the bar bell clang as they entered. Leslie unlocked the front door, and a stream of eager diners swarmed in. Leslie was swallowed by the sudden crowd as everyone scrambled to claim a table. The noise level immediately rose to a buzzing new height. It reminded Sarah of the stampede. Her heart began to hammer, and her palms were slick with sweat. "I don't know if I can do this."

"Sure, you can." Alien gave her a gentle push. "Just get things started. It'll go from there. We're all friends. Besides, I'm here to back you up."

Sarah entered the dining room on leaden legs like a zombie. Willpower was the only thing keeping her moving. It was tough, but she was going to face this down. She was through running away from lies. She reached for a fistful of laminated menus just to have a something to hold onto, a prop. As she did, the conversations around her died like a silent ripple, and the roomful of speculative faces turned in her direction. Butterflies battered Sarah's stomach. Her knees began to wobble as her mouth went bone dry with fear. How did she get into this? Did she have the courage to face this crowd?

"Sarah! There you are!" Steve slapped the bar, breaking the spell. "Glad you could make it. Crissakes! You should misbehave more often. Look at my business! I want to hire two more of you."

"Get after it, girlfriend." Anna-Marie breezed by carrying an already loaded tray. She pointed with her elbow. "That policeman friend of yours asked for one of your tables."

"Thanks, A-M." Policeman friend? Sarah glanced across the room. She felt a shock of recognition to see John sitting at table three. What more could he want from her? She swallowed her fear. There was only one way to find out.

He sat patiently, his hands clasped on the table. He was wearing a turquoise polo shirt with khaki chinos. Sarah had seen so much of him in his uniform lately that he looked weird wearing civilian clothes. The disparity played with her head.

"Hello, again. How are you this evening?" he asked.

"I'm fine." Sarah cleared the frog in her throat. "I'm surprised to see you here. Didn't you get enough answers out of me yesterday?"

He smiled, and Sarah's heart did a little flip. When John smiled, he looked like a different guy, not at all so focused and grim. She regretted her snappy retort. Yesterday, in spite of his questions, he had treated her with kindness, and some gentlemanly respect.

"Actually, I'm here because I'd like some supper. May I see a menu, please?"

"O-kay." She handed him one and pointed her pencil at the second setting. "Are you expecting someone else?"

"No. I'm alone this evening. Sadly, it's a table for one."

"Would you like something to drink?"

"Yes, please." He closed the menu and leaned forward. "I'd like a Sam Adams with a glass of water. Tap water is fine. And I'll take the steak and salad special, please. Steak medium rare, house dressing on the side."

"You got it." Sarah scribbled his order. "Won't take a minute. I'll be right back."

She checked her other tables before heading back to the kitchen. Sure, John could have stopped in to grab some dinner but still, she felt wary of his motives. He had seemed satisfied with everything she had said yesterday, but the experience hadn't blossomed into anything like a higher level of trust. He kept asking her the same questions three or four times in different ways in what seemed like an effort to catch her telling a lie. The curious thing was, she hadn't done anything wrong but still, Sarah felt like she had dodged a bullet, and she didn't know why.

Steve stepped out of the storeroom carrying a case of beer. He ripped the cardboard box open and felt a bottle with his hand. "Crissakes! These beers are moving so fast, I can't keep them cold. What can I get you?"

"One Sam Adams, two vodka tonics, four Amber Lights."

"Coming up."

A-M cruised back into the waitress station. "Holy heck! What a crowd. This is brutal. Steve? I need another bucket." She pushed her bangs back with her wrist and took a breather. "Hey, I saw you talking to John. He's a decent fellow. I used to babysit for his family. You should give him a chance. There's something to be said for decent, you know. Most men are jackasses. When you find a decent one, you should grab him, and hang on."

Steve laughed. "Most men are jackasses, huh? That explains why you've been married three times."

"Like I said, jackasses." A-M pointed to the karaoke stage, where Sally was already reviewing a playlist with D-Buzz. "Take that one, for instance. Her first husband was a complete jackass. Woke her up the morning of her fortieth birthday, no flowers, no card, nothing. Said he wanted a divorce because she was getting too old. Now that she was turning forty, he wanted to trade her in on two twenty-year olds. Jokes on him, jackass. Sally takes it seriously, and she files for divorce first. Cites mental cruelty. Judge Coffin sees it her way. He gives her all the marital assets plus half of his business, then she ends up married to Seth Poldridge. He dies, and leaves her that fine beach house. Her first husband, what a schmo. I bet he wishes he never opened his big fat mouth."

"Who was Sally's first husband?" Sarah asked.

"I was." Steve slid the fresh bucket across the bar. "It was me."

A-M hefted the beer. "Hope you enjoy listening to her singing up there now, boss. Heck, I bet she'd even sing you '*Happy Birthday*' if you asked her right."

"Get stuffed. Haven't you got enough to do?"

Sarah felt shocked. Steve was Sally's first husband? No wonder Sally had the run of the place, she was part owner. Nantucket was turning out to be like the three degrees of Pittsburgh, where everyone was either related or they knew each other from church or from work. She quickly loaded her tray and moved back to servicing her tables, setting down platters and drinks as she went. As she neared the stage, Sally was tapping her lips and considering her selection carefully.

"What's your pick, D-Buzz? Should we try some Vin Malone on these philistines tonight?"

"I love the man, lady, but which song? The cat wrote over a thousand. You pick the song, and we'll play it."

"Let's go with something jazzy, and wake these people up. How about '*Secret Lover*'?" Sally turned. "Oh, Sarah! Wait a minute. You've certainly had some adventures since I saw you last. I hope our friend Kurt hasn't gotten you into any real trouble, has he?"

"No," Sarah lied. She wasn't going to give Sally any ammunition to use against her. "There was a misunderstanding, but it's been straightened out."

"Good girl! But a word of advice. Be careful around Kurt. He's not the man he seems to be."

"Thanks, but I need to go. We're really busy tonight."

"I can see that. Carry on. We'll catch up later."

Sally clambered up on stage in her red stilettos. Malcolm adjusted a knob on his light board and flooded her with a spotlight as she glided toward the microphone. Removing the mic from the stand, Sally shook the cord loosely and gave Malcolm a wink. He tweaked a second knob and the mic hummed into life. Sally scratched it with her thumbnail to make sure it was on.

"Good evening, ladies and gentlemen. Welcome to the remodeled Tap Room. Doesn't it look fabulous?" She cupped her breasts and gave them a playful push. "We can all use a little work now and then." A diner snorted, and Sally laughed. "As you know, Monday night means karaoke at The Tap Room. We're delighted that you've decided to join us. Now, I know that some of you are a little shy about singing in public, but I'm hoping that once some of Steve's booze kicks in, more of you will come up and join me on stage. Until then, why don't I go first?"

She flicked the cord like a whip. "I'd like to dedicate this song to a very dear friend of mine, Lieutenant John Jarad of the Nantucket police. Hello, John. I can see you over there, hiding in the shadows. Folks, let's give John a hand for all that he does to keep us safe." She shielded her eyes from the spotlight. "And who is that very pretty young lady serving you that beer? Why, it's Miss Sarah Hawthorne from Pittsburgh, Pennsylvania. Hello, Sarah. I have to say we've certainly been hearing a lot about you, lately."

The spotlight raced across the tables. Sarah froze, exposed by the sudden brilliant light. Damn that Sally! Why couldn't she leave her alone to do her job?

Sally waited for the crowd's laughter to die down before she gave Malcolm a nod. He returned the spotlight to the stage, a violin melody began to fill the room, and Sally began to sing.

It may be true, my dear, we may never love again
But I still hold you in my dreams.
Our shared embrace, that fevered kiss
That proved what love could mean.

You may have found a new lover now
I may have found one, too.
Never forget, darling, what we once had
Our embrace, that single touch, our sweet kiss.

Sally shimmied across the stage, laughing delightedly at the audience's reaction. She pointed the mic directly at John, and then deliberately and lewdly flicked her tongue over her upper lip.

Sarah glanced down. John was blushing to the roots of his hair. "Don't mind me asking this, but is something going on between you two?"

"In her mind, not mine. Sally likes to stir things up. She always has. I can't imagine what folks are going to make of this."

"It kind of a strange feeling, isn't it? When you know you haven't done anything wrong, and people still look at you funny?"

"Point taken." He straightened his knife and fork. "Actually, I wanted to talk with you about that. Sarah, I've reviewed your statement, and I think you caught a bad bounce. I don't believe you were actively involved in Billy's homicide, but I do think Stockton is using you. You should be careful around Stockton. I don't think he's safe."

"Really?" John's admission broke through Sarah's clouded mind like rays of bright sunshine. If John believed her, then maybe everything would be okay.

"Yes. And I'm sorry if I came off badly yesterday. That wasn't my intent, but I needed to get at the truth." He swallowed. "Damn this is hard. What I'm trying to say is that I'd like to make amends. I know you have to work, but I thought we could make a date before your shift starts. I'd like to show you Nantucket, the real Nantucket, if I could."

Sarah clutched her tray as her heart soared. Was this really happening? After that fiasco with Kurt, John was giving her a second chance? "You mean, like do lunch?"

"I was thinking of something even earlier, like a picnic breakfast aboard a sailboat. How about that idea?"

"I think that sounds pretty terrific."

"Great! How about tomorrow morning? Could you be ready by nine? We could catch the tide. Or is nine o'clock still too early for you?"

"No, nine is fine." Sarah flinched. Crissakes! Now she sounded like Dr. Seuss. Why did talking to John have this effect on her? "I can be ready by nine."

He relaxed. "I'll swing by and pick you up. Don't worry about bringing a thing. I'll cover supplies. You be just ready by nine, and we'll take it from there."

"Thank you again, John. That sounds like fun." Sarah reached into her apron pocket. It was hard, but she needed to keep her eye on the essentials. "Oh, and one more thing. This is for you."

He looked up, surprised and curious. "What is it? A love note, already?"

"Nice try. I'm sorry, no. It's your check."

She cruised back to the bar with a new spring in her step. John believed her story and he had asked her out again. She was filled with fresh hope. This time she was not going to screw things up again. She slid into the waitress station, and bumped into Alien, who was busily loading her tray.

"I saw you talking to John out there. Sarah, are you in more trouble? What did he say?"

"Believe it or not, Alien, he asked me out again."

"By God, I hope you said *yes* this time!"

"I did. We're going sailing tomorrow. A picnic breakfast."

"Good girl." Alien stacked some glasses. "Now that sounds more like it. I never did like you going out with that train wreck."

There was a scuffle at the door and the sound of raised, protesting voices.

"Speak of the devil," Alien said.

The line parted and Kurt stumbled into the dining room. Kurt looked disheveled, and he was arguing with Leslie, who was furiously standing her ground.

"Sir, please! These people have been waiting in line longer than you have."

"I said I don't want a table! The bar rail is fine. I only wanted a drink." He spotted Sarah and hurried over. "Sarah! Sweetheart! Thank God I found you. We need to talk."

Alien grabbed her arm. "Don't go over there, Sarah. Seriously, he's not worth it."

"Alien, it's okay." She checked her resolve and it held firm. From now on, she was going to tackle her problems head on. "Let me see what he wants. Cover my tables, will you? I'll only be a minute."

Kurt ambled up, smiling. He wrapped his arm around her waist and guided her into the dim bathroom hallway. "How are you, sweetheart?"

"Jesus, Kurt." Sarah unwrapped his arm. "You smell like a distillery."

"So I've had a few. I deserved it. Those fuckers kept me at the station all day long. Honey, they think I killed Billy Bear. They think I ran him down."

"It was your car."

"Yes, but I didn't drive it, and I can prove it. I was with you last night. You backed me up on that, right? Isn't that what you told the police?"

Sarah felt torn by indecision. How much should she tell him? Yes, she had been in Kurt's house, but she hadn't been with him all night. Had Kurt slipped out while she slept? And how to explain the fresh cut on his arm? "Kurt, you were upstairs, alone. I was downstairs, in the den. I don't know, I'm not sure. You might have snuck out, after I fell asleep."

He gripped her elbow. "Is that what you told the police?"

"Let go of me. You're hurting my arm."

"I'm sorry." He released his grip and leaned wearily against the wall. "Sarah, you've seen the layout of my house. There's no way I could have come downstairs without you knowing it. I'm counting on you to remember that."

"Tell me this. How did you cut your arm?"

"It must've happened when that picture fell." His fingers traced the bandage under his sleeve. "We just didn't notice it at the time. You do remember that happening, right?"

"Yes, I do remember the picture falling but no, I don't remember you cutting your arm."

He pushed off the wall. "What are you saying?"

She stepped back. "I'm saying I'm confused. I'm confused because it was your car. If you didn't run Billy down, then who did? Do you even remember that you hid the car keys from me last night?"

"Ohmigod, I forgot about the keys." Kurt pulled her deeper into the hallway. "That has to be the answer. Sally is setting me up! She's the only one who has my spare keys. I gave her a set years ago, but I'll bet she still has them. She took my car, and she ran Billy down and now she's trying to frame me for it. It's the only answer that makes sense!"

"Why would Sally do that?"

"Sweetheart, you don't know Sally. She's ruthless. She thinks like a man. Sally plays by her own set of rules, and she always has. She's not afraid to do whatever it takes to get her way."

"Kurt, you haven't answered my question. Why would Sally try to frame you?"

He took a deep breath. "Something happened awhile back, something bad. Sally was a part of it, and Billy was, too. I think she killed Billy to shut him up, and to protect herself. Sally killed Billy, and now she's trying to get rid of me at the same time. This sounds exactly like something she'd do."

Sarah felt chilled by a dark well of doubt so deep, it felt subterranean. "Kurt? What was so bad that she had to kill Billy?"

"Something happened, years ago." He grabbed her wrist. "We had some trouble with a girl. I can only tell you what happened afterwards, when I woke up. Sally kept saying that everything was fine, but even then, I knew it wasn't, but I was too afraid to ask Sally what really happened, because I didn't want to know, and now she's trying to frame me for it. It's Sally, I'm telling you, it's Sally and it always has been. You've got to believe me. I'm afraid of what she'll do next!"

"You need to go to the police, Kurt. They're the only ones who can help. If Sally did kill Billy, you might be next."

"She won't do that. You don't know her." Kurt closed his eyes and shook his head. "She needs me alive to take the fall. Once the police arrest me for Billy's murder, she'll get off scot-free. I know Sally. I know the way she thinks. This is exactly what she has planned -"

"Excuse me, Sarah?"

John stood on the threshold, outlined by the dining room's slightly brighter light. "Is everything alright? I wanted to say goodnight."

Kurt stepped forward. "I've got some questions for you now, Jarad. You police are so fucking stupid. It's all right in front of your face, and you can't even see it."

"Can't see what, Stockton? What's right in front of my face?"

"Let me ask you this." Kurt dangled his keychain. "Did you find any keys in my stolen car?"

"You know we didn't. We've already talked through this."

"Did you ever wonder why? I still have my set. Did you fuckers stop to think that maybe someone else had a set of my car keys?" He pointed at Sally. "Because she does."

"Let me get this straight. You're suggesting that Sally stole your car last night, and used it to run Billy Bear down?"

"Fucking A. That's exactly what I'm suggesting."

"Alright." John crossed his arms. "I'll consider the possibility if you tell me why Sally would want to do such a thing."

"Why don't we ask her?" Kurt snapped. He pushed past and stepped into the dining room. "Sally? Could you come here a minute?"

"Certainly, Kurt. What is it?" Sally strolled over. "Hello, John, Sarah. What's up?"

Kurt stuffed his fist in his pocket. "Sally, do you still have the set of keys I gave you?"

"Keys?" Sally frowned. "Which keys?"

"You know which fucking keys! The spare set of car keys I gave you a few years back."

"No, Kurt, no." Sally regretfully shook her head. "You never gave me a spare set of car keys. You did give me a spare set of house keys, in case you ever got locked out during another one of your drunken stupors, but no, you never gave me a spare set of your car keys."

"You lying bitch!" Kurt slammed his fist against the wall. "Look at her, Jarad! She's lying straight to your face. Can't you see that?"

Sally raised both hands. Twin vertical creases appeared between her eyebrows. "No need to get violent, Kurt. What's this about?"

"Mr. Stockton believes that you possess a set of his car keys," John said.

"That is pathetic. I've said it before. I do not have a set of Kurt's car keys. I never had a set of Kurt's car keys. The man is so pickled, he couldn't possibly remember what he did or did not give me 'a few years back.' "

"I know what you're doing, you bitch! You're setting me up!"

"Calm down, Stockton."

"I will not calm down! I know what this is. You two are in this together! You're trying to set me up! But it won't work, because I didn't do anything wrong."

Sally continued to observe Kurt dispassionately as he stormed off for the bar.

"I don't know what Kurt's been telling you, John, but if he keeps this up, I will have to contact my attorney. Kurt's been a raging alcoholic for years. Now, he's starting to sound seriously unstable. If he starts spreading scandal, I will press charges." She interlaced her fingers. "Are we through here?"

"For now. I may want to talk with you later."

"I look forward to it. Enjoy your evening, darlings. I plan to." Sally smoothed her silk blouse over her hips. "Now where was I?"

Sarah released her pent-up breath. She was in awe that John had stayed so calm and so focused during such an emotional exchange. How did he do that? She felt wiped out, as limp as a dishrag. She glanced into the dining room. She wanted to stay with him, but her tables were waiting. "I'm sorry. I need to get back. Steve'll wonder where I've gone."

"I'll say good night then. See you in the morning?"

"Yes. And thank you again. I'm really looking forward to tomorrow."

She slipped back to the waitress station and retrieved her tray. A young couple was looking hopefully at newly vacated table three. Sarah straightened her shoulders. Time to get back to it. Hearing the distinct clink of glass on glass, she turned. Kurt was leaning bodily over the far end of the bar. Reaching down into the well, he fished a bottle out and snatched it up, hiding it under his sports coat. Thinking that no one had noticed, Kurt turned and headed for the door.

"Shit!" Steve scowled from the storeroom. "There he goes again. I hate it when he does that."

"Aren't you going to stop him?" she said.

"Why bother?" Steve started washing glasses. "I'll just add it to his tab, like I always do."

Sarah remembered her terror during the nightmarish drunken drive to Wauwinet. Kurt was a menace, and she would never do that again. "At least we know the streets are safe tonight. Kurt will have to grab a cab to get home."

Steve looked up. "And why is that?"

"Because the police impounded his car."

CHAPTER TWENTY SEVEN

John leaned the carton of supplies against his truck. He'd been in such a rush to get ready for their picnic that he hadn't really thought the proper execution through. He should have lowered the tailgate first before carting the groceries from the A&P. Doing it ass-backwards like this felt like he was playing a losing game of Twister. He paused long enough to laugh at himself. Why did the idea of seeing Sarah again so mess with his head? What was he afraid of? It was only a date. As he slid the carton into the truck bed, it occurred to him that he hadn't thought about Ava in weeks. John straightened up, astonished. Was that right? Was he finally cured?

His cell phone rang. Pulling it from his pocket, he recognized CJ's number.

"Good morning, CJ. What's up? I left you in charge. Couldn't you start the day without me?"

"John, you need to get out to Wauwinet, stat. Sally Poldridge is dead."

"What?" The bottom dropped out of his day. "What?"

"Yes, her cleaning lady called it in. It's bad, John. Someone beat Sally to death."

He slammed the tailgate shut, scrambling to put a base under this new emergency. "Who's with you?"

"I've got Ted and Sam. Paul is on his way. I can't find Hank. I don't know where he is."

"Lock it down, CJ. I'll be right there. Give me twenty minutes."

John ended the call and stood in the parking lot, stunned by the news. Sally was dead? How was that possible? His brain couldn't seem to process the idea. CJ said she had been beaten. He recalled the heated argument between Sally and Stockton at The Tap Room last night. Stockton, Stockton, everything always came back to Stockton. The man was a threat, but was he a killer? He needed to get to Wauwinet ASAP. Glancing up Main Street, he saw Toby directing church traffic. He waved Toby over.

"Yes, Lieutenant?"

"Come with me." John turned on his heel and ran for the Easy Street basin. "We need to get to Wauwinet. We're taking the cruiser."

"Why Wauwinet, sir?" Toby's boots drummed the dock as he ran alongside. He skidded to a halt, reaching down to tug the mooring line free. "What's happened?"

"Sally Poldridge is dead." John leapt into the boat. He flipped the blower switch and started an impatient sixty-second delay count in his head. "We've got another homicide." He gestured Toby into the boat and pushed the throttle forward, spinning the wheel to starboard as the powerful Johnson twin 250s bit in. The cruiser quickly began to plane as they roared toward the head of the harbor. John ignored the bobbing 'No Wake' signs and pushed the cruiser even harder. Waders at Jetties beach pointed as they flashed by. He was going to hear about this one. Suddenly, John remember his date with Sarah. "Shit! Toby, take the wheel."

"Yes, sir."

Toby slid into the captain's chair as John unlocked his phone. Thumbing through his contact list, John hunched his shoulder and tried to protect the speaker from the whistling wind. There was no answer as the dorm phone continued to ring. Shit! Why didn't someone pickup? His call rolled to voicemail.

"Sarah? It's John. I need to cancel our date. Something's come up." What else was there to say? John grabbed a windshield strut as Toby cranked the cruiser around Polpis. "Give me a rain check. I'm sorry, but this shit happens. It's part of the job. I'll call you later, once we get clear of it. I hope you understand."

He felt completely lame as he ended the call, but John knew he was right. He was a cop, and this was the kind of shit that happened. It was a stern rule, but duty always came first. If they were going to date, Sarah would need to learn to put up with it. John wasn't happy about it, but that's the way it was. Tapping Toby's shoulder, he took the wheel.

The shoreline raced by as the cruiser roared up to Sally's dock. John was surprised to see that where Sally's glass house was immaculate, her boathouse looked derelict, its walls missing shingles and its single window shuttered and barred. The dark boathouse door was frozen open, and he could see a small runabout moored inside. Sam was waiting for them on the rotten dock. John throttled back, and spun the wheel hard to port to fishtail the cruiser, and Toby quickly tossed Sam a line.

"This is bad business, sir." Sam slipped the line through a dock ring and tied it off. "Glad to see you. That coroner fellow's been asking for you."

"Did we find Hank yet?"

"He's here now, sir. Got in about five minutes ago."

"Good." John trotted up the slope toward Sally's house. "Establish a perimeter, Sam, and grid it. Start a ground search. Toby? Come with me."

Sam halted by the garden gate. "Yes, sir. Will do. By the way, sir. Nice legs."

John glanced down at his civilian shorts and bare knees. Crissakes! He'd forgotten what he was wearing. Everyone addressed the tension and horror of a crime scene differently, and Paul and Sam liked using humor. He was going to catch holy hell for his wardrobe choice this day.

Pocketing his sunglasses, John crossed the garden and paused at the patio door. CJ was tucked into one corner of the rumpus room. She was wearing a one-use Tyvex suit and framing a mid-range shot with her digital camera. CJ had already taped out an evidence grid, and tagged the scene with dozens of small yellow placards. Evidently, she had also drafted Hank into helping her. Hank was standing flat against a wall, grappling with a notepad and scribbling frantically. Paul was also wearing a Tyvex suit. He was pacing the perimeter of the hot tub with his hands behind his back. His forehead was puckered into a field of thoughtful wrinkles. He caught John's shadow, and looked up.

"I can already tell you she put up one helluva fight."

The carpet squelched as John stepped into the room. "Did she drown?"

"Won't know that until the autopsy. I do know that the actor beat her with a blunt object. I can see the contusions on her arms and face."

It was time. John clenched his stomach and prayed he wouldn't vomit. Sally was floating in the tub with only the side of her face and the tips of her elbows breaking the water's reflective surface. Her body bobbed gently, and her hair floated in perfect suspension around her skull like a blonde halo. Hot acid splashed the back of John's throat and he fought it down. Sally's once surgically perfect nose was broken, and her bloodshot eyes gleamed dully through the slits of her blackened eyelids.

"Did we find the weapon yet?" he asked.

"No, not yet." Paul tapped his lips with his gloved hands and frowned at the acquired taste. "I do know it was something square, with an edge to it. A section of two-by-four, mebbe?"

"How long has she been in that water?"

"Long enough for rigor to pass and decomposition to start, probably accelerated because of the temperature in the tub. Usually, a cadaver sinks as soon as the lungs fill with water. Then, once methane and hydrogen sulfide inflate the torso, the cadaver rises, trailing the head and limbs behind the rising chest, as you can see."

"Dead man's float," John said.

"Exactly." Paul *tsked* the way a knitting woman does when she drops a stitch.

"What you're really saying," CJ lowered her camera, "is that's a big bowl of germ soup."

"The girl in the bog wasn't floating face down," Toby said. "She was face up, like she was trying to swim back into the light."

"That's a solid observation, Toby." Paul reset his glasses. "Probably a secondary effect of the bog water. No oxygen in the water means no methane. That particular vic never started the decomposition process."

"Not to mention she was anchored to a cinderblock," CJ said.

"I've been dreaming about her a lot lately," Toby said. "Gives me the wicked creeps. It's like she's a mermaid, and she wants me to join her."

"Here's an odd thing, John," CJ said. "The front door was bolted, but the patio door was wide open. The alarm system was activated, but the open door didn't trigger it."

"It wouldn't. Sally never locked the patio door. It wasn't on the circuit."

CJ blinked. "And how would you know that?"

A creeping blush warmed John's neck. "It's common knowledge. Did you bring a kit? Let's get started on prints and DNA swabs before we pull her out of there."

"I'll try," CJ snapped on a pair of gloves, "but I wouldn't expect too much from this evidence, since evidently half the men on Nantucket have walked through that door."

John turned to Paul. "The housekeeper found the body? Where is she?"

"In the bedroom, lying down. It's Emily Parrish, Pilar's mom. I know she has a heart condition. I'm sure finding the body this morning came as quite a shock."

"Is someone with her?"

"Ted is in there. He's some kind of cousin."

"Aren't we all? Toby? Come with me. I'll run the interview. I want you to take notes." John rapped a knuckle against the door and entered the serene blue room. "Mrs. Parrish? It's Lieutenant Jarad. We need to ask you some questions."

"I know who you are, John Jarad. Come on in here."

An older woman built as stout as a wharf piling pushed up off the silk chaise lounge. Her face was as creased as dried salt cod, but her cocoa brown eyes were sharp. Five feet tall and nearly three feet wide, Mrs. Parrish was dressed for work in a flowered housecoat and a ruffled apron. Elastic support hose ribbed her knees. Her feet were stuffed into sensible black shoes. Her ankles overlapped her shoes and the flesh on her upper arms flapped as she struggled to rise.

"I went to primary school with your father," she said. "Oh my, but you look just like him."

"Please, Mrs. Parrish, don't get up." John pulled a chair forward and acknowledged Ted sitting nearby on a gilded boudoir chair. Toby leaned in the doorway and held his notebook ready.

"I don't mind taking a load off." She cocked her thumb at the rumpus room. "I will say it was some kind of shock, finding her like that in there this morning."

"I'm sure it was. We appreciate any information you can give us."

"Ask away." She settled her hands across her stomach. "Since evidently that's what I'll be doing this morning instead of scrubbing floors, which will make for a nice change."

John was surprised by her cavalier attitude. Evidently, Mrs. Parrish wasn't going to mourn her dead employer. He tailored his approach accordingly. "What time did you arrive for work this morning?"

"Seven-thirty sharp, same as always. I'm not complaining, mind you, but I do have to say it cuts into my day, getting started so early, but you know how it goes." She rubbed her thumb and fingers together, making a *money* gesture. "She liked keeping the house tidy, and she never slept in. Liked to go for a run first thing in the morning while it was still fresh. Led herself quite a life, you know, and not always sleeping alone with just one man—or one woman, neither—if you catch my drift."

"So we've heard."

"You'd be surprised at some of the cars I found parked outside her door some mornings." Mrs. Parrish pulled a cheap penny notebook from her apron pocket. "I've kept a list of the license plates of all the cars I found parked in the driveway when I came to work. You'd be surprised to learn who some of these fine folks were. Funny her car's not out there now."

John couldn't believe his luck. "We'll need a copy of that notebook for our investigation."

She clutched the notebook to her bosom. "Oh, no. This is mine. I won't give it up. This was privately meant, and something I was only doing for myself, as a hobby. Gossip does get around. I wouldn't want word of my little hobby getting out. It's going to be hard enough finding another job at my age, but I will say I do know when to mind my tongue, not like some others I could mention, like that nasty Enid Gardiner, for one."

John held out his hand. "We'll keep it strictly confidential, and return it to you once we've made a copy. You have my word."

She slowly handed the notebook over. "Don't forget that is my property."

John flipped through the pages. There were dozens of plate numbers, some of them out of state. There was no way to narrow this down in a hurry. Direct questions would be quicker. "Did you find anyone parked in the driveway this morning?"

"No I didn't, and that was strange, and I got here right on time, too. You won't find a tardy bone in me. I'm as steady as the tide."

John passed the notebook to Toby, who handled it with the awe befitting the Holy Grail.

"How long have you worked for Sally Poldridge?" John said.

"Ever since that Marty fellow died, and she moved into this fine house.

Sally was no housekeeper, no sir, that was plain enough to see from the very beginning, and she had no interest in it, neither. Kept herself busy with other interests, if you catch my meaning, but I was happy to do the housework. She was a good employer, you know–fair, and always paying in cash like I asked for and never a problem about getting my money, neither, and right on time. Not like some of these other rich folks I do work for! You wouldn't believe how tight some of them are with their money–cheap skinflints! They want you to work for next to nothing, and they hold onto your pay and make you practically beg for it like you didn't earn it fair and square in the first place–and don't never take a check from them, neither, not without calling the bank first to make sure that the check is good. Oh my, yes! I've learned from my mistakes. It's cash, nothing but cash, cash on the barrelhead because those checks do bounce, but I have to say Sally wasn't like that, no, sir!" She paused for breath. "Always paid me in cash and never a complaint out of her about it, neither, if I missed a day or two because of my sore knees." She rubbed the offending body part with her roughened hands. "Rheumatoid arthritis is such a sad trial for a women in my profession, but easy work it was here, you know, mostly sheets and towels, if you catch my drift."

"Thank you, Mrs. Parrish, that's helpful," John interjected. He felt swamped by the tsunami of information. He checked to see how Toby was keeping up with it. Apparently, Toby had mastered some competent form of shorthand, because he stood poised and ready for the next informational onslaught.

"Was the front door was locked when you arrived for work this morning?"

"Locked up tight as a clam, as always."

Mrs. Parrish pulled a key ring from her pocket. John was surprised to see that the heavy steel ring held literally hundreds of keys of all shapes and sizes. The keychain looked like it weighed five pounds. Judging from the evidence before his eyes, Mrs. Parrish had been entrusted with a house key to half the homes on the island.

"Like I said, see, I usually start dusting upstairs, but this morning I heard that tub bubbling away the minute I stepped through the door, so I came down here first to turn it off. No sense in paying for electricity you don't need, as pricey as it is, and that's when, that's when–" She shuddered. "That's when I found her floating in that tub, dead and drowned something horrible with her beautiful face all smashed in and this room busted up like you see, and I called you police."

"You did exactly right, Mrs. Parrish." John placed his elbows on his knees. "Can you think of anyone who might have done this horrible thing?"

A sly, foxy look flitted over her face. "I'm sure there's a list as long as my arm of some *wives* who might have done it, but if I had to put a man at the top of my list, I'd look no further than that artist fellow who lives next door, that Kurt Stockton. He's been nothing but trouble to her for years, plus he's one of them crazy drunks that gets mean whenever he drinks too much, and since the man lives to drink, that's pretty much all of the time." Her fingers rubbed her forearms. "Lord knows I've had to clean up more than one of his messes after he's pitched one of his fits. I never did know why she put up with it, but I think mebbe they knew each other from back before when they were young or sommat. Mebbe that explains it, but I will tell you what every single time that man got himself in trouble, he'd come running over here begging for her help." She shook a finger at the room. "Wrecked his car more than once, too, don't you know, and she had to help him with that Irish girl from next door when he got her in trouble, too. Sally sent her packing back home to Ireland, and God only knows what she did when she got there. I know those Catholics are wicked strict about that sort of thing." The curls in her perm bounced with indignation. "I don't understand these men. My husband Henry led himself a wild kind of life before he took his vows and settled down with me, but he's walked the good path ever since, God bless him. Sometimes, I swear, some of these men think with their dicks."

Ted ripped a snort at her remark, and even Toby cracked a smile. Pushing out of the doorway, Toby stepped fully into the bedroom for the first time. Catching sight of the portrait gallery hanging over his head, he turned. Amazement registered on Toby's face as his eyes traveled from row to row, taking in the array of painted images. Suddenly, his jaw dropped, and all the color drained from his face. The notebook fell from his limp fingers to the floor.

"I don't get it. Sir? What does that mean?" Toby stared at the portrait of the girl riding her bike down the country lane. "I swear that's my sister Bess up there. How can that be?"

"That's one from that painter fellow I've been telling you about," Mrs. Parrish said. "He painted most of the pictures you see up there. I have to say I have a damned hard time cleaning all of them frames, too. Can't lift the sweeper near 'em."

Toby bumped into the bed as he stepped back to gain a better view. "I swear to God, sir. That's my sister Bess. It has to be Bess in that picture."

"It could be almost anyone, Toby," John said. The mind could play tricks, and people saw what they wanted to see. "Stockton didn't paint her face."

"But that's the exact outfit Bess was wearing the day she was killed. It can't be a co incidence, sir. It can't be! Stockton must have seen Bess that day. How else would he have known how to paint her clothing that way?" Toby scooped up the notebook and rapidly flipped through the pages. He turned on Mrs. Parrish so quickly that she squeaked in fear. "You said

Stockton kept wrecking his car. When was that? When did Stockton wreck his car?"

"Just about every summer, like as not. Probably drunk as a skunk when he did it, too. You cops should've taken his license away years ago. Terrible thing, drinking and driving. Gets people killed that way."

"Think about it, sir!" Toby turned. He looked half-crazed. "Stockton is the one who ran Bess down. He's the one who killed my sister!"

"Toby, we don't know that." John pulled the CSO away from the terrible wall of pictures. "You need to listen to me. Maybe Stockton did, but that's not why we're here today. Toby! We need to focus on this investigation. We need to build a case that will stand up in court. I swear, we'll reopen your sister's case once we're clear of this one, but we need to collect the evidence for this one, first."

"But, sir! I know Stockton did it!"

Going off half-cocked never did an investigation any good. John scrambled to come up with a reason to remove Toby from the red-hot center of this one. "Go help Sam search the grounds. That's an order."

Toby's face turned beet red. "By God, sir! Don't do this to me. I'm not leaving!"

"That's a direct order, CSO Talbot. I will not let you jeopardize this investigation."

Toby stood, ashen-faced as he struggled with the conflict of obeying a direct command or following up on the fate of his sister. Duty won out. His shoulders slumped as Toby firmed his mouth into a grim line. "Yes, sir. Lieutenant, sir. I understand completely, sir."

They both looked up as CJ entered the doorway. "John, we need you out here. I think we found the murder weapon."

They crossed the littered rumpus room and headed out the patio door. Sam, Hank, and Paul were huddled in a circle, gazing at an empty liquor bottle cached in the thicker side yard grass. Sam looked up, and beamed.

"Found this in my sweep, sir. The grass under it is still green, barely crushed. The bottle still has blood smears on it."

"Possible DNA from saliva, too." CJ lifted her camera. She fired off a string of long-range shots to establish the chain of custody, and looked hopeful. "We might raise some prints off of it, too, even with the dew."

"They might be right, John," Paul agreed. "This bottle would fit the contusions I mentioned earlier."

"Good solid glass," Sam noted. "Funny it didn't break. The label says it's not for retail sale. Must've come from a private club, or a bar."

"Shit," CJ said. Using a pen, she lifted the bottle, and dropped it into a paper evidence bag. "I hate even saying this, but Steve Barnett owns a bar, and he was Sally's ex-husband. Most homicides on women are committed by the men they know from a domestic situation."

Steve Barnett? Really? John knew the barman reasonably well, they were fishing buddies. Had Sally's taunting behavior finally pushed Steve over the edge? Could Steve have battered and killed Sally so viciously? John recalled the previous night's argument between Sally and Kurt Stockton. Stockton seemed the more likely homicide candidate, but the bottle evidence tipped the scale, because only Steve had both motive and access to a retail bar supply. In any case, it was time to cover the bases. "Email me that barcode shot, CJ, then take Ted and bring Stockton in for questioning. By God, we'll get to the bottom of this. But watch yourselves! I'm not sure Stockton is stable. Paul? Get Sally out of that tub. I'll need your report ASAP. Council will go bat shit crazy once they hear about this one. Sam, Hank, lock the site down and head back to the station. I want your reports on my desk by noon. Toby and I will take the cruiser back to port."

"Why?" CJ coughed. "Where are you two going?"

John studied the bottle lying in the grass. "We're going to talk to Steve Barnett."

CHAPTER TWENTY EIGHT

For the tenth time in as many minutes, John touched the copy of the bottle's bar code in his pocket to make sure he hadn't dropped the bit of paper in the street. They had swung by the station long enough for him to change into his lieutenant's uniform, print the email file CJ had sent, and retrieve his service piece. John had felt so unsure of Steve's innocence that he had strapped his .32 ankle holster on as backup, too, just in case.

"What's the plan, sir?" Toby asked.

John felt fissured by doubt. They were standing outside The Tap Room, finalizing their approach. Every investigative entry was different, and you needed a Plan B in case things went awry, because when things did go wrong, they went wrong fast. Even though they had fished for stripers too many times to count, how well did he really know Steve? Could he have murdered Sally? Did he hate his ex-wife that much? This case was making John feel paranoid about the very people he thought he knew.

"Follow my lead. Keep your eyes open, and keep on your toes. Make sure you know where all the exits are located." Pushing on the door, John stepped inside.

Steve was hunched over a newspaper spread open across the bar. He looked up and, lowering his coffee mug, tapped the newspaper with a finger. "They didn't waste any time. Special edition already hit the street. At least they spelled my name right." He reached for the coffee pot. "I was wondering when you'd show up, John. Fancy a cup?"

"Yes, please. Pour me a big one." John slid onto a barstool. "It's been a rough morning."

"So I've heard." Steve filled a white china mug and slid it over. He raised the pot. "Toby?"

"None for me, sir." Toby scanned the empty room. "No, thank you."

"Alrighty then. John, let's not be awkward about this. Sally's dead and I'm in a pickle, and I know it." Pulling a bottle of Irish whiskey off a shelf, Steve slopped a dollop in his mug. He used the bottle to gesture his next

220

question.

"None for me, thanks, no. I'm on the clock."

"Figured as much," Steve shrugged. "I'd appreciate it if you told it to me straight. Are you here to arrest me?"

"No. We just wanted to ask a few questions."

"But still, this is official police business?"

"Yes, I'm afraid it is."

"Fair enough. Let's get to it. I've done nothing wrong, and I've got nothing to hide. What do you need to know?"

John pulled the bar code from his pocket. He flattened it against the bar. "We need to know if this bottle came from your bar."

"Easy enough to check. Is that from the bottle that killed her?"

John felt a tightening in his guts. They hadn't released the bottle information yet. "Where did you hear that?"

Steve shrugged again. "In the Hub, when I picked up the paper. The woman at the counter said a liquor bottle was used to beat Sally to death. I'm Sally's ex-husband, and I run a bar. Two plus two equals four. It doesn't take much math to know that you'd be in to check on me." Steve flattened the creased paper between his palms. Moving to the storeroom, he held the bar code under a red laser scanner and then checked an inventory list on a clipboard. "Yep. It's one of mine. Case lot 046B-7, received on May the eighth of this year." He slid the bar code back across the bar using his fingertips. "Would it do any good to say I saw Kurt Stockton steal that bottle out of my well on Monday night?"

John felt an electric snap of possibility. Had Stockton stolen the bottle? Was he Sally's killer? That tidbit of information changed everything, as motive and means re-aligned. "Did anyone else see Stockton take it?"

"Sarah did. She was standing right next to me. She'd remember seeing Stockton take it. We even joked about it."

"I'll follow up with her. Do you have an alibi for Monday night?"

Steve flushed an angry red. "I wasn't aware that I needed one. Besides, that's a tricky question. I'd rather not say, if I don't have to. There's a lady friend involved. I'd rather keep her out of this if I can. She's in the middle of a nasty custody battle over her kids, and her future ex-husband is a real dick. I wouldn't want to drag her into any more trouble."

"We'll do our best to keep it quiet, but we really do need to know where you were."

"Ma'am?" Toby pushed on the swinging doors. "Why don't you come out here and join us?"

"He was with me." Leslie stepped into the dining room. She looked reproving and furious. "Steve Barnett was with me all Monday night, if that's really any of your business."

"Honey, you don't need to say anything-"

"Yes, I do." Leslie slid her arm around Steve's waist and raised her chin. "We haven't done anything wrong. I separated from my husband months before I started dating this good man, and I'm not afraid to say that in front of anyone. Steve was with me all Monday night from the minute we closed until the first thing on Tuesday, when we started prepping the kitchen. I hope my word is good enough for you, John Jarad."

"Sweetheart, thank you for that, but it really doesn't matter. I'm pretty much hosed either way. Sally put me through the wringer once before, and even if John does find her killer, people are still going to point me out because I'm her ex-husband. The funny thing is, anyone who knows me, really knows me, knows that I could never have killed Sally. I loved her. In a way, I still do."

Leslie dropped her arm and stepped back.

"Yes, I still do," Steve repeated. "I know that sounds nuts, because I'm the one who fucked it all up, but it's the truth. Sally could never forgive me for it, but I know, and she knew, too, that losing Sally was the biggest mistake of my life." He wiped his eyes with his fingertips. "Do you remember Sally from when she was young, John? When Sally was still in high school?"

"No. She was in my brother Pete's grade."

"Oh, that's right. Pete Jarad. I know him. Nice guy." Steve closed his eyes. "You should have seen Sally then. She was the most beautiful thing you ever saw. Dressed in her tennis whites, out on the court, all slim and tanned, Sally looked like an angel come to earth." He reopened his eyes and blinked the memory away. "Sally always did get a lot of attention from the guys, and from some of the dads, too, even when she was only fourteen. Sally was an angel, a pure, pure angel, and she said she loved me."

"Sally Poldridge was a cunt, and a bitch, and you men were always too stupid to see it," Leslie snapped. "She loved causing trouble and she knew *exactly* what she was doing. That bitch is laughing at all of us from Satan's side in Hell, and that's right where she belongs. At least Satan should be happy now. He got his pet bitch back."

"Jesus, Leslie! That's a little harsh, don't you think? Sally's dead."

"And good riddance to her is all I have to say."

"I'll need statements from you both," John quickly interrupted. Sally's venom was still reaching out to cripple good folks from beyond the grave. Who would it poison next? "I'll need to see you at the station later today, and Steve, you'll need to tell us of any plans you make to leave the island."

"I'm not going anywhere, John. Nantucket is my home. I've weathered worse than this before." Steve reached for Leslie, but she avoided his arm. "Honey? What's wrong?"

"Pardon me." Leslie snapped a bar towel over her shoulder. "Nothing's wrong. I need to get back to work, since evidently that's all I have going for me here."

Poor Steve. John knew Steve well enough to know when the guy was lying, and nothing in their interview had even hinted at an untruth. But Leslie? John didn't know her at all. He needed to dig a little deeper before he completely trusted her alibi. But what if their combined statements held up? If they could prove their alibi, then that threw suspicion back on Stockton. It had been obvious last night that Sally was willing to give Stockton up to the police as the suspect for Billy's murder. Had Stockton's protests last night about Sally been true? Had she been setting Stockton up as the fall guy? And if so, had Stockton decided to strike first, and take Sally out while he still could?

It was easy enough to check on this new line of reasoning. John pulled out his cell phone and speed-dialed CJ's number. She picked up on the very first ring.

"Did you get him?" he asked. "Did you arrest Stockton?"

"No, we didn't." Frustration added a vibrant timbre to CJ's voice. "Stockton's not at his house. Ted and Sam triple-checked it. I'm at his studio on the Wharf now. It's locked up tighter than a drum. John, we don't know where Stockton is. We've BOLO'd the ports. Where could he be?"

"Tell the team to keep looking. Stockton is looking like our person of interest." John rang off. With a sickening sense of dread, he realized that in his zeal to pursue the investigation, he had failed to deliver a single word of warning to the one person who mattered the most. "Where's Sarah?"

"She should be upstairs, in her room." Steve followed him around the corner of the bar. "Her shift doesn't start until four-thirty. Why?"

"I need to apologize. I broke a date. Toby, give me a minute. I'll be right back."

"Sure thing, Lieutenant," Toby grinned.

John stiff-armed the double doors and sprinted across the foul alley. Somehow, in the midst of all this investigative chaos, he needed to find Sarah, to make things right again. His feelings for her had morphed. He couldn't begin to imagine a future without her in it. "Sarah!" he shouted, running down the hall. "Sarah?"

The woman from Altar Rock—Alien, that was it—sat on a bed in the last room, painting her toenails blue. "Hello, handsome. Sarah's not here." She batted her eyelashes. "Is there something I could do for you?"

"Where is she? Where's Sarah?"

She noted his confusion. "She said she was going to the art supply store. Why?"

"Can you text her?" He pointed to her cell phone. "Tell her to meet me here?"

"I would if Sarah had a phone. The house phone is all she ever uses. Hey, what's going on?"

"I need to find her. If Sarah comes back, tell her to stay put. Ask her to call me." John wrestled his spinning thoughts back into some kind of order. "Where is this art store?"

"Somewhere on Old South Wharf, I think."

Premonition rattled John's bones like a tremor. Stockton was out there, at liberty, roaming free. He needed to find Sarah, to wrap her in his arms, to know that she was safe. Fate could blast pathetic human hopes in the blink of an eye, and John feared that he was already too late.

CHAPTER TWENTY NINE

Sarah quickly crossed to the sunny side of the street to avoid a pair of dog handlers who held a half a dozen wiggling charges on a spider web leash.

"Oops! Make way. Sorry!" The red-haired girl in leggings said, "We're not really in control of this flea circus, I'm afraid."

"Not a problem," she replied easily.

"When my sister called this morning, I couldn't believe she was dead," her partner continued shrilly. "You know that bitch only got what she deserved -"

The day was getting on. Sarah sipped her vanilla latte and paused to admire the morning sky. It was a clear cerulean, such a contrast from the persistent Pittsburgh overcast she knew as Pantone 442. Bright sunlight was shining over the tops of the buildings across the street. The sun had already burned the dew off the mossy brick sidewalk under the elms.

It was a perfect day for a sail on Nantucket Sound, but that wasn't going to happen. Alien had been waiting for her when Sarah had returned to their room from her shower.

"Hey, girlfriend. Bad news. John called. He had to cancel. Something came up."

Sarah had felt torpedoed by doubt. Was it a real emergency, or had John decided that she was a load of trouble that he didn't need? She had hoped that they understood each other a little better than that, but men were fickle. In any case, Sarah had shaken those bleak thoughts off. She was through being a pawn in someone else's drama. She couldn't control what other people did, but she could control her responses, and she was determined not to fall back into the pit of despair. She would find something else fun to do.

She had considered the ninety bucks stashed in her duffle, and decided it was time for some retail therapy. What did she want to buy? A new purse, or a pair of fun, kicky sandals, perhaps? A suggestion suddenly sprang to her mind that was so perfect, she sighed. She would start buying her collection of new sable brushes. It was time to start painting again.

That decision had led Sarah to the art supply store this morning. She tossed her empty cup into a curbside recycle bin, and picked her way across the buckled sidewalk. A tinny bell rang as the shop door opened. Kurt paused on the stoop, and when he saw her he laughed.

"What the hell! Instant karma. Here's the one person I most wanted to see."

"Kurt! What are you doing here?"

"I needed more flake white." He scratched his day's growth of beard. He also sported a new war wound, a fresh purple bruise on his forearm. "Can't do any new work without it. What I really need, though, is a Bloody. Too bad the bars aren't open yet." He trotted down the steps. "Last night was a disaster. I don't know what your policeman boyfriend is up to, but he's barking up the wrong tree. I had absolutely nothing to do with Billy's death."

"You know that's because they found your car at the crime scene. We've been through this."

"I do know that, but that was Sally's doing, not mine." Kurt slyly pulled a keychain from his pocket. "Turnabout is fair play. I took Sally's car last night. Woke up in it on Jettie's beach this morning." He massaged his neck. "I don't recommend sleeping in cars. Leave that for the teenagers. They're more flexible."

He glanced at the Jaguar parked in the alley. "I wanted to talk to you, Sarah, but let me put this stuff in the trunk first. Somehow, I have to convince you that I'm an innocent man."

"You don't need to convince me, Kurt, you need to convince the police. Like I said, it was your car they found."

"No, no, no." Kurt popped the trunk. "You're still talking about Billy. I'm not worried about that. Even the police know that I didn't kill Billy. No, I'm worried about Sally now. Sure, we had our differences, but Sally was a beautiful woman. I'm an artist. I cherish beauty. Beating Sally like that was the act of an animal."

What the hell was Kurt talking about now? "What do you mean, beat Sally?"

"You don't know about Sally yet?" He whispered, slowly closing the trunk.

Sarah felt a sudden chill. Kurt was staring at her, his eye sockets as hollow as a railway tunnel. Looking into their depths, she saw something inhuman twitching in there. She was looking at a monster. She had seen this before.

"You don't know. You don't know. You don't know." Kurt's words rustled like leaves before a sudden summer storm. He leaned against the car. "Sarah, can I trust you with my life?" He closed his eyes and shuddered. "I love you like I've never loved another woman before. I see you in my dreams. There is something about you that is still pure. You still believe in hope." He leaned back and dragged his fingers down his face. "There is so much crap in my head but Katie, I swear to you, if you go with me I could start over. We could go places most people only dream of. I know people, powerful people, in Europe, Dubai, in Asia. We could rule the art world. We could be the next Picasso and Marie-Thérèse, but I need you, Katie, to be my muse. My beautiful and incomparable muse."

Kurt was insane. He didn't even know who she was anymore. Oddly, instead of fear or panic, Sarah felt a crystalline sort of calm she couldn't explain. Was it shock? In any case, a line had been drawn in the sand, and it was a line she would never cross again, because this time she knew where she stood.

"You beat Sally to death," Sarah said.

"No, I did not!" Kurt leapt up. "I only went over there to talk to her, to make Sally see reason, to make her stop lying." He stroked the bruise on his arm. "But she said she was going to feed me to the pigs. She got hysterical, so I slapped her." He stared at his hands. "I slapped her, and she wasn't hurt then, no, no, not really, but she wiped her nose and then she sneered at me. She sneered at me. *'I've got you now. This makes it assault. Everything you paint from now on belongs to me.'* That's when I hit her. I hit her, and I hit her, and I hit her again, until she shut up."

"You killed Sally, Kurt. You killed her. There's no getting around that."

He looked up. "So that's the way it is? Sally didn't mean anything to me, but I need you."

Sarah felt the power of conviction sparkle through to her fingertips. Maybe something good had come from surviving Mason, after all. She had learned to stay super calm, and to reason against Mason's madness. Would that work on Kurt, too? They were on an island, thirty miles to sea. Where could Kurt go? She had to hope that somehow, John would find them.

"You need to talk to the police, Kurt," she said. "It's the only way this will stop. You can't get away. They'll be watching the airport, and the ferries."

He laughed mirthlessly. "I'll bet those fuckers never thought about using a boat! Sally left a nice little runabout all gassed up in her boathouse. I've already borrowed her car. Sally won't mind if we take her boat, too, because, well, because she's dead."

He had called her bluff. Sarah stepped back. "There's only one thing wrong with that, because I'm not going anywhere with you."

"Oh yes, yes, you are." He pulled a steel canvas cutter from his pocket. Kurt slid the lethal razor blade open with his thumb. "Get in the car, bitch. This time we're going all the way. I'm never letting you leave me again."

CHAPTER THIRTY

John raced for the art supply store. His lungs were on fire with the effort, but he wasn't going to stop running until he knew that Sarah was safe. Toby kept pace with him step for step as they dodged through the moving cars and SUVs on the authority of their uniforms.

"Stockton is our killer," John said. "Sarah Hawthorne is in danger. We need to find her, make sure she's safe."

"Where are we headed, sir? Stockton's studio?"

"No. CJ checked it. Sarah's at some art supply store on South Wharf." John skidded to a halt, unable to believe his eyes. Sarah and Stockton were in Sally's white convertible, making a left turn onto Federal street.

"Bugger me, I never thought of that! He's using Sally's car to get around." John grabbed his cell phone. "Watch the Jag. I'm calling for backup. We'll never catch them on foot."

"They've turned left on Orange Street, sir. They must be heading for Wauwinet. It's the only place they can go."

"We'll get there faster by boat. Tina? Stockton's taken Sarah Hawthorne hostage. He's driving Sally Poldridge's white Jaguar convertible. Pull the plate, and share it with the team. Tell them to meet us at Stockton's house in Wauwinet. Exercise every precaution. Stockton may be armed. Toby's with me. We'll switch to ship-to-shore, once we get to the boat."

They ran for the boat basin, and raced down the floating commercial dock. It jounced with their every step. John jumped in the cruiser, cursed the blower, and fired the twin engines up. Toby snapped the lines free of the dock rings and leapt aboard as the propellers bit deep. John spun the wheel, and the cruiser roared out of the basin toward the inner harbor.

Toby clung to an aluminum strut like a limpet. He had to shout to be heard over the noise of the twin engines. "I know Stockton's a killer, sir. I stopped by Fink's last night. Stockton brought his car in for service six years ago. Stockton said he hit a deer, but they bondo'd his fender and polished red paint off his hood. That paint came from Bess's bike, sir, I'd bet my life on it."

"I told you to leave that case alone, Toby, until we could tackle it together."

"But it'll help us get Stockton, sir. We have to stop him. We have to."

"We are going to stop him, but we need to make sure Sarah is safe first." John thumped the throttle with the heel of his hand, hoping for even more speed. Cranking the volume control on the radio, he reached for the handset. "Tina? Where the hell is my backup?"

"They've passed Monomoy, sir." Her voice crackled over the connection. "ETA, nine minutes."

"Remind them to lock the Wauwinet gate. Seal off land access. I want Stockton penned in."

"Roger that."

The prow started to toss spray as they roared around Pocomo Point, and John turned the wiper blades on. Pocomo beach was a popular spot for kite-boarders. The last thing he wanted to do was to run one of them down in his hurrying need to reach Wauwinet.

The landscape began to flatten out. He caught intermittent glimpses of Wauwinet Road on the right.

"I don't see their car anymore, Lieutenant," Toby said.

"Neither do I."

The color of the water in the harbor shifted from green to golden yellow. John hated to do it, but he powered down. The cruiser needed at least thirty inches of water to clear the bottom, and he could see the sand coming up to meet them. If they grounded the cruiser on a sandbar at top speed, the boat would flip. Pointing the bow at the shoreline, John scanned Stockton's property for signs of life. Stockton's house looked deserted. He checked his watch.

"Where the hell did they go? There's no way we beat them here. Stockton had a head start."

Toby pointed. "They're over at the Poldridge place, sir. I can see the Jag."

John dropped the cruiser into reverse and noted with satisfaction that CJ and Ted had arrived. Two speeding units were cruising down the shell lane, lights flashing. His satisfaction quickly faded when he noted that both cars were kicking up plumy dust trails that could be seen for miles. They had lost the element of surprise. Stockton would know they were coming.

"Toby, when I go up to the house, I want you to stay with the boat."

"But, sir!"

"That's not open for discussion. You're unarmed. I can't cover you and take care of this situation at the same time."

"Then let me have your backup piece, sir," Toby pleaded. "I know you have one." He squared his jaw. "I'm either a member of the force, or I'm not. Which is it going to be?"

Toby had a point. He had a carry permit, and he had certainly earned his place on the force, first with The Whistler capture, and now with this response.

"Take the wheel." John unsnapped his ankle holster. Checking to make sure the clip was secure, he handed over his .32.

Toby tucked the gun in his waistband. "Thank you for trusting me with this, sir. You won't regret it."

"You're still staying with the boat," John said. "We'll deal with any CSO fallout later."

Toby fishtailed the cruiser against Sally's decrepit dock. John tilted his sidearm forward and releasing his holster lock. He was through taking chances. Sarah was at risk. He would put Stockton down without question if needed. Keeping his knees bent, John rode the lapping wake, and clambered onto the rotten dock boards.

Cupping the Sigma with both hands, he rolled his weight forward until his thighs took the strain and his balance felt right. CJ and Ted had blocked the driveway. All of the action was now trapped inside Sally's house. John took a steadying breath, and released it slowly. "Cover me, Toby. I'm heading up."

"Yes, sir." Toby dropped the cruiser into an idling neutral, and climbed onto the dock. He ran a line loosely through a rusty dock ring, holding the line in one hand and the .22 in the other. "Be careful up there, sir."

"You stay put." John focused his attention on the path leading up to Sally's house. Sarah was in that house now, at the mercy of a monster he had unleashed. He was fully in the zone, and he locked his resolve. He was going to walk into that house, win this situation, and bring Sarah out alive. He had never felt so intensely focused before in his life. Raising the Sigma, John stepped forward.

The oar swept out of the doorway, and slammed into the side of his head. He was blinded by an explosion of pain as bolts of lightening flashed across his eyes. The Sigma dropped from his suddenly nerveless fingers, thumping a two-beat as it hit the dock. John dropped solidly to his knees and toppled over, landing on his shoulder, hard. Paralyzed and helpless, he rolled off the dock into the harbor with a splash.

Spitting saltwater off his tongue, John struggled to rise. Toby was still frozen on the dock in a half-crouch, holding the line to the bobbing cruiser in his hand as Stockton stepped out of the darkened doorway. Stooping quickly, Stockton retrieved the fallen Sigma. Toby dropped the line with a thump and straightened. Toby's eyes looked as wide as saucers. He raised the .32.

"No, I really don't think so," Stockton said. And he fired.

The sound of the shot echoed across the water. The impact shoved

Toby off his feet. He stumbled and fell back into the boat, both arms outstretched. Blood burst from the gaping wound in the center of Toby's chest. The cruiser bucked sideways under his sudden weight, and the momentum kept Toby going. He skidded along the deck until he collapsed against the transom.

John groaned. He needed to get to his feet! Saltwater seared his lungs, and his whole right side felt unresponsive and numb. His feet scrabbled futilely for purchase against the murky bottom. He continued to flounder as Stockton reached back into the boathouse and dragged Sarah out into the light. She was trying to fight, but Stockton had duct taped her hands together and taped her mouth shut. Stockton threw her bodily into the boat. Sarah bounced off a chair and fell out of sight and Stockton jumped in after her. Wrenching the wheel around, he shoved the throttle forward, and the cruiser roared in response.

Ted ran onto the dock, aiming his Glock for a kill shot, but Stockton ducked low over the wheel and gave Ted nothing to aim at. Ted howled in frustration as the cruiser sped away.

The cruiser's wake pushed John underwater, and everything turned seaweed green. John was helpless to resist it. There was a sudden, tremendous splash, and he felt grappled by a bear.

"I've got you now, sir." Ted gripped him in a ferocious fireman's carry. He hauled John bodily ashore. "Take it easy, sir."

"No." John rolled over. His brain was still buzzing, but he could flex his fingers again. He made it to his knees. "We've got to stop them. We've got to go."

CJ jumped off the dock onto the sand. She knelt, and examined the bloody welt already swelling over his left eye. "John, you've done enough. Stockton took the cruiser. The Coast Guard cutter will pick them up in the Sound."

"No." John stood. His legs were quivering, but he was back on his feet. "He's got Sarah. He shot Toby. I'm going to get that sonofabitch." He pointed at Sally's runabout moored in the boathouse slip. "We'll take that one."

Ted did a quick double-take. "Fuckin' A, Lieutenant!" He roared. "Semper Fi!"

CHAPTER THIRTY ONE

Sarah couldn't breathe. She gagged at the coppery smell of all of the blood. She was lying in a hot pool of it, and her clothing was soaked. What had Kurt done? He had killed the young cop from the station. Toby? That was it.

She ripped the duct tape off her mouth, and spat out the dusty burlap sack trying to clear her tongue. Kurt was focused on the horizon. Using her teeth, Sarah started to shred the tape that bound her hands.

"We just need to get to New York," Kurt muttered. "That's all we need to do. Get to New York and hop a plane. Hop a plane, and those fuckers will never catch us."

She twisted her hands free and scrambled to her feet. Kurt caught her movement from the corner of his eye. He swiveled the captain's chair, and leveled the Sigma at her head. It was like looking down the Fort Pitt tunnel.

"My, my, my, my dear. You do look a fright. Why don't you come up here and join me?"

Sarah was sticky with blood, and she stuck to the upholstery when she sat. The radio emitted a burst of static, and then a woman's voice. "Dispatch! Officer down! Notify the Coast Guard. Block the harbor at Brant Point. Stockton shot CSO Talbot. He's taken the cruiser. He has Sarah Hawthorne hostage. Consider Stockton armed and dangerous. Repeat that. A&D. Warn them to take every precaution."

"Roger that." The radio clicked. "Standby."

Sarah's heart quavered. What about John? They hadn't mentioned him. Was he alright?

"Block Brant Point, my ass!" Kurt laughed. "Come and get me, motherfuckers! They'll never be able to scramble in time. Have fun catching us out in the Sound."

A commercial trawler loomed ahead. *T. GARZA & SONS* was painted on its red side in bold white capital letters. The trawler crawled to a stop, and with a loud, clanking, mechanical hum, it began to lower its triangle spars and to set its nets.

Kurt bolted upright and peered over the windscreen. "What the fuck does that Portagee think he's doing? He can't set his nets in here! He's still inside the harbor–wait a second, I know what he's doing, but it won't work!" Kurt cranked the wheel one hundred-eighty degrees and spun the cruiser on its tail as backwash slopped over the transom. "Go ahead and block the harbor, motherfucker! I bet you never thought to cover the spillway."

Sarah clamped her jaw shut so hard she heard her teeth crack. Kurt wasn't going to get away, because he wasn't from Nantucket. He hadn't heard about the new spillway breakwaters installed over the winter, because he spent that season in Connecticut. It was within her power to make Kurt pay for all of the evil he had done. All she needed to do was to find the courage to not say a word.

She eased her fingers under her thighs, and sat on her hands. He wasn't going to get any warning from her. Kurt was a killer, and he was about to meet up with some very concrete justice when he tried to run through the spillway. She tried not to think of what that meant for her, too.

"You're going to enjoy meeting my friends," he shouted. "Or I should say they're going to enjoy meeting you. Sweetheart, I'm going to teach you some of my darker tricks. It should be quite a show. Hell! I might even sell tickets."

Sarah began to weep. Kurt was such a monster. How had things gotten so messed up? In any case, it would all be over soon.

She looked at Toby's body, huddled against the transom. Toby was dead, and he was even younger than she was. Where was the justice in that? It was such a waste, such a sad, sad, waste. "I'm so sorry, Toby. This was all my fault."

Toby opened his eyes at the sound of his name. A bubble of bright blood burst across his teeth. "Jump," he wheezed. "You have to jump."

Even as he said it, the first pair of crimson warning buoys flashed by. They bobbed madly in the cruiser's reckless wake. The spillway entrance was only seconds ahead. Sarah could already see the sluggish ocean rolling through the concrete gates in heavy green waves.

"Jump," Toby repeated. "Jump for him."

There was no time to think any of this through. It was now or never. Gathering her strength, Sarah pushed off the chair and leapt.

The water was like ice. She sliced into it, arching her back to return to the surface as quickly as possible. Sucking in a great lungful of air, Sarah started pulling for the nearest buoy, deliberately blanking her mind to the idea of Kurt pointing the gun at the back of her head. She only knew that she needed to reach the buoy. Saltwater blinded her eyes, and she plowed straight into it. The buoy tipped and rang as she scrabbled for a handhold, a grip, the merest lip of anything she could hang onto. Her fingernails scraped through the slime, and she found a narrow weld where the buoy's base had been soldered to its hollow steel top. It was enough to hold onto. Sarah dug her nails into it and lifted herself from the water. Sweeping the hair from her eyes, she searched for the madman.

Kurt had circled the cruiser around. He was idling nearby, amused by her desperate act. He casually waggled the gun at her. "And where do you think you're going?"

Sarah moved around the tiny rim, hand over hand, doing her best to use the buoy as a screen. "I said I'm not going anywhere with you!"

Kurt eased the throttle forward. "And I said you weren't allowed to leave."

The bullet punched a hole through the sheet metal above her head. The buoy thrummed and bobbed, and pushed her underwater. Sarah scrabbled to keep her grip, and when she pulled free of the water again, Kurt had maneuvered the cruiser even closer.

"Katie, Katie, do come out and play," he sang lightheartedly. "What's the matter, Katie? Don't you like this new game?"

"I'm not Katie!" She screamed as she crabbed over to the far side of the buoy. "I'm Sarah! And I told you to fuck off!"

"Oh, that's right," Kurt frowned. "Sally hit Katie with that paint can, when she found out about the brat. That's why Katie died. Why can't I ever remember that?" He shrugged, and raised the gun. "Oh, well. They're both gone now. I think it's time for you to go, too."

She felt the impact of the shot in the same instant that she heard it. The bullet punched her left elbow and then zipped off through the water like a bottle rocket. Sarah fumbled her grip, and began to sink. Reaching up, she struggled to find the weld again, but her nails only scraped more algae off the side of the clanging buoy.

Giving a hard kick, she swam back to the surface as the pain in her arm woke up. Sarah screamed and sank again, losing her precious air in a bobbing line of fat, silvery bubbles. She gave another hard kick and reached for the buoy with her good right hand. In spite of the pain, Sarah was focused, and boiling mad. Kurt might take her out, but she was a Hawthorne woman, dammit, and no one ever called them quitters.

She tucked her left hand into the waistband of her shorts, and clung to the buoy with her right. Kurt was standing at the wheel with his back to her, peering down the main channel. He suddenly scrambled to sit and spun the wheel around. The cruiser sped off toward the spillway gates. Sarah pulled herself up to see what had scared Kurt off. Were the Garza's still coming? She glimpsed an oncoming boat, and with a pure sense of disbelief, she saw John behind the wheel.

He looked dreadful. John's face was bone white, and he had a bloody T-shirt wrapped around his head. Ted was standing at John's shoulder, pointing at the buoy and shouting something unintelligible. Sarah had never seen anything so completely wonderful before in her life. John brought the boat straight in. There was a big splash, and a muscular arm gripped her waist.

"You take it easy now, missy," Ted sputtered. "We've come to take you home."

* * * * * * *

John throttled the boat to idle, and reached for Sarah's hands. "Are you alright?"

"Are you?" she asked.

"Watch her arm, Lieutenant. She's been hit." Ted clung to the side of the boat. He gave Sarah a terrific boost.

John pulled Sarah aboard, and wrapped her in his arms. He couldn't believe his luck. She was alive. "Thank God you're safe." Unwrapping the T-shirt from his head, he carefully began to bind her arm. "This is going to hurt a little."

"But Kurt's getting away!"

"We'll catch Stockton later, and make him pay for Toby. The important thing is that you're alive."

"But Toby's still alive, too!"

"What?" John couldn't believe his ears. "What did you say?"

"Yes! Toby's the one who told me to jump."

"Good God, sir." Ted fell back. "What are we gonna do? Stockton's still got the kid."

John straightened. Duty directed him to secure the civilian, but Toby was down because he had lost control of his service weapon. Which one was the greater responsibility? Which one did he choose? "Sarah, I need to know. Do we take you back to port, or do we go after them?"

"Are you kidding me?" She tugged the T-shirt tighter and flared with anger. "Toby saved my life! Of course we need to go after them. What kind of a question is that?"

"By God, babe," Ted stared awestruck. "You're the bomb."

"Hang on." John leapt for the wheel. He slammed the throttle, reset the trim and turned for the spillway, asking the little runabout for everything it had. The boat was underpowered, and the cruiser had the Johnson twin 250s and a solid, three-hundred meter lead. There was no way to catch Stockton and Toby. Or was there?

The seawater turned from green to golden yellow as John turned the runabout hard to port, and sped directly toward the shore.

"Excuse me, Lieutenant?" Ted peered uneasily over the side. "Where are we going, sir?"

"Stockton needs to keep to the channel to stay deep, because of the cruiser," John shouted. Banking hard to starboard, he began to parallel the beach. "This inboard only draws a foot, foot and a half max. We can go shallow and trim the distance that way."

Ted looked unconvinced. "Only draws a foot and a half, you hope, sir."

"I know what I'm doing, Sergeant Parsons. I can work this harbor blindfolded."

"I hope you're right about that, sir."

"Why are you always arguing with me, Ted?"

"Because that's what I do, sir," Ted grinned.

They closed in on the cruiser, working a direct line toward the spillway gates. Ted worked his way forward and wedged his hips between the dashboard and the passenger seat. He unlocked his Glock, and held it at the ready.

"Get me less than fifty meters, sir. I need less than fifty meters."

"This is as good as it gets," John yelled. He was all out of tricks. Stockton turned and caught sight of their pursuit. The cruiser growled as Stockton sped up.

"Kurt doesn't know about the new barriers," Sarah shouted. "He still thinks he can make it through those gates."

"This ain't going to be pretty," Ted warned.

Kurt ignored the final pair of warning buoys floating outside the massive concrete bunker. He must have thought he had it made, because he never even slowed down. There was a horrible screeching howl when the cruiser's fiberglass hull met the first breakwater, and then the bow hit something big. It made a drawn-out, hollow, thumping crunch.

The resultant fireball was spectacular. Coal black smoke feathers were thrown into the air, tossed up through gold and tangerine flames. The spillway exploded into a fat, gray burst that looked exactly like a young mushroom cloud.

It began to rain small pieces of boat. Some of the pieces were metal, some were fiberglass splinters, some were flaming bits of teak. They all hissed when they hit the water. It made a kind of music.

"Toby," John said.

CHAPTER THIRTY TWO

FOR IMMEDIATE RELEASE
UNITED NEWSFLASH INTERNATIONAL
DATELINE: WEDNESDAY, JUNE 15, 2011
SPECIAL REPORT FILED BY PATIENCE FORTESCUE-ELLIOTT
NANTUCKET, MASS

FEDERAL HAULOVER SPILLWAY PROJECT PERMANENTLY DISABLED TODAY BY MASSIVE EXPLOSION. UNDERWATER TURBINES IRREPERABLY DAMAGED.

SENIOR ENGINEER ANTHONY LENNON REPORTED QUOTE: THE SPILLWAY WAS NEVER DESIGNED TO OVERCOME AN IMPACT OF THIS MAGNITUDE. WE PLANNED ON FREAK TIDAL SURGES, MULTIPLE CAR ACCIDENTS, EVEN A FORCE FIVE HURRICANE. THERE WAS NO WAY TO PLAN FOR AN EVENT LIKE THIS. ONLY A FREAKING LUNATIC WOULD TRY TAKING A BOAT THROUGH THERE. UNQUOTE.

GOVERNMENT SOURCES REPORT THAT THE SPILLWAY WILL BE DISMANTLED BEGINNING THE FALL OF 2011. DEMOLITION FUNDING WILL BE PROVIDED BY THE FEDERAL DEPARTMENT OF OBSOLETE PORK BARREL PROJECTS. EVERY EFFORT WILL BE MADE TO RETURN THE SITE TO ITS ORIGINAL PRISTINE CONDITION.

ISLAND PRESERVATIONISTS HAILED THE DECISION AS A RETURN TO SOLID YANKEE VALUES AND PLAIN COMMON SENSE. THE NATIONAL WILDFOWLERS ASSOCIATION HAILED THE DECISION AS A VICTORY FOR PIPING PLOVERS EVERYWHERE.

NANTUCKET RESIDENTS BRACED THEMSELVES FOR AN IMMEDIATE THREE-FOLD INCREASE IN ELECTRICAL UTILITY RATES.

Chapter Thirty Three

Father Duffy sipped his flute of dry champagne, and considered the idea that maybe it was time to retire. He'd been marrying people on Nantucket for fifty-three years, and he'd never see another wedding party as beat up as this one was.

The tiny 'Sconset backyard was brimming with rented tables and rows of white folding chairs. Bridal tulle was gaily looped through the boxwood hedges, and tied in big, casual bows. Wedding guests stood clustered around the lawn, chatting, dressed in their finest festive apparel. He noted the familiar hot pinks and lime greens, mixed in with bright plaids and classic Nantucket Red. A few of the senior Jarad ladies had worn hats to the ceremony. Father Duffy approved. Even outside of the church, one should show respect for tradition.

The groom stood by the garden gate, greeting friends and relatives as they entered. John Jarad still sported his eye patch, and he looked about as happy as a successful pirate king. Sarah Hawthorne Jarad, the stunning mainland bride, was wearing a vintage Jarad family lace gown that had been split down one side seam to allow for her cast, with the seam stitched back up using Velcro. She was helping her bridesmaid, an oddish young woman named Alien, and two Jamaicans set up an electronic monstrosity called a karaoke machine, next to an even more monstrous display of homemade pastry called a cookie table.

Father Duffy shook his head. Kids these days. He wished them all the best of luck, but they had no idea of what they were getting themselves into.

ABOUT THE AUTHOR

Martha Reed is a Pittsburgh-based crime fiction author who is busily developing her John and Sarah Jarad Nantucket Mystery series. She serves as Chapter Liaison for Sisters in Crime, Inc., coordinating the efforts of SinC's more than 50 chapters. Her short stories have appeared in *Pearl 26*, *Spinetingler*, *Mysterical-e*, and *LUCKY CHARMS, 12 Crime Tales*, an anthology produced by the Mary Roberts Rinehart Pittsburgh chapter of SinC. Martha also serves as a Corporator for the historic Allegheny and Homewood cemeteries, and is a creative writing mentor for Mercersburg Academy's Program for Global Studies (MAPS). She loves great coffee, big jewelry, and is committed to renovating her 128-year old Victorian home, which she has affectionately nicknamed The Bottomless Money Pit.

Excerpt from the second John and Sarah Jarad Nantucket Mystery

THE NATURE OF THE GRAVE

*2006 Independent Publisher (IPPY) Honorable Mention
for Mid-Atlantic Best Regional Fiction*

CHAPTER ONE

12 Macy Lane
Wednesday, January 11, 2012

The island was flat, and the wind howled across the moors like a living thing. With no trees for protection, no hills or valleys to channel it away, it blasted into the weathered clapboards of the house, shooting icy drafts through the meager insulation, a malevolent banshee trying to force its way in.

Sarah Jarad snuggled deeper under the covers, deciding firmly that nothing had prepared her for winter on Nantucket.

Like all newcomers, Sarah had learned quickly that heating oil was an imported and precious commodity. Each morning she woke with only the tip of her cold nose showing outside the comforter. She slid out of bed, leaving the warmth of her sleeping husband, and scrambled into layers of fleece-lined clothing.

The kitchen was the only truly warm room in the house. Her grandfather from Vermont, wise with sixty years of New England winters, had shipped them a wood stove as a wedding present. Back in September, Sarah had scoffed, but now the stove held a place of honor, enthroned on the blue slate hearth. She lit a handful of driftwood sticks, bleached brittle and white like ghostly fingers. Wood was another expensive concern. A cord here cost twice what she had paid for it on the mainland, and since they were saving every dime toward the down payment on a mortgage, Sarah had taken to the beach, scavenging. John had thrown a fit when he found out what she was doing, until Sarah had proved they were saving a third of a month's pay just on fuel. John had given in, grumbling that he had married his mother, whose thrift was legendary.

Overhead in the loft, Sarah heard John stumble out of bed. He bumped down the narrow stairwell, struggling into a rough woolen sweater. Planting himself in a chair, John ran his fingers though his hair, putting it in order. Sarah cheated the coffeemaker and set his mug on the table. As she did, he wrapped his arms around her waist and pulled her, un-protesting, onto his lap.

"I woke up, you were already gone." He worked his face into the folds of Sarah's bathrobe, inhaling deeply.

Sarah lifted his face in her hands and kissed him. "And good morning to you, too."

"Is there a hurry? I don't have to report to the station until nine."

"I wanted to get to the bank, first thing." She rose, retying her robe and pulling a check from her pocket. "Meredith sent me a commission."

"We're not hurting for money." John sat back in his chair. "The rent's not due for another two weeks."

"I know that, but I like seeing the money in our account. I sleep better, knowing it's there."

John smiled. Getting used to married life was hard enough, without discovering–after the wedding–that your wife had a phobia about bouncing checks. He had tried to explain to Sarah that the town's automated payroll deposit system had worked without a glitch for years, but she would have none of it. She had been footloose, a gypsy, for too long; she didn't believe the money was real until she held it in her hand. John sighed. There would be no fooling around before work this morning. He had learned to recognize that gleam in his wife's eye. She was on a mission.

Sarah raised the coffeepot. "Touch-up?"

"Just a little," he agreed, pushing his mug across the table. They had only been married four months, and he still found the whole idea of *having a wife* pretty amazing. Sure, there had been girlfriends before, and serious ones, too, but no woman had ever rearranged his life like Sarah had. She had blown into town last May, and wham! Everything had changed.

"Must be love," he muttered, pushing back from the table and finishing his coffee over the sink. "Don't run any water for a minute, okay? I'll jump in the shower."

"You got it," Sarah agreed. It amused her they were still working on house rules.

She fixed herself a second cup and went to the window to check on the weather. Another picture perfect January day: clear and crisp. Fresh snow had dusted the bayberry and wild rose bushes that filled their yard, or what passed for a yard on Nantucket, for no one here really had a yard, or even tried growing a lawn. People in town kept trim brick walkways and clipped boxwood hedges; outside of town they built their homes in the middle of isolated sandy clearings, leaving the remaining property pretty much as they had found it: pitch pine, poverty grass, broom crowberry.

Sarah had asked John why people built their homes this way, and he had given her a one-word answer: ticks.

It had proved to be another example of misguided human kindness. Passing sailors had rescued a deer swimming across Nantucket Sound, and released it to run wild on the island. Years passed, other humans worried the buck might be lonely, so they imported mainland does. The does brought deer ticks as a housewarming present, the ticks carried Lyme disease, and as result, no one on Nantucket ever walked in tall grass anymore.

No matter, Sarah shrugged. I'll take this island as it is. From the moment the ferry had entered the harbor around Brant Point, and she had seen the quaint gray palette of a town spreading out before her, she had known that this place was home. And it was home for her without apology; home in the corny, old-fashioned sense of the word.

Sarah was the first to admit that her choice made no sense. She certainly had no ancestral claim to this part of the world. One-half of her family had stepped off the boat from Ireland, the other half was Eastern Shawnee. Claiming County Cork or the Ohio River valley made a whole lot more sense than loving an isolated elbow of sand thirty miles to sea. But home for her had always been a matter of heart, and her heart had never been ruled by common sense. Nantucket was her home in everything from the way the salt breeze stirred her hair to the muted colors she discovered in the lapped layers of tidal sand.

Upstairs, she heard John drop the soap, and curse. *Husband.* Now there was an idea for you. But, just as Sarah had instantly known this place was home, she had also known that this man was her husband, from the first moment she had laid eyes on him. Love at first sight was a comic proposition, a bedroom farce, until it happened to you.

Of course, nothing had happened easily. They had met during the course of a rigorous homicide investigation, and there had been weeks of chance encounters and stammered, blushing replies. Her ex-roommate Alien hadn't hindered matters either, leading the cheer from the sideline. But somehow, even in the whirling, magical confusion of that time, Sarah had known that everything would work out; that this decision, required of her, would by its very nature need to be a leap of faith, a demonstration of blind trust in her own judgment, and in her hopes for the future.

So, one languorous Tuesday afternoon, four short months ago, on a sailboat in the middle of Nantucket Sound, she had looked up into John Jarad's hopeful brown eyes, taken a deep breath, and said: *Yes.*

And now, here she was. A *wife.* Sarah shook her head at the thought and climbed the stairs to their bedroom loft, smiling as she caught the sound of John singing tunefully in the shower. She grabbed her jeans hanging on the footboard of their bed, judged them clean enough, and selected a heather-blue sweater from the dresser. She wasn't planning on taking her coat off in town anyway. Her shower could wait until later.

John hit one last lingering note and shut off the water. Sarah retraced her steps to the kitchen to wait. She finished the coffee, rinsing the pot and setting it in the dish rack to dry. Deciding that a grocery list was a good idea, she spent a further five minutes rummaging through the junk drawer looking for some paper and a pen that worked.

"Someday, when we get our own house," she vowed, "I will have a place for everything, and everything in its place."

"I heard that," John called down over the buzz of his electric razor. "This place isn't so bad. At least it's cheap."

"Twelve hundred a month is not cheap."

"It is for Nantucket," he clattered down the stairs, straightening his tie. "We could always move in with my mother. You know that she offered."

"We've already been through that." Sarah tested a pen. "We're too old to be living at home, especially you."

"Seven years is not that much of a difference, and Jenny does have a point. We would be saving more toward a down payment, if we didn't pay rent."

"Just because you're right doesn't mean I have to agree with you." Sarah paused to admire her husband in his police Lieutenant's regalia. John in uniform always brought a wickedly evil grin to her face. The uniform made him look so official, so authoritarian, such a contrast to the gentle man she loved. But she had to admit, once he put on his mirrored sunglasses and became *The Man with No Eyes,* Sarah felt a thrill, a *frission,* of raw desire.

"Don't look at me like that if you want to get into town this morning," he warned.

She gave herself a shake. "You're right, sorry. Listen, I need to use your truck today, but I'll pick you up after your shift."

"Fine," John grumbled. Married life sometimes involved painful compromise. "But I'm driving."

The distance from their rented house to the South Water Street station was only a short hop, the sole advantage to living in town. John handled his truck with the unconscious skill that followed complete familiarity. Turning the corner on Chestnut, he noticed a pedestrian muffled to the ears in a red-striped scarf, and gave him a two-finger salute.

"Who was that?" Sarah asked idly.

"Mike Hussey. We played league soccer together. Eighth grade."

"Ah." It came as no surprise to her that John knew the man on the street. As a native, and a cop, John seemed to know everyone. It was one of the hardest adjustments she had to make. Her husband could walk into a party full of people and glad-hand every single one of them. Sarah still found herself at a disadvantage, rifling through short-term memory, desperately trying to connect a name to a face. Or even worse, trying to connect an insider childhood nickname to a face. She grew indignant at the thought. How were you supposed to remember the business affiliation for a man introduced as *Puffy*? Or, that your insurance agent's given name was Helen Marie, when everyone called her *Jinx?*

"What's your game plan for today?" John asked, putting the truck in park.

"First stop the A&P. I'm hungry for roast pork with applesauce. Then lunch with your mom." Sarah scooted across the seat, and took his place behind the wheel. "I'll call you later, and let you know how it went."

John leaned back in through the open door. "Honey, my mother likes you, you know."

"I know she does. I just can't help it though, sometimes I wonder."

"Wonder what?"

Sarah struggled to explain. "Your mom's only known me for what? Six, seven months? All your other girlfriends, well, I mean, they were cousins; I'm sure Jenny knew plenty about them. Sometimes, well, sometimes I think she still wonders who I am."

"That is not true." John zipped his coat. "I never dated any of my cousins. They wouldn't go out with me."

"You know what I mean."

"Yes, sweetheart, I do know what you mean." John chose his

next words carefully. "And I know you've been asked to make a lot of adjustments lately. We both have. And Sarah, I'm counting on you to make them. Just let me know if it gets to be too much. Sweetheart, that's why I'm here. And please stop worrying about my mother. Consider her side of things. Her thirty-year old son walks in the house one day, announces that he's just met a girl in a bar, and he's going to get married." John grinned. "Part of this is my fault, I accept that. I did not break *us* to my mother in the right way. But sweetheart, you'll have to forgive me, because I wasn't thinking clearly at the time."

Sarah laughed. "Is that really how you told Jenny about us?"

"It was worse than that, actually." He scratched his jaw. "I remember telling her you were the only woman in the world for me: my one, true, only. I was probably a complete fruitcake about it. But you have to give Jenny some credit; once she sat down, she said if that was how I truly felt then I was not allowed to let anyone or anything stop me. And you can take that to the bank. My mother does not lie. If Jenny says she likes you, she does."

"Well, she'd better, because I'm not leaving."

"That's the spirit." John relaxed. Somehow, with Sarah, finding the right words came easy. "I'll call you later. Enjoy your day."

She drove along Main Street, delighting in the brick storefronts with their festive displays of holiday greenery. The town of Nantucket was deserted this time of year, such a difference from peak season when finding any parking was impossible. As Sarah turned right, the truck's worn tires slipped on the wet cobblestones, and she slowed, crossing a speed bump into the public parking lot.

She was in luck. It was still early, no one was out yet. Sarah pulled a cart from the corral and headed in. Grocery shopping was her least favorite chore, but if she followed her list and kept her focus, she would be home in plenty of time for a shower and lunch with Jenny. Dinner was simple: slice an onion, toss the pork roast in the crockpot, and she would have the whole glorious afternoon free to paint.

She dug the list from her purse and steered through the produce aisle. The aisles were narrow and the shelves overstocked, and if there was a floor display, forget it, you could get trapped behind your cart for life. The meat counter ran along the back wall, deserted. She tore a number off the paper roll and waited patiently for some sign of activity. Sarah waited one more minute, and then thought: *nuts to this*, and rang the bell.

The butcher backed through a swinging door carrying a chrome tray. "Morning, miss. What can I get for you today?"

"A three or four pound pork roast?"

"I've got a nice one in the back. I'll go get it."

She scanned her list one more time, double-checking, because there was nothing worse than getting all the way home and realizing you had forgotten that one thing. And there was always something. It didn't matter how organized you were, how super-efficient, there was always that one thing that you forgot.

"Gangway!" Sarah heard a woman shout. She had no time to react as a runaway cart smashed into hers, snagging it and carrying it away.

"Oh, lady, I'm so sorry! Are you okay?"

Sarah turned to answer, and caught herself gaping instead. Standing before her was a middle-aged woman in a worn Navy pea coat. The woman had straggling gray hair, a look of concern in her periwinkle blue eyes, and a curling, almost pubic, blond beard.

Sarah struggled to catalog this last item intellectually. *More of a goatee, really*, she decided.

"Thought I surprised you!" The bearded woman announced, her voice a strong, nasal monotone. "Turned around and my cart was gone! They really need to level this floor."

"That's alright." Sarah retrieved her cart and wheeled it to one side. "No harm done."

"You're not from around here, are you? You're a coof. I can tell it from your voice."

Coof? Sarah didn't recognize the word, but it sounded dubious. She added it to her *ask John later* list. "I've been living on Nantucket since May."

"Near anything counts, nowadays. Used to be you had to live here *years* to call yourself a Nantucketer. Now they're letting anyone come over. I saw a yacht pull into the harbor that was bigger than the ferry! And they drive trucks inside the ferry." The woman lowered her voice. "Who are those people, d'you think? Foreigners from New York, maybe? Or Hollywood movie stars?"

"I'm sure they could be both."

"Let me mend my manners." The woman stuck out her hand. "We're going to be friends. I'm Addie Simpson."

"I'm Sarah Jarad. Nice to meet you, Addie."

"Does Stan know that you're here?"

"Yes, he's getting a pork roast for me."

"I'm here for corned beef. Mom's making Boston boiled dinner for supper. I love boiled dinner, don't you?"

"Absolutely. Especially the buttered cabbage."

"Well, that's good, but corned beef is better. With yellow

mustard, too. It's got to be yellow mustard, not brown - "

"Here we go," Stan interrupted, pushing through the door carrying a neat, paper-wrapped package. "One four-pound pork roast. Ah, good morning, Addie. Didn't see you standing there."

"Stan, Mom wants a corned beef for supper."

"And I'll help you pick out a good one, as soon as I'm through with this lady. Will that be all, miss?"

"Yes, thank you."

"Nice to meet you," Addie repeated. "Sorry again for the trouble."

Stan glanced uneasily between his two customers. "Did something happen while I was in back? Was there an accident?"

"It was nothing, Stan," Addie said. "Weren't no problem here. We bumped carts, that's all. You don't need to worry about that."

The butcher looked relieved. "Alright, then. Come on, Addie, let's pick you out a corned beef."

As Sarah pushed her cart toward checkout she caught Addie's reply.

"Pick me out a good one, Stan! You know I *LOVE* corned beef!"

And I *LOVE* living here, Sarah admitted. Every day is an adventure.

Back out on the sidewalk, she patted the commission check in her pocket and considered: maybe it was time for a splurge. She'd been working hard lately. The splurge didn't have to be big. Something small, but special.

It was a part of Sarah's nature to immediately think of splurging on John. But she knew once she bought him a present, he would want to buy her something, too. John was overly generous that way sometimes, and the last thing she wanted to do was start them on a spending spree. *What to do? What to do?* She wondered, tapping her fingernails on the steering wheel.

Then she smiled. She had it. The perfect bonus for them both. She would stop at the packie and pick up a bottle of wine, not too expensive, but festive enough. Then she would take the time to prepare a real meal: set the table, light some candles, pick out some tunes, the works. With a little effort, she could turn a regular Wednesday night into a romantic evening they would cherish forever. John was a closet romantic; he would be delighted with her surprise. It was perfect. She was brilliant.

She pulled the wheel around and turned for Nantucket Spirits on Washington Street. Not only did Sarah love the name of the store, but it was as multipurpose a packie as you could want. She read their sign as she parked the truck: Beer, Wine & Cordials. Yes, Sarah agreed, give the girl a little pocket money and she certainly started feeling cordial.

A tinny bell rang as Sarah pushed on the door. She still felt so adult when walking through the racks of wine, admiring the graphics on the labels, glancing peripherally for yellow sale tags. Hand-written notecards announced Wine Selector ratings: this Chilean red had earned a 98, the Rioja from Spain an 87. Keeping their budget in mind, she moved toward Domestic.

"Can I help?" A silver-haired saleswoman stood up from a chair behind the counter. "Looking for something special?"

"Yes. I'd like something nice for dinner. I was thinking about a Merlot."

"We have a very nice selection of Merlot." The saleswoman led the way down the aisle. "These Californians are some of the best in the world." She glanced surreptitiously at Sarah's outfit. "Did you have a price in mind?"

"Less than twenty?"

"I have just the ticket." The saleswoman chose a bottle from the rack, and cradled it gently. "This one is nineteen, and you won't find a better wine for that price on the market. It's woodsy, with nice depth, and just a hint of cherry finish."

Sarah dug for her wallet. "Sounds perfect. I'll take it."

"You'll be pleased." The doorbell chimed again. The saleswoman looked up, and frowned. "Oh no. Here we go again."

Sarah turned to see who had entered and realized what the saleswoman was up against. Shuffling through the door was a gaunt, elderly man, John's great-uncle, Ethan.

Ethan Jarad ignored their presence, intent on reaching the vodka. Both women watched the elderly man pause before the inventory, drawing himself up to his full, rawboned height and eyeing the display. His fingers trembled past the top shelf, descending toward Kossak on the bottom row. He tipped a plastic bottle off the shelf, and caught it with eager hands.

"We go through this every other day," the saleswoman confided *sotto voce*. "You'd think he'd buy it by the case. It would save him a trip into town."

"I'm sure it would."

"You know," the saleswoman continued, "there is something just plain wrong with that family. Must be tainted blood or something. Every generation one or two of them goes right off the deep-end. I've seen it myself."

She doesn't remember who I am, Sarah realized. Unable to resist the tease, she whispered: "What do you mean?"

"You stay here long enough, miss, and you'll see what I mean. Any trouble on this island, you look close, and you'll find a Jarad somewhere near the middle of it." The saleswoman drew herself up, shrugging apologetically. "Sorry to trouble you, but I need to see some I.D."

This should be interesting, Sarah grinned, and she handed her driver's license over.

"Yes, that's fine. Uhm, oh my." The saleswoman was so mortified, she blushed maroon. She returned Sarah's license and retreated into formality. "That'll be nineteen dollars, even."

Sarah handed her a twenty. As she waited for her change, Uncle Ethan shuffled up with his vodka. Even arthritic and bent with age, he still stood a head taller than Sarah's five-foot eight. She waited until he put his bottle on the counter before speaking. "Hello, Uncle Ethan. How are you?"

The elderly man looked over with rheumy, bloodshot eyes. "Ah, Sarah Jarad. Didn't see you standing there."

"Too busy looking at your bottle," the saleswoman muttered.

"Excuse me? What was that you said?" Uncle Ethan slid his purchase across the counter. "I thought I heard you say something."

"I said that'll be twenty-one fifty."

"Sack that double please. Paper." He turned to Sarah. "John treating you alright?"

"Of course he is. We're very happy together."

"Good. He always was a good boy. A little stubborn, maybe, but I call that grit. Are you going to put that in a sack, or do I have to stand here all day?"

"I said," the saleswoman replied indignantly, one hand on her hip. "I need to see twenty-one fifty, first."

"Got it right here." Ethan Jarad dug into a pocket and retrieved a roll of bills wrapped in a thick rubber band. "There's a ten, and a five, another five, and a one." A handful of coins were dredged up from another pocket, and snapped one-by-one against the countertop. "And two quarters makes fifty. There, now. Satisfied?"

"We do deliver, you know." The saleswoman's voice squeaked with disapproval. "It's not like it would cost you anything."

"Do you know where I live?"

"I haven't the foggiest idea." She double-sacked the bottle angrily. "To tell the truth, I don't really care to know, either."

The old man grinned. "Then how would you deliver?"

"Ethan Jarad, take your bottle and get! And I don't mind saying, if I were the manager here, you'd be taking your business elsewhere! Even if it did mean losing steady custom!"

He slowly gathered his package. "But I like it here. I find service with a smile."

"Get!" The saleswoman pointed at the door, her strident voice following them both out into the cold. "And I feel sorry for you, miss, for marrying into that family! Good luck to you, is all I can say! My mother warned me: *marry in haste, repent at leisure!*"

The storm door slammed. Uncle Ethan grimaced, and shuffled uncomfortably. "Marion didn't upset you with that last remark, did she?"

"It's nothing I haven't heard before. But I'll bet she remembers who I am the next time."

He chuckled. "Marion's an old battle-axe, but she can't help it. She inherited her Irish temper." His deep cough sounded wet, but he waved it off. "I can remember Marion as a girl. Hair as red as a fresh copper penny." He coughed again, then winked. "Least then she gave some warning."

"I take it you two have been carrying on like this for awhile?"

"Oh, I give Marion something to talk about, true enough. It's one of the reasons I still visit this store. Marion doesn't know it, but she's going to miss me when I'm gone."

Sarah shook her head. John had warned her this great-uncle of his was a character, but she realized now John might have shaved the truth. Thoughtfully, she paused. It would interfere with her morning, but she knew Uncle Ethan didn't drive, and he was family. "Can I give you a lift?"

The elderly man looked both surprised and pleased. "Why, no, no thank you. My ride will be here soon enough."

"Are you sure? It's no trouble," she pointed. "The truck's right there."

"No, no, Eddie'll be along. He knows I'm waiting."

Sarah paused, feeling unsure. She could sense her precious painting time ticking away, but she couldn't just leave the man standing on the curb, it was freezing out. His lips were turning blue. She had a sudden, inspired idea. "Why don't we wait in the truck, until your friend gets here? It'll be warm. I'll blast the heater."

Uncle Ethan started to protest, and then surrendered to the promise of warmth. He waited patiently as Sarah unlocked the truck, and then climbed stiffly in. "I appreciate the offer. Won't be but a minute before Eddie gets here. Took some training, but he's learned to be prompt."

11

She started the engine. It was still warm. "No problem. Don't mind the bags."

The elderly man rubbed his rough knuckled hands before the dashboard vent. "Ah, that feel's nice. I don't know why, but I can't seem to get warm today. You'd think, after eighty-seven years, I'd be used to it, but this damp cold cuts right through to my bones."

"Maybe it would help if you put some meat on them," she suggested.

He looked at her wide-eyed. "Young woman, are you usually so outspoken?"

"Pretty much," Sarah admitted.

"Humph. Must be my day to hear from opinionated females." He wheezed. "Well, since we are being so outspoken, then let me ask you a question."

"Sure, shoot."

"Are you and John planning on having a family? Any children, I mean?"

Sarah was surprised by the question. Sure, she and John had talked about kids, but they certainly hadn't made any plans. "I'm sure we will, someday, when we're a little more settled. I'd like to be in our own house first, but saving for the down payment is going to take years."

Uncle Ethan shuddered through another deep bronchial cough, and groped for his handkerchief. "That's good to hear. There's nothing better than family." He wiped his eyes, and announced: "Job, 15:7: *'For there is hope of a tree, if it be cut down, that it will sprout again, that the tender branch thereof shall not cease.'* "

"That's rich, coming from you. If I remember right you never married."

"No, that's true enough, I didn't; but not every man is cut out for family life. Look at King Solomon. He had a thousand wives and he was still unhappy. Perhaps divine Providence saved me from error." He smiled weakly. "Besides, I never lacked for family. My brother Ike put a whole pack of 'em on the ground. I've got more nieces and nephews, and grand-nieces and grand-nephews now than I can count."

"I met most of them at our wedding, but I'm still getting to know everyone."

"That was a fine party you had. It was good to see the whole family together. Some of them I never see anymore, from year to year."

"Maybe we should have a reunion next summer. A picnic or something?"

12

Uncle Ethan's eyes grew misty and distant. "I can remember a time when the family met up for no reason at all. There'd be a clambake or a taffy-pull, some such foolishness, more for the fun of being together than getting any real work done." The old man sighed. "Those were good times, no doubt about it. And so many kids you couldn't move without stepping on one of them."

"Do you remember John from when he was a boy? What was he like?"

Amused by the question, Uncle Ethan scratched the stubble on his chin. "Oh, those boys had the devil in them, no doubt about it. But I always said, better a boy with spirit than one without. I'll never forget, one summer Tindy had a picnic, and those two boys disappeared. We should have known right then it meant trouble. But by the time we went looking, they had pulled all of Tindy's fancy Japanese carp out of her fishpond! You never saw a prouder pair of fishermen than those two boys with all those dead carp lined up on the patio. Tindy pitched a fit, of course, but I mean, how could you get angry? Boys will be boys."

Sarah smiled. "Was John your favorite?"

He suddenly scowled. "What makes you ask such a foolish question? My past is none of your business! Job 27:6: 'My righteousness I hold fast, and will not let it go: my heart shall not reproach me so long as I live.'"

"Sorry if I hit a nerve, Uncle Ethan. I didn't mean anything by it." Uh-oh, Sarah realized, Marion was right. Uncle Ethan had a bone to pick, and here she was, stuck with him in the truck. She started hoping for his ride.

He turned to face her. "You remember this, Sarah Jarad. Life is as fragile as the sand we build on, and God's implacable hand guides the incoming tide." His quavering voice rose, booming inside the cramped truck. Foam flecked the corners of his mouth and he continued on, blindly: "Job 19:10: 'He hath destroyed me on every side, I am gone: my hope hath he removed like a tree!'"

"Uncle Ethan," Sarah started. "Take it easy -"

The elderly man rattled on, heedless. "Daniel was the judgment of God! Job 5:17: 'Happy is the man whom God correcteth! Despiseth not the chastening of the Almighty!'"

As Sarah watched in horror, Uncle Ethan's face turned battleship gray. His eyes rolled back into his head, and he slumped onto the passenger side door, releasing his purchase. The bag rolled down his leg and thumped against the floorboards, snapping Sarah out of shock. She reined-in her panic, opened her door, and raced back inside. "Marion!" she yelled. "911! Call 911!"

The saleswoman looked up, surprised and irritated, from behind a wine rack. "What are you saying? Hey, wait a minute! You can't go back there."

Sarah grabbed the telephone and started punching numbers. "Uncle Ethan's had a stroke, a heart attack, or something out in the truck. Hello? Hello! Yes, we need a paramedic. Marion! What's the address here?"

The saleswoman looked stunned. "Number 10 Washington Street. But they'll know that -"

"Did you get that? Number 10. Yes, outside in the parking lot. A white pickup truck. Yes, yes, I'll wait for you there." Sarah hung up the phone and clawed her way back around the counter.

"Where did you say he was?" Marion followed, buttoning her cabled cardigan. "Ethan's in your truck?"

"Can you help me? I'll try CPR." Suddenly, Sarah felt woozy. The adrenaline pounding through her system was making her feel nauseous. She stumbled on the gravel and wondered: *maybe I should've taken him straight to the Cottage Hospital; they could have helped, it's only two minutes away.* She sucked in a deep, ragged breath. "Marion, we need to stretch him out flat. I'll grab his shoulders. Can you get his feet?"

"I'll try." Perched on the curb, the older woman hesitated. "Dear sweet Lord, have mercy. Look at that, the poor dear man." As they drew even nearer, Marion moaned.

It was a nightmare image. Uncle Ethan's sightless white eyes stared through the fogged window. Sarah clawed for the handle. The passenger door swung open, propelled by the weight of his body. Sarah grabbed the collar of Uncle Ethan's pea coat. "Marion, are you ready? Grab his feet. I need you to grab his feet."

"I'm right here, I've got him. Oh dear sweet Jesus. Mind his head. Don't drop him."

"I've got it, there, that's good." Sarah staggered as Uncle Ethan's body slid heavily onto the gravel. He hadn't made a sound during the transfer. "Help me stretch him out. We need to get him flat."

Abruptly, Marion let go and stood up, twisting both hands. "Child, why don't you leave him be? Can't you see that he's passed?"

Sarah knelt in the wet gravel, fighting the obvious. Marion was right. She knew it, yet Sarah still felt compelled to try to do *something.* "Maybe we can save him," she argued weakly.

The older woman clutched Sarah's sleeve. "Child, leave him be. Ethan Jarad's been waiting on death longer than you've been alive.

You won't be doing him any favor saving him now. This is between himself and God." She drew a string of rosary beads from her cardigan pocket. "Sweet Jesus, have mercy on this poor man's troubled soul."

And as the EMS van arrived, sirens wailing, Marion closed her eyes and silently began to pray.

Made in the USA
Charleston, SC
18 January 2015